# OATHS

AND

# OMISSIONS

SAV R. MILLER

Copyright © 2022 by Sav R. Miller

All rights reserved. No part of this book may be reproduced or used in any manner without written permission of the copyright owner except for the use of quotations in a book review. For more information, address: authorsav@savrmiller.com

This is a work of fiction. Names, characters, businesses, places, events, locales, and incidents are either the products of the author's imagination or used in a fictitious manner. Any resemblance to actual persons, living or dead, or actual events is purely coincidental.

FIRST EDITION

Cover Design: TRC Designs
Editing: Ellie McLove, My Brother's Editor
Proofreading: Rosa Sharon, My Brother's Editor

# AUTHOR'S NOTE

Oaths and Omissions is a dark, contemporary romance inspired by the Helen of Troy and Trojan War myths.
It is not fantasy or a retelling.

Oaths and Omissions is the third interconnected standalone in the Monsters & Muses series, and contains material that may not be suitable for all readers, including explicit sexual scenes, graphic violence, and other unsettling images and themes.

**Reader discretion is advised.**
**Full content warning list can be found at savrmiller.com**

*Because slaying your real life demons is often frowned upon.*

*Nothing has more strength than dire necessity.*

— EURIPIDES

# PLAYLIST

"Please Notice" — Christian Leave
"Happiness is a butterfly" — Lana Del Ray
"All I Want" — Kodaline
"Lover of Mine" — 5 Seconds of Summer
"Church" — Chase Atlantic
"Daddy Issues" — The Neighborhood, Syd
"like you're god" — mehro
"Look After You" — The Fray

# PROLOGUE

## Lenny

*Twelve Years Ago*

Mama makes the best vegetable lasagna on Aplana Island.

Possibly the best in the world.

It's blue-ribbon worthy, which is proven at the county fair each year when she takes home first place in the headlining cook-off.

People travel from the mainland just for a taste.

That's what Daddy always says.

Daddy has a habit of exaggerating, though, according to

my big brothers Cash—short for Cassius, which he *hates* to be called—and Palmer.

But I don't think either of them really likes Daddy, so sometimes it seems like they make stuff up just to get me on their side.

Cash used to say that if he had to pick between wrestling a gator with his arms tied behind his back, or saving Daddy from drowning in the ocean, he'd pick the reptile, no questions asked.

I would rather die myself than let either of our parents drown.

Palmer says that's my problem.

*Siblings are supposed to stick together*, the twins tell me. Even though they have no problem leaving me at home every Friday night, taking the ferry to one of the other islands and staying out until the sun comes up.

Ever since I was pulled out of school and we moved from Savannah to Aplana, the only people I see aside from our family are Primrose staff. Private tutors, housekeepers, chefs, and gardeners are the only ones allowed on our property.

So, why wouldn't I side with the people I spend most of my time with? Cash and Palmer are practically glued at the hip, and Mama says I ate my twin in the womb, so my parents are my only other option.

My stomach growls as I glance down at my fingers, coated in marinara sauce and ricotta cheese.

Okay, so there's one other option.

*Food.*

But I can't really do *this*—stand at the kitchen island, shoveling cold bites into my mouth—every day. At least, not when people are around.

Which is why I'm up at midnight, hiding in the dark.

Everyone else is asleep, and I'm downstairs getting sauce on the bright yellow Easter dress Mama made me wear to Sunday service.

There are probably worse things I could be doing.

Palmer always says no good comes after my bedtime, and stuffing my face feels pretty lame compared to the stories I've heard and the shows I've seen on television.

But for some reason, I still feel like I'm doing something wrong.

My fist is halfway to my mouth, a flat piece of pasta dangling between my thumb and index finger, when a dull thud somewhere on the other side of the house makes me freeze.

Glancing up, I catch my stained reflection in the giant mirror hanging across the room, and a hot, sticky feeling washes over me.

*Gross.*

Still, I don't move, bracing myself for an intruder.

A soft glow spills in through the rounded archway leading out of the kitchen, and my heart smacks against my ribs.

*Crap.*

Voices drift down the hall, echoing off the tall ceilings of our far-too-big house.

They're getting closer.

*Double crap.*

*I'm in so much trouble.*

If *anyone* sees that I'm the one always ruining Mama's dishes the day before a fair, I'll be grounded for a month.

And since I already don't have many privileges, I'm not really looking to get more taken away.

Staring at the lasagna dish with its plastic cover half-torn off, I scoop it into my arms and duck down on the side of the island. Balancing the glassware on my knees, I pull them tight against my chest, forcing a swallow through the dryness in my mouth.

The iron handle on the white cabinet door digs into my back as I press into it, trying to make myself as small as possible. My breaths come in quick bursts, making the plastic flap against my fingers.

My belly rumbles the second footsteps thud on the tiled floor.

Curling my fingers around the dish, I bite into my bottom lip, trying to keep my breathing soft.

Sweat slides from my hairline to the tip of my nose. I watch the droplet, eyes crossing, and for a second I forget that I'm in danger.

My vision blurs and the drop rolls, falling onto the plastic.

I stop breathing altogether.

A groan echoes through the air, and I lean out past the counter to peek at the source. The toes of Daddy's favorite pair of loafers stick out from the other side, and I let out a little sigh.

He's much less likely to punish me.

With a little grin, I decide to aim for cuteness as I reveal myself, hoping to sway Daddy's anger with my best puppy dog eyes.

But when I stand and set the lasagna on the floor, rounding the corner of the island, I'm met by a head of dark, graying hair as Daddy lies on the ground.

Bleeding from a hole in his skull.

# 1

*A* WIRE TRANSFER *has been made to your account.*

Swiping the notification from my phone, I send a quick thumbs up to Alistair and pocket the device, slightly more enthused about carrying on with the evening now that he's paid me for it.

Some of my brother's political adversaries put up more of a fight than others, and the city manager he fucked yesterday seems less willing to die than I'd anticipated.

No matter, though.

The screams of my targets no longer deter me.

My house sits on a stretch of green, grassy land on the

north end of Aplana Island, a little patch of rock floating just outside the Boston Harbor Islands, with a permanent population that's grown from a mere couple hundred to several thousand in the last few years.

Before that, we were mostly relegated to tourist country and rich families interested in hiding their illegal activities in mint and crab exports or developing the infrastructure to attract more residents.

Essentially, Aplana acts as an independent, partially impoverished version of The Hamptons. With far more crime, its own little airport, and sprawling acreage split by small roads.

It's not the kind of place I would've picked for myself, but my family moved here from London when I was a boy, and I never left.

My house is separated from the buzzing array of attractions and shops downtown; with no neighbors for miles, things can get as loud and messy as they want.

Normally, I try to avoid loud and messy. Clean hits mean clear consciences, and I'm not a man who wants even a modicum of guilt weighing down his shoulders.

There will be time for guilt on Judgment Day, and not a moment sooner.

Switching off the faucet, I spin on my heel and dry my hands on a dishrag. Kevin glares at me from behind the packing tape I've wrapped around his head, his mouth accessible through a tiny gap left in the binding.

"It's a shame things have to end this way," I tell him, eliminating any hopes he may have of leaving this earth with dignity.

Slowly, I approach the chair he's tied up in, noting the beads of sweat percolating along his hairline. Flames from the stone fireplace lick at his back, heating the room and turning the exposed skin at the nape of his neck into a web of purple welts.

Crouching down, I slide a metal rod from the wall-mounted fire iron hook, holding the shaped end against the flames. It flares orange, sizzling, and I can't stop the excitement from thrumming through my veins when Kevin whimpers.

Standing up straight, I pull the rod from the fire and shove it toward his face. It skims his cheek, and he squeals like a stuck pig, rocking back until his chair almost tips over.

"Have you anything to say for yourself?" I ask, even though there's no way he'll answer. "I'll admit, I've no idea why Alistair asked me to take care of you. It's been a while since he had me do any eliminations, so he must be planning something *grand*."

Kevin groans, and I'm sure he'd be in tears if not for the tape.

Hooking my ankle behind one of the chair legs, I lean in, gripping Kevin's shoulder in one hand. The rod glows as I wave it between us, tsking at the fear frozen on his tired face.

"Come on, mate. Throw me a bone here." The gold cross around his neck catches my eye. "You're Catholic, yes? So you believe confession absolves you of your sins, or some other bloody nonsense. Well, now's your chance. Tell me what you've done, and maybe God will have mercy on your soul."

This time, he doesn't even try to say anything. Sighing, I swipe the poker across his jaw, reveling in the absolute terror radiating off him.

The head of the iron is shaped like a W and engraved with intricately woven vines and roses. It's an heirloom passed down from my grandfather to my father, and then to me—though I suspect I'm the first to use it in this manner.

Then again, my father's lack of creativity in this line of work is likely what got him killed in the first place. If he'd stuck to his hidden talents and not tried to align himself with Primrose Realty, perhaps he'd still be alive.

I glance at the silver Rolex on my wrist and frown when I realize what time it is. Alistair will have an aneurysm if I show up late, so I'd better make this quick.

Pity.

Prolonging the inevitable really is the best part of my job.

Kevin trembles in my grasp, and satisfaction funnels through my nerve-endings, lighting me up like the night sky.

"I thought for sure when my brother had his cock up your arse, it meant good things for you. Though, I suppose he has his methods of torture..."

Biting back a smile, I push the W-shaped end of the branding iron against his cheek, letting him thrash and scream as much as he can. The smell of burnt flesh reaches my nostrils, and I inhale deeply, allowing myself a breath to revel in the depravity.

The Wolfe family insignia looks delightful etched into his face, and once I'm content with the severity of its presence, I move back and fit the letter between his lips.

"...and I have mine," I finish, one flick of my wrist shoving the iron into his mouth. He has no teeth left to block the entry, so the end reaches the back of his throat on the first try.

He jerks some as I hold him in place, but the struggle dies off quickly as his energy evaporates. When he goes limp, I punch my arm forward more forcefully, until the end of the iron pops out the back of his neck at an awkward angle.

Blood gushes from his lips and the exit wound, spilling onto the floor. Some of it splatters onto my leather shoes, and I sigh as I bend down, wiping it away with the handkerchief in my breast pocket.

Refolding the tissue, I stuff it into my leather jacket and clean up, wrapping Kevin's body in a tarp and placing him temporarily in the deep freeze on my back deck.

Later, when I arrive at my pub, The Flaming Chariot, my brother sits in a booth in the very back, watching patrons writhe around the dance floor with a blank expression on his face.

Smoke from a Cuban swirls up around him, tangling with his neatly coiffed jet-black hair, and the navy trousers and suspenders he wears make it clear this isn't an establishment he frequents often.

Icy blue eyes meet mine as I slide in across from him. A moment after I'm seated, a red-headed waitress named Amber puts a pint in front of me, refills Alistair's water, and then scurries off.

"Surprised you wanted to meet here," I say, raising my voice slightly so it's audible over the music.

He takes a drink, balancing his cigar against the glass. "Yes, well. Figured it might be easier to come to you. No one bats an eye at the mayor visiting a seedy pub if they think he's just being diligent."

"But they'd question my presence at the mayor's house, I suppose."

"Precisely." Placing his glass down, he sucks on the end of his cigar, inhaling deep. On the exhale, he leans forward. "And what of our dear friend, Kevin?"

"Taken care of." I sip my beer. "Though I hope you have a

better reason for wanting him gone than the possibility of someone finding out about your... *trysts.*"

Alistair chuckles. "My sexual preferences are no secret at this point, little brother. That I enjoy the company of a man as much as a woman's is hardly the revelation you'd think."

"The press would spin it, regardless."

"Oh, I've no doubt. The press just has very little influence on my decisions, is all."

Tapping the edge of the wooden table, I blow out a breath and scan the room quickly. Booths line three of the four walls, with the bar front finishing the square. In the middle sits the dance floor, though on the days we open early, it's just extra room for single tables.

Nothing spectacular to look at, but it's mine.

Spend a little time in jail with nothing to your name, and the concept of property becomes incomparable.

"Surely you haven't come here to discuss your sex life," I say, finishing off my drink.

Slowly, he reaches into his suit and pulls out a black card. *You're Invited to Primrose Manor* is in gold, embossed lettering at the top, and he places it flat on the table.

My stomach flips, my gut twisting as I think about the last time I set foot in that house twelve years ago.

Silence stretches thin between us, and I hook my ankle over the opposite knee, waiting for him to continue. "You're not planning on going to that, are you?"

He frowns, not moving his gaze from the card. "For the first time since they bought their estate, Tom Primrose is opening it up to the public. I'd say every major dignitary and socialite from here to Boston will be in attendance, desperate just to see inside his home."

I don't respond.

"It would be untoward of me not to attend. I hear the daughter is looking for a *partner*." He sets the card down, something haunted lining his irises. I uncross my legs, not particularly interested in meeting his ghosts.

I have plenty of my own.

An image of Tom Primrose's brunette puppet pops in my head, though it's been ages since I paid attention to her in a magazine or elsewhere.

Nodding, I lift a shoulder in acknowledgment. "Better you than me."

A strange feeling settles in my gut when Alistair doesn't say anything more. I look down at the placard, watching as he spins it around with his index finger.

Slowly, my gaze lifts to his. He catches it and holds fast.

My nostrils flare. "No."

His fingers drum on the table. "I wasn't asking, Jonas."

Then again, he rarely does. Alistair grew up traveling the world with his Scottish mum and a silver spoon lodged up his arse, and no one ever taught him manners. He takes without remorse, which I'd admire more if it wasn't constantly being used against me.

Aplana Island, though relatively small in permanent population, has always had a very heavy and extensive presence of crime. It's not specifically organized, but there are competing branches of underground societies that operate on the south side or in the less habitable, underdeveloped parts.

Everyone always thinks the criminal networks are exclusive to big cities, but in truth, it's much easier to corrupt the smaller tourist towns.

Tightly knit communities are less likely to rat, and there's far more at stake if they do.

That's how my brother came to hold any sort of political influence in Aplana; his association with high-powered criminals might make him a lot of enemies and not the public's biggest fan, but hijacking an election is fairly simple. He didn't even have to do any of it himself.

My fist comes down on top of the table, and I clench my jaw until my molars ache.

"You're aware that the Primrose family hates me?"

Justified, some might say, considering I tried to kill the patriarch.

But he started it by killing my father.

"All of Aplana is aware, yes." Alistair shrugs, tapping his nails on the card. "Which is exactly why no one will be expecting you."

# 2

## Lenny

The knocking never ceases.

Someone is always standing on the other side of my closed bedroom door, rapping their knuckles raw. Desperate for a crumb of my attention, or in need of my face for a PR stunt, or a signature for some endorsement or sponsorship.

Going along with whatever Daddy asks of me is my shtick, at this point. I've done it for so long with a smile on my face that no one bats an eye when my lips start to fall.

The facade cracks and my sunny disposition turns sour, but they don't notice.

They just keep coming to me with new things to do.

More people to meet. More ways to make Primrose Realty—and, by extension, Daddy—look good.

Eventually, you have to learn to master the art of multitasking. You turn the pages of an art history magazine with your feet, while a team of makeup artists come to slather your face in creams and glitter.

You paint with a longer sable-hair brush, perfecting a fine-tipped watercolor piece while people pin your hair to your head, unaware of the strands being torn from your scalp.

And while you're stuffed into a cocktail dress for a party you're not remotely interested in attending, you admire the soft, crimson material and dream of blood.

Mama's the first to greet me when I make my way down the split staircase in our foyer, brown eyes twinkling as I get to the last step.

Tonight, for the first time ever, Daddy's throwing a soiree to celebrate my return to our compound. At least, that's the official slogan.

I know better. Men's heated gazes gravitate toward me as I curl my hand around the banister, and the women in the room look like they'd like to rip the bobby pins from my updo. Half of Aplana Island must be here, and they're all intent on one thing: figuring out who Lenny Primrose, the favored Primrose child, wants to date.

As if Daddy would actually let me have some sort of choice in the matter.

Mama reaches out, twisting my shoulders as she inspects my dress. "Well, aren't you just pretty as a peach?"

Her white-blonde bob bounces at her chin as she tilts her head, studying, and I can't help the beads of sweat that percolate along my hairline. Even though I'm sure every hair is in its particular place and my makeup isn't running, my insides squeeze tight, sure she'll find something to nitpick anyway.

My fingers pull at my polyester dress, hiding in case I didn't scrub them clean enough. Before coming down, I held them under the scalding water in my en suite bathroom until my skin felt raw, but I can still feel paint everywhere.

Reaching between us, Mama hooks her pinkie in the little loop of my zipper, which runs all the way down the middle of the dress. Tugging upward, she clicks her tongue, attempting to hide my cleavage.

My entire body tenses up, afraid she'll see the angled paintbrush I have tucked between my breasts.

I don't go anywhere without one, just in case inspiration strikes.

*Just in case.*

The zipper pauses as she releases it, then slides back into its original place, leaving a good portion of my breasts on display without revealing the bristles.

Sighing, she shakes her head and moves back a step. "I guess we'll just have to make do."

Part of me wonders if she's waiting for me to offer to change, even though this is the dress *she* sent with the housekeeper to have me wear tonight.

"You look tired, Helene. Are you not sleeping well?"

A knot forms in my throat. Resentment burns in my lungs—she and Daddy are the only ones who call me by my full name, and I loathe it. "I'm fine, Mama."

Her fingers slide beneath one of my dress straps, hiking it higher up my shoulder. "It looks like you've lost weight, too. Maybe we should send you back to that specialist. What was his name? Dr. Goldstein?"

"No," I say quickly, slipping away from her hold. My heel presses into the step behind me, and I clear my throat as Mama frowns, clearly confused. "I mean, I'm fine. I don't need to see anyone."

"But you look sick—"

"It's probably just nerves from the party." Forcing a smile, I push past her and hop off the steps. "Come find me in an hour and I'll be as good as new."

Part of me believes that when I say it. Or, at least, part of me *wants* to believe it.

Sixty minutes later, though, and I'm plastered against Daddy's side as he regales a crowd of business partners with stories from his undergrad years at Berkeley, more uncomfortable than ever.

My eyes stay on the massive oil portrait hanging above the marble fireplace in the family room. It's an impressionistic view of our immediate family, with me sitting in the middle between my brothers, and our parents behind us looking larger than life.

If I'd known when I'd painted it that one day I'd find their presence suffocating, perhaps I would have shrunk them instead. Every piece of them since, especially of Daddy lately, barely includes his full figure at all.

As if I can change perception and influence with brushstrokes.

A baby grand piano sits off to the side of the fireplace, and a silver-haired woman in a beige gown plays softly, staring out past the crowd. I wonder what the party looks like to those standing on the manicured lawn outside, still waiting to get in.

If the facade is visible through the single-paned windows

lining the downstairs, or if the ocean views beyond our property distract from the ugly reality.

"Of course, I gave up those wild days for the kids," Daddy tells the men, yanking me tighter against his side.

One man cocks an eyebrow, leering at me. He smirks around his beer bottle, and when he leans in, I can't shake the tendril of discomfort that wraps around my spine.

There's something familiar about him. Something off.

I swallow it down, attributing my unease to anxiety. Or maybe it's the fact that I just got done shoveling half a sheet of red velvet cake into my mouth before I got ready, and I'm afraid someone might be able to tell.

"They're hardly kids anymore. Darling little Lenny's all grown up," the man says, nudging my father with his elbow. He licks his lips, and nausea curdles in my stomach.

"Oh, don't remind me." Daddy laughs. "Can you believe she turned twenty-three this year? Had a party while she was off sowing oats in Vermont. First one I didn't get to throw for her."

A snort pushes past my lips, but no one seems to hear.

Or maybe they just ignore it. As usual.

Still, I don't remember the last time Daddy threw me a party, and I hardly count my escape to my aunt's as "sowing oats," when most of what I did there was work at getting rid of nightmares and learn self-defense.

But whatever it takes to keep the Primrose image intact.

"That is unbelievable." The dark-eyed man chuckles, taking a sip of the drink in his hand. "How *was* Vermont, Lenny?"

My throat tightens, a strange feeling wedging between my ribs at the way his gaze seems laser-focused on me, as if waiting for a slip-up.

I can't help but wonder what he knows.

If my father told them everything and is only pretending now.

The answer I give is vague, but it seems to satisfy him nonetheless; after peppering me with a few more questions, they lose interest, and I'm shuffled from one room to the next, greeting everyone we come into contact with.

Daddy keeps his hand tight around my shoulder, or my waist, like he's afraid the crowd might swallow me whole. Frankly, the way they congregate around us like hyenas desperate for scraps makes me think he's onto something.

Deep down, I wish I didn't know why my parents decided to throw the party. It'd be so much easier to enjoy if I wasn't concerned with over-analyzing every eligible bachelor we meet, aware that my father's lifelong threat of pairing me off with someone is coming to fruition before my eyes.

He introduces me to politicians, CEOs, and foreign leaders. Men that any woman would probably feel lucky to have the attention of, and yet after each conversation all I feel is grimy.

These men run in the same circles as my ex, Preston, and no doubt are aware of the scandal that sent me to Vermont months ago. They don't necessarily understand the nature of everything that happened, but I don't think they'd care, anyway.

They're just interested in getting Lenny Primrose in the sack. Testing her to see how far she bends before she breaks.

Eventually, Daddy goes off to mingle with some of the Primrose Realty board members, and the weight of everyone's judgment in my own home bears down on me. I'm not a stranger to having the attention of the public, but for some reason right now it feels a thousand times more intimate.

And a million times more terrifying.

A sharp, sudden pang rips through my chest and settles in my gut as the crowd watches me. Their eyes are peeled, as if waiting for me to crumble.

I bite down on the inside of my cheek until the taste of copper floods my mouth.

*Two breaths in, three breaths out.*

Silently, I curse my older brothers for not bothering to attend the party tonight. Mass surveillance would be easier to navigate if they were here, but the boys get off scot-free when it comes to family duties.

Straightening my spine, I stalk from the room, feigning nonchalance as I make my way through the house.

When I was younger, the blue-gray walls and stuffy white furniture felt like a maze, and I spent a lot of my free time tracing my steps from one hall to the next, trying to memorize the massive square footage.

Like other houses in the area, ours always seemed far too big for just five people. Even the forced coziness brought on by nautical themes, bright hardwood floors, and balconies off every bedroom couldn't erase the overwhelming emptiness.

Then again, maybe that was why my parents bought the mansion in the first place. It's much easier to ignore your demons when you're not running into them on your way to the bathroom.

Passing quickly through the chef kitchen off the corner of the west wing, I push through the door into a hidden stairwell. It winds up four stories, and I come out onto one of the two towers decorating the house.

Salty sea air smacks my face as I step out onto the balcony. Leaning up against the wooden railing, I scan the length of our property slowly, letting my eyes rove over every inch of the landscaped acreage.

Pockets of light from solar lamps illuminate the grounds, and I watch people mingle below, blissfully unaware of the immense unhappiness that exists within the halls of the mansion. Like ghosts, bound to haunt the living for all of eternity.

I'm not sure how long I stand up there before a shuffling sound draws my attention, and by the time I whirl around, a shadowy figure is lunging at me, hands seizing my throat.

Panic swells in my chest, stealing the air from my lungs as the attacker squeezes, leaning so I'm bending backward over the balcony railing. Harsh gasps tear from my mouth as I try to suck in oxygen, but the person increases the pressure until my vision darkens.

"You think you can run from us?" the attacker growls, shoving his pelvis against me. I feel something hard against my hip, and the presence of it sends my heart into a frenzy. "Darling little Lenny has debts to pay, and I'm gonna make sure you stay fucking put this time."

It takes me a moment to recognize the voice as the man from my father's earlier circle—and a second longer to remember him from the night my entire life flipped over on its axis. Fear invades my bloodstream like a virus, and I renew my struggle against him, kicking and scratching at his hands on my neck.

One drops to the zipper of my dress and yanks hard, baring my breasts to him. He cups the right one with a meaty paw, squeezing my nipple so hard I cry out from the pain.

His free hand slaps over my mouth, and I bite down on whatever part of his palm I can fit between my teeth;

swearing under his breath, the man jerks back, releasing me just enough to shove me onto the ground.

I land on my hands and knees, the force of my fall knocking the wind from my chest. The paintbrush slips out from between my breasts, clattering to the floor, and I only have a second to consider my impulse before it turns into action.

"I'm gonna enjoy fucking you up again," the man says, chuckling darkly behind me.

Fisting the paintbrush, I break off the end on the concrete floor, leaving the handle jagged.

Hands grab my shoulders, and then he's tugging roughly, turning me over to face him. I roll with the movement, letting him think I've lost the will to fight.

When I'm on my back, I grip the brush tight, lift my arm, and drive it into his neck with every ounce of strength I can muster.

Blood spurts immediately from the side where the brush protrudes, and the man's eyes go wide, his hands coming up to touch the site. My chest heaves, and I stare up at him while he gapes, trying to place him in my memory.

I can't, and it infuriates me even more.

A choking sound comes from the back of his throat, and I use his shock to shove him away, squirming out from under his weight.

The man collapses onto his side and yanks the brush out, placing his hand over the wound as if that might help. If anything, it just seems to make the blood pump out faster.

Chest heaving, I reach down and pull my zipper back up, adrenaline racing through my veins. I'm covered in crimson like some sort of psychotic murderer, and all I can do is stare at the man and wonder what the fuck I've done.

"Oh god oh god oh god," I chant softly, blinking over and over, as if that might change the reality before me.

"Seems a bit counterproductive to be praying now, love. Don't you think?"

My head snaps up as a tall man in an all-black suit steps onto the balcony, hands in his pockets and curly, dark brown hair blowing slightly with the wind.

But it's his eyes I focus on. Deep violet one step and impossible, angry blue the next.

For some reason, I recognize them.

Recognize the British accent.

And I know I'm in trouble.

# 3

SEA FOAM green eyes stare up at me, wide and unfocused like two shards of opaque glass.

Strands of golden-brown hair have fallen from the intricate bun at the nape of her neck, and her red dress sits awkwardly on her tits. Her chest heaves, a high tide waxing and waning as she gulps down mouthfuls of air.

Deep red stains mar her chest, painting her skin like a serial killer's wet dream.

But as I step closer, it's not panic I see.

It's *excitement.*

Or at least a close cousin to the emotion, radiating from her tanned skin in harsh waves.

I'm not exactly sure what I've just stumbled upon, but I'll admit I'm no longer cross over the detour I took to get here.

On a reflex, my arm extends, fingers spreading outward. She blinks.

Doesn't move.

I clear my throat and withdraw my offer, adjusting the necktie at the collar of my suit. All black, like Alistair suggested, to keep me as inconsequential as possible. Makes it far easier to hide in the shadows and prey on the unsuspecting.

"Well, this is a bit awkward, isn't it?" My brows arch, and I wait for her to respond. After a few more moments of stillness, I exhale, step over the corpse, and lean against the balcony. "Not every day you witness a murder. Which of us do you think should tell the party downstairs?"

Tapping my fingers along the wooden beam, I scan the landscaped yard. My eyes rove over sprawling green grass, circling around the cobblestone courtyard and the maze of hedges that lead to a secret garden and the beach beyond.

You can't access the shore unless you scale the stone wall surrounding Primrose Manor, but it's there, nonetheless.

Most of the guests linger inside, where they're more likely to uncover family secrets.

I'm not interested in them.

I already know them all.

What I want is *revenge.*

And while I'd planned to make patriarch Tom my target, I don't necessarily mind starting with his beloved daughter instead.

This path promises much more *fun.*

Heaving a long sigh, I bend so my forearms rest on the rail. The girl exists in my peripheral, still mostly unmoving, although now I see she's staring at the dead man. Studying him like some sort of science project.

"It might behoove you to have a witness explain the turn of events." Pausing, I wait for her to refute this. Still, she doesn't. "Although, I can't be *certain* of what transpired before you stabbed the lad. Perhaps it's best if you make the announcement. Party's yours, after all."

From the corner of my eye, I see her chin jerk in my direction; the movement is infinitesimal. Something you'd miss if you weren't paying the utmost attention.

But I can't possibly see anything else.

"How do you know who I am?"

Frowning, I turn around. "Are you saying you don't know who *I* am?"

Again, she just blinks.

My eyes narrow, something irritable percolating in my gut.

Taking a step forward, I reach up to stroke my chin, letting my sleeve ride up a bit. A leather corded bracelet is tied around my wrist, pinned together by a black W-shaped charm.

If she recognizes the Wolfe family insignia, she doesn't let on. For some reason, that irks me far more than her previous silence.

She was there the night I almost finished her father off. The ensuing arrest and trial were quite publicized on the island, and my face was plastered everywhere for years to keep the general public informed about the monster living among them.

Thing is, they don't know even the bloody half of it.

"You're damaging my ego, love." Blowing out a breath, I crouch down and inspect the body. Blond hair sticks to his face, perpetually frozen in shock. "Here I'd been hoping our little tête-à-tête would be informative, but it appears you enjoy lying too much."

"I'm not lying, and I don't really give a shit about your ego."

"Well, that's terribly rude. My ego could save your pretty little arse right about now."

Turning my head, I meet her soft gaze.

"I don't need saving." Her eyebrows knit together, a glare contorting delicate features.

One side of my mouth curls up. "Don't you?"

Pushing to my feet, I circle around her slowly. Each crunch of my boots on the concrete has her curling into herself.

Almost like a lioness preparing for an attack.

"It was self-defense," she says, and I see her right hand twitch.

Just once, then again in the direction of her victim, and for a moment I wonder if she's finally cracking. Going back to the scene of the crime and experiencing fear without the barrier of surprise.

I pause at her back, my eyes drifting over the length of her body; in this position, she's practically presenting herself to me on a platter, and I'm man enough to admit that her gentle curves in that tight red dress affect me.

Unwilling to entertain the lust even as it scrapes at my esophagus, I force my gaze to the back of her head. It shifts slightly, and I can feel her searching. Seeking me out so she can keep up her defenses.

Perhaps Tom Primrose's puppet is more self-aware than the tabloids give her credit for.

"Who's going to believe you?" I ask, reaching down to brush a strand of hair off her shoulder. I shouldn't touch her at all, but my arm feels compelled to see if she's as soft as she looks.

My chest tightens as the silken lock brushes over my fingertips.

*Even softer.*

"Maybe if you'd rammed the heel of your hand into his face or pushed him off the balcony. People would have a much easier time swallowing that tidbit as truth." Tilting my head, I glance at the broken paintbrush lying on the ground beside the man's hand, having rolled out of it when he lost consciousness. "But you came *prepared.* The move was calculated... at least, what I saw of it. Unfortunately, they'll find that far more fascinating than the nature of your encounter beforehand."

Her breathing becomes less labored as the seconds pass. Soon, the music from the party downstairs filters through our air, drowning out nearly everything else.

My shoulders lift in a half-shrug. "It's okay to admit you were out for blood tonight, Ms. Primrose. I know I was."

More silence. Makes the air thick, rife with omissions.

I suppose she's back to ignoring me.

The sound of her fingernails scraping against the ground isn't audible, but I feel it in my spine, nonetheless. With a smirk, I walk as lightly as possible in the direction she's inching, zeroing in on the weapon so our timing connects.

My shoes halt directly in front of the brush just as her fingers wrap around it. They curl tight around the handle, and she's already mid-strike when the toe of my boot swipes out, pressing down on the back of her hand.

Securing it to the ground and trapping the brush beneath.

"I wouldn't do that if I were you."

Tipping her chin up, she glares. Flames whip violently behind her irises, darkening the glassy hues. When she tries to pull away, I push down harder.

She winces, though I'm not applying enough pressure to do any actual damage. "If you're going to kill me, just do it."

"Why would I do that?"

A pause. Her lips part, her tiny pink tongue darting out to wet the bottom one.

Growing weary of her refusal to answer my questions, I pinch the side of my slacks and crouch down, draping my forearms over my knees as I meet her at eye level. My foot stays, keeping her hand in place and her on her knees.

Hatred burns through her features as we stare at one another, and my cock jerks behind the zipper of my slacks at the rawness of it all. She doesn't even know how much she *should* hate me; it's pure instinct at this point, something primal that drives her to react so strongly to my presence.

"I lied."

My eyebrows arch, surprise etching into the planes of my face. "Oh?"

Folding her lips together, she gives a tiny nod. "I know who you are."

The breath stalls in my lungs, and I wait for more. Unsurprisingly, it doesn't come, and I'm starting to wonder if this woman offers anything unless held under extreme duress.

"I see." My foot slips back, sliding away from her hand, which remains on the paintbrush. "And?"

She looks up. "And what?"

"Aren't you afraid?"

I'm not sure what I expect her to say, but it's certainly not what I get. Her head tilts, as if considering my question, and then she's pushing to her feet. Dusting dirt from the front of her dress and adjusting the way her tits sit in the fabric.

The movement is slow. Discerning.

Anxiety floods my nervous system, washing out rationale where this girl is concerned, and I'm not even sure why. Something about her is bloody unsettling.

I move as she does, unfolding myself so I'm still towering over her.

She takes a step forward, shoulders straight, and comes toward me until our bodies are almost touching. Notes of vanilla and something whimsically floral waft around me as she reaches out, taking my hand in hers.

It takes me a moment longer than it should to realize what she's doing.

Uncurling my fingers, I'm trapped inside her hypnotic gaze while she presses something into my palm. Then she's folding each digit back and pressing my fist to my chest.

When she releases and steps away, it feels like she takes all the air with her.

"It may be your word against mine," she says, her lips curving upward. "But my word holds *much* more weight than that of the man who tried to kill my father. I don't think anyone will have a hard time believing you're the culprit, especially now that your fingerprints are everywhere. The victim, the scenery..."

Trailing off, she cocks a brow and nods her chin at my hand. "The *weapon.*"

Glancing down, I unroll my fist to see she's tucked the paintbrush inside, effectively tying me to the crime scene as much as she is. And while technically I could scrub it clear of me before she even had time to return to the party, I have to admit I'm intrigued by the little puppet.

I point the sharp, bloody edge of the brush at her. "I could just kill you. My word against that of the recently departed."

Taking another step back, she shrugs, smoothing her hands down over her stomach. All confidence, except for the slight tremor racking her fingertips.

"You could," she concedes, even as she puts more distance between us. Reaching the door to the stairwell, she grips the knob in one hand and twists, pushing it open. "But that's not why you came here tonight, is it?"

# 4

## *Lenny*

Narrowly avoiding contact with guests lining the halls on the main level of the house, I make it back to my bedroom.

Somehow.

By the grace of God, maybe.

Locking the door behind me, I flatten my back against the wood and let out a laugh of indignance.

*Sure, Len.*

*More like the grace of Jonas Wolfe.*

A man not known for mercy or softness. Who literally just threatened to take me out of this planet's rotation when he realized I intended to stab him the same as I did my attacker.

It wouldn't surprise me if Jonas fancies himself God. All the men in that world, the criminal underground that he and a small percentage of our island thrive in, have that complex. Humanity is expendable to them, and they toy with fate just because they can.

My father is one of those men.

Always has been.

Twelve years ago, I didn't understand why someone had broken in and shot Daddy. Why they left him on the floor in his office to bleed out from the wound instead of trying to get him help.

When he crawled from the east wing of our house to the kitchen, staining the carpet beneath him to the point where it would eventually be replaced with expensive polished wood, I didn't know what was happening.

I was terrified. Of losing him, of his attacker coming back to finish the rest of us off.

Now, though, I get it. I've had a front-row show to the sort of things Daddy is involved in, and the company he keeps. I don't know the specifics, but I'm aware enough to know Primrose Realty is hardly your run-of-the-mill investment firm.

Even if he tries his best to keep business separate from family, it bleeds over because the weight of evil is too much to contain.

Should I have left my attacker's dead body with Jonas, knowing who he is and that he likely came by tonight with the express intent of trying to ruin my family?

Probably not. But what was I supposed to do, lug the corpse around myself?

I'm certain that anything I did with the body would only arouse suspicion. If they find it after Jonas disposes of it, Daddy's much less likely to care. For some reason, homicide is common in his circle.

Kicking my Louis Vuittons to the corner of the room, I unzip my dress and shake out of it. The drapes in front of my windows and balcony door are drawn, so I hobble quickly to the shower in my en suite bathroom, pausing to look in the mirror hanging between the double porcelain sinks.

My chest grows tight as I take in the blood splashed across my skin. Tingles shoot down my spine, electrifying my nerve endings.

They say murder changes you. Fundamentally.

Makes you a completely different person.

As I step into the shower and scrub the evidence away, I can't help but wonder what the indifference buzzing through my veins means.

*"It's okay to admit you were out for blood tonight, Ms. Primrose. I know I was."*

Jonas's words from the balcony whisper down my back, goose bumps chasing their gentle caress. His violet gaze flashes across my mind, brilliant and striking as he looked right through me. Down to my core, eyeing the dirty soul I keep stuffed where no one can find it.

Not only did he find it, but he witnessed me at my most vulnerable and compromising. On my knees, covered in someone else's blood.

And he didn't even wince. Just stumbled upon us and accepted the situation as it was, albeit tauntingly.

Maybe that should unsettle me more, but for some reason it was sort of… comforting, being discovered like that. Like cracking yourself wide open and letting someone see the ugliest parts of you, and them not running away in fear or disgust.

Fascination seemed to spark in his gaze as he stalked around me, exactly like the predator everyone says he is.

I'm not sure what to do with the fact that it didn't terrify me in the least.

After getting out of the shower, I change into a pair of silk pajamas and climb into my upholstered sleigh bed, yanking the white down comforter to my chin. My hand slips beneath one of the pillows, feeling for the box of charcoal pieces and sketchpad I keep hidden there.

Just as I go to pull them out, the door swings open, and my heart sputters as the man I loathe strolls right in.

Closing the door with the heel of his leather loafers, Preston drags a hand through his blond hair, brown eyes seeking mine immediately.

Sitting up, I hold the comforter to my chest and scoot back. "What the hell are you doing here?"

One of his hands comes to his chest, feigning offense. "Are you not happy to see me, bug?"

The nickname makes my stomach cramp. I grit my teeth and cross my arms, scowling as he continues to advance on me. When he reaches the edge of the bed, he braces one knee on the mattress and unbuttons his gray suit jacket.

My toes curl, and not in a good way.

"Don't call me that," I snap, "and don't come any closer. I told you I didn't want to see you."

Preston sighs. He *always* sighs, like I'm an inconvenience to him even though he's the one who invited himself in.

"Come on, *bug*, it's been months. Guantanamo Bay deals in less excruciating torture."

"I don't *care* how long it's been. That's the entire point. We broke up, we aren't supposed to see each other."

My lungs constrict, squeezing until pain flares, making it difficult to breathe. Being this close to him dredges up *everything* I'm otherwise able to pretend I don't remember.

*Hands on my body, roving and stroking. Too many to keep track of, although I'm sure it's more than I agreed to.*

*Damp breath scraping across the back of my neck and the insides of my thighs.*

*Pain. Excruciating, mind-bending pain. They swear I won't feel anything, or that I won't remember, but I want to know which one it is. I'd prefer the comfort of both, but even that feels like grasping at straws.*

In the end, neither was true.

I felt everything, and the memories remain.

Preston's hand finds the footboard of the bed, fingers curling around the cushioned edge as his features darken.

His mouth mashes into a thin, firm line, and he glares at me.

"We aren't broken up, Lenny. I didn't agree to that."

"Yeah, because it wasn't up for discussion." Slipping one leg off the bed, I let myself balance in limbo between fight or flight. Prepared for either but trying to wait for him to make the first move.

His eyebrows draw in. One finger taps against the bed.

"How many times do I have to apologize?"

The comforter comes with me when my other foot finds the carpeted floor. I clutch it to my chest, keeping the barrier between us. In the five years I've known him, Preston Covington has always maintained an air of unpredictability about him.

It's not uncommon for him to be fine one second and

utterly unhinged the next, nor is it uncommon for him to take the switch out on the people around him.

For three years, I withstood the constant changes silently. Daddy loves him, and for a time I thought I loved them both, which meant putting up with a lot of shit.

Until *that night*, when my endurance finally ran out.

Favors turned to manipulation.

*Evil.*

Wrapping one arm around my waist, I press my fingers into the soft tissue of my abdomen, just below my belly button. Trying to soothe the pang of despair Preston's existence causes.

"There isn't an apology in this world big enough to cover what you..." My voice catches, pitching high and tight, and I clear my throat. "You can't say sorry and erase what happened."

"I'm not trying to erase it, baby."

Fire surges into my throat, singeing my tongue and stealing the words from my lips.

He steps around the bed, eyes softening as he extends his arms. "I'm just sorry. I'm tired of being without you."

My stomach flips, and my eyes burn. "Stop."

His frown deepens. "No, Lenny. I won't. You think I'm gonna stand here and watch while your father pairs you off with someone else? You're supposed to be with me."

"How do you know that's what he's trying to do?"

Preston scoffs, still moving toward me. I back up, hitting the wall and wishing I could disappear into it.

"The guys downstairs won't shut the fuck up about it. Everyone wants to tame Lenny Primrose, make her their bitch and get Tom's company in the process. It's all about status and money for them, and your father's eating it up, letting them vie for a shot at your hand."

He stops just in front of me, and I smell it when the toes of his shoes touch my bare feet: alcohol. Preston's greatest vice.

I grit my teeth as his vodka-laced breath assaults my face, trying not to grimace.

Reaching up, he curls a loose strand of my hair around his middle finger. "They can't love you like I do, Lenny bug."

"Get out." I flinch when he tugs, hating myself for showing weakness.

A small snort comes from his nose. "Don't say that. You don't mean it."

My hands come up, dropping the blanket and shoving at his chest. I'm not sure if I catch him off guard, or if he's more loaded than I realized, but whatever the case, he stumbles with the push, and I glide past him.

Darting to the other side of the room, I grab the doorknob in my hand and yank it open, standing to the side so he has enough room to leave unimpeded.

For a moment, he just stays there. Staring. Disbelieving, if his wide eyes are any indication.

"You want to date one of those fuckers downstairs, don't you?" He scoffs, moving to where I'm standing without getting too close. "Still nothing but a dirty fucking slut, I see. Guess you don't need me to help with that anymore."

A chasm breaks open in my chest, sucking in all my internal organs and crushing them into dust when it closes. I pinch my eyes shut, steeling myself against the way his words hurt.

Refusing to give him any more of my time, or tears.

"Leave." Straightening my spine, I peel back my eyelids and raise a brow. "Now."

The vein in the center of his forehead bulges, seeming to throb with every passing second. I know the heir to a pipeline fortune isn't used to not getting what he wants, but I'm no longer in a position where I care.

An image of blood and death crosses my mind, giving me pause as he steps out into the hall. Classical music drifts up the split staircase, indicating the party still rages below, and I can't help but wonder if Jonas has disposed of the body by now.

What I wouldn't give to kill him all over again.

To kill every single fucker who laid a hand on me months ago. Made one night into something twisted and changed my life for good.

The urge to start with Preston is almost overwhelming.

My hand clamps down around the doorknob until it aches.

Sighing, Preston shakes his head and exits, pausing at the threshold. "Your father will give you back to me if I ask. I didn't think it'd have to come to this, but I'm not letting you go, Lenny. You belong with me."

I don't say anything, and after a moment, he rolls his eyes and finally leaves. Slamming the door behind him, I turn the lock and suck in a deep breath, willing the tears away. The memories flood my brain, playing on repeat until it feels like I'm suffocating.

Clutching at my chest, I tear my pajamas off, trying to get air. To cool down before I combust as fear and misery culminate in my soul, ripping it apart limb-by-limb.

Ducking into my walk-in closet, I shove aside a dozen pairs of shoes and dig around for the box I keep hidden in the back. Removing the lid, I exhale as my fingers meet familiar cellophane, and immediately get to work removing the contents from each little baggie.

It's been a while. Years, in fact, since I indulged in multiple urges in a single night.

But right now, the temporary rush feels worth it.

# 5

ALISTAIR SPOTS me almost immediately as I rejoin the foray.

He stands in a corner of the great room, holding a crystal tumbler with two fingers while a man with a scraggly goatee repeatedly claps him on the shoulder, spittle flying everywhere as he speaks.

Double-checking myself in a hall mirror, I tug at the lapels of my suit jacket and greet them. My brother's eyebrows raise, perhaps intrigued by my sudden return, though he still looks thoroughly unimpressed by everything else.

I have to admit, the party isn't what I'd been imagining,

either. Save for the grandeur of the Primrose mansion with its glittering chandeliers, luxury furniture, and the massive windows covering three-fourths of the grayish walls, the place manages a complete boredom that I find myself growing quite tired of.

Or perhaps I'm craving a certain level of excitement, and any hope of recapturing what happened on the balcony has already been squandered.

"Brother." Alistair nods at me, then points his glass at the other man. "Mr. Rafferty, my brother Jonas. Rafferty owns the marina on the south end, and you've probably heard of Jonas's pub, The Flaming Chariot?"

"Ah, yes. The infamous bar owner." Mr. Rafferty tugs at his goatee once before extending his hand. I don't take it, and he shifts his weight, dropping it back to his side. "I'm surprised to see you here, though. Without a pair of handcuffs, that is."

"I can assure you my bedroom habits have nothing to do with what parties I attend."

Mr. Rafferty's face flushes, and he glances at my brother. "That isn't what I meant—"

Alistair chuckles. "Jonas was my plus-one. It's a bad look to show up to these events without them, wouldn't you say, Lionel?"

The two men stare at each other for a beat, and Mr. Rafferty clears his throat, apparently uncomfortable with the direct spotlight.

"Well, I wouldn't bring *competition*." Mr. Rafferty shakes his head. "Aren't you worried you'll be pitted against each other for the Primrose girl's hand?"

"Neither of us are interested in dating a Primrose," I say.

"Of course, *you* aren't," Mr. Rafferty replies, laughing.

"Tom would probably rather sell her to the mob than let her date the likes of you."

My jaw clenches, but I force it to relax. It's obvious the man is trying to rile me up, though I'm not sure why.

Nor am I sure why it's working.

Stuffing my hands in my pockets, I steal a quick glance around the room. "She should be so lucky."

"She would probably do wonders for your bid for senator, though," Mr. Rafferty tells Alistair, once again clapping him on the shoulder.

For a split second, Alistair winces. It's fleeting, almost imperceptible, but his mouth seizes up and his shoulders stiffen enough that I notice. Taking a sip of his drink, his stature returns to normal, though he refuses to meet my gaze.

"I'm more interested in how you'll help my campaign," Alistair tells the man, raising an eyebrow. "Have your assistant call my office Monday morning, and we'll set something up."

My body hums, aware that meetings with my brother usually go one of two ways. The fact that he's bringing it up with me around tells me everything I need to know about its nature.

Rafferty hesitates, glancing at me from the corner of his eye. "About that... I'm not sure aligning myself with your cause is in my best interest currently, as I'm seeking to expand ventures into the political sector myself."

Alistair frowns, and I let go of the unease his grimace caused, pushing it down and welcoming what I know comes next. Rocking back on my heels, I smother a grin, trying not to let the excitement bleed through.

If I can't exact my revenge on the Primroses tonight, at least I get something out of attending.

"We had a deal, Lionel."

A hand goes to the back of his neck, and Mr. Rafferty has the gall to look sheepish. "I understand that, Alistair, but—"

"Your Honor," my brother corrects.

"What?"

"*Your Honor*," Alistair repeats. "I'm your mayor, Mr. Rafferty, and you can address me as such. Just like you can keep your end of the deal we struck moments before my brother's presence made you antsy."

My grin breaks through, and I take a step closer. "Do I make you nervous, Mr. Rafferty?"

"O-of course not."

"You *sound* nervous."

Even though we're surrounded by party people, Aplana Island's elite, no one else seems to notice me. I can't tell if I like the lack of recognition or not, but when fear sparks in the other man's dark gaze, contentment bursts through my insides like a raging rapid.

Reaching out, I clamp my hand around his shoulder the way he keeps doing to Alistair, and I squeeze until the man shifts, biting his lip as he tries to get away.

"And you should be. If you fail to show up Monday, I shall find you. Deliver you personally."

The man gulps, his Adam's apple bobbing beneath layers of excess skin, but finally nods.

I pat his cheek harder than necessary, reveling in his grimace. "Good boy."

We leave after that, getting into my brother's town car before anyone happens to notice the unwanted guest in their midst. As we exit the curved drive's porte cochere, I glance out the rear window and scan the Cape Cod-esque home front one last time.

Its pale blue siding and gray rooftops don't show as well this time of day, but their image lingers with me regardless.

A window on the second story catches my eye, and I look up just as a silhouette appears behind the curtain, barely visible in the pale moonlight.

I've spent years memorizing the layout of the house, so I know the owner of the window immediately. Even if I didn't, though, I think I'd recognize her figure anywhere.

It's the kind that burns itself into your memory, like an invisible brand you can never dig up.

"Where'd you disappear to tonight?" Alistair asks, not looking up while he types something on his phone. "I noticed Tom Primrose was alive and well when we left."

"For now," I say, drinking my fill of the silhouette one last time before our driver leaves through the wrought iron gate, obscuring my view. "Didn't feel like explaining why I killed the host to Aplana's best and brightest."

He doesn't say anything else, and I don't offer more. Besides, he'll find out where I ventured off to when they find Richard Stiles's body hanging from the rafters in the Primrose's five-car garage in the morning.

GROWING UP, my father cultivated a myriad of aspirations.

Keeping a wife wasn't one of them, so Alistair's mum raised him on her own, and mine vanished not long after we moved to the States.

Criminal activity, though, he excelled in, using his pub as a front for whatever organizations he was involved with.

From political cover-ups to actual organized crime, The Flaming Chariot catered to many sleazy operatives over the years, and the general public steered clear of it.

When my father died, ownership of the pub—and his criminal dealings—was passed along to me, though I lost the plot a bit when my stint in jail threatened everything the Wolfe family had spent centuries building.

Luckily, a man known to be far more dangerous than me decided to have mercy, for once in his life. He bailed me out, got my sentence reduced, and rescued the pub before it could be collected in civil assets forfeiture.

Unfortunately, that meant I owed the man, and I don't like debts. So, for years I worked as Dr. Kal Anderson's associate, part fixer and part private investigator, while he figured out a way to extract himself from the Mafia.

Eventually, he did—by stealing his don's daughter and forcing her to marry him.

But that's not my story to tell.

In the five years since, I've never seen the bloke happier. Or, as happy as he allows himself to appear in public. Even now, sitting in the booth across from me sipping a Jack and coke, his features are drawn and guarded, his black hair swept back neatly over his head while his dark eyes scan the article in front of him.

The black trench coat he wears and his permanent scowl make him look like the formidable god of the Underworld that everyone sees him as. But there's a softness to him, too. Something gentler, or less irritable as the pub music pulses around us, that wasn't present before he got married.

You'd never guess the man has a young wife and two kids at home by just looking at him, but after being his closest—

and only—confidant for most of my adult life, I can certainly see the signs.

Kal Anderson is happy, and he bloody well deserves it.

Setting his glass on the wooden table, he throws an arm over the back of the red leather booth, looking up at me. "So, the party was a success, I take it?"

I cock an eyebrow. "Tom Primrose is still alive, isn't he?"

"We both know that isn't going to last, if the message you left in his garage is any indication." Tapping the edge of the article, he shrugs. "Couldn't have been all bad if you found time to cover up a crime for someone else."

My chest tightens, and I blow out a breath, reaching for the cigar resting by my elbow. Taking a slow puff, I let the smoke fill my lungs before releasing it slowly, watching it billow up in front of us.

"What do you mean?"

He gives me a pointed look. "Man found hanging in the Primrose family's garage, even though no one saw him leave the main house? That has you written all over it."

"Right. So, why a cover up?"

"Multiple lacerations to the face and scalp, as well as a likely fatal one to the throat." He rubs his chin with his palm. "You don't leave that many variations of trauma for the public to see. Either you're sending a message or covering something up."

"Can't it be both?"

Palming his drink, he brings it to his lips, nodding as he gulps the amber liquid down. "I guess, but that still begs the question: why? You were in Tom's house, I can't think of a better opportunity for you to strike."

When I don't reply immediately, losing myself in the memory of my actions the other night and how I thought waiting was a good idea, a slow shit-eating grin spreads across Kal's face.

"*Oh.* I see, then." His glass hits the table, impossibly loud, and one of my waitresses, Amber, comes over to refill it, before scampering away. "So, what's her name?"

I suck on the end of my cigar, scoffing. "Who?"

"Come on, Wolfe. Men like us don't abandon our plights for just anyone. She must be special."

It's true—at least, it appears that way. I've certainly thought of little else but Ms. Lenny Primrose since the party, allowing myself to entertain the image of her tits caked in the blood of her enemy while emptying my cock at night.

But I didn't *abandon* anything for her. I just... postponed.

"I don't even know her well enough for her to *be* anything but a nuisance."

"Let me guess," he says, bracing his elbows on the table. "Brunette, killer figure. Young. Draws the attention of the room without even trying?"

My eyes narrow, and I balance my cigar on its ashtray. "How in the bloody hell can you possibly know that?"

His grin widens, threatening to show teeth. "Because I think she just walked in."

# 6

"This is a bad idea."

"So you keep saying." My brother Palmer tosses me an irritated look. He reaches up, adjusting the collar of his boyfriend's plum button-down shirt. "You need a new catch-phrase, swan."

Troy grins at the nickname, nudging me with his elbow. "Swan?"

"Len did ballet before we moved to Aplana, and they put on a production of Swan Lake one year," Palmer answers. "Broke her ankle the night of curtain call and ended up not being able to perform."

"Naturally, my brothers have been making fun of me for it ever since."

Troy laughs, leaning against the bar top. "Your brothers are assholes, Lenny. But I like it. *Swan*. It suits you, 'cause you're, like... graceful and shit."

I hold up my hand. "Don't even think about adding it to your vocabulary. I'd suggest forgetting the nickname right now, actually."

"Yeah, or she'll peck your eyes out," Palmer snickers, pressing a kiss to my temple as he shuffles around.

Sliding onto the stool beside me, Palmer waves the bartender over, then combs a large hand through his sandy locks. If not for the shoulder-length hair and the hoop piercing in his left nostril, it'd be easy to mistake him for his identical twin, Cash.

When they were younger, they were practically interchangeable, which they took advantage of by switching places. We had a constant stream of private tutors replacing one another over the years because of the prank; while my brothers were identical in both appearance and interests, their personalities and academic abilities differed greatly.

Palmer had a mild case of dyslexia, and Cash struggled with algebra. Tutors were always getting mixed up and frustrated because they couldn't keep track of what the boys were learning individually.

Eventually, they were shoved together and taught that way while I remained alone in my studies.

Serves me right, I guess, for gravitating toward my parents over them.

The bartender pauses in front of us, bracing his palms on the counter. The bottom half of an anchor tattoo peeks out from the sleeve of his Deftones T-shirt, and he cocks an eyebrow.

"What can I get ya?"

I open my mouth to decline anything, but Palmer interrupts. "Two shots of tequila, and a raspberry margarita."

Nodding, the bartender doesn't even spare me another look for confirmation before he spins away, heading to the other end to speak to more customers.

"What part of 'I'm not drinking tonight' did you not understand?" I ask, glaring at my brother.

He chuckles, brushing some lint off his acid washed denim jacket. "If you don't drink, you're not gonna be any fun."

"Very brotherly of you to peer pressure me."

Daddy's words from before we left this evening echo in my mind—his insistence I pick one of the men from his list, so he can move on with cleaning up my image—and I wonder if the men in my life are capable of doing anything *but* pressuring me.

Rolling his eyes, Palmer twirls his phone in his hands. "I'm just *saying.* You've been wound so tight since the party, you're bound to explode any second if you don't let loose a little. What better place than here, with your big brother and his lover to watch over you?"

My nose scrunches up at his use of the word lover, but I don't argue. He's not wrong, anyway. The events at the party the other night, coupled with Richard Stiles's postmortem discovery and the whole dating situation, has left me on edge.

And not in a good way.

The bartender comes back and slings our drinks down, leaving a mason jar with pink liquid in front of me. I grab it with both hands and bring it close, if only to keep anyone else from touching it.

"Bottoms up," Troy cheers, tilting his head back and downing his shot in one gulp.

Palmer mimics the action, pulling Troy in for a sloppy kiss to celebrate. My brother threads his fingers into Troy's dark, braided hair, grinning into him. When they pull apart, they turn and look at me expectantly.

Chewing on my bottom lip, I scan the crowd again, searching for any semblance of recognition. A phone aimed in our direction, whispers between friends hidden behind hands—something that will not only alert our parents that I'm out being a delinquent, but Preston, too.

Not to mention the fact that we shouldn't even be in *this* bar at all; The Flaming Chariot is strictly off-limits to Primrose family members, and after my encounter with its owner the other night, I have double the reason not to patronize.

"What happened to you, swan?" Palmer slides his arm around my shoulders, pulling me into his side. "You used to be fun. When did you become such a dud?"

*Eight and a half months ago.* "Probably around the same time I broke my ankle."

"Jeez, Palm. She's not a dud for wanting to be responsible." Troy reaches across my brother, patting my hands.

Palmer waves him off, leaning into me. "Whatever. Tell me you're at least hooking up with someone tonight."

I just stare at him.

An exasperated sound escapes his throat, and he spins around on his stool. "I might as well have dragged Cash out."

Like Cash would ever come out the night before he's due in court.

Offering a sympathetic smile, Troy takes Palmer's hand

and tugs him into a standing position. "I'm gonna take this one to dance and blow off some steam. You okay over here on your own?"

Nodding, I watch over my shoulder as the couple disappears into the smoky atmosphere, blending in with the twisted limbs in the middle of the bar. A country song crackles over the loudspeaker, and I smother a grin when Palmer breaks free from Troy's grip to begin a line dance.

Bringing the mason jar to my lips, I take a small sip. The acidic, fruity flavor bursts on my tongue, and I swallow it down before it has a chance to settle in.

If I let myself think about how much I enjoy it, I won't be able to stop after just one drink. Out here, surrounded by people chomping at the bit to sell a story about Lenny Primrose losing control in public, I can't afford to indulge.

*See, Daddy? I* can *control my urges, after all.*

I'm alone for approximately two minutes before I get bored, and the margarita becomes far more enticing than sitting here watching the dance floor.

A year ago, maybe I'd interact with the others sitting at the bar with me, but right now all I want to do is temporarily forget the bad shit in my life. If I talk to other people, the subject of my demise is bound to come up.

Normally I refrain because it makes me feel like Preston, but maybe it wouldn't hurt to let loose a little. It's been a *long* time, and I think after everything I deserve to have a little fun.

Three drinks and two shots later, the bartender comes over to check on me, and I feel him hesitate as he looks me over, maybe just realizing who I am now that I'm by myself.

"Your friends leave?" he asks, and even in the dim lighting I can see the striking blue of his eyes.

Lifting a shoulder, I nod. At least, I'm pretty sure I do. "Not exciting enough for them."

"Now, I doubt that." He grins, leaning a deeply tanned forearm on the counter. "You look like you know fun, but it's probably not the kind they're into."

"Oh?" The room spins a little, and my mouth feels impossibly dry, but I want to listen to him talk anyway.

"I can spot a club-goer a mile away, and you have wallflower written all over you."

"Could I record you saying that? Because the general public has a completely different opinion."

Smirking, he shakes his head. "I'm Blue."

He extends his hand, and I take it with a tentative smile, grateful that my night may not be confined to wallowing while my brother and Troy have the time of their lives.

"Lenny," I offer.

I can't even remember the last time I interacted with a stranger of my own will, much less one who didn't immediately want to talk about rumors or Preston or Primrose Realty.

His head tilts to the side. "Let me guess. You're an artist."

My tongue feels heavy as I let out a little laugh. "Something like that."

"So, you'd probably rather be out painting a sidewalk or vandalizing the side of a building right now. Like that Banksy guy."

"Well, not really." I tuck a piece of hair behind my ear and take another sip of my drink. "My parents would murder me if I ever defaced public property. Wouldn't look good for their brand."

"Ah, yes. *Your* brand of criminal activity looks a bit different, doesn't it, love?"

Surprise seizes my throat as the British accent that's haunted my dreams since the party rumbles in my ear. Liquid catches in my esophagus and I sputter trying to clear an airway.

*I knew this was a terrible idea.*

"Oh, my." A hand finds my back, barely touching as it smooths a circular pattern that seems to scorch me through my clothes. "Jumpy little bird, isn't she?"

The question is clearly directed at Blue, who plasters a tight smile on his face. "Boss. Didn't know you were in tonight."

"Clearly. Otherwise, maybe you'd be doing your job instead of flirting with drunk customers."

My fingers squeeze the mason jar glass until they're numb, and goose bumps prick the back of my neck like a million little needles.

"I'm... not drunk," I insist, spinning around on the stool to prove it to him.

Except I misjudge his proximity, and my knees knock into his side as I turn. The impact throws me off-kilter, and my hands lurch out, grabbing his hips to keep from falling.

The room continues spinning. I stick my tongue to the roof of my mouth, concentrating on getting it to stop.

Jonas Wolfe stares, those violet eyes piercing straight through me. God, he smells good. Like tobacco and coffee, smoldering in a leather jacket and ripped jeans right before me.

"*Right.*" Gripping my shoulders, Jonas forces me upright. "And I'm not ten seconds away from firing my best employee for over-serving."

"I didn't over-serve her," Blue snaps, folding his arms over his chest. "Apparently she's a lightweight."

"*She* is right here," I say, trying to jerk out of Jonas's hold, only to have him dig his fingers into my bare biceps. "It's inappropriate for you to be touching me."

"It is," he agrees, a spark of amusement flashing in his heated gaze.

*Or is the heat coming from me?* My face feels warm suddenly, and I feel a bead of sweat chase the line of my spine beneath my pink corset.

Swallowing through my dry mouth, I lift my chin.

"Maybe you should stop."

"Maybe I should."

But he doesn't.

If anything, his grip tightens, and then he's hauling me to my feet. I can't stop staring at the sharp curve of his jaw, hidden beneath a thin layer of stubble—less facial hair than he had at the party the other night.

My fingers buzz in tune with the beat of my heart, and I reach up to see if it's as rough as it looks.

Coarse strands poke my skin, and his brows raise. A small smile tugs at the corner of my mouth, and I feel liquid when he grasps my wrist.

I giggle at the size of him wrapped around me. "Your hands are *huge*."

Jonas scowls, glancing at Blue. "Was her drink unattended at any point?"

"I... I don't know." Blue shifts, scratching at his elbow. Someone calls his name down the counter, and he holds up a hand to them. "Maybe? I just came over a few minutes before you showed up."

Fingers pinch my chin, and Jonas jerks me into him, tilting my head back as he inspects my eyes. It feels like I'm swimming, struggling to stay afloat as his irises fade from that bright purple to dark, stormy blue.

"Your eyes keep changing colors."

"Trick of the lighting. Who are you here with?"

"Why?" I ask, poking him in the chest. "Jealous?"

For some reason, the word just tumbles out, unbidden. Even though I don't know this man, nor does he have any reason to feel *anything* when it comes to me.

I'm flirting with danger, standing at the edge of a cliff and trying to convince myself not to take the plunge, even as my foot steps into the air.

If Daddy and Mama saw me right now, tangled up in the enemy, they'd have me committed for sure. Part of me should be concerned about the other people in the bar and the things they'll whisper online before I've left tonight, but my mind is too muddy for me to concentrate on any consequences.

Jonas's frown deepens. "Believe me, love. You couldn't handle it if I was."

My eyes widen, and my lips part to refute that, but then he's shifting and pulling me away from the bar. Heads turn as we make our way to the back of the room, past filled booths and sweaty bodies, and my entire body feels like it's on fire as he leads me into a locked room.

Before, I was only contemplating jumping off the cliff. Now, I've launched myself off the edge, and am free-falling out of control.

Closing the door behind us, Jonas brings me to a leather sofa against the far wall of the room, and I sit down slowly, taking in the scenery around me; a large desk and filing cabinet sit in the middle of the room, and there's a hutch against the wall across from me with a glass decanter and bowl of grapes on top.

I sink into the leather and let out a sigh. Jonas brings a plastic cup over and shoves it in my face.

"Drink."

My eyes narrow as I take it. "How do I know you haven't drugged it?"

"I'm pretty sure someone already beat me to it."

Snorting, I lift the cup and sniff twice before taking a sip. "Why would someone drug me?"

Jonas moves backward, discarding his jacket and leaning against the corner of the desk. It takes me a moment to realize we must be in his office, and again I'm cursing my brother for dragging me here of all places.

"Because you're a girl, and you're alone at a seedy pub?"

Balancing the cup on my knee, I scoff. "I'm not a *girl.* I'm twenty-three."

"Still far too young for me."

I'm not sure why, but that stirs something in my gut. It warms despite the ice water, and I press my hand against my abdomen to try and tamp it down.

"Good thing I'm not trying to ride your dick, then." The words escape before I can bite them back, and I regret them almost immediately.

Not because anything shifts in the air. In fact, Jonas seems completely unfazed by the comment at all, and somehow that makes me feel worse.

"Who were you with tonight?"

My head lolls back, resting against the sofa, and my eyes fall closed even though I know better. I shouldn't be letting my guard down at all right now, especially in the presence of a stranger I *know* has evil in his bones, but I can't seem to help it.

As if weighed down by an invisible force, my body slumps at once, and I fit the cup between my knees.

"I need you to stay awake, love." He sounds closer, but I can't open my eyes to check. "Talk to me. I've never seen you at my pub before tonight. Who brought you?"

"My brother," I say—at least, I think I say it. The words sound garbled to my ears, and I can't really feel my lips.

"Staging some sort of Primrose family coup?"

Laughter bubbles in my chest. "No, nothing like that." I pause, gathering my thoughts as they float around me. "People saw us together tonight, though. You and me."

"That's probably true."

"They'll talk, you know. Exaggerate and make things up."

He hums. "I suppose we'll deal with that when the time comes."

My stomach twists at the thought of my father hearing that I was canoodling with the man who tried to kill him—who may have succeeded, if not for my presence in the kitchen that night.

Stupidly, the notion of his disappointment weighs heavy in my soul for a beat. Like I'm his perfect little angel again, willing to do anything and everything to keep him in good spirits and to retain the admiration of the public.

He would probably die if he could see me right now.

My eyes spring open, interest weaving through my limbs. Jonas stands above me, muscular arms crossed over his broad chest, an expression of suspicion lining his gaze.

I blink up at him, an idea forming like a lead balloon in my mind.

A *bad* idea, I'm sure. But what do I have to lose?

"What if we didn't have anything to clear up?"

Jonas shrugs, adjusting the corded bracelet on his wrist. "In a perfect world, I suppose—"

"No," I interject, my eyelids drooping as I try to sit forward. "What if we just... told everyone we're dating?"

The last word has barely escaped my lips before all I see is black.

# 7

"Not a bloody soul leaves this establishment until you've searched everyone. Got it?"

Blue nods, slipping almost seamlessly into soldier mode as he comes around the bar, starting in on the crowd gathered at the front exit.

Malevolence drives the beat of my heart, pumping chaos through my veins as I stalk back to my office to check on the girl. She's sprawled out on the leather sofa, mouth parted slightly as she lets out a soft snore.

I have half a mind to just trap everyone inside and set fire to the building. Put the *flaming* in The Flaming Chariot. But that isn't something I would be able to recover from financially, after having already sunk my life savings into restoring the place and buying Kal's shares.

Plus, that would be too extreme a course of action, given the fact that I loathe the Primroses. Defending Lenny's honor certainly goes against the immoral code I've lived by for the last decade; even keeping her in my office now so she can sleep peacefully feels like a mistake, but it's too late to backtrack now.

"This seems like an overreaction." Kal's hand comes down on my shoulder, and he shakes me as he glances past me.

"Yes, well, you certainly have experience in that department, Anderson."

He chuckles, letting his arm drop. "Indeed, which is why I'll be the first to tell you to tread lightly."

"That your official prescription, *doctor*?"

"No. Retired, remember? All the advice I give now is strictly below board."

Pausing, he adjusts the collar of his suit jacket, revealing the small pomegranate tattoo on his wrist. I cock a brow at the ink, aware of the Hades and Persephone dynamic he and his wife indulge, but don't question it.

"Give her two Tylenol when she wakes," he says, reaching around to rub the back of his neck. "Whatever made her blackout will likely give her a headache when she's conscious again. If you want answers, make her comfortable first."

"Comfortable." I scoff, disgust filling my chest. "I should dump her arse out on the street. Would serve her *daddy* right for letting her come out tonight unattended."

"Still plenty of opportunity for you to be the bad guy." He

heads to where a waitress guards the back exit, lifting a single hand in goodbye without turning back.

The crowd grumbles as they hear a door shut, and I glare harder at the unconscious girl taking up space in my life. As if the complications she created that night at her party weren't enough, now she's quite literally bringing trouble to my fucking doorstep.

*And what was that about pretending to date?*

There wasn't even time to point out the absurdity of the notion before she'd passed out. Though I can't be sure if it was her suggestion or the drugs.

Scrubbing a hand down the side of my face, I step inside the office, letting the door fall shut behind me. Swiping a bottle of Jameson from the sideboard against one wall, I prop up against the wood drawers, unscrew the cap, and take a swig.

The moment the glass mouth touches my lips, Lenny's green eyes pop open. She doesn't even seem confused as our gazes connect, something weighty and silent ebbing between us like an electric tether.

Her comfort sends a jolt of unease through me, wrapping around my sternum and refusing to release.

Almost as if she *isn't* surprised to find herself in my office. Like that's exactly where she planned on being all along.

"See? Would a drugged person be awake already?" she asks, her pink lips barely moving.

"Depends on the dosage."

She shoves her hands beneath her cheek, studying me with a thoughtful expression. "Have you ever drugged anyone?"

Bringing the bottle back to my mouth, I suck down another gulp instead of answering.

"Are you going to kill me?"

My jaw clenches. "I'm debating it."

Sighing, she rolls onto her back, smoothing down the material of her cream-colored skirt. She folds her hands over her chest, and I inch toward her, inexplicably drawn to the aloofness she radiates.

People tend to be many things in my presence. Petrified, resentful, or perhaps even aroused.

Ambivalence is not something I see often, and I find that alarming.

The whiskey bottle is heavy in my fist as I stop mere centimeters from the sofa. Her gaze is fixed on the ceiling, her lush tits threatening to spill from the cups of the lace top she wears. I trace the curvature of her cleavage, trying to rectify this seductress with the modest, proper girl always shown in the tabloids.

It's almost as if she came dressed for temptation, and I wonder if the party at Primrose Manor was some sort of trap. Perhaps Tom expected me to show up, and she revealed my identity the second I left the property.

Maybe he's the one who reported the body and paid to have the autopsy results sealed. By the time I'd sent one of my guys over to make sure the manner of death wasn't released, all evidence pointing to anything but suicide had been taken care of.

"You don't intimidate me," Lenny says after a stretch of silence passes between us.

I blink, my eyes snapping to hers. "What?"

"If that's what you're trying to do. It won't work."

Her shoulder is right in line with the hand at my side; all I'd have to do is lift a finger, and it'd brush against soft skin.

My pinkie twitches, as if pining itself.

"Why would *I* be trying to intimidate *you*?" I ask, hooking my fingers inside of my trousers pocket instead. "Need I remind you that this is my pub, and I didn't invite you here?"

"Yeah, and that must ruffle your feathers. I bet you're used to snapping your fingers and having people fall over themselves to do your bidding. Does it bug you that you can't tell me what to do, Mr. *Wolfe*?"

The sound of my name rolling off her tongue does something wickedly violent to the state of my wellbeing. A single syllable dancing in the thick air around us, teasing the hair on the back of my neck.

Pushing her feet off the side of the sofa, Lenny pulls herself into a sitting position, turning and extending her legs so the black heels she has on slip between my boots. She arches her back, swiping those golden-brown locks off her shoulder, and peeks up at me through hooded lashes.

My feet turn inward, trapping her ankles between them. "You'd do well not to make such antagonistic assumptions, little puppet. Just because I haven't killed you yet doesn't mean I won't. I'm more than happy to rearrange my plans."

Defiance flashes in her glassy gaze, and her hand sweeps out, snatching the bottle of whiskey from me. She tips it back against her mouth before I can stop her, throat working as she guzzles the amber liquid.

The opening of the bottle is slightly larger than she seems to expect, though, so some of the whiskey escapes, spilling down her neck and cascading across her chest.

Try as I might not to look, I can't bloody help it; my eyes flock to her dampened flesh like a prepubescent boy's would, and she catches me. Lifts her free hand and drags her manicured fingers through the mess, before licking the tips clean.

My cock stiffens, pressing against the fly of my trousers. The entire situation is so wildly inconceivable that I give myself a pass for finding weakness in such an obvious gimmick.

What possible reason is there for the way she's acting, other than being sent by her father to seduce and destroy?

"Explain yourself." Being this close to her cinches the nerves in my chest, squeezing until it's difficult to breathe. "Why are you here?"

"Well, because you dragged me away from the bar." She giggles at that, sobering a bit when she notices I'm not joining her. "I *told* you. I came out with my brother and his boyfriend. Neither of them give a shit about your beef with Daddy."

Moving closer, I kick her legs apart and stand so my shins are flush with the sofa. Her skirt rides up slightly, revealing more of her toned thighs, but her hand comes down to keep it in place.

Gently, I reach out and remove her fingers from the neck of the whiskey bottle. One by one I pluck the vessel free, ignoring the smooth texture of her skin as I do so. She cranes her head, fixing her gaze on mine as I take the bottle back.

Surprise registers momentarily on her face as I slide one of my hands under her chin to cup her jaw, tilting her head back so she's bent almost at a ninety-degree angle.

"No guards? I find it hard to believe your father would let you come out unattended."

"Clearly you don't know him."

"Tell me," I say, holding the mouth of the bottle inches above her parted lips. My heart ricochets around my chest, bouncing uncontrollably against my ribcage. "How would *Daddy* feel if he knew where you were right now? If he knew the man who once held his life in the palm of his hand was currently cradling your cheek and fantasizing about just how *wet* he can get you?"

The first splash of alcohol dribbles down over her upper lip, disappearing through the seam of her mouth. She jerks in my hold, but doesn't otherwise demand release, and I find that *peculiar*.

Among other things.

"I imagine he'd get over it once he learned of the nature of our relationship," she says, her tongue darting out and swiping her skin clean.

"Our *relationship*?" The movement of her tongue makes me dizzy, and I inadvertently tighten my grip on her.

"People saw us tonight," she breathes, her warm gaze tangling with mine. I feel her pulse jump beneath my hand, and I press back against it, chasing its beat. "We didn't see them, but if I've learned *anything* in my life, it's that someone is always watching. Daddy's gonna find out either way that I was here, and it won't take very much digging for him to find out we also… interacted at the party."

"So?"

I tip the bottle again, allowing a droplet to land in the slight dimple in her chin; my thumb inches up, feathering out over her lips before brushing it away.

"*So*," she continues, "what do you think the gossip blogs are gonna say? That nothing happened between us? They'll make up whatever wild stories they can think of for a quick payday. Primrose gossip sells well, for some reason."

After a moment, my hand drops, and I step away with the bottle at my side. "I fail to see how any of this is my problem."

Lenny pushes to her feet, crossing her arms over her

chest, which still glistens from the whiskey. If she *was* drugged, her ability to recover is impeccable.

If she *wasn't*, then I'm back at square one wondering what the hell she's on about.

"You like your cushy little life, right? Enjoy your privacy and freedom? I'm sure being in the spotlight would make your... line of work difficult, right?"

Unfortunately, she's not wrong. That's the main reason I refrain from interacting with my brother in certain spaces; politics and murder only mix well in the shadows. If Alistair didn't double as my benefactor, I doubt I'd ever see the bloke at all.

Lenny doesn't wait for an answer. "It's a lot easier to control a narrative when you're two steps ahead of its driving forces. If we announced that we're dating, they'd have no reason to come running out of the woodwork for a story."

*This again.* "You don't think they'd be concerned at all, given our history?"

"Not if we give them breadcrumbs. Let them fill in the gaps themselves." Walking over to my desk, she runs her hand over the leather material of my jacket, pursing her lips.

"We don't even know each other," I say, moving to set the whiskey bottle down. "And I don't date."

I sidle up behind her as she stares down at the fire-breathing Minotaur patch sewn into the jacket sleeve, keeping enough distance between us to refrain from doing something I might regret.

"All the more reason to *fake* date," she mutters. "No chance of catching feelings."

One of my hands raises, sweeping over the soft ends of her hair and the curve of her lower back. "What's the incentive?"

"Bodily autonomy." A shiver racks through her, and I bite down on my tongue to stave off the satisfaction it gives me. "If I don't pick someone, my father's going to set me up with one of his business buddies. Or worse."

"Worse?"

She doesn't answer. "You'd get *good* publicity, for once. It'd convince Aplana Island that you've buried the hatchet with my family."

I swallow. "And what's to keep your father from simply refusing to accept me as your boyfriend?"

A long pause ensues, and I fix my gaze on the wall beyond; there's a circular indentation in the plaster from where I rammed someone's head into it just this morning and haven't had time to repair it. Blood coats the cracks like a thick paint, and I can't help wondering if Lenny sees it.

If she notices, she doesn't say.

Licking her lips, she spins around and leans against the desk. Those big green eyes blink up at me, reminding me of that night at the party.

Something flares behind her irises, bright and full, but I can't allocate it exactly. It doesn't *feel* like fear, but that same thread of excitement I found when she crouched on the floor covered in a dead man's blood.

"He won't say no," she tells me, straightening her spine, "because he's terrified of you."

# 8

## Lenny

THE NEWSPAPER CRINKLES as my brother lowers the edge beneath his chin.

"You did *what*?"

Cash has the highly coveted corner office in his building, an environmental law firm just outside the Boston city limits. The glass walls around us give the illusion of transparency that people seek out in their legal counsel but keep all the sound inside.

Sometimes I wonder if they gave him the room so he can yell at his clients and not disturb his colleagues.

Popping another chocolate mint into my mouth, I lean

back in the plastic chair in front of his desk. Maybe if I pretend that I've got everything together, he'll believe it.

That's the only good thing about having a lawyer as a brother; he operates on a strict need-to-know basis. And right now, all he needs to know is that I fucked up.

"What do you mean, you're *dating* Jonas Wolfe? I wasn't even aware you knew the man."

I give him a skeptical look. "Hard to know who my friends are when you live off the island and never visit."

Cash removes his wire-rimmed glasses, wiping the lenses with a tissue he pulls from a drawer. "Fair enough, but doesn't associating with him go against several *legal* pretenses?"

"He was asked to stay away from *us*, not the other way around."

"So, you approached him? You sought him out?"

Pressing my lips together, I nod once. "Yes. That's exactly what happened."

Cash groans. "You're the worst liar, Len. What the hell are you not telling me?"

Blowing out a breath, I run my fingers along the edge of the desk, taking a moment to sit back and study him. Like his twin, Cash's personality seems to be wholly wrapped up in his physical appearance: neat, dark blond hair that he doesn't let grow past a certain length; crisp button-downs and dress pants with the intentional pleating; a clean-shaven jaw and emotionless brown eyes.

Even his *name* denotes what the man prioritizes, and the fact that he's trying to lecture me about honesty feels ironic.

"Buried body clause."

His mouth forms a terse line. "No, Lenny. Damnit, not again."

I reach for another mint. "Buried. Body. Clause."

Sighing, Cash slumps in his chair, defeated by his own principle. During undergrad, he learned about these lawyers back in the seventies whose client confided in them about the murder and burial of two women.

The lawyers found the women but kept their discovery a secret, and later hinged that decision on confidentiality duties to their client.

Cash lives by that clause, which is the only reason I'm here and not paying someone else money for legal consultation.

Not to mention the fact that if Daddy saw me pay a law firm or take out a large sum of cash, he'd be on high alert. And right now, I need him in the shadows.

As I explain how the current plot of my life came to be, starting with the party the other night and ending at Jonas's bar, Cash's face grows increasingly more haggard with each passing second. I'd feel a little bad for confiding my darkest secrets if I wasn't so fucking sick of shouldering them alone.

Placing his glasses on the desktop, he lets out a low whistle when I'm done.

"For fuck's sake, Len. I didn't think you were invoking an *actual* buried bodies clause. What have you gotten yourself into?"

My stomach lurches, because in truth I don't know.

When I came back from Vermont, I wanted change. Kicking Preston and his evil out of my life was the start of that, though I wasn't expecting such a quick and volatile progression.

Sitting forward, Cash slides a yellow legal pad from under his laptop stand, watching as I take *another* mint from the dish in front of me. I chew slowly and he uncaps a pen, waiting.

"So, what's the plan? You need a contract, yes?"

Swallowing, my brows hitch. "You're gonna help me?"

"If I don't, you're gonna get yourself killed." He pauses, tapping the pen against the desk. "That's not your goal here, right?"

Acid burns in my throat as I think back to what my response would've been a few months ago.

The pit of despair I managed to crawl out of, and the hours spent biding my time, waiting for an opportunity to separate myself from the girl I was and the girl I had to become in order to survive.

Sometimes, the best revenge is just moving on. Thriving, while the men who ruined my life sit back and have no say in anything.

If you'd told me a year ago that Jonas Wolfe would somehow play into that, I would've called you a liar. But here we are.

Sort of.

I shake my head, and Cash starts jotting something down. He keeps his case notes handwritten and locked in a safe, and though I don't understand why an environmental lawyer takes such extremes to ensure his privacy, right now I'm grateful.

Daddy's proven to be lethal when it comes to getting what he wants, and I have no doubt that if he caught wind of a scheme brewing under his nose, he'd hack into any technology necessary to nip it in the bud.

"Okay, well, do you think we can get Jonas here to sign his portion of the contract?"

Toying with the paper wrapper in my lap, I clear my throat. "Well, that's the thing. He hasn't exactly agreed yet."

Cash pinches the bridge of his nose, then turns to his computer and begins typing. Ten minutes later, he sends me on my way with a notarized document and a simple request: get Jonas Wolfe to sign.

Which would be a bit easier if he hadn't banned me from his stupid bar.

I catch the ferry back to Aplana and a cab to the house, staring out the window as summer on the island whips past.

Small oak and cedar trees line the concrete sidewalks of The Square, our version of a downtown on the north end of the island. Storefronts with vibrant flowers and rustic signage are peppered in between government buildings and restaurants, and the contrast between this half and the half where The Flaming Chariot operates is like night and day.

Jonas's bar sits on the border, stuck in a turf war between the north and south ends. Somehow, the spot works, though, because people from all over flock to it, though that could have more to do with the fact that it's the only landlocked source of nightlife we have.

We pass the building on our way, but only because I ask the driver for the scenic route. The windows are boarded up, and the place looks completely desolate—though I know there's likely *someone* inside.

If the rumors are true, Jonas himself is probably in there right now, skinning someone alive for whatever secret organization he works for. The Mafia or some cult-like terroristic group, nobody seems to know, but people on the streets are always whispering about it.

Suddenly, my proposal to him feels like a colossal mistake.

Not that it matters, I guess, since he hasn't even agreed.

And really, why should he? The only incentive I've given him to pretend to date a stranger is *publicity*, which is probably the last thing a man like Jonas Wolfe wants.

When I arrive home, I lock myself away in my bedroom. Mama and Daddy are gone on a business trip, so aside from the regular staff and the security detail I keep ditching, I have the house to myself.

Dragging my easel outside to the balcony, I set up a small canvas there and finish up a sketch project. My mind isn't fully immersed, though, and keeps drifting to thoughts of Jonas and his bright purple gaze.

His hands in front of me, gripping the bottle of whiskey and pouring drops onto my exposed skin.

How I shouldn't have fed into it, given *everything*, but the alcohol seemed to spur me on.

*Or maybe I really was drugged.*

The tip of my pencil breaks off onto the page as my mind wanders farther, and the reality of my situation turns into terror. Memories from months ago come flooding back, and I can no longer focus on anything except the volume of my heart beating in my throat.

A sick feeling pounds around inside my skull, like a screw being drilled into the bone. Sobs form in my lungs but don't escape, as if they're stuck in a sort of limbo between my despair and coping mechanisms.

Toes curling, I sit back against the French doors and try to distract myself from the urge swelling inside of me. It builds and builds, a tidal wave ready to crash against the shore and destroy everything in its path, and when it crests in my brain, I snap.

I shuffle to the kitchen in a daze, driven by visions of

food as they flash before me. I'm not even fucking hungry, but I find myself tucked in the corner of the walk-in pantry, shoving Little Debbie zebra cakes into my mouth until I'm almost choking on the artificial flavoring.

My throat struggles to take it all in, and my stomach aches in protest, but goddamnit if the agony doesn't dull in the wake of indulgence.

# 9

"I THINK YOU SHOULD DO IT."

Wiping the sheen of sweat from my forehead, I glance over my shoulder at Alistair as he lounges on my suede love seat. His suspenders are unhooked, limp at his waist, and the top two buttons of his burgundy undershirt are undone, revealing a corded necklace that matches the bracelet I wear.

Both gifts from our father, just before his death.

Aside from the pub, it's the only tangible connection we have left.

Working another heap of fat and muscle into the vintage

meat grinder, I focus on making sure the mechanism doesn't clog, keeping the funnel straight.

"You think I should date the daughter of our family's mortal enemy?"

Alistair chuckles, pointing at me with a brown beer bottle. "*Dad's* mortal enemy. I'm not sure your mum would possess the same rivalry."

"Yes, well, my mum isn't exactly here to contest my resentment, is she?"

The last of the meat pushes through, leaving me with the dirty bones of some former CIA agent my brother asked me to track down. I'm not sure what his motives were, nor did he give me anything to ask before I sliced through the man's carotid artery, and I don't particularly care.

Since I kicked her out of my pub and told her not to return, my little puppet has given me an endless string of headaches over the last few days. I'm sure she thinks I'm oblivious to the fact that she leaked our lackluster rendezvous to the press, but the timing was just too coincidental not to be her doing.

And now there are people loitering around my pub *all the bloody time.*

Lenny's asinine proposal makes me leery of her in general, and it's having the opposite intended effect.

That night in my office, maybe I was right tempted to take her up on the offer. Perhaps sweeten the deal by making sex one of the conditions.

I would've taken her right there on the desk. Fucked her 'til our arrangement felt *real*, and then pumped her full of cum just to spite dear old daddy.

*Jesus.* The image of her thighs and juicy little cunt

sprayed with my seed sends a spark of arousal through me, rolling down my chest as I continue scrubbing.

*Imagine the look on her father's face when he realized I'd soiled his precious baby girl. Tainted her soul and marked her as mine.*

Her desperation—and the alcohol—told me she would've been willing.

Now, though, I wouldn't mind tying her to a cement block and sending her to the bottom of the bloody Atlantic, mob-style.

It would be the least she deserves for fucking my life up so spectacularly.

"I'm just saying. Dating the Primrose daughter is probably your best shot at getting back at Tom."

Alistair stretches, throwing his arm over the back of the love seat. His blue eyes crinkle at the corners as he watches me switch to the bones at my side, cleaning them so they're easier to dispose of in the vat of limestone I keep in the backyard.

Pausing, I squeeze the scrub brush in my hand. "Who says I want to get back at him?"

"If you don't, that's news to me." He hooks an ankle over his knee and shrugs. "Fine, don't do it for revenge. Do it for me."

"You."

"Having the backing of a Primrose would help *immensely* when I campaign for the Senate."

"And the fact that I make most of my living as a *hired killer*... you think that's something everyone will just overlook."

"I'm overlooking it right now."

"You're the one *paying* me." Dropping the brush, I get to

my feet and brush my hands on my jeans, irritation spreading through my limbs like tree branches. "I don't even know the bloody girl. She could be a fucking prop, and you're encouraging me to partake in her little scheme?"

Alistair rolls his eyes, checking the bulky watch on his wrist. He stands, swiping his black suit jacket from the arm of the love seat, and moves to the kitchen to toss his bottle in the recycling.

Bracing his palms on the counter, he steels me with a look. "The fact of the matter is, we know I barely got this mayor gig, and I can use all the political support I can get. Maybe if the public thinks the Primroses and the Wolfes are moving on, they'll be more likely to support one in office, and I won't have to resort to such... drastic measures to keep my rightful place."

I don't say anything, because deep down, I think we both know that isn't true. Once you get a taste of power, of bloodshed in the *name* of power, you don't ever look back.

Our father certainly didn't, and it cost him his life.

There is no world any longer in which Alistair won't spill blood. Even if he only hires someone else to do it.

Fingering the pendant on my bracelet, I consider his points. "And what if I decide to just kill Tom Primrose, once and for all?"

"I trust you'll make it untraceable." He shrugs. "Get the public support first, and you can do whatever the fuck you want afterward."

THIS TIME when she shows up at my pub, I'm fully prepared to indulge in her presence. Everything happened so quickly the other night that I didn't get to appreciate what her being in my midst really meant.

For some reason, even though she was possibly roofied the last time she came, Lenny shows up alone *again.* As I watch a weekend bouncer stamp the back of her hand on the security monitor from my office, I doubt she even has an actual bodyguard in the first place.

When I look her up online, I'm met mostly with pictures of her and her father, darting to and from events. His arm is always around her shoulders, as if afraid she might float away, and she always has a bright smile plastered on her face and a hand lifted in greeting.

Fucking *greeting* the slimy paparazzi.

My chest winds tight as I continue through the gallery of photos, annoyed by Tom's face in so many. The spinning ceases altogether when I get to those of her attending red carpets and cozy restaurant dates with some preppy-looking douche.

Something akin to rage spirals through me, shooting through my veins like white-hot flames, and I keep clicking through, seeking an end. Both to the two of them together—his hands on her hips, her neck, the underside of her breast where they definitely don't fucking belong—and to the insane, fiery sensations zipping through my bloodstream.

I wasn't putting her on when I said I don't date. My adult life leaves very little room for such adventure, and I find most people so dreadfully *bland* that the idea of keeping their company makes me want to blow my brains out.

It shouldn't be any different when it comes to Lenny Primrose, and yet I can't stop thinking about her. She's occupied the majority of my thoughts since I found her on the balcony at her family's party, and even though I'm pretty sure something is off with her motivations, the desire to find out for myself takes precedence.

When a random patron approaches her as she makes her way to the washrooms, I push out of my desk chair and head out front. Violence thrums against the ventricles of my heart, and I locate her immediately, glaring as the wide-shouldered frat boy traps her between himself and the wall.

Rational thought doesn't register in my mind as I reach the two. My actions are driven entirely by primal instinct, some natural resistance to other people toying with the things that belong to me.

*Bloody hell.* I don't entertain that notion, grabbing her wrist and tugging her into me.

"Hey, man," the frat boy complains, his eyebrows drawing in as he turns with her. "We were having a conversation, dickhead."

"And now you're not. Find someone else's girlfriend to snog before I beat seven shades of shit out of you."

Lenny's eyes widen as if in question, and I wish I had an answer for her. Wish I could explain the sudden need I have to make known that she's here for *me*, even if they don't know it's pretend.

My hand slides up the column of her neck, my thumb pressing beneath her chin while my fingers curl into her soft flesh. It's demented, this urge, but I'm in too deep now to stop it.

When I lean down and press my lips to hers, the entire background of the pub seems to melt away. My tongue prods the seam of her mouth, and it opens on the softest sigh, beckoning me to explore.

And right then, I know.

*I'm fucked.*

# 10

Lenny

*Okay, Len. Don't panic.*

*Everything is fine.*

*So, a psychopathic assassin has you pressed against the wall of his bar while he defiles your mouth in ways you didn't think were possible anymore.*

*That's not cause for concern, right?*

*Especially since his lips are incredibly soft, and he tastes like bittersweet candy.*

Jonas wrenches himself from me as soon as the lurker with a bad crew cut scampers off, tail tucked between his legs. His large fingers twist in the strands of hair at the base of my skull, somehow keeping me close and distant at the same time.

My body hums, dissatisfied with the loss.

"First thing you should know," he says, or *breathes*, rather. Like the kiss we just shared dragged the air from his lungs the same way it did mine. "I don't share. Ever."

*See, Len? Already off to a better start than you were with Preston.*

Even as his words send frissons of heat through the chambers of my heart, I can't help but poke the beast anyway.

"*Ever*?" I bat my lashes, feigning innocence. "That's a shame."

His eyes narrow, shifting from that unique violet to angry blue. They're electrifying, impossible to look away from, and I momentarily consider the mistake I've made involving him.

I'm way in over my head, and I think Jonas Wolfe might capitalize on that.

One of his thumbs catches on the swell of my bottom lip, and he plucks against it like a musician tuning his favorite instrument; slowly, deliberately. As if he's the only one who knows the right pitch.

"The only sharing I'm interested in when it comes to you, is ensuring my cock gets as much time with your cunt as my lips. Believe me, love, when I say you won't require more than that."

My breath hitches, warmth pooling in my stomach and expanding lower, like heated jelly between my thighs.

"I don't think that's a very good idea," I say, because in spite of the butterflies erupting in my chest, there's an undercurrent of unease that digs its claws into me, too.

"No?" Jonas tightens his grip, sending a flurry of sharp

pain across my vertebrae. “It sounds good to me. I could take you to the back. Have you stripped and ravished before you can even bloody blink.”

Some memories are like vampires, sinking their fangs into your vulnerable flesh and draining you until they’ve transformed you completely. A year ago, I might have been able to handle the flirting. Might have even taken him up on the offer.

Now, all I feel is weary.

Uncomfortable in my own skin.

The hairs on the back of my neck stand straight, and my heart hammers inside my throat. I swallow over the sudden dryness coating my tongue. “Sex wasn’t on the table.”

“Well, no, I suppose it doesn’t have to be.” He shifts, brushing his hips against mine, and my muscles tense up. “I’d be just as happy to bend you over the bar and make you see stars, little puppet.”

“Glad to see my attitude hasn’t actually hampered your ego at all.”

Smirking at the reference to the night we met, Jonas slowly lets his hands fall from me, taking a step back. I wipe my mouth with my palm, trying to erase the imprint of him on my skin, and he tosses a quick glance around the room.

Most of the people are going on with their night like we aren’t even here, but there are occasional outliers who find it necessary to gawk. Like they’ve never seen two people make out in a dark alcove before.

Pressing my palm to my stomach, I try to relieve the ache flaring in my gut; something twisted and anxious, warning me of trouble to come.

“Maybe we should talk in your office?”

Jonas dips his chin, looking down his nose at me. "No, I don't think so."

"What? Why not?"

There's *something* about this man—it's wicked and dangerous, tainted by evil doings, but he somehow maintains a certain charm despite that.

Mama would say it's his accent, deep and silken that confuses Americans and makes them putty in a Brit's hands.

I've heard our staff members whisper that it's a curse on the Wolfe family. That being likable is their penance for generations of corruption.

Standing here with him though, all that charm seems to evaporate, leaving just the husk of a criminal behind.

"I accept your proposal."

My shoulders sag as relief flushes over me. "Really? Oh, my god, that's great. We can—"

Lifting his index finger, he presses it against my mouth, silencing me. "Ah, ah. There are, as you can imagine, stipulations. Three of them, specifically."

The corded bracelet on his wrist is rough as it rubs my chin, the W-shaped pendant catching my attention. Another reminder that my impulses aren't to be trusted.

"If we do this, we *do this*. Dive into fantasy a hundred and ten percent, and we don't let up until both of us get what we want."

It feels like an elephant sits on my chest, crushing my lungs beneath its weight. "Okay..."

"We'll move you out of Primrose Manor."

My eyebrows shoot to my hairline. "We said nothing about living arrangements—"

"We're saying it now. It's already a far-fetched story. The idea of a whirlwind courtship is much more feasible if we live together. Gives us time to fabricate stories and a connection. The public will eat it up, and more importantly, well…" He trails off with a shrug. "Your father will hate it."

Most likely, he won't allow it. But I'm not in much of a position to argue. "Do you even have room for another person in your house?"

"We won't be staying in my house, love. Far too many *things* for you to see that you have no business shoving your nose in."

"I know what you do for a living."

"No, you only *think* you know. I can assure you that whatever morsels of gossip about my life you've been fed over the years, they're either greatly exaggerated or completely off the mark."

Someone shuffles past us, knocking into Jonas as they stumble to the bathroom; he slides closer, lining the hard ridges of his body with the soft contours of mine, and I don't exactly hate the way it feels.

I don't love it, though, either, and find myself trying to disappear into the wall behind me.

"There's one thing to clarify here before we go any further. Murder is my default setting, and I charge handsomely for it." One of his brows quirks, as if waiting for me to object or voice concern.

Like that wasn't a deciding factor in me asking for his help.

"I don't bloody well trust you. I'm not sure what your aim is, but make no mistake, little puppet. If you're scheming for your father, I'll find out. And I don't play nice when threatened."

Linking my fingers together behind my back, I nod. My

ulterior motives have nothing to do with him. "What's the other demand?"

"It's simple, really." He reaches up, bracing his forearm on the wall above my head. "You want my help, love?" His mouth morphs into a sinister curve, incinerating good intentions. "Beg for it. Right here, right now... where everyone can hear."

My eyes dart to the bar, where a couple of girls in distressed jeans and cropped t-shirts are standing, staring. A man in the corner has his phone propped in his hand, angled perfectly at us.

They're *always* watching. Waiting for the next moment they can document my descent into depravity.

Months ago, I had no say in my very public falling out as Aplana and Tom Primrose's angelic socialite. Liberties were taken, and Preston Covington played his hand immediately in order to absolve himself of his debts.

Debts I'd agreed to help him pay off, though not the way I ended up doing so.

The assault wasn't even the most traumatizing part of it all, but what came after with my father.

A choice was ripped from me then, too, and while the media rejoiced thinking they'd witnessed my fall from Heaven, all they'd really seen was an orchestrated tale of destruction.

But I have a choice right now. Sort of.

It's not an ideal one, but I'm willing to do whatever it takes to force Daddy's hand the way he's always done me.

Aligning myself with Jonas Wolfe may prove reckless and impulsive, but as I slowly sink to my knees in front of him, the dirty floor grating against my joints, I accept this as my fate.

*It's only demeaning if you let it be.*

His face screws up as I blink at him, and his nostrils flare. He looks angry, but I'm not really sure why.

"Please," I say, my voice steady, though I don't know if he can hear it over the music. "*Please* help me."

# 11

With a grunt, I straighten my spine, letting the memory foam mattress slip into the platform bed frame. Across the room, Alistair sips from a porcelain teacup, watching me with barely contained amusement.

"I'm glad you find this funny," I say, hitting a button on the wall. First the black-out curtains swing closed, and then the metal bars I installed on the windows last night follow, locking automatically once they meet.

Fitting my finger against the scanner, I activate the alarm for the master bedroom's balcony window and move on to the shared washroom across the hall.

Staying at the beach bungalow was a last-minute decision; my mum's final big *fuck you* before she ditched my dad and I isn't a place I frequent normally. Would've had it condemned years ago if Alistair hadn't convinced me not to part with it for "sentimental reasons."

As if the bloke is capable of sentience himself.

With its cracked foundation and the overgrown weeds barring entry to much of the property, I almost don't even need to implement a security system of my own. However, I don't trust Lenny Primrose, and I certainly don't trust her vile family, so I'm considering the installation an insurance clause.

She won't find it in that blasted contract she brought over, but it'll be there, nonetheless.

"You're looking at the situation all wrong." Alistair comes to the doorway, leaning against the frame. "It's another hit, Jonas. You're just... playing the long game."

I kneel against the bathtub, reinforcing the padlock on the frosted window above the tile. "Except that no one has any idea when this arrangement might end. It's indefinite, left up to interpretation, and I don't know how much of Lenny Primrose I'll be able to withstand."

Alistair scoffs. "Right. I'm sure there's nothing you can think of to help ease your time spent."

"What, you think I should just hop into bed with her?"

"If that'll relieve your stress about the circumstances."

"Sounds like a bloody recipe for disaster." A delicious recipe, but disaster, nonetheless.

"Or an *adventure*."

He's on my heels as I exit the bathroom and head down the stairs. The small foyer and hallway open up directly into a sunken living area and kitchen on one side, and a home office on the other, and unfortunately, I can see bits of my mum in the rooms.

Unsealed paint cans sit on the light hardwood floor of the office, and a tarp stretches across the room, but it doesn't appear as though she ever touched the beige walls. Half-finished and abandoned, just like everything else in her life.

"I'm not going to fuck her."

Snapping the strap of his suspenders against his chest, Alistair points at me. "But you'd like to."

Moving down the hall and into the kitchen, I shrug. "Wouldn't the whole island like to?"

"If you believe the tabloids, the whole island already has." When I don't say anything, Alistair cocks a brow. "You *don't* believe the tabloids, do you?"

I don't *want* to, but the evidence to the contrary is damning. And the thought of anyone else putting their hands on the little puppet, when she's only been my possession for a short time, blinds me with fury.

"My beliefs don't bloody matter," I snap, pulling the metal cage above the kitchen windows closed. "I'm doing this for *you*, and that's all there is to it."

And because Tom Primrose deserves to pay *somehow* for the things he did to my father. If not an eye for an eye, I'll take the daughter instead. Make *Daddy* think she's all mine, and strike when the iron is hot.

He studies me as I take a bottled water from the fridge and unscrew the cap, drinking the contents in seconds. "If you say so, brother."

Later, long after Alistair leaves and I spend too much time pouring over inventory receipts at the pub, Lenny still hasn't shown up.

She requested I not go directly to Primrose Manor to

retrieve her and swore her lawyer brother was more than capable of bringing her to me.

And yet...

I wait until Blue shuts down for the night, and the only thing left to occupy my thoughts is the question of her whereabouts.

Certainly, the little puppet hasn't given up already. Not when she was so adamant about requesting my assistance.

Finally, around four in the morning, I take it upon myself to investigate. Irritation lodges in my chest as I drive through town, turning down the gravel road that leads to the ocean-front Primrose property.

If I thought she was trouble before, the fact that I'm having to become actively involved in this arrangement does not bode well. For either of us.

A security guard sits in the gate kiosk, and he says something into a walkie-talkie as I pull up. Winding the window down, I swing my arm out and smack my palm against the side of my Range Rover to get his attention.

Eyes wide, the scrawny guard leans to peer through the glass. "M-Mr. Wolfe."

"Ah, perfect, you're familiar. Care to let me in, mate?"

"Uh..." He trails off, rubbing the back of his neck. His immediate discomfort makes my blood hum, even though I find the hesitation bothersome. "I'm afraid I'm not able to do that."

The smile on my face twitches. "Why not?"

"You don't have clearance." Flipping through a little notebook on the counter in front of him, the guard cringes. "Actually, I'm supposed to contact the authorities if you show."

Inhaling slowly, I reach over and uncover the Glock sitting in my passenger seat. "Better get on that, then."

Smoothing my fingers along the barrel, I bring it to the steering wheel and let it rest, cocking a brow. The guard's face falls, and he slides off his stool, panic flaring in his gaze. *Fucking hell.* The panic.

Looks just as sweet on your hundredth victim as it did on the first.

Seconds later, I'm granted access through the gate. Wiping blood spatter from my chin, I exit and leave my vehicle there, tucking the gun into my waistband. It's the middle of the night, so I'm not expecting anyone to be up; in fact, half of me anticipates finding the manor completely empty, convinced Tom would steal his family away in an effort to distance them from me.

Unfortunately for him, I'm quite invested in this family.

One member, anyway.

The light beneath the porte cochere is on, and there are figures standing under it. Their shadows cast on the ornate front doors, warped in the wood so they look massive.

I recognize one of the forms immediately and glue myself to the hedges before they notice my presence.

"Lenny, come on now. You're being ridiculous." A male voice, pinched and slow, as if deliberately reviewing each word before he says it.

"So what if I am? It's my right to be, and I don't remember asking for your opinion."

"You're just gonna leave without telling anyone? Think about your father, bug. This will crush him."

She doesn't come right out with it, but "*good*" is implied through the heavy silence anyway.

"What do you even know about this guy? Aside from the

fact that he tried to kill your father. Or is that something you're conveniently forgetting?"

"No one *conveniently* forgets attempted murder, asshole."

I glance up at the second story of the mansion, curious to see if anyone else is watching the spectacle. All of the windows are dark, though, and I wonder where Lenny's brothers are. Her security guards.

If she's so precious and dear to her father, why is there never anyone around to protect the little puppet?

"Then what the fuck are you doing? If you're trying to hurt me, congratulations, it's fucking working."

His tone takes a dark turn, developing a sharp edge, and it raises alarm in my gut. Pushing off the hedge, I shove my hands in my jacket pockets and continue to where the pair stands, my face growing hot when I see how they're tangled together.

A man stands in front of Lenny, his hands clutching the brass knobs of the front doors. My chest tightens, watching as she shoves at him, and he takes the opportunity to move closer. One hand leaves the door and snakes up her side, cupping just beneath her left breast; his grip is so taut that it pulls the T-shirt she has on flush with her tit, and I can see the outline of her nipple all the way over here.

"*Stop it*, Preston." She squirms, her fist balling at her side. "You're not my dad or my boyfriend, you have no say in where I go or what I do."

"But I have a say in *who* you do," the man—Preston, apparently—says, releasing her shirt to capture her chin instead. "And your father already agreed to let us date again."

He forces her to look up at him, and I see her hand slip into her shorts pocket. My chest draws tight, somehow knowing what she's doing before I even see the end of a paintbrush poke out from her fist.

She fiddles around, and as my shoes hit the cobblestone walkway, her gaze flickers to me. It might be a mistake, but I swear I see a flash of relief before she steels herself and glares at the man, retracting her hand.

"You're psychotic. I'd rather drink bleach than date you again."

I can't suppress the smirk that tugs at one corner of my mouth.

"*God*, okay, bug. I fucked up, I know. Let me... I'm trying to make it up to you, okay? Just... don't fucking *go*. Don't tell me you're moving on and living with someone else."

Desperation reeks as it wafts off his lean body, smacking me in the face and instantly souring my mood even more. The toes of my boots meet the backs of his boat shoes, and silently, I slide the pistol from my waistband, fitting the cold mouth against the back of his neck.

He freezes, his shoulders drawing in.

It gets completely still, like the calm before a storm. Satisfaction settles hard and heavy on my soul as his fear seeps into the air, and I let my index finger brush over the trigger, relishing in the shiver that racks him.

"Would you rather I tell you, mate?" I pause, tapping him forcefully. "All right, here it is. I've come to collect my fiancée, and I don't appreciate you putting your dodgy hands on her. I suggest you remove them now, or I'll be forced to make you my third victim on Primrose property."

Nobody moves for a moment. Lenny's eyes remain on me while mine stay on the little shit, afraid of what I might find if I look away.

Fiancée wasn't what we discussed, and yet for some

reason, it's what fell out of my mouth. Once the first syllable passed my lips, it was too late to backtrack and not look like a bumbling idiot.

"Get your fucking hands off me," he says finally, breaking the silence and ripping me from my spiral.

"You first."

His grip on Lenny's chin becomes harsher, and she grimaces. My nostrils flare at that, violence seeping from my bones and getting swept into my bloodstream. With a sigh, I pull my hand back, trying to reel in the anger coursing through my nerve endings before I scar the girl for life.

Rearing my elbow back, I flick my wrist forward, turning at the last second so the butt of the gun connects with the guy's ear. The familiar crack of metal colliding with bone rings out, and immediately his hold falls away as he stumbles to the side, clutching his head with a sob.

He falls to his knees, moving his hand to look at the blood pooling from a small cranial laceration. It covers his fingers and drips down his wrist, and perhaps I shouldn't add insult to injury, but I've come too far at this point to stop before it gets good.

I glance at my little puppet as she pushes off the door and combs her fingers through her hair. "Are you all right, love?"

She nods, stepping up beside me.

"Holy *shit*. Lenny, he just fucking *hit* me. You're gonna go off and live with this freak?" The man cradles his head, hissing under his breath.

"Maybe if you—"

The front door swings open, interrupting her reply as a burly figure fills the space. "What in the Sam Hill is going on out here?"

Even though she's standing inches away, I can sense Lenny's body tense up, and I feel slightly responsible. Something close to guilt scrapes at my spine, trying to burrow in my marrow, and I don't bloody like the sensation.

As if driven by its own train of thought, my free hand finds the small of Lenny's back, and I hook a finger in the hem of her shirt. She doesn't relax, exactly, but she leans into the gesture, as if she needs the support.

Then her father steps outside, holding the flaps of his plaid robe closed. He frowns as he inspects the injured creep, and then freezes altogether when his gaze swings around to me.

A grin threatens at my mouth for a brief second, before breaking free.

"*Thomas.* Long time, no see."

# 12

## Lenny

Mama paces across the room, and each time she turns to walk in the opposite direction, I wring my hands together, ignoring the way my stomach growls. Not because I'm hungry, but because my body wants a different kind of discomfort.

By the time Preston comes out of Daddy's office, my fingers are turning purple, and I rub my hands together as I shoot to my feet.

"Helene," Daddy calls, and I avoid looking at my ex, even as he pauses at the threshold of the door.

Waiting.

For what, I can't be sure. Maybe an escort, in case Jonas—who was ignored after the initial shock of his presence wore off—assaults him again.

My eyes stay fixed on the grandfather clock just visible in the office, and eventually Preston gives up, turning on his heel and disappearing down the hall. I watch as he goes, my stomach flipping with delight when I notice his swollen ear and the bandage just above the cartilage.

His footsteps echo as he gets farther away, and Mama puts a hand on my bicep, squeezing tight. One of the pink curlers falls from where it's pinned to her scalp, but she ignores it as she tries to comfort me.

"Everything will be fine, dear."

I don't believe her, but then again, I knew there would be absolute hell to pay for my actions.

In truth, that was a major part of the appeal.

"We can't help who we love," she continues, tucking a strand of hair behind my ear. The sympathetic smile on her face tempts me; the truth teases the back of my throat like vomit, but I swallow it down because Mama can't keep secrets.

Probably why she doesn't know what really happened with Preston and Daddy.

Once upon a time, I thought she'd want to be included. The night I found Daddy bleeding out in the kitchen, I ran and told her immediately, seeking some sort of comfort from her. When they took him away in an ambulance, though, she only complained about the inconvenience.

As if his attempted assassination was a given, and she was just upset she had to acknowledge it.

To this day, I'm not sure what Daddy could've done to

warrant an execution, but I suppose I'm past the point of getting answers.

Besides, it's much easier to enjoy life when you've got your head buried in the sand.

"*Helene.* Now, please."

Mama gives me a gentle push in the direction of the office, and I walk in with my fingers interlocked. Wishing like hell that I had a bagel or something sweet in my palm, so I could distract myself from the anxiety knotting in my internal organs.

He's seated in one of the oversized armchairs across the room from his desk. Bookshelves line the wall behind them, collecting dust like most of the things in this house that no one's ever around to use. The only difference is that housekeeping isn't allowed in here.

With a sweep of his hand, Daddy gestures for me to take the chair in front of him. He crosses one leg over the other and drinks from a crystal tumbler I got him for Father's Day when we lived in Savannah; a fake bullet pierces one side, and mine and the twins' names are engraved on the opposite.

Swirling the dark liquid in the glass, he studies the detailing silently.

My face heats, my unease notching higher with every tick of the grandfather clock. Mama comes in after me and takes her usual spot behind Daddy, rubbing his shoulders as she attempts an encouraging smile.

When Daddy speaks, it's like a whip cracks through the air, lashing against my skin.

"Are you trying to ruin me, Helene?"

I swallow, folding my hands in my lap. My stomach rumbles, and I realize that it's almost five a.m., and most people will be waking up for breakfast soon. God, I could really go for a jelly-filled donut or two right now.

Or maybe an omelet. There's a restaurant on the boardwalk that serves theirs with grilled chives and sour cream, and they always overdo their portions, so there are leftovers no matter what.

That would be good right now. Better than sitting here, for sure.

"...not even fucking listening." Sitting forward, Daddy shakes Mama off and snaps his fingers directly in front of my face. I jerk back to reality, and he lets out an angry huff.

"I'm listening," I say, straightening my shoulders. "Not everything is about you, Daddy. Least of all my dating life."

"Dating life," he scoffs, setting his tumbler on the coffee table between us. "You don't even have a dating life. Or you *didn't*, which was the decision you made when you chose not to reconnect with Preston after Vermont."

"I don't want to date Preston."

"Well, that's just too damn bad." His fist comes down on the arm of his chair, and Mama jumps. "You're a goddamn Primrose, Helene, and you'll do what I tell you."

"Thomas," Mama chides gently, the way you might try to calm a spooked horse. "She's an adult. We can't control every aspect of her life."

"Oh, spare me, sweetheart. An adult who's never paid for a damn thing in her entire life. Never had a job, or a real friend. Just sits in her room painting and stuffing her face, thinking people won't notice the way her weight fluctuates every time she's pictured in the papers."

He pauses as if checking to see if the blow landed, and I hate the way his words slice my skin wide open.

Clearing my throat, I push to my feet. "If that's all you wanted to say, I think I'll be going."

Daddy springs from his chair, his big hand wrapping around my arm. His grip is harsh, a lot like it was months ago, and I have a sudden flashback to that night. The anger on his red, ruddy face and the agony ripping me apart inside.

The circumstances now are slightly different, but I feel no less miserable.

"I'll have him arrested again," Daddy says when I manage to wriggle out of his hold. He's right behind me as I exit the office, and I can feel each swipe of his hand as he tries to grab me.

"For god's sake, Thomas." Mama trails close, like she's afraid to leave him alone with me.

*As she should be.*

When I reach the front door, I pull it open right before Daddy fists my hair, yanking me back. Jonas is leaning against one of the pillars just outside, seemingly relaxed as he waits.

I don't miss the way his gaze snaps to me, though, and then slides slowly to where my father holds me close.

Or the way his jaw clenches, the muscle beneath thumping like a pulse point.

"If you leave right now," Daddy says, his face by my ear, "I'm cutting you off. No allowance, no connections, no inheritance. Your association with the Primrose family leaves the second you go with that *criminal*."

*Takes one to know one*, my insides scream.

"Ah, still not averse to using threats to exploit the people in your life." Jonas shakes his head, taking a step in our direction. "Glad to see you don't change, Tom."

Daddy ignores him, waiting on an answer for me.

For a moment, I'm tempted. He's not wrong about my lack of real-world experience, though that's also his doing. Best way to keep someone at your disposal is to ensure they depend on you for everything.

Once upon a time, I wouldn't have even minded. If you'd asked the eleven-year-old hunched over her dying father in the kitchen if one day she'd be disgusted by his very presence, she would've laughed in your face.

Then again, that eleven-year-old didn't know better.

Didn't know what he was capable of.

And I owe it to her to stop letting him win.

When I don't reply, Daddy growls and releases me with a shove, and I go tumbling outside. My arms flail, prepared to catch myself on the ground, but I hit a different kind of hard surface instead.

One that's somehow smoldering and ice-cold at the same time.

"We're done here," Daddy announces. The hatred lacing his words makes me feel about ten feet tall, but I ignore it, pulling away from Jonas.

"On the contrary, we've only just begun," Jonas says, smoothing a hand over my back. It hovers at the nape of my neck, as if checking for damage, and I can't stop the little shiver that skates down my spine at the contact.

Our kiss lives rent-free in my mind, and right now I wouldn't care to recreate it, if only to thank him for showing up tonight.

Daddy slams the door in our faces, even as Mama tries to facilitate some sort of common ground between the three of us. The last thing I see before it closes is a pained expression on her face, and then we're shut out from the house entirely.

Clasping my hands together, I force a smile and turn to Jonas. "Well, I think it's safe to say we don't have to worry about holidays at my house. Hopefully your parents are more welcoming."

"My parents are dead."

Nodding, I reach for the rolling suitcases Preston upturned earlier. Part of me regrets telling Cash to stay in Boston, but the other part is glad to have gotten all of that over.

It went a bit better than expected, at least.

Assuming Jonas is parked outside the gate, I start in that direction, not waiting to see if he follows. The crunch of his boots on the driveway closes in on me, and he appears at my side, taking the suitcases by the handles from me.

"You don't have to do that," I say.

He doesn't look over. "What kind of fiancé would I be if I didn't carry your luggage?"

My face heats and the inside of my mouth feels like cotton. "Yeah, about that..."

A black Range Rover sits just beyond the security building at the gate, and I search the window for Matt, the guard Daddy hired about a year ago to replace one who retired.

I slow to a stop, my eyes glued to the glass. Jonas continues around me, popping the trunk of his vehicle and lifting my suitcases, tucking them into the hatch.

"What about it?" he asks, his voice slightly muffled.

Streaks of red decorate the windowpane, and my stomach twists into a giant, concrete knot. There doesn't appear to be a single sign of life inside the brick room, and I inch closer, anxiety igniting at the base of my spine and spreading outward.

The trunk slams closed, and I jump as a presence materializes at my back. Dread slithers down my limbs, immobilizing me as I see the top of Matt's head, pressed against the interior corner of the floor.

Jonas's breaths are heavy as they brush against my scalp. I swallow, trying to even mine out so he doesn't notice how labored they've become.

A cramp seizes my stomach. He brushes some hair off my shoulder, and I feel his lips on my ear.

"What did you do?" I whisper. Afraid to do more than that.

"I won't be kept from you," Jonas murmurs, his words hot and damp as they send a flurry of goose bumps across my skin.

Even as my terror spikes, flaring like an infection in my veins, there's something else, too. Something that keeps me from fleeing.

*Excitement.*

# 13

"SO... THIS IS IT."

Lenny glances up at the beach house, nodding as if she can see beyond the flickering porch light. She extends one suitcase handle, tilting her head as she inspects the immediate surrounding area.

Unfortunately, there's not much to see. An abandoned townhome complex sits a little ways down the shoreline, but other than that and a farmer's market about a mile away, we're the only structure on this one-lane road until you get back to town.

"How'd you get an oceanfront on such short notice? I

thought they were usually booked for the season by now." She starts up the front walk, pausing on the first porch step. "Oh, god, did you kill the owner?"

"Why? Afraid of ghosts?"

"Not afraid. I just happen to think they shouldn't be disturbed."

She stands behind me as I unlock the door, letting the scanner beside the knob calculate my fingerprint before it unlatches. As I push it open, Lenny steps inside, dragging both suitcases along the ceramic tile floor.

"Was the person who lived here before also completely paranoid, or did you install stuff especially for me?"

Flipping on lights as I go, I try not to think about how much smaller this space is in comparison to the mansion she's just left. Turning, I study the slope of her narrow shoulders and the tightness of her cheek muscles, trying to gauge her impression of the home.

For some odd reason, I want her to approve.

"It belonged to my mum a lifetime ago," I tell her as she moves through the hall to the office, then onward to the kitchen. The downstairs just loops around the carpeted steps, which sit across from the back sliding glass door. "She inherited it from her Armenian immigrant parents, and even after she met my dad and moved in with him, she kept the place."

Lenny drags a finger over the black-and-white granite kitchen island, not responding.

"Don't worry, though," I rush out, needing to fill the silence all of a sudden. "She didn't die here, or anything."

Glancing at me, Lenny lifts a shoulder, letting the neckline of her oversized T-shirt expose some of the smooth skin of her collarbone. "Doesn't *need* a ghost to be haunted."

I suppose she has a point, though I'm positive the only one my mum's haunting is me.

Grabbing her luggage, I take it upstairs and into the master suite. Lenny follows, pausing with raised eyebrows as she enters the room.

"Was your mom a psychiatric patient at any point?" she asks, walking to the canopy bed.

"Bloody well should've been." I've already told her too much about the woman, but I can't seem to stop.

Her fingers wrap around one of the metal posts, twisting the sheer fabric draped over the frame, and I consider Alistair's comment about bedding her.

Frankly, it was tempting before this, and now that she's standing inches away from a mattress and we're all alone, the idea of pressing her into the surface until the springs squeal from our weight is becoming vastly more appealing.

Sure, it might complicate things, but what about our situation isn't already?

My footsteps are slow. They carry me to her in an almost deliberate fashion, stopping just behind her as she looks at the covered windows.

I lift a hand, ignoring the way it trembles, and follow the outline of her spine beneath the cotton of her shirt.

"Now that you're here," I say, my voice so low that it feels more like a rumble in my chest, "I can't very well allow you to leave."

"Oh?" The single syllable is barely more than a whispered breath, and I wish I could taste its essence on my tongue. "Am I your prisoner now?"

Swallowing a groan, I shift forward, letting my thighs graze the backs of hers. Behind my zipper, my cock lengthens, throbbing with an intensity that's almost painful. I move again, pressing my hips into the swell of her arse through her silk sleep shorts and trying not to blow just from the contact alone.

My fingers find the nape of her neck, sliding down and tracing the ridge of her collarbone. "Would you like to be?"

I hear her sharp intake of breath, and it sends a violent spiral of warmth throughout my body. Then she lets out a yawn, her hand coming up to stifle the moan she makes. I snap out of the haze of lust that her floral and vanilla scent sends me into, taking three massive steps in the opposite direction.

Sheepishly, she turns to face me, wrapping her arm around the bedpost and using it as a crutch. As she blinks, I notice for the first time just how tired she appears, and it sets something foreign in me ablaze.

It's the exhaustion that's been building, that carves itself into the purple bags under your eyes, and Lenny seems to be one yawn away from passing out.

Scrubbing at my beard, I rock back on my heels. "You should get some sleep. We'll continue the tour in the morning."

I can tell she wants to protest, but after a moment's hesitation, she seems to think better of it.

She climbs in bed, shuffling down beneath the covers, and then rolls to face me. For some reason, I haven't moved, even though my brain is begging me to retreat. To not fall for her pretty face and round tits when she's the goddamn daughter of the man who orchestrated my father's ruin and death.

Who's to say what I witnessed back at the house wasn't a staged coup meant to throw me off, so Tom can exact his own revenge on me now that his restraining order isn't doing the trick.

She may be too bloody beautiful and wicked for her own good, but if I can't trust her, I certainly can't shag her.

Shoving Alistair's suggestion to the back of my mind, I try to refocus on my original reason for agreeing to fake date her. Remind myself that I need the reputation boost—rather, Alistair needs it, and the whole point is to use the relationship with the Primrose family to help him climb the political ladder.

Pausing before I leave the room, my hand grips the doorframe. "You were going to kill him, weren't you? The one manhandling you?"

Lenny presses her lips together. For a moment, she just stares, like she isn't sure how to answer.

I don't need an answer, though. I already know.

Saw the *thirst* in those soft, green eyes.

Pulling back the covers, she reveals a medium-sized paintbrush lying prone at her elbow.

"I wasn't going down without trying," she mutters, her words loud in the quiet room. They're slow and focused, rolling off her tongue without preamble, and it makes me wonder how many bodies the little puppet has left behind.

TWO WEEKS PASS RATHER UNEVENTFULLY, before I realize I've not a clue what to do with a fiancée, fake or not.

Unfortunately, my assertion about not dating was less of an attempt at deterring Lenny from pursuing me, and more of a confession.

I *don't* date. Never quite understood the appeal of intertwining your fate with someone else's, especially in the temporary sense that most relationships seem to exist within.

I'd like to think the aversion has nothing to do with my parents' failed marriage, but in truth, I'm sure the majority of my issues can be traced back to them.

Still, with the terms of our agreement set in stone and centering around our relationship being *known*, it feels wrong that I've pretty much relegated the girl to the confines of the beach house.

Though, she certainly hasn't complained. Not that I've seen much of her in the time since, unwilling to compromise my end goal for a single night spent between her thighs.

If I'm around her too much in the house, I know I'll have no choice but to strip her bare and lick her raw. She's always in these tiny sleep shorts or lacy, low-cut tops, feeding my depraved imagination with every little sigh or grunt of frustration.

One day, I get home from the pub late on account of having to take contractual business to the cellar. There's a tear in my jacket and what feels like clumps of hair missing from my head because the bastard fought until I squeezed the last breaths out of him.

My bad for not restraining him beforehand, but I thought for sure a man double my age and half my size wouldn't require such dramatics.

Lenny sits in front of the closed door to the office, where she's set up some sort of makeshift craft studio. Tins of paint and canvases, blank and half-finished, line every available surface in the room, while plastic tarps stretch over the two dark gray cabriole sofas angled before the electric fireplace.

Since she isn't allowed back at Primrose Manor currently,

her older brothers dropped her belongings off, and her material possessions now fill the house.

I don't particularly mind her making the space her own. Especially given that I'm rarely here, and she has quite literally nothing else.

What I *mind*, however, is the fact that she's stark fucking naked. Sitting with a pillow under her knees, Lenny's entire bare backside is plainly visible to me and the entire ocean, since the lights are on and the curtains are drawn.

"Bloody hell." Averting my gaze out of courtesy, I stare at the marble mantle and try not to look up at the mirror hanging on the wall above it.

From my peripheral, I see her head turn to the side. "Oh. You're back."

"Do you often paint in the nude?"

"Yes. I find clothes restricting."

Pulling my cheek between my teeth, I clamp down until the flesh breaks, flooding my mouth with the taste of copper. "Well, unless you want me to take that as some sort of invitation, I suggest not prancing around where other people might see you."

She pushes to her feet, tossing a little black crayon into a bucket by the pillow. I feel her come nearer, and my body stiffens when she stops just in front of me.

Nostrils flaring, I let my gaze fall to hers, refusing to look farther down. The heat from her body emanates wildly, brushing the surface of my skin the way the sun warms the sky.

"I don't mind if you look," she tells me, lifting a brow. "My live-in fiancé should probably have a pretty intimate knowledge of my body, anyway."

"Who's going to ask about that?"

She snorts. "Clearly, you don't know the paparazzi. And besides, it's not about them asking. It's about knowing your *character*."

"So, what? You consider this research?" A lump lodges in my throat, and I struggle to swallow around it.

"Something like that. Trust me, I did ballet when I was younger. The performance goes better when there's authenticity behind it."

Considering this, I let my gaze dip. Just a fraction, slipping past her chin for a peek.

Just a peek, and just for a second.

The swell of her tits rises and falls slowly, in tune with each breath that comes from her. I can already feel my cock stirring, arousal unspooling like a cut thread at the base of my spine.

My mind wanders, envisioning how it might look to fit myself between her flesh and decorate it with organic paint.

Clearing my throat, I drag myself back up, cataloging the flutter of her lashes as I do so and wishing I could imprint her own reactions to the backs of my eyelids.

Grinning, she tosses her ponytail over her shoulder and traipses back to her workspace.

"How long have you been an artist?" The words spill from me before I can even determine if I'm interested in them, and something lights in her eyes. Something hopeful that I haven't seen in her before, so I can't take the question back.

She picks up a piece of what appears to be charcoal, resuming her sketch. "I think to consider yourself an artist, you have to have sold some of your work."

"And you haven't?"

"Nope."

I glance at the fast-growing collection of her work in the room. "Why not?"

One shoulder lifts, and I keep my eyes on her face. It's completely serene as she creates, almost as though she's entered an alternate universe with her craft where she can relax and just *exist*.

"When I was little, my parents made me and my brothers do a lot of extracurricular activities. Mama said that it was important we had a variety of interests, so we'd be able to entertain important guests as we got older. Before we moved to Aplana, I did *everything*: synchronized swimming, ballet, knitting. Cooking classes and painting lessons. My brothers were lucky, but as the only girl, for some reason, I had to be *extra*."

My face pinches. "That's demented. You were a *child*."

She shrugs. "Mama and Daddy were my best friends, and when you're close with perfection, it takes a lot to keep up." Pausing she glances at the closed office door, a faraway look in her eyes. "But when we moved here, a lot of the stuff I enjoyed back home became more difficult because I wasn't allowed to go out and do stuff anymore."

"You weren't?"

"They hired private tutors and security guards the same year. By the time I turned sixteen, I'd practically been de-socialized."

Though she's not seemed awkward or inept at any point thus far, I can't help wondering what kind of work that would take, to reintroduce yourself to society after being locked up inside for years.

My parents, for all their faults, had at least ensured I experienced the world in its natural beauty. Even if that meant learning things the hard way.

"*Anyway,*" she says. "I had a Calculus tutor who also happened to teach art history once upon a time at Purdue, and she would sneak me in old magazines and textbooks and give me brief lessons between math courses."

"And since you were already familiar with painting..."

"I took it back up, and the hobby stuck." Looking over her shoulder at me, she gives a soft smile. "Making money off your art is a modernist way of thinking. I didn't learn from the modern artists, though, and I guess I just don't think a price tag adds value. I think the quality, the *passion*, is what matters. That's what lives on, long after you're gone."

Leaning against the counter, I watch silently as she gets lost in her medium, smudging patterns with her thumb and creating intricate line work.

"Some of my favorite artists died as the starving archetype." A pause. "Van Gogh, Eva Hesse, Gericault. If they didn't have to sell their work in their lifetimes, why should I?"

"Wouldn't you like to turn passion into a hobby?"

She glances up. Narrows her eyes. "Do you have hobbies, Jonas?"

The question catches me off guard. "Ah... woodworking? Homebrewing, though I haven't done that in a while."

*Murder?*

"And are you planning on becoming a carpenter?"

"Well, no, but—"

"Then you get it. Passions and work don't have to equate. That's not why I do this."

Snapping my mouth shut, I nod to myself, supposing she's right. Passion and work don't *have* to line up, but it certainly makes life a bit easier when they do.

# 14

## Lenny

My brothers were an accident.

I was planned.

Strategically created for the benefit of Primrose Realty, and the company's benefit alone.

My whole life, I sat glued to my parents' sides, touted around as their miracle so they could gain sympathy with the public and humanize themselves. The company seemed like a family-first business, and my face was what all of our PR revolved around.

When the miracle baby spiel grew old, they chiseled away at my personality. Sculpted and sanded until all that was left on the surface was sunshine. Things the general public enjoyed looking at, enjoyed seeing in the magazines and on blog sites.

Because if the public was happy and invested, that meant they'd throw their support behind the business.

Everything—my relationship with my parents, my slow descent into madness, Daddy's attempted assassination—came back to the business.

Primrose Realty.

The real baby of the family, and at the end of the day, the only thing that actually matters to them.

Which is why I'm not at all surprised when Daddy sends a courier invite to brunch. Even though I've been ex-communicated for a short time, I'm sure the media is having a frenzy once again trying to determine where I went and what happened.

I step out onto the front porch to retrieve the invitation and almost mow over a familiar-looking woman standing at the threshold, a fist frozen mid-air as if reaching to knock.

An unflattering squeal peels out of me, and the woman reaches up, wrapping her palm around the head of a dark-haired infant strapped to her chest.

"Jesus," she says, letting out a ragged breath as she checks the child over.

Despite the scowl marring her forehead, she doesn't appear to be much older than me, with dark brown hair spilling down her shoulders and sharp, hazel eyes. They lift, roving over me slowly, and I suddenly feel very exposed in my slinky satin pajama set.

"You're not Jonas." Her voice is soft and slightly raspy, and there are faint yellowish-purple splotches at the base of her neck that disappear beneath the neckline of her black top.

"Uh..." I force a nervous laugh, running my hand over my hair. "Not last I checked, no."

She tilts her head, studying me. "Well, as much as I'd love to stand out here and play the guessing game, do you mind letting me in to pee? If I don't go in the next minute, we're going to have a very serious situation on our hands."

I shift awkwardly, pulling at my blue top. Jonas's warning about not letting strangers inside rings through my mind, and I'm not sure what to say. *I* don't know this woman, but she clearly knows him, and I'm not sure what the rule on known visitors is.

"Okay." Stepping aside, I grant her access, and she immediately swoops in. "There's a half-bath next to the—"

She disappears around the stairs, and a second later a door slams. For a woman holding a baby, she moves fast.

Walking to the stairs, I glance into the kitchen and note the mess I was elbow-deep in when the courier dropped off the invite. Slapping the stationary on the island counter, I quickly scoop the discarded cellophane wrappers and empty boxes from a variety of junk food, ignoring the discomfort in my gut as I consider eating more before she comes back out.

I've cleared about half of the counter when the woman reappears, hiking her distressed jeans higher on her hips.

"Why does no one talk about the postpartum changes in your bladder?" she asks as she comes to a stop in the doorway. "I swear, six years ago I could hold it all night long, now I'm lucky to get from the Asphodel to Kiko's Bakery downtown."

*The Asphodel.* I blink, trying to figure out why that name

sounds so familiar as I push the last evidence of my binge into the garbage, tucking the bin back into its cabinet.

My gaze falls to the infant, and pain solidifies in my stomach, sending a ripple of agony up my spine. I grip the island to keep from doubling over, and clear my throat, looking away.

As if sensing my discomfort, she offers a little smile, rubbing the top of the baby's head. "I'm Elena, by the way. I guess I probably should've started with that."

It clicks, finally: Elena Anderson, wife of the notorious doctor who owns part of Aplana Island. His house, a renovated hotel on the south side, is a piece of property Daddy's tried to obtain for years, with the intention of turning it commercial, but Dr. Anderson's resolve is unwavering.

Like Jonas, the man has a reputation on the island, but *unlike* my fake fiancé, no one dares speak of it. At least, not where anyone can hear.

"By the look on your face, I'm assuming you've just realized who I am," Elena says, pointing a finger at me with a little wink. "Or who my husband is, in which case you're probably scared shitless."

I shake my head. "I'm not scared. Just… confused."

"Well, that makes two of us."

The back door shimmies open, and a moment later Jonas pops through, his pistol drawn and aimed in our direction. When he registers the people in his kitchen, he frowns and curses under his breath.

"*Blimey*. I thought I told you not to let anyone in the house," he snaps at me. The skin around his eye is three different shades of purple, and the white part inside is tinged with red where one of the blood vessels popped.

"To be fair, I basically threatened to pee myself if she didn't," Elena says.

He slips his gun back into his jacket, then walks over to the kitchen sink and runs a washcloth under the faucet, cleaning his hands with the material.

Leaning against the counter, he glares at me with his good eye. "Still shouldn't have let her in. You think those bars on the windows are here to keep you inside?"

My eyes narrow, his terseness unnerving me. "Since that's pretty much what you told me they were there for? Yeah, that was my assumption. Call me fucking crazy."

"You're bloody insane," he grumbles, turning away to dab at his face.

Elena's eyes volley between us, and she raises a brow. "Jonas, introduce me to your guest."

"She's not my guest." A pause, as if considering what he should reveal.

Annoyance stabs at my heart as I wonder how close they are. Since she felt comfortable coming here to use the bathroom and seems totally unperturbed by his state of being, I wonder if he tells her other secrets.

"She's my... fiancée," he admits finally, and a strange sensation washes over me with the lie.

She lets out a half-laugh. "Very funny."

Jonas lifts his head, meeting her gaze. "I'm not joking."

Silence blankets the air for several beats, and then Elena sputters. Shrieks. Covers her baby's ears again.

"You got *engaged*? When?"

"Doesn't matter."

Her head rears back like she's been smacked. "It absolutely matters, dick. Does Kallum know?"

"Anderson isn't my boss anymore, so no, I didn't feel the need to tell him."

Elena's mouth falls open, and I can tell she's shocked by his response, though I'm not sure why. She looks at me, and I shrug.

"It's a recent development," I tell her, ignoring the dirty look I can feel Jonas sending my way. Instead, I focus on the baby, my throat closing up as it lets out a little yawn.

"Well, color me offended." Her eyes narrow, and she looks down at my fingers. "Where's the ring?"

I swallow. "It's... *really* recent."

"Recent," she repeats slowly. "Or fake?"

My muscles lock up, and Jonas groans, driving the heel of his hand into his bruised eye socket. His knuckles are cracked and caked in dry blood, and I wince on his behalf with the pained hiss he releases.

"You want proof, Elena? What? Want me to fuck her while you watch? I know you and Anderson are into that voyeurism shit."

A choked sound comes from her throat. "No, I'm just—"

He cuts her off by stomping over to me, grabbing the back of my neck, and dragging my lips to his. The pressure on my spine doesn't lessen, even as I lean up on my toes to try and relieve it. My hands come to his chest, twisting in the soft material of his shirt beneath his jacket, my nails scraping lightly at his skin.

One of his palms smacks against the counter behind me, and the sound makes me jerk, almost losing my balance. He shifts, trapping my hips with his, and a broken gasp bubbles inside my chest at the feel of him against me.

*All* of him.

Sliding his hand around to the front of my throat, I feel

his fingers curl slightly, gripping tight. Not stealing air, but enough that a little thrill races through my nerve-endings, and a tiny moan escapes me as he parts my lips with his tongue.

I taste coffee and mint, and a little hint of blood. My tongue explores, teasing and touching, deprived of sexual gratification for so long that making out with this murderer in front of a stranger doesn't seem like a half-bad idea.

Jonas grunts, his hips grinding once, *hard*, and the friction between my thighs multiplies, a sudden jolt of electricity zapping my pussy.

"*Okay*, I get it." Elena's voice barely penetrates through the fog, and I wrench my mouth from Jonas's, glancing at her from past his shoulder. "I think I just got pregnant again watching that."

Breaking away from me like I've burned him, Jonas nods to her and clears his throat. "Next time, don't doubt me."

She rolls her eyes, and he follows as she exits the room. I try not to eavesdrop as they walk down the hall, but their whispers are loud enough that I don't even have to strain to listen. Blinking at myself, I wipe my mouth with the back of my hand, then drag my fingers through my hair.

He asks what she came by for, and she said she was at the farmer's market and needed to use the bathroom, and that her husband had happened to mention he was staying here. She assures him no one else knows, at least not because of her, then they say their quiet goodbyes, and the house falls silent again.

Jonas doesn't speak when he returns, just goes to sit at the island with a heavy sigh. I walk to the refrigerator and wrap an ice pack in a dish towel, then bring it over to him.

Sucking in a sharp breath as the pack touches his

bruised skin, he scowls at me. I can tell he's tempted to push me away, but he doesn't.

"Bad day?"

He shrugs. "I've had better."

We stay like that for a couple beats, neither of us saying anything else. His lips are swollen from our kiss, his beard rubbed raw, and I wonder if he's still thinking about it.

I want to ask what happened. How he knows Elena, or her husband. Technically, we're supposed to be getting to know each other, but the secret, dangerous life he lives doesn't seem to leave much room for that. It's been a while since I moved in, and yet he's only been here every night long enough to sleep on the couch.

He's always gone before I wake up.

And while I know that this is what I signed up for—a fake relationship in public, not in private—I can't help wondering what the point is. We're not really pretending if no one's around to see.

My hand slides to the middle of the counter, and I slowly pull the discarded invitation over. He watches the movement, shoulders stiffening as he seems to read the font.

"I have an idea."

Jonas closes his eyes. "I'm listening."

# 15

Alistair crosses one leg over the other.

Uncrosses them.

Takes a sip of his tea.

Drumming my fingers on the arm of my chair, I sit forward, waiting. "Did you summon me here just to stare at me, brother?"

He snorts, running a hand through his coal-black hair. It's unkempt and longer than it was just a few short weeks ago, and I try not to think anything of it not being perfectly in place.

It's the middle of the night, after all, and none of my business what he does in his free time.

"Can't a bloke invite his brother over for a spot of tea?" Placing his cup on the round wooden coffee table between us, he folds his hands in his lap. Throws an ankle over one knee, gripping the joint with his hand.

"Sure, but I don't drink tea, nor do we sit around gossiping like old hens."

Humming, he lets his gaze wander around the living room, and I follow, glancing at the outdated wallpaper with the little boughs of holly printed on it, and the wooden molding that surrounds us.

Not at all the kind of decor Alistair is accustomed to, but being mayor means accepting tradition, and unfortunately, the interior of Aplana's mayoral housing hasn't been updated since the turn of the previous century.

"It's blasphemous that you refuse to drink tea, you know."

Clenching my jaw, I exhale, trying to stifle the urge to bust his kneecaps with the knuckle-dusters tucked in my jacket pocket. "Probably blasphemous that I ask people to give me their confessions before I put a bullet in their skull, too, but here we are."

"Here we are, indeed."

Pushing to my feet, I give him a little salute. "I'm not really in the mood for games right now."

"For Christ's sake, relax, Jonas. I'd have thought now that you're bollocks-deep in the Primrose girl every night, you'd be a wound a bit less tight."

My ears heat, irritation simmering in my bloodstream. I've been on edge ever since Elena showed up at the beach house and questioned the sanctity of my relationship with Lenny.

Rightfully so, maybe, but the kiss I sprang on my little puppet wasn't.

In fact, it was undoubtedly selfish.

Inane.

And I haven't stopped thinking about it since.

Settling on the edge of the armchair, I fold my arms over my chest. "Like I told you before, I'm not shagging her. Too messy."

"I'm certain it could be." He grins like it's the funniest joke, but I just stare at him. Finally, he sighs, pushing a suspender strap off his shoulder, and reaches into the breast pocket of his white button-down. "Okay, fine. I have a request."

"I'm still in the middle of your previous request."

"*Okay.*" Holding a folded piece of paper between two fingers, he lifts a brow. "This one comes from the Great Beyond."

"What are you on about?" Leaning with my forearm on my thigh, I snatch the paper away, untucking the corners. Smoothing it out on my leg, I clear my throat, scanning the page.

The tendons in my neck grow taut, tension slithering along them like a thick sludge.

I look up. "This is Dad's handwriting."

Alistair nods.

Reaching the end, I flip it over, certain there's more. A note, instructions, anything. "It's just a list of names."

"A list of *whose* names?"

My mouth dries up, and I don't respond.

Can't, really.

"Surely you didn't think it'd been me funding your extracurricular activities all this time." Picking his teacup back up, he takes a drink. "I'm merely the messenger."

Crumbling the paper in my fist, I glare at him. "Why am I just now getting the message?"

"If we're aligning destinies, I figured it was time. Now that you're deep in the trenches with the Primrose family, why not use that to your advantage, and get your revenge on the people who helped bury Dad?"

My father's face flashes before me, bright and smiling even when his world was falling apart. Blame was crowned on his head, and the weight of his associations came crashing down, resulting in his death at the behest of Tom Primrose.

Tom didn't act alone, but it would've been much easier on everyone if that were the case. The list in my hands proves otherwise, though I've worked through the majority of them over the years already.

The realization is almost disappointing. Had I known they'd played a hand, I might have enjoyed their demise a bit more.

Still, I don't like the idea of Alistair driving the ship. "I told you, I'm not after revenge."

"I know what you said, brother." He shrugs. "If that's the hill you want to die on, fine. But I don't believe you."

I leave not very long after that, and not before he reminds me about protecting his image, placing the responsibility of our family's honor squarely on my shoulders again.

Like that worked out so well the first time around.

Part of me is tempted to head straight home. Maybe take some comfort in the liveliness that Lenny provides, even if she does tempt me in ways I can't begin to comprehend, given that I'm supposed to loathe her existence.

Lust doesn't compute with hatred, though. My dick appears to think feelings are invalid, so long as there's the promise of getting it wet.

Since I've made such a big deal at this point about not bedding her, I pass up the turn to the beach house and wind up outside Primrose Manor instead. I sit there for so long, reliving the night everything changed over and over until I'm disgusted with myself all again.

All I had to do was get in, make the hit, and get out.

Back then, the Primrose family didn't fully understand the scope of danger they were surrounded in; Tom invested in far more than just property, though, which is how he came to know my father in the first place.

Getting in was simple. A quick scale over the stone wall, the clipping of a cable connecting the security system to the internet, and the picking of the lock to a side door off the chef's kitchen.

I'd practiced breaking and entering dozens of times at that point. Trained extensively with my father and his mates, before his death. Even so, I knew deep down that I wasn't prepared.

But I was fueled by anger. Broken and bleeding from the loss of the most important person in my life, and so I let my emotions cloud my judgment.

Didn't think about how getting caught would affect my family—at that point, my only family was Alistair, and he was just a political science major. I had a modeling job that I'd secured a few years earlier, mostly print work for national corporations and sponsorships, that gave me a certain level of fame on the island and something to do when I wasn't committing crimes.

We were nobodies, though, in the grand scheme of things. I certainly hadn't realized my getting caught would change that.

But it did.

Now, over a decade later, I'm wondering what might have happened had I not been so hasty in my need for revenge. If I'd waited for the right time to strike. Maybe there'd be no Primrose empire today, operating as if they don't have more blood on their hands than I do.

I still don't know what went wrong, and I think that's what bothers me most.

*My failure.*

The lights on the front lawn flicker on, and I take that as my cue to leave. No sense in continuing the war now, when brunch shall be far more interesting.

Again, I consider going to the beach house. Even get to the fork in the road and sit with my blinker on, knowing a good fiancé would be home with his woman more.

Luckily, I'm not the real deal.

Sighing as I pull away from the turn and start back up the road, I wonder why that doesn't absolve me as much as it should.

Parking in a paid lot a couple blocks from downtown, I get out and walk the cobblestone streets, looking into dim storefronts as I pass, ignoring the crazed reflection looking back. Hardly anyone is out this time of night, but the buildings remain lit, as if that's truly an effective security measure.

If darkness wants in, it'll find a way.

A newspaper stand on one stoplight corner catches my eye, and I pause, picking it up and scanning the front page.

*Wild Socialite Settles Down with Outlaw: Aplana's Very Own Romeo and Juliet.*

I scoff, tossing the paper back into the stand. The journalist is grasping at literary straws, unaware that ours is a tale as old as time itself.

Lenny isn't Shakespearean blank verse; she's a Greek tragedy waiting to happen.

She just doesn't know it yet.

Wandering until my feet begin to cramp, I end up in front of an old mattress store across from a petrol station. The place is boarded up, even though I'm well aware of the activity inside.

Aplana isn't known for much, but their network of underground criminals is extensive, and growing each day.

My father had a direct hand in that growth.

Eventually, so did Thomas Primrose.

Just like he had a hand in my father's death.

Still, he wasn't the only one. At the top of the list is a man who frequents the prostitution ring being run out of the basement, and call it a gut feeling, but I know before I even step inside that he's here tonight.

My fingers find the knuckle dusters in my pocket, slipping through the holes and making a fist. I pull my hand out, turning the metal piece to admire the Wolfe family brands accenting the top.

When I beat him to a bloody pulp, I'll leave the imprint as a message for whoever comes to retrieve his body, letting them know I'm nowhere near finished.

# 16

I'D LIKE to think I'm cool under pressure. That the years I've spent in the direct spotlight, learning every trick to appearing unaffected and aloof in public, have eroded the nervous energy that plagues the human condition.

I'd be wrong, but I'd *like* to think that.

Instead, as I stand in line at a thrift shop waiting to pay, all I can think about is the million other things I'd rather be doing. Painting the sun as it stretches high in the blue sky. Eating the block of gouda cheese in the fridge at the beach house until it makes me sick, because even that would be better than existing under a microscope.

The people in the store don't speak to me, but they watch. Like they somehow think it's better to speculate than it is to just come right out and say what they're thinking.

When I get to the front, the cashier's eyes widen as I drop the armload of items on the counter. "Retail therapy?"

I give her a half-smile. "How'd you guess?"

Swinging her blonde ponytail from side to side, she holds up a rose quartz, swan-shaped pencil holder and a pair of fuzzy socks with the original tags still on. "All about the combinations. You definitely didn't come in here with a list, but you're leaving satisfied anyway."

As she starts ringing me up, I chew on my lip, trying not to think about her comment. The total climbs as she bags items, but the usual rush never really comes.

It tries, but stalls out on the ascent, like a roller coaster whose hydraulics are shot and can't make it up the first hill.

Glancing out the front window of the store, I see a swatch of curly dark hair. Jonas stops just outside, toying with the bracelet on his wrist, oblivious to the people who pass him.

Their reactions are mostly two-fold; the most common is the initial notice of the very tall, devastatingly handsome man standing on the sidewalk. Then recognition, and either the gawking intensifies, or the decision to create a wide berth is born.

Most people move to the other side of the street, as if they're afraid the man might accost them unprompted.

My stomach knots as I stare at the numbers on the register. I can almost feel Jonas's attention shift inside, his focus making my entire body heat up.

"...rejected Preston so she could run off and elope with that freak."

A whisper reaches my ears, and I look to my right before I have a chance to pretend I didn't hear it.

Two girls, probably not much older than me, stand at a clothing rack near the dressing rooms, sifting through hangers. They aren't even looking at me as they discuss my life, as if my presence is completely inconsequential to them.

I'm entertainment.

Not human.

"Can't believe she'd throw away such a bright future," the one in a turquoise tank top says.

*Bright future.* I smother an eye roll. Living beneath the authoritarian rule of someone else doesn't leave much room for interests, let alone a future in which I would ever be happy with.

The one with bronzed skin and braids snickers. "Well, she made her way through the men in her circle."

"True. Plus, have you seen Jonas Wolfe lately? I guess I'd be slumming it up, too."

Sucking in a deep, sudden breath, I remind myself that they don't *know*.

People judge what they can't understand.

Running a hand through my hair, I twist the ends around my fist while the beeping from the scanner gets louder.

At least, I think it gets louder. Blood rushes between my ears, embarrassment hot and thick as it washes over me, dulling my other senses.

I don't even need any of the things I'm buying. Don't really have room for them at Jonas's house. Shopping was just always the easier urge to indulge, because it was one Mama understood well.

But the serotonin from it doesn't last. Doesn't even seem to exist anymore.

Reaching out, I put my hand on top of the pile. The cashier pauses, cocking her head in confusion. "On second thought..." I say, swallowing down the nerves that surge into my throat. "I don't think I'll be getting any of this."

She blinks. Hesitates. Looks me up and down, before frowning. "*You* don't want to complete the purchase?"

I can't blame her; I've never left a store without something in hand.

"Well, I left my wallet at home."

Her eyes fall to the vegan leather clutch hanging off my shoulder. "What about credit? I'm sure the owner would vouch for you."

"That's okay." Shaking my head, I take a step away, narrowly avoiding bumping into the man behind me. I certainly don't need them billing Daddy right now. "Maybe I'll come back later."

"Uh... okay." She stares at the pile of clothes and other random items. "Do you want me to—"

Not sticking around to hear the rest of her question, I bolt from the store, colliding with Jonas's sturdy chest the second my feet cross the threshold.

"Whoa, love, where's the fire?"

His hands find my biceps, goose bumps popping up beneath his touch, and I jerk back to tug at the hem of my skirt. "No fire. Just... overheated inside, a little. One thing you can't thrift is air conditioning, I guess."

My forced laugh does little to change the look of suspicion on his face.

"Right." He releases me, looking down at my empty hands. "You didn't get anything?"

"No, I was just looking."

His frown deepens. "I thought I saw you with your arms full."

*How long had he been at the window?*

I shrug, feigning innocence. "Must've been someone else."

For several erratic beats of my heart, Jonas just stares down at me, those violet eyes searing a path straight to my soul.

Biting down on the inside of my cheek, I resist the urge to confide in him, knowing that's not what this arrangement is about.

We're on a need-to-know basis. Even that seems to have its limits.

"I reject the notion that I'd notice anyone but you," he says quietly, piercing my heart with the tenderness of his words.

*"Where's the fire?"*

Right fucking *here*. Can't he feel it?

My brows furrow, confusion and lust etching itself into my brain. The feeling grows when he slides his hand down my arm, locking our fingers together as he begins tugging me down the street.

Disbelief colors my features, muddying my thoughts as he drags me along. I can't stop looking at where we're connected, trying not to let my heart beat too heavily.

Finally, I steal a glance around, noting the photographer stationed by the bushes at the corner of the street. His attention is on us, documenting our every move, and the little thrill from before deflates into nothingness all over again.

I want to kick myself for entertaining anything beyond our contractual duties.

The two kisses we've shared have clearly fucked with me,

and my long-buried desires are making everything look like *more*.

But Jonas isn't capable of more, and he's made that evident from the beginning.

More doesn't appeal to me, anyway. That's not why I'm here.

He drops me off at the house a little bit later before speeding off to "take care of shit," and I busy myself with some sketches. Palmer calls a couple hours after I get home, and I take a towel outside and stretch out in the sand while he peppers me with questions.

"But you're coming to brunch tomorrow, right?" my brother asks, and I hear his boyfriend shout something in the background. "Even *I* got an invite, and we both know Mama and Daddy don't ask me to come to anything."

Cringing, I reach up to untie the strings of my bikini top, letting the warm sun rays beat down on my back. "I hate to say it, but that feels like a trap."

"Of course, it is. But you can't deny that it'll be exciting."

"Exciting is definitely one word for it." Rolling my head to the other side, I gasp as a figure down the beach appears in my peripheral.

Sitting up, I cover my breasts with my forearm, squinting into the distance.

"What? What happened, swan? Are you okay?"

Palmer's voice barely reaches my ears as I stare out, unease notching at my sternum. The shore is empty, practically a ghost town, but I *swear* I saw someone.

Clearing my throat, I brush it off. My mind has been known to play tricks on me, so maybe that's all this was.

Maybe someone from the farmer's market got lost, or a tourist stopped to wet their feet.

"I'm fine," I tell my brother, even though the tightness in my chest indicates otherwise.

I used to see things a lot more often. Shadowy, malignant figures everywhere I turned, waiting to push me down and force themselves on me no matter how many times I screamed no.

For a while, it was difficult to even leave my bedroom. The nightmares were frequent, forcing me to relive that night over and over. To expect it every time I came into contact with someone.

That's why I went to Vermont. A fresh start.

To get away from the trauma.

I thought I'd moved on.

The attack at Daddy's party weeks ago should've been my first indication, though, that I haven't. Not fully, anyway.

*I didn't even flinch when I killed Preston's friend.*

Someone who's doing well would have likely had a different, more appropriate reaction.

Sighing, I let Palmer ramble about past events for a while, using his voice as a balm to my nerves. Eventually, I tell him I need to get a shower, and he grumbles but lets me go anyway, making me promise to text him when we've left in the morning.

My lungs compress as I get to the top of the stairs, a sob catching in my chest. It bubbles, refusing to come out, and I cover my mouth with my hand until I make it to the bedroom at the end of the hall.

The door swings open, and I freeze in place.

A pile of shopping bags sits on the floor in front of the bed, their handles twisted together. Stepping closer, I scowl, recognizing the thrift shop's logo on the reusable packaging.

Pulling the first one apart, I see the pink crystal swan from earlier, and my heart thumps loud against my ribs.

Reaching into another bag, I pull out the fuzzy socks I had in hand at the checkout counter. A cashmere sweater, a porcelain tea set with lilies painted around the rim of the cups.

Everything I had at the store but chose not to buy.

My throat constricts, and I put the items back, sitting cross-legged on the floor.

One thing's for certain: if no one else, Jonas is watching.

Paying attention.

For some reason, I find that as exhilarating as it is terrifying.

# 17

THE WATER MORPHS into a reddish brown as it pools at my feet, disappearing into the shower drain. Turning around to brace my hands on the wall, I let the harsh spray work over my tired muscles, massaging out the kinks that come with a labor career.

I reach over my shoulder, pressing down on a particularly stubborn knot caused by Sergeant Gonzalez's nightstick, another name I've crossed off the list after questioning turned to retaliation.

Can't blame the bloke for trying.

Unfortunately, I've had much longer to sit with my

demons, and their festering can't be cured except by bloodshed.

Every time I come back worse for wear, I can tell the little puppet sleeping in my bed wants to ask about it. Her sweet eyes light up, like she's fascinated by the things that should horrify her, and her mouth poises around unspoken questions.

Perhaps it's just boredom fueling her interest. Aside from lounging on the beach and the endless hours she spends painting or drawing, Lenny doesn't seem to have anything else to do.

It's almost as if she revolved around her family's company and the PR relations she was forced to maintain, and now that she's somewhat free of those shackles, she doesn't know how to spend her time.

With each passing day, she seems to grow more despondent. I thought dating a socialite meant being dragged from event to event, and yet our shopping trip was the first time we've been out as a couple in the weeks since she moved in.

On the one hand, her despair fills me with a sick sort of gratification.

Revenge by proxy.

Alistair's words echo in my mind, his insistence on keeping up appearances reminding me that while I don't necessarily want to care about Lenny's happiness, at least while we're pretending to date, I'm supposed to.

I'm trying to convince myself that that's why I went back to the thrift store and asked the cashier to find everything Lenny left behind. I knew she'd been lying when she said she was just looking, though I didn't fully understand why.

The cost barely amounted to pocket change, so I can't imagine that played a factor.

It doesn't matter, I suppose, although I would have liked to see the look on her face when she realized I'd gone back. The idea of a smile gracing her delicate face because of something so bloody simple makes my cock hard as a fucking rock.

Reaching down, I palm my shaft, closing my eyes to relive the kiss we shared the other day. I've thought about it so often at this point that I can practically feel her soft body against mine, desperate to open up and let me inside.

My jaw slackens at the thought, my fist jerking in harsher movements as I envision her spread eagle beneath me, lush tits and plump little cunt on display. Wet and wanton. I'd grab the back of her neck and haul her up, just enough so she could watch me sink in.

She tastes like absolution, but I'll bet she fucks like damnation.

Arousal draws my balls up, winding a heated spiral up from the base of my spine, and release surges through me. For a moment, I consider the fact that I told myself I wasn't going to entertain these thoughts anymore, but all that does is make me come quicker.

The acknowledgment of the forbidden has me spilling all over my fist, a pained grunt tearing from low in my throat. Sticky semen drips down my fingers, and I brace a forearm on the shower tile, trying to convince myself that she's out of my system now.

I can stop letting her occupy my every bloody thought.

When I step out of the bathroom a few moments later with a towel wrapped around my waist, though, it's clear that's not going to happen.

Lenny stands in the hall, her golden-brown hair pulled back into a single braid that falls off one bare shoulder. Bare, because she insists on wearing those fucking tiny pajama tops with the equally tiny shorts, and every time I see them I'm tempted to tear them down the middle, just to show her how easy it would be.

Her arms are crossed over her chest, pushing her tits up obscenely, and she's scowling. If she's at all startled by the fact that I'm in nothing but a towel, she does a fantastic job covering it.

"Can I help you?" I ask, turning my chin down to meet her gaze. "Shouldn't you be getting ready for brunch?"

"What are you doing?"

My eyebrows knit together. "Ah… I believe we call this bathing?"

"No, I mean…" She trails off, walking backward to the partially closed bedroom door. Pushing it open with her bum, she sweeps her arm to the side, brows arching into her hairline. "With all of *this*. Why did you go back and buy this stuff?"

Following her into the room, I look at the bed where she's emptied the contents of the thrift store shopping bags. Articles of clothing and trinkets are piled up in the middle of the duvet, and the bags are discarded on the floor.

She clutches the receipt in one hand, shaking it in my direction. "Honestly, Jonas, what the fuck?"

Holding my towel closed, I narrow my eyes at her tone. "Are you seriously mad right now? Over a kind gesture?"

"Was it just a *kind gesture*?" She hooks her fingers, putting air quotes around the last two words. "Or are you trying to bribe me into sleeping with you?"

The question catches me so off guard that my chin actually snaps back, like the recoil on a bobblehead toy. She's seething, her tanned skin flushed and clammy, genuinely pissed off that I bought the stuff she'd been halfway through ringing up before she fled the store.

According to the cashier, at least.

Taking a deep breath, I hold one hand up in her direction. "You've got it all wrong, love."

"People don't just drop hundreds of dollars on *strangers* for no reason," she snaps, balling the receipt up and throwing it at me.

The wad of paper bounces off my wet chest, and she blanches as she watches it fall, her eyes seeming to get stuck on my exposed skin. Clearing her throat, she crosses her arms again, cocking a hip as if waiting for an explanation.

Amusement filters into my blood, and I inch closer. "Still strangers, are we?"

She swallows. Hard. I track the movement, my eyes desperate for the image.

"We… our circumstances don't mean we're close."

One of my brows arches. "Perhaps we don't know each other's favorite songs and worst nightmares, but you can be soulmates and still not be aware of those things. Some connections are physical, love. Tangible. You know them when you feel them."

I walk closer, and her jaw tenses. Spine straightens.

*Bloody hell.* Defiance lines the rims of her irises, blazing like tall flames in her gaze. They lick at my skin, scorching a path to my cock that leaves me a bit lightheaded.

"For instance," I say, lifting my hand slowly. She watches the motion from the corner of her eye, keeping her face forward even as I skim her side, smoothing my fingers over the silk material of her top. "Do you feel hollow when we kiss?"

"What?" she breathes.

"The other day in the kitchen, when you had my tongue in your mouth. Did it *feel* like kissing a stranger?"

Circling her like she's a deer and I'm the hungry wolf, I stop just behind her, letting my voice dip an octave as I bend to speak in her ear.

"When you were thinking about grinding your sweet little cunt on my cock, did that feel foreign? Wrong? *Strange*? Or was it just right, just crazy enough that you were as tempted as I was to spread your thighs and let me bury myself between them?"

"I don't know what you're talking about," she says. "It was just a kiss."

"Just a kiss," I repeat, chuckling darkly. My fingers find her hip, and my thumb draws slow circles over the waistband of her sleep shorts. "So, you don't think about it when you touch yourself at night?"

Silence. My thumb pauses, slipping beneath the elastic to seek warm skin. Behind the flap of my towel, my cock jerks to life, despite having been drained less than ten minutes ago.

"No." Lenny draws in a shaky breath. "I don't think about that."

"Right." I hum, moving forward so my pelvis fits against her backside, the shift causing me to flatten my hand and press lightly against her hip. "What do you think about, then?"

"I-I don't," she stammers, her breathing growing shallow. My thumb flicks against her skin, my hand sliding up until I can feel the weight from the underside of her breast pushing back. The swell rests against my forefinger, and my thumb twitches, grazing the edge of her nipple.

She gasps, and I want to crush her to me. Cover her

mouth with mine so every sound she makes after this belongs to me, as well.

But I don't.

I resist, despite the ache in my balls and the lust twisting my gut.

"You're lying."

Scraping my teeth over the shell of her ear, I let my fingers curl into her flesh, squeezing her tit and reveling in how it's the perfect size for my palm. Like she was bloody made for me.

Her back begins to bow, her hips pushing into me as if searching for friction, but then she catches herself. Clears her throat and tries to relax. Closes her eyes.

"I wouldn't need to bribe you."

"No?"

"No," I agree. "You're as desperate for my cock as it is for you, you just don't want to be. I bet if I slid my hand into your shorts right now, I'd find all the evidence I need."

Teasing the peak of her nipple until it's puckered and angry, I let my tongue trace the outline of her ear. Wordless, she cranes her neck—just barely, but I seize the opportunity and continue my trek down the side of her throat, lapping at her pulse.

"Oh, my god." The words are a hiss, and she reaches up, covering my hand with hers over her top. Guiding me, she kneads and pinches, though her eyes stay shut.

"Admit it, love." My lips latch on to her neck, sucking hard before releasing with a wet pop. "Admit you think about me."

"I-I... *fuck*, I do."

"What do you think about?" Laving my tongue over the

red splotch, I move up, repeating the action just below her ear.

She moans. "About you. Us. What it would be like..."

My free hand glides up, hooking in the band of her shorts and shoving them aside.

When I do, her entire body locks up, and immediately I know I've taken it too far.

Lenny's eyes spring open, and she drops my hand like it's a scalding dish fresh out of the oven. Wrenching away, she wriggles from my grasp and darts to the bed, glaring at me with renewed rage.

"See what I mean?" she huffs, pointing at me.

I smirk. "That wasn't payment, love. That was me proving a point."

She rolls her eyes. "What point was that?"

Gripping my towel tight, I don't even bother trying to hide the outline of my cock behind the cloth. Glancing down, she notices, and the bob of her throat is almost enough to make me come again.

"I've seen how you react when a stranger makes sexual advances toward you," I tell her, backing up so I'm straddling the doorway. "I'm still breathing, aren't I?"

Reaching for the doorknob, I toss her a wink before I turn to go and get dressed.

"We aren't strangers."

# 18

## Lenny

SPINNING in the mirror one last time, I smooth my hands down my rose-pink dress, already dreading what Daddy will have to say about it. In truth, compared to the corsets and miniskirts I wear, the off-shoulder crepe dress is fairly modest, but I can feel in my gut that Daddy will pick a fight regardless.

Every bone in that man's body screams vindictive, and he wonders where I get it from.

Heading downstairs, I pause at the easel in front of the office, plucking a clean brush from my collection, something thin that tucks easily.

Fitting it in my cleavage, I take a deep breath and force myself to relax. The sooner we get this over with, the sooner we don't have to interact with my parents again.

Jonas is waiting by the Range Rover when I exit the house, and I almost swallow my tongue when I see him.

The night we met, he was wearing a suit, but I didn't really get a good look at him then on account of the murder clouding my judgment.

Now, he's in an all-black slim-fitting suit with a deep red tie, his dark curls tamed with some sort of product. Seeing him dressed has me thinking back to when he stood half-naked in the bedroom and had his hands all over me.

For the first time in *months*, I didn't mind someone touching me. Didn't feel like my universe was collapsing in on itself, even with the depravity he spoke in my ear.

In fact, I wanted him to do more. Take it further.

Which is how I knew I was in trouble.

As I approach, he drags those violet-blue eyes over me slowly, starting at my Givenchy heels and stopping at the lacy white choker around my neck.

Lifting a brow, Jonas lets out a low whistle, and I try not to make it obvious that I'm thinking about what happened upstairs.

*I can still feel his short beard against my cheek.*

He opens the passenger door for me and I climb inside, tension threading through every one of my muscles. They pull tight, and it feels like they're being shredded one by one like confetti.

Sliding behind the wheel, Jonas starts the vehicle and pulls away from the house. I stare out the side view mirror, my cheek resting on my knuckles.

Movement in the foreground catches my attention, and I

swear I see a shadow on the beach again. But when I sit up and turn, glancing out the back window, there's nothing there.

The lack of large vegetation on this part of the island means there really isn't anywhere for someone to hide, so maybe I am seeing things. Stress-induced figments of my imagination.

Settling back in my seat, I feel Jonas's eyes on me. They're hot where they roam over my skin, and I meet his gaze to try and force him away.

*Mistake.*

Instead, he captures and refuses to let go, even as he continues driving down the one-lane road. His fingers tighten on the steering wheel, knuckles bleaching, and I press my thighs together as I remember the feel of his calloused palm cupping my breast and massaging my nipple.

Moisture pools between my legs, and I cough into my fist to cover the flush crawling up my chest.

"You should probably look where you're going."

A muscle in his jaw jumps, but he turns back around. Drapes a wrist over the wheel, like we're on a leisurely drive and not en route to disaster.

"Any suggestions for dealing with your family?"

"I'd say be yourself, but they kind of hate you."

"Rightfully so, I suppose." The leather bracelet on his wrist peeks out beneath a big, silver Rolex, and I see the little W charm dangling from it. I don't think he ever takes it off.

We travel in silence for a little longer, and I lock my fingers together in my lap, trying to think of something to say. A way to bridge the awkward gap between us, so my family buys the story of our engagement.

Because if they don't, Daddy will certainly try and rip me away.

"I'm a Cancer," I say finally, propping my knee up so it's in the seat with me.

Jonas frowns. "That's no way to talk about yourself, love."

"What?" My face twists up. "No, not like *that*. My zodiac sign. My birthday is June twenty-fifth."

"November fourth."

Scoffing, I shake my head. "You would be a Scorpio."

"I can assure you, I have no idea what that means." Turning onto the gravel drive leading to my family's mansion, he glances in my direction. "Thirty-three-years old. Moved here from London as a kid, had a brief modeling stint as a teenager, allergic to shellfish."

"Yikes. You live on an island outside the Boston Harbor, and you're allergic to shellfish?"

"Quite the conundrum, I know."

"What about college? Friends?" Pursing my lips, I raise an eyebrow. "Jail time?"

His eyes flicker to me as we roll to a stop at the security building outside the stone gate. The window has been replaced, and Matt seems to have been replaced with someone new—a burly, bald man who just glares at us from behind the glass.

If I didn't already suspect that Daddy's into shady practices, the lack of alarm and intrigue around the blatant murder of his party guest and employee would've been a red flag. But what I've learned in the last year is that no one is who they say they are.

Least of all my father.

I give a slight wave, and the gate unlocks, sliding open. Pulling through, Jonas drags a hand through his hair, tousling the strands so a few curls droop down over his forehead.

"Never went to university," he says, parking behind a line of vehicles in the circular driveway. "Wasn't a very good student, so the thought of going into debt for a degree I wasn't interested in never really appealed to me. Took a couple courses in business management and biotech at Roxbury after I got released from... well." He pauses, a thin smile stretching over his face. "I don't think *you* need a rundown of my criminal record."

My fingers toy with the door handle. "Is there a record? I mean, you told me once that the stuff the media says about you isn't true, so... what is?"

Leaning over the console, Jonas balances on the armrest between us, one hand coming up to capture my chin. He tugs, forcing me to look up at him. The tip of his thumb swipes across the bow of my bottom lip, and he smirks when my nostrils flare at the contact.

"How did I propose?"

Flustered with the subject change, I shake my head. "What?"

"Something tells me your mum will want to know. So, how'd I do it?"

"Um." I pull away, flattening my clammy palms on my thighs. "I don't know."

"Come on, little puppet. Level with me here. What did you dream about as a girl?"

Pressing my lips together, I shrug, too embarrassed to admit that there's a binder full of wedding ideas stuffed away in my old room somewhere, collecting dust like all of my other memories here. Pink and white color schemes, bouquets of lilies and dahlias, and a host of Mediterranean destination venues come to mind, but I realize that isn't what he's asking for.

"I didn't dream about a proposal," I admit, and the surprise that registers on his face makes my heart sink to my stomach.

"Not at all? I thought that was commonplace for girls."

"Guess I was a little busy being married to Primrose Realty."

"You don't work for them."

"Wrong." I smile, hooking my fingers in the handle and pulling until the door pops open. "All I've *ever* done is work for them."

Cash and Mama greet us at the door, which I find alarming right away. Normally, she likes to be set up somewhere inside that the guests have to find her. It's disorienting to people who have never been to a venue before, which is how she asserts her dominance.

Otherwise, she'd never have any.

She's in a green dress that makes her blonde hair somehow brighter, and she beams as Jonas and I exit the vehicle, clasping her hands together.

"My, look how you've grown!" Pulling me in for a tight hug immediately, she retreats just enough to give me a once-over, rubbing her cool palms up and down my biceps.

I force a laugh, anxiety swelling like a rain cloud in my stomach. "Mama, I haven't grown since I was fifteen."

"Well, that's just not true. Vertically, maybe, but you didn't always have C—"

"Mrs. Primrose, I presume?" Jonas interrupts, stepping forward with his hand extended. He stops at my side, just close enough for discomfort, and Mama releases me to put her hand in his. "Jonas Wolfe. It's a pleasure to finally meet you."

Her mouth flattens for the briefest second, and then she seems to shake it off, plastering a wide smile on her face. "Pleasure's all mine, sweetheart. Not every day you get to shake hands with the man who almost took your husband from you."

Cash and I exchange a look, and he reaches up to tug at the collar of his red sweater.

"Our relationship did start off a bit rocky, didn't it?" Jonas removes his hand from hers, then wraps his arm around my waist, fitting me against him. His fingers dig into my hip, tiny sparks of pain resonating down the length of my leg.

"Just a tad." She looks between us.

"*But*," Cash adds, throwing his arm around Mama's shoulders. "We're willing to look past that, aren't we? The Primroses are a very forgiving sort."

"When pressured." Daddy's voice comes from behind us, his large frame filling the front doorway. His jaw clenches when he sees me, and his face grows red when he notices Jonas's arm.

"Maybe if we didn't have our fair share of fuck ups, we could afford not to be." Cash steps away from Mama, stuffing his hands in the pockets of his gray dress pants.

"Yes, yes, we've all made mistakes. Some pay more extensively than others, but that's a story for another time."

"The *important* thing is that Mr. Wolfe makes our baby girl happy. Right, Thomas?" Mama says, nudging him with her elbow.

But he won't even meet my gaze. "Certainly, Erin." Clearing his throat, Daddy throws open the front door, revealing the empty foyer. "Let's eat while it's hot."

He holds his arm out for Mama, and we follow them through the house to the courtyard in the back. A wave of nostalgia turns my stomach on its axis, the realization that I went from never leaving this house to not seeing it in weeks making me long for simpler times.

"What do you think that'll cost me?" Cash asks, hooking his arm in mine to mimic our parents.

Jonas trails close behind, his presence a constant source of heat at my back. The only thing keeping me from puking all over the floor right now.

"Be prepared to lose your inheritance," I tell my brother.

"About time I join the likes of you and Palmer."

I snort. "Where is Palmer, anyway?"

"Running late, I'm sure. You know how he loves his grand entrances."

When we get to the glass doors off the dining area, the nostalgia evaporates and gets replaced with violent disgust.

Preston Covington sits at the end of the long, rectangular patio table, a cloth napkin tucked into the collar of his polo shirt. Surrounded by a hoard of men in varying states of dress—two in suits, and two who look like carbon copies of my ex.

Men I wish I didn't recognize, but that automatically send my body into a state of frenzied panic.

They aren't the only non-family guests, either. In fact, that table is among several others, all with chairs filled. Strangers, but by the looks of it, important people in Daddy's life that I'm sure he's invited for publicity's sake.

Jonas's hand finds my lower back, guiding me to the seats we're instructed to take.

Right across from Preston.

# 19

## *Lenny*

"So. How's business?"

Daddy's question makes the rest of the table pause, looking up from their plates. It's directed at Jonas, who smirks behind the lid of his champagne flute.

As if anything about this situation is funny.

Placing the flute on the table, Jonas clears his throat. "The pub is doing quite well, actually. More consistently in the summer and fall months, but there's not been a shortage of patrons throughout the year in a long time."

Wiping his mouth with a napkin, Daddy nods. "I see. And your other business... ventures? Surely, you're aware that my little girl is accustomed to a certain lifestyle. How do you plan to manage that on a bar owner's salary?"

Even though I haven't touched my food, I choke anyway, sputtering into my hand.

Jonas rubs my back, then reaches for my mimosa. I take it from him and sip slowly, letting the bubbles distract from the volume of people watching my every move.

"While I'm sure I'll have no issues *satisfying* Lenny," he says, and I choke again, mimosa dribbling down my chin. The groove in Preston's forehead deepens, and at the other end of the table, Palmer and his boyfriend snicker. "I'm not at liberty to discuss my other ventures because of NDAs and contractual boundaries. You know how it is."

A dark cloud descends on the table, the unspoken meaning behind Jonas's words clogging the air. Daddy's fingers tighten around his fork, and he spears into the quiche in front of him.

"Where'd you two meet, anyway?" Preston pipes up, leaning back in his seat. "You don't really run in the same circles."

"The Flaming Chariot," I say, finding my voice once I've dried myself. Everyone stares blankly, and I internally roll my eyes. "His bar?"

"*Helene*," Mama chides, and I see Jonas's eyes widen slightly at the name. "Since when do you go to bars?"

"Since Palmer started dragging me to them."

My brother freezes, his fork suspended with a bite of frittata on it. "Hey, that was only a couple of times. Not my fault the recreational options on the island are limited. You guys would've died if I'd brought her to the city."

"Boston?" Mama's face screws up, and she signals for one

of the caterers to top off her merlot. "Oh, no. There's nothing for Helene there but trouble."

"She seems to do a good job of finding that in Aplana," Daddy says. He follows it with a chuckle, but the dark look he gives pins me with shame, and I wring my hands together to keep from getting up and letting violence take over.

Rage funnels into my stomach, sifting into my bloodstream until my vision is decorated with splashes of red. The urge to strike is hot and prevalent, making my hand twitch.

I twist harder.

At my side, Cash tries to redirect the conversation. "Personally, I think it looks good for the Primrose name to see Lenny outside the compound. Makes her seem more relatable."

Mama scoffs. "The media loves her."

"That's right." Daddy snaps his fingers, drawing the attention of a man in a sweater vest at the table behind us. "Paulie! Remember those commercials we shot back in the day? All Lenny had to do was smile at the camera, and people ran to their phones to invest or donate, or whatever else."

"She single-handedly raised thousands of dollars in relief funds after the hospital fire a decade or so ago, remember?" Paulie says, tapping a spoon on the table. "The ad copy for that practically wrote itself."

I see Jonas tense up from the corner of my eye, though I'm not exactly sure why. It's not *him* they're talking about like he's not here.

"Just 'cause the media loves her, doesn't mean the *people* do." Cash shrugs. "Her popularity is what gets the brand deals and sponsorships."

"Which she hasn't had in years," Palmer adds, like that's helpful.

Frowning, I gulp down a breath. Release it too quickly, so the air rushes out and I'm left dizzy. "It hasn't been that long. I took a break when I went to Vermont and haven't accepted any since my return, because I've been focusing on me."

"Do you have any idea how bad that looks on the company?" Daddy snaps, his frustration mounting along with the crimson shade of his face. "Withdrawing from society is one thing, but now you're shacked up with a goddamn criminal, and—"

He cuts himself off, seeming to recall too late that there are more guests than family here. One of the suited guys beside Preston shifts, rubbing the back of his neck as if uncomfortable, and a few people from other tables lean in to whisper to each other.

My anxiety skyrockets, bile teasing the back of my throat as I glare at my plate. Wishing I hadn't agreed to this in the first place.

"It's a big change, is all," Mama finishes, giving a placating smile to the crowd. Some people jot down in their little notebooks, and I wonder if they're reporters or gossip bloggers. "Letting go of your baby girl is never easy."

Tears form in her eyes, and the child in me wants to believe her. Wants to think she means it, that she misses me and is having a hard time losing me.

But the truth is, my moving out wasn't a catalyst. It was the final straw. A symptom of a much larger issue that'd been going on under Mama's nose for months, and she chose not to pay attention.

Chose to take Daddy's side without even listening to what I was trying to tell her.

"Anyway," Palmer says, plucking a piece of fruit from Troy's plate. "When's the wedding?"

Neither Jonas nor myself answers, apparently too lost in the fog of our own thoughts. I feel the weight of speculation and look up, noting that the entire table is staring at us.

Shifting, I unclasp my hands and stretch them, before tangling them together in my lap again.

"We haven't really discussed it yet," I say.

Preston's jaw almost unhinges. "*What*? You're engaged, and you haven't even talked about your wedding?"

I shrug. "The engagement is still relatively new, and—"

"When we dated, we had everything planned. Down to the guest list."

Jonas's eyes snap to mine, and warmth floods my cheeks. It's not like it was a secret, and yet for some reason, there's a flash of betrayal in that violet gaze, and it feels like a lead weight's been dropped directly onto my chest.

Across the table, Preston grins, elbowing his buddy as Jonas sits taller in his seat. "What, did you guys not talk about that either?"

My fingers go numb with how tight I'm twisting.

He tips his head back and laughs, the sound drowning out whatever Mama tries to say next. "Classic bug. Too embarrassed to admit how you used to get ridden hard and put away wet every—"

It feels like my chest caves in, his words making my stomach churn. The brush between my breasts digs into my ribcage, and I consider how much effort it would take to launch myself across the table and drive it into one of his eye sockets.

Daddy's fist comes down on the table at the same time a hand finds my thigh. I swallow a gasp when the rough fingers pull mine apart, slipping beneath and keeping me from inflicting more damage.

My fingers ache, and I track the hand as it travels up, finding it attached to a thick wrist with a corded bracelet. Jonas scoots closer, his arm hidden by the white satin tablecloth, and his thumb smooths circles over my knuckles.

"Goodness, Preston," Mama says, casting a nervous look around the tables. Her composure is hanging by a thread, unspooling with each minute that passes.

"Oh, come on. Not like it's anything the whole world doesn't already know." He grins at me, that stupid fucking grin I found charming years ago. When I didn't know the insidiousness behind it.

"Impolite to bring up peoples' sex lives at brunch," Palmer says. "Unless we're all sharing?"

Mama's eyes widen, and she quickly looks away from him and Troy. "No need, darling. It's enough that you're here at all."

That comment seems to slice through the tension in the air. It doesn't get rid of it, just splits it up into more manageable, bite-sized pieces. I let out a breath, my lungs on the verge of collapse, as Jonas's hand slides farther inward.

My eyes shoot to his. Dark blue irises stare back, rage and desire swimming in their depths.

"Keeping secrets, little puppet?" His voice is a low rumble I feel on the back of my teeth.

I shake my head, watching Preston from the corner of my eye as he tries to eavesdrop. "More like embarrassments."

"Hmm." My nostrils flare as his hand continues its ascent, slipping under the hem of my dress. His eyes rove over my face as if studying for the slightest changes in my reaction, and blue fades to violet when he grazes the lace edge of my thong, coaxing a sharp breath from me.

*God, I'm gonna be sick.* Only this time, for entirely different reasons.

"I don't think I like the idea of you not sharing things with me."

Laughter collects in my throat. "Get used to it, *Mr. Wolfe.*"

A low sound emits in his chest, something half-human and half... not. My pulse kicks up, intensifying between my thighs as his fingers inch closer and closer.

Jonas leans in, and for some reason, I look at Preston, regret filling my blood almost immediately. He and his friends are watching, eyes narrowed, and I wonder if they can tell what Jonas is doing.

Then I wonder why I *care.*

Hooking his thumb in the fabric covering my pussy, Jonas somehow manages to yank it aside enough, finding my clit and pressing hard.

I jolt in my seat, my hands gripping the edge of the table.

"Are you all right, Helene?" Mama asks, furrowing her brows.

Nodding, I reach for my mimosa, bringing it to my lips to hide the fact that they won't close.

The first swipes against my swollen flesh are slow. Lazy, almost, like we're not at brunch with my family and a bunch of strangers, but somewhere private we can enjoy each other.

His breath is hot in my ear. "You didn't even tell me your real name."

"It was on the contract," I say.

"I didn't read the bloody contract."

"*What*?" The word is far too loud, mixing with a strangled gasp as he speeds up his strokes, fitting the pad of his finger so it hits *just so*, and setting my nerve endings on fire. My stomach heaves, tension knotting the organs and drawing the muscles in my body tight.

It's obvious that I've been neglecting myself as he silently works, dipping lower to gather some of my arousal and spread it over my skin.

"You want to come while he's watching?" Jonas whispers, and I almost spit out my drink. "Show him, love. Prove to him who you belong to."

"I don't belong to you," I say back, just as soft.

His chuckle trickles down to my core, sending a spiral of arousal up my spine. "You do right now."

Once again, I find myself staring at Preston. His eyes darken, brows drawing in as he clears his throat. *He knows. Oh, god, he knows.* Moving his arm slowly, he drops his fork to the ground, and right when he bends beneath the table to grab it is when Jonas forces my thighs apart and impales me with two fingers.

"Jesus, Len, you're pale as a ghost." Cash grabs the pitcher of ice water from the center of the table, pouring some into an empty glass and pushing it toward me.

"I'm f-fine," I manage, taking the water just so I have something to do with my hand other than bite it the way I want to.

Jonas doesn't let up, angling himself even closer so he can massage the inner walls of my pussy with ease. I don't fully understand what's happening, or why he's doing this here, but one thing appears certain: Jonas Wolfe is a man of action, and he does not take well to threats.

Face red and pinched, Preston sits back up. He glances at Daddy, as if debating whether or not to mention what he just witnessed.

A broken sound catches in the back of my throat at the thought of getting caught so publicly. At Preston's rage, floating freely inside of him where it can't be doused.

The way I've carried mine for so long, because of him.

Reaching across my plate, Jonas grabs a blueberry scone from a silver platter and brings it to my mouth; it probably looks romantic from the other side, like someone feeding their lover an affectionate bite, but in reality, he shoves the pastry between my lips to keep me from making another sound.

I'm basically gagged at breakfast, and even when I try to tear off a piece to thwart him, he just pushes more inside.

*And I kind of like it.* Being stuffed, helpless and unable to peep.

It's exhilarating at his command.

Blueberry bleeds onto my tongue, and my orgasm approaches slowly, building and building; when it breaks, it's like a pipe bomb exploding. Shockwaves roll over my skin, drawn out by Jonas's unrelenting friction both inside my pussy and against my clit.

"Spectacular," Jonas hisses in my ear, the sound just barely breaking through as I fall apart. "You're soaking me, love. Doing such a proper job drenching my fucking fingers. I have half a mind to add more, stretch you apart right here and see how well your juicy little cunt takes it."

I clamp down hard, stars flashing across my vision, my hips shifting mindlessly even as he tries to keep me in place.

"Shh," he says, and the chatter of the people around us starts to filter in, making me hyper aware of the fact that we're in public still. He slides the scone from my lips, then takes a giant bite himself, and I almost pass out. "Be a good girl and don't draw any more attention while I'm inside you."

My mouth is dry as I quickly chew and swallow, and I want to quip that he shouldn't have his fingers in me in the first place, but then he withdraws, wiping himself on the inside of my thigh and righting my underwear.

"Are you fucking kidding me?" Preston growls, his voice too low for anyone else to hear, except maybe the guy with a crew cut beside him.

Smirking, Jonas brings his hand back up above the table, though he doesn't bother moving away from me. My stomach drops when I realize his fingers still glisten.

With his opposite hand, Jonas grabs his champagne, lifting it in the direction of my parents, who don't seem to have been paying attention to us until now.

"To new discoveries," Jonas says, pinning Preston with a solemn look, before raising his free hand and sucking on the tips of his fingers. Sucking *me* off of him. "And delicious brunches."

# 20

KISS FOR THE CAMERAS! *Just a little peck!*

The chants echo around me as I run my thumb over my bottom lip, watching Lenny disappear inside with her mum and brothers. We'd obliged for the photo op, and the strangled noise that came from her as she tasted herself on me was far more intoxicating than I'd ever anticipated.

A few weeks in and I can clearly see my plan for abstinence crumbling.

Then again, how could I have accounted for the fact that Lenny would be like an intravenous drug? One hit of her could leave me addicted as easily as it might kill me.

As soon as the glass door shuts, leaving me outside with the bloke my little puppet used to date, I spin on my heel, searching the grounds for Tom.

"She's never gonna love you the way she loved me."

Cursing inwardly, I turn my head in the direction of the prep school prick who doesn't seem to know when to keep his gob shut. He's lounging on a chaise by a dormant fire pit, leaning back on his elbows with a smug grin on his irritating face.

Two men sit on another chaise behind him, one watching our exchange while the other types on his phone.

Shoving my hands into my trouser pockets, I take a single step toward Preston Covington. If I'd thought to pay any attention to Lenny over the years, perhaps I would've recognized the heir to an oil pipeline. As it is, I've been quite busy, and the lad never seemed to be of very much consequence.

Clearly, the fact that they're now broken up just proves that theory.

"I should certainly hope not," I tell him, pasting on a wide smile of my own. It's all teeth, stretched so it makes my lips ache. "Given that she's no longer with you, mate."

Preston rolls his eyes, sitting forward and steepling his hands between his parted knees. "That's just 'cause she scares easy."

"Oh?" My smile falters a bit. Lenny, *scared*? That certainly isn't the girl I know.

*How much do you actually know about her?* A tiny voice screams in my mind, reiterating the fact that I've been a shitty boyfriend, fake or not. Studying the subject is no substitute for experiencing it.

"If she hadn't run off to Vermont the first chance she got,

things would've been different. I was hooking her up with art dealers and gallery shows all around the country. Trying to get her to do something with her life."

My mouth opens to question the value of her paintings. Not because they're *bad*—what the bloody hell do I know about art?—but because she's said she isn't interested in selling them. Canvases just seem to pile up at the beach house, her muse more active than her desire to turn them into something useful.

Granted, Lenny also seems keen on keeping things from me, so perhaps business is yet another one of her secrets.

"Yeah," one of Preston's mates says, running a hand over his platinum blond hair. "Some of the deals he had in the works for Lenny would've made her a big fucking name in the art world. My boy has *connections.*"

"And you think I don't?"

"I think your brother's not as well-liked as he wants everyone to believe, and that your connections are probably the sewer rats behind your bar." Preston tilts his head to the side, then reaches up and pulls the Ray-Bans off his head, fitting the black frames over his nose.

Dull amusement prods at the back of my neck. "I'd tread lightly when speaking about the people in my life, Mr. Covington. I don't believe you know me well enough to voice your opinions."

"I'll talk about whatever I want where Lenny is concerned." He pushes to his feet, heading back to the house. As he passes by me, he says, "If she'd stop letting her nasty pussy do all of the thinking, maybe she'd realize you're just using her."

There's a split second where I refrain. A singular moment suspended in time where I don't immediately react.

In the grand scheme of things, the pause is infinitesimal, because in the next second I've got the pillock pinned to the wall. One of my hands wraps tight around his throat, and I use the leverage of the house to lift so his feet just barely scrape the ground.

Preston claws at my wrist, drawing blood in his attempt to free himself. Regret floods his gaze the moment he realizes he's broken my skin, and I reach into my pocket and slowly pull out the switchblade tucked inside.

Lenny asked me not to bring any weapons, but I declined to enter the lion's den unprepared.

Flicking it open, I can't suppress my grin when he flinches. His eyes search over my shoulder, and I hear the two sets of footsteps shuffling toward us, trying to save their friend.

The tip of the blade fits itself at Preston's pulse, pushing in just enough to hurt.

"I'm not sure who you think I am," I tell him, noting from my peripheral that his saviors have stopped in their tracks. "But I won't ask you again to keep my fiancée's name out of your mouth. Her life, her decisions, her *snatch*—none of that concerns you any longer."

Removing the blade from his neck, I swipe the tip through some of the blood he left behind on my wrist, then press the flat of it against his jaw, leaving my mark behind.

Branding him would be preferable, but I suppose this will do.

His face grows red and splotchy, and with the slightest jerk of my wrist, the knife slices through his skin, creating a very minor flesh wound across his cheekbone.

"You're fucking crazy," he spits, a tear gliding down to mix with his blood.

"And you'd do well to remember it."

Releasing him with a violent shove, I step back and put my blade away as Preston crumbles to the ground. His friends rush to his side, trying to assist him, but he shakes off their grip and pushes to his feet on his own, before stalking off around the side of the mansion.

The two men stare at me for a beat, and I grip the lapels of my suit jacket. "Gentlemen," I say, nodding once, and then moving on.

Tom's garage sits on the southeast side of his property, the five-car building dwarfed in comparison to the main house. Each overhead door is latched shut and secured with a heavy-duty padlock, a far cry from the way it looked just a few weeks ago.

I suppose finding a dead body in storage is as much a reason as any to upgrade security.

At the back corner of the building, the single side door is wide open, as if he'd expected I'd come find him.

Stepping inside slowly, I do a quick scan to make sure the bastard isn't trying to ambush me. The immediate area is mostly boxes and plastic bins, and only two of the five stalls are filled, one with a steel gray Aston Martin and the other with a cherry red Maybach.

Neither car looks as if it gets any use, though the Maybach is exactly where I find Tom sitting on his haunches, polishing the aluminum wheels.

He pauses his task as I come up behind him, letting out a sigh that seems like it's been held in for years.

"She was supposed to be off limits."

The statement catches me off guard. "I hadn't realized we were in negotiations."

Tossing his rag to the ground, Tom stands and turns

around. He folds his arms over his chest and leans back on the car, staring off into space for a moment.

I wonder if he realizes how easy it would be for me to kill him right now. To finish what I haphazardly started twelve years ago and put my father's ghost out of his misery.

"You don't go after a man's family." His dark eyes meet mine, aged and weary, though no less sinister than the last time we were alone in a room together.

"You went after mine."

"Helene has nothing to do with whatever game you're playing here."

"Well, to be fair, I've gone after other people. Surely, you didn't think that body showed up in your garage on its own."

He scoffs. "I *knew* it. You're a sick son of a bitch, Wolfe. I want you to stay the fuck away from my daughter."

Walking past him to the vehicle, I drag my index finger over the matte hood; the movement causes a loud squealing sound, and Tom cringes.

"What are you suggesting, Thomas? That my intentions with your daughter aren't pure?"

"*She* isn't pure, you know."

My brows hitch, nearly disappearing into my hairline. I stop walking, my face pinching with disgust. "Are you really trying to discuss your *child's* virginity with me? You do realize that's not the commodity it once was?"

He doesn't say anything. Just watches as I circle the vehicle, searching the workshop against the wall that has an array of cleaning supplies and power tools.

My fingers wrap around the rubber handle of a sledgehammer hanging above the wooden counter. "In any case, her purity doesn't interest me. I happen to like the fact that she's positively *dirty*."

Tom shifts, leaning farther into the car as I turn back around. The sledgehammer rests against my thigh as I continue my trek around the vehicle, studying him for any sudden movements.

"I could have you arrested. Two casualties on my property, plus you're in violation of the restraining order."

"You could." Tapping the tool against my knee, I shrug. "But I'm sure there's a reason you haven't. Could it be you're doing something worse behind the scenes, and don't want the attention?"

Silence. Then, "What do you want, Wolfe?"

"Oh, I don't know. Perhaps the same thing I came for twelve years ago."

Stopping at the trunk, my eyes glue to his mouth as it parts, hopeful that this time I'll get an answer. That maybe he's softened with age and become less prone to lying, although I know better.

Men like us don't lie less; we just get better at it.

His pudgy fingers pull at the collar of his shirt. Disappointment spews from his mouth as he says, "My answer hasn't changed, damnit. I don't *know* what happened to your father."

Nostrils flaring, my elbow jerks, the bulky head of the sledgehammer rising and falling in a whip-like fashion. It connects with the left taillight, and the plastic cover cracks, sending shards of acrylic flying.

Tom flinches, raising his arms in a blocking stance.

"Who knows then?" I prod, coming around the vehicle. "If not you, whose side my father worked at diligently for years, then *who*?"

"He had a host of enemies—"

Rushing over to him, I bring the handle of the sledgehammer up, pinning him to the car with the rubber end against his windpipe. He wheezes, eyes bulging as I increase the pressure, but he doesn't really try to fight me off.

*Pity.*

"You were one of those enemies. Kept him close so it'd be easier to pin your fuck-ups on him." His back bows as I push harder, and now he does resist. Bringing his hands up, he tries to pull the hammer away, but I've got a good forty pounds of muscle on him and the benefit of youth. "Did it even matter that he considered you a friend? Or that he had two sons who weren't ready to be orphaned?"

A blood vessel throbs beneath his eye. "I had nothing to do with what happened—"

"*Tell me who*!" I roar, spittle flying from my mouth into his face. He squeezes his eyes shut as the droplets hit, trying to hide from them. "All of a sudden after you moved to the island, he started acting different. Saying people were out to get him, and that he was in trouble. Then, shit started happening around town and he was getting blamed. Companies were tanking and buildings were being destroyed. All that had ties to Primrose Realty, but you want me to believe you had nothing to do with any of that?"

"*No*, I didn't—"

"Lying won't make it hurt less." Gripping his jaw in one hand, I turn his face to the side so I can see it. The evidence of my emotions getting the best of me and causing me to ruin the vengeance I'd been planning for so long.

The W is partially hidden in his sideburn, the mangled flesh having healed enough over the years that you don't even notice that it's there at first.

I can still smell his skin melting away, the metal of the

fire iron ensuring that whoever found him that night would know who did it.

For some reason, I thought my father would be proud. Looking down and smiling from wherever he is in the afterlife.

Stupid, really. Might as well have turned myself in.

Tearing away from Tom, I drop the hammer to my side and take a step back, letting the sound of his frenzied gulps of air seal the cracks in my heart. Cracks he helped put there in the first place.

"When I come for you, it's not going to matter if you've confessed or not. I'm going to make sure you suffer. And I'll take your daughter along for the ride in the meantime."

Lifting the tool, I bring it up and grip the base with both hands. Tom's mouth drops in horror, and he curls into himself as I swing down.

He screams, the sound blood curdling as it echoes off the walls, and the hammer lodges into the top of the car, landing right beside his head.

It doesn't touch him, but as I step back, I see the dark stain forming in the crotch of his pants. A gasp rips from his chest, and he hunches over the hood, struggling to calm down.

I leave him there with the knowledge that I could've done more but chose to have mercy.

This time.

# 21

"YOU PROMISE you'd tell me if he was hurting you?"

Hiding my laugh behind a fake sneeze, I glance over at Mama as she flits about my old room. Her hands rove over picture frames and ribbons won from art competitions back in Savannah—things I left behind because I didn't want the reminder that our lives were ever good.

It's easier to sacrifice yourself when there are memories to ground your hurt in, and I refuse to do that.

"Yes, Mama. I'd tell you if I were being abused and held against my will."

She turns, fiddling with one of her earrings. A skeptical

look crosses her face, pulling her mouth to the side. "You never told me what happened with Preston."

Sitting on the edge of the made bed, I tap my fingers together in my lap. As she comes to sit beside me, she pushes a glass, heart-shaped frame into my hands.

Inside is a lightly crinkled photo of Preston and me at one of the Primrose Realty awards banquets a couple years ago. He's in a gray suit, gripping my hips tight as I sit diagonally on his lap, one of my arms around his neck to keep from falling to the floor.

I remember having to do that because he wouldn't let me have my own seat, and he was constantly moving around as if his goal was to see me slide off and humiliate myself.

My knuckles blanch as my hold on the frame tightens, disgust welling up inside of me like a funnel cloud.

"Preston and I just... didn't work out." I hand the picture back, and she frowns at it as if trying to see past the snapshot. "We had different ideas of what a relationship should look like, and they weren't compatible."

Nausea presses along the lining of my stomach, the lie barely even registering on my tongue as I say it. I've repeated the mantra to myself so many times at this point that it's almost believable.

"Couples sometimes grow apart. But he was good for you, wasn't he? Kept some of your... impulsive behavior at bay." I bite back a retort about how he only amplified them, and she shakes her head. "Plus, your father sure does love him. It would've been so good if you'd married into an oil family."

The fractures in my heart seem to deepen, threatening to break the organ up entirely. "Good for who?"

For a moment, she doesn't say anything. Leaning

forward, she places the frame on the bed, then reaches over and wraps her hands around mine. I don't even realize how tight my fingers are tangled until she threads hers through them.

"I know you can't see it now, but everything we've ever done has been in your best interest. If we seem reluctant to let you go with this... Wolfe boy, it's only because we know how dangerous he is. You know what he did to your father."

*Yes, but no one knows* why. My knowledge of the man is limited, and yet he doesn't seem to be the sort of person who leaves any loose ends, so the fact that he allowed Daddy to live and *also* got caught seems suspicious.

Like he's been dragging it out all this time. Causing Daddy to live in a constant state of paranoia, afraid of when he'd come back.

Or maybe there's a greater force at work here. Maybe none of us know what really happened at all that night.

Meeting her gaze, I lift a shoulder. "Preston's not any less dangerous. Jonas is just more vocal about it."

"If something happened..." Pausing, Mama swallows. "If he hurt you—"

"Mama, I'm fine. Honestly, you're worrying for no reason." Ripping my hands from hers, I gesture manically at myself, forcing a tight smile. Hoping it looks less fake than it feels, because I don't want to talk about what she's trying to dredge up.

Don't want to think about it.

Dwelling brings the nightmares, and the nightmares bring the *urges*. In the last few weeks, I've been controlling them a bit better, and I don't want to backpedal now.

Though even as I brush her words off, the memories resurface, scraping against my brain like the sharp bristles of a hairbrush. My stomach gurgles, cramping around emptiness, and I'm once again glad that I didn't eat during brunch because it would be making a reappearance now.

"Okay," Mama concedes, sitting back on the bed. "If you say so, dear."

~

Jonas is quiet on the drive home, which makes me feel about two feet tall. I'm not even sure how to drum up a conversation, considering the last moment we had together before leaving the house involved him being knuckle-deep in my pussy.

Getting me off while Preston glared.

If I'd been thinking clearly, I wouldn't have let him do it at all.

Probably.

I think.

In truth, my body seems to like having Jonas Wolfe's hands on it, and if he'd told me to get up on the table and spread my legs so he could fuck me in front of my ex, I don't think it would've taken much convincing.

The sheer rage in Preston's eyes would've been worth it.

Still, I can't deny the fact that Jonas is the first man I've *let* touch me since before I went to Vermont.

The first one whose fingers on my skin don't fill me with a profound sense of horror, spurred on by memories.

His comment about us not being strangers resurfaces in my mind, and I glance over at him as he pulls in front of the beach house, studying his stoic profile. The muscles in his jaw seem tight, and as his tongue presses into the bottom of his cheek, warmth floods my core, crawling up my stomach and spreading over my neck.

Slowly, deliberately, his eyes swing to mine.

My breathing stalls, and I feel like a star on the verge of collapse.

"Stop looking at me like that."

The rough, gravelly tone of his voice cinches my chest tight. My heart ricochets around my ribcage, excitement thrumming under my fingertips.

"Or what?" My tongue peeks out of my mouth, wetting my bottom lip.

Jonas sits forward, balancing his elbow on the console. He pinches my chin between his thumb and forefinger, violet flashing in his gaze as it grows heavy.

Heady.

*Hungry.*

Moisture pools between my thighs, leaving me sticky where they meet under my dress. I shift, and he tracks the movement, scraping over the seam of my mouth.

"Or," he murmurs. "I might be tempted to finish what we started earlier."

Desire slinks through my nerves, a thick sludge I'm starting to drown in. Maybe it's odd to go from what happened with Preston and his friends to *this*—a quiet sort of desperation for my fake fiancé—but at the moment, I can't find it in me to care.

All I know is that I want more.

"What if I want you to?" I challenge, capturing the tip of his digit with my lips as he swipes in the opposite direction, smearing my nude gloss.

Liquid heat flares in his irises, and he looks down at my

mouth. Pushes more of his thumb inside, pressing the flat of it against my tongue.

"I'm very different without an audience," he says. "You'd take a lot more than just a couple of my fingers, love."

Reflexively, my thighs clench together.

One side of his mouth lifts. "You like the sound of that?"

I nod.

Just once. Just *barely*.

But it shifts something between us. Knocks a tectonic plate out of place, sending hot arousal rippling through the air.

"Tell me something, first."

Pulling back, I let him remove himself from my mouth. "Okay."

"What's the deal with you and Preston Covington?"

The blood in my veins turns to poison, and I seize up at the question, sitting back in my seat. "What do you mean? He's my ex-boyfriend."

Jonas drops his hand. "Right. And yet the animosity he demonstrated today indicates there's something you're not telling me."

I stare out the windshield of the Range Rover, my eyes fixed on the beach behind the house but unfocused. Blue and white swim in my vision, trying to blot out my thoughts.

Hooking my pinkie in the hem of my dress, I shrug. "I don't know what to tell you. That's just how he is. Borderline psychotic and spoiled."

"What in the world possessed you to date him, then?"

Turning my head, I look at Jonas. "The same thing that told me to proposition you."

His face tenses, an unreadable expression passing over

his face that has my stomach dropping to my ass, though I can't quite pinpoint why.

"And what was that?"

I consider lying again and giving the spiel about Daddy making me date someone. About being my own person and wanting to make decisions for myself that have nothing to do with Primrose Realty or publicity.

But the truth is that my decision to enter a fake relationship with him wasn't a *choice* at all.

It was an impulse. A split-second action driven entirely by the part of my brain that refuses to let me do what I *want* in the first place.

So, instead, I give him this.

Because I want more from him.

"A whim. I didn't think about it, I just... did it because something in my gut told me to."

# 22

My brother rubs his temple with a knuckle, watching as I kneel in front of Carl Campbell, the acquisitions manager at Primrose Realty.

Once a CPA in his hometown of Pittsburgh, Carl's background in finance and experience with embezzlement made him the perfect candidate for Tom's shady corporation.

On the surface, Primrose Realty was merely a company interested in building its portfolio by obtaining large commercial properties and selling them for profit. The reality, however, was a far more common practice for many businesses; the purchasing of real estate acted as a veil, keeping the facade of legitimacy up while they were busy extorting and laundering, and sometimes, trafficking.

That aspect was where my father, Duncan Wolfe, came in. His connections and associations put him at the center of fostering a mutually beneficial relationship with the Primroses, who used generational wealth to buy up half the island.

According to Carl, my father's direct involvement with both parties made him the perfect scapegoat, which is exactly what Tom and co. turned him into.

The list Alistair gave me doxes those involved in the framing and the cover-up, and Carl sits relatively high up because, supposedly, the initial plan was hatched in his brain.

How perfectly ironic that he's currently in so much agony, he can't seem to *hatch* a coherent thought, other than plead for me to stop.

Pushing the ignition on the handheld propane torch, I tilt the W-shaped end of the steak brand—a gift from Alistair one Christmas, and what I keep at The Flaming Chariot—and let the flames heat the metal. The silver tip glows orange, extreme heat radiating off of it and warming my face.

Carl twists in the chair he's strapped to, sobbing into a dirty rag. Tears stream down his face, which only makes him cry harder as the salty droplets seep into the wounds gracing both cheeks.

"I do believe the W is my favorite letter. It's so perfectly symmetrical and looks *delightful* when burned into one's flesh. Wouldn't you agree, brother?"

Turning the blow torch toward Carl, I let the flame scorch his bare knee. The smell of singed flesh permeates the office, and part of me considers the logic in bringing work to my pub during business hours.

Oh, well. Carl's fault for patronizing the place, anyway. It was much easier to take care of him here than chase him down and make a whole *thing* about it.

Alistair snaps one of his suspender straps against his chest, blowing out a breath. "I don't have particular feelings about any letters in the alphabet, Jonas. Can we please get on with this? Some of us have meetings to attend."

"It's almost midnight," I point out, reheating the end of the brand.

"I didn't say it was an official meeting."

Rolling my eyes, I push into a standing position and set the torch on my desk. Carl's wet whimpers are music to my ears as I push the rod into his left pectoral, lining it up so it matches the mark on his right.

A hissing sound erupts from the sight, and his head rears back in agony.

Even when done properly, branding runs several risks. At its best, the direct contact of the heated element to skin results in nerve and cell damage, which is the exact reason I began implementing its use in my hits over the years.

No matter how you do it, the brand bloody hurts, and though I'm not typically interested in torturing my targets, their pain is satisfying, nonetheless.

Plus, there's the added benefit of their anger when they realize the mark is likely permanent, leaving a piece of the Wolfe family with them forever.

As his screaming subsides, I reach forward and tug the rag from his mouth. He pants, glaring at me for a long moment before twisting his mouth up and spitting.

He hasn't been hydrated in several hours and has cried,

sweated, or pissed most of his body's natural lubrication out, so the spit doesn't get far. It drops on the wooden floor, joining the blood and urine pooling beneath our feet.

I click my tongue in disapproval, increasing the pressure on his chest. "That wasn't very nice."

"You're... an... asshole," Carl chokes out, gasping maniacally as the brand pushed deeper.

"And you're about three seconds from me sodomizing you with this rod." Yanking back, I give him a moment's reprieve. "Tell me what else you know, and I'll consider overlooking that little tantrum."

"I don't have any more information," he grits out.

"Don't see how he can think at all with you mutilating him."

My head whips toward Alistair. "Do you have a problem with my methods, brother? Because I've certainly never heard you complain when it benefits you."

Alistair runs a hand over his face. "I don't care if you bleed the man dry. I'm just saying it's hard to formulate a train of thought when your brain is also focusing on the pain receptors in your body. That's just science."

"Okay, fine."

Dropping the iron to the ground, I walk over to the safe in the wall, dialing the pin so it unlocks. Inside, there are two handguns, several clear vials with tape labels, and stacks of cash shrink-wrapped and stuffed in the back.

Grabbing a vial with a blue piece of tape stuck to it, I shut the safe and reach into the cabinet next to the built-in bookshelf behind Carl. Pulling out a syringe, I take a step back, swiping a cloth and a tube of burn ointment, then walk back over to him.

Squeezing some of the cream onto the cloth, I hold it up

for Carl to see. "This is probably going to sting, so I'll need to numb the area first."

The man doesn't say anything, which I take as tacit compliance. Not like he can stop me, since his hands are cuffed behind him and his feet are taped to the chair legs.

Turning the vial over, I stick the tip of the syringe into the soft top, extracting the liquid slowly. Pocketing the glass container, I flick the tube to get rid of bubbles and point the needle at his bare bicep.

He groans as I inject the liquid, slathering the ointment over his chest at the same time.

"There," I say, giving the lad a smirk. "I've scratched your back, perhaps now you can answer my bloody questions."

Carl nods, and I move to the other pec, applying the cream there as well. "Look, kid, all I know is that your father was nosing around back when Tom started involving himself with other figureheads. Technically, Tom was under oath to work exclusively with your father and his organization, but he started other business deals anyway. Your father didn't take kindly to it."

"Who was Tom working for?"

"How the hell should I know?" Carl snaps, letting out a strangled cough. He smacks his tongue against the inside of his gums. "They were top secret. I don't even think he knew."

Pursing my lips, I consider this. While my father's criminal ties shifted to me when he died, by proxy, I'd never been able to ascertain an identity behind them. Just knew that occasionally, they'd send me someone to take care of or investigate, not unlike the things I did for Kal Anderson and my brother.

My gaze slides over to Alistair, who's lounging on the

sofa, one arm thrown up over the back as he stares up at the ceiling.

*I wonder if he knows.*

If my father gave him the list of people he wanted implicated, perhaps he also told him about Tom's involvements.

Bitter resentment hollows out in my chest, threatening to undo all the progress I've made with my brother over the last decade.

"He... Tom knew what... would get your father in trouble." Carl's words become less frequent and his breaths shallow. "He set him up... but that's all I know."

Frankly, that's all I need to know.

Alistair gets to his feet. His forehead scrunches as he walks over, studying Carl with a blank expression.

As Carl begins struggling to inhale and exhale, he grows panicked, though his body is too drained to do much. Paralysis takes him slowly, and I notice the exact moment he catches on, looking up at me with a hint of betrayal in his eyes.

Within a half hour, he's dead.

Sighing, Alistair walks to the sofa and grabs his suit jacket. I take the tincture from my pocket and hold it up, shrugging.

"Saxitoxin."

"Naturally." He pauses. "But why? You could've threatened him, continued with the torture. You didn't even figure anything out."

"He had over a decade to come clean, and my patience for secrecy is fast-running out. It's not always about the information. I'm clearing Dad's list, regardless."

Staring at the man's lifeless body, I can't stop a twinge of disappointment stabbing at my chest. I'd been hoping for a clear-cut confession. Something saying Tom killed my father directly, so that his inevitable demise wouldn't feel like a complete waste.

Action without answers is a simple, hollow victory.

One I'll take but won't enjoy nearly as much.

Alistair leaves as I begin cleaning up, ridding myself of Carl's body by draining his blood, dismembering and packing him into stiff storage containers, and delivering him to Tom's security team under the guise of it being something his secretary had special-ordered.

When I get back to the beach house, I don't immediately go inside. The lights are on downstairs, though the curtains are drawn so I can't see in.

Not that I need to. At this point, several weeks into our little arrangement, I have Lenny's daily routine down to a bloody tee. Since the brunch at Primrose Manor, we've gone out on a scourge of public outings, satisfying the interest of those who seem to have nothing else going on in their lives.

It's impossible to go anywhere and not see our faces plastered on a blog site or gracing a television screen. While the attention makes me incredibly uncomfortable given my personal life, Alistair at least says his poll numbers are increasing.

I'm three-quarters of the way done with a fifth of Jameson when I see a shadow on the porch. It moves slowly, sticking to the white siding of the house, as if trying to peer inside.

My brows furrow and I sit forward, looping my wrist over the steering wheel. Taking a swig from the bottle, I watch as it comes closer to me, wondering if Lenny's come to investigate my whereabouts.

The shadow freezes at the porch steps, like a deer in

headlights. I can't tell if they're looking at me, and that's why they've stopped, or if there's something else out there.

Something sinister that I can't see.

Fiddling with the door handle, I try to get out, but my vision clouds and my hand doesn't seem to want to cooperate with my brain. I struggle for what seems like hours before I finally latch on and shove it open, stumbling out of the Range Rover with a grunt.

When I look up, the silhouette is gone.

Chuckling to myself, I start up the front walk. My chest warms at the thought of Lenny running and hiding from me, possibly punishing me for leaving her alone in the house more often than not.

Part of me hopes that's what she's doing. Being the defiant, fiery girl I met at that party, so I have an excuse to fuck it out of her.

I get to the front door and push it open, spotting her on her knees across the room. I don't even pause to consider the fact that she's naked, or that it doesn't seem possible for the shadow from the porch to have made it back inside to hunch over a canvas that quickly.

My feet carry me to her like a sailor being lured to his death at sea.

# 23

## Lenny

JONAS'S BREATHS come in short, scattered bursts as he throws open the front door.

He stands at the threshold, eyes wild and his dark curls tousled like he's been running his hands through the strands for hours. Casting a look about the foyer, he takes a moment as if to gather himself before stepping inside and slamming the door.

One hand on the wall, he stumbles slightly, his leather jacket squeaking as he leans into the plaster.

Keeping my eyes on him, I slide the empty box of frozen

French bread pizza to the side, pushing it under an end table, pulling my brush away from the canvas before me.

Tripping over his boot, Jonas clutches the wall, kicking the shoe off and across the room. It hits the fireplace in the living room, landing in front of the couch. He grumbles under his breath, bending down to unlace the other; after nearly toppling over, he gets frustrated and punts the other off as well.

It crashes against one of the massive windows behind me, the sound echoing through the house.

I dip my brush into my cup of water, then gently into a light blue paint tin. He comes over, staring hard at me as he grabs the doorknob to the office. Almost as if he can't stand upright on his own.

My eyes narrow. "Are you drunk?"

"Are you naked?"

Glancing down, I resist the immediate urge to cover myself. In all honesty, I'd forgotten until this moment that I'd taken my robe off in the first place. There's something innately calming about painting, especially since I moved to the beach house, that allows me to get fully absorbed in the work so I forget reality.

Though with the way he looks like he wants to swallow me whole right now, I'm kind of wishing I'd paid more attention.

"I've told you. I like to paint naked."

"Yes, yes. It's *freeing*, or whatever nonsense you say." Scrubbing his hands over his face, he stalks over to where I'm kneeling, stopping just in front of the plastic tarp I use as my workspace.

"I've been doing it since I was little. Can't change the process now." Shrugging, I bring my brush down on the painting, creating a watercolor sky across the top of the page. "If you don't believe me, you should try it sometime."

The weight of Jonas's stare burns into the top of my head as I work, adding subtle pinks and oranges with no actual vision of what I'm creating. My art has never worked out that way; it's always an idea, a foggy concept that pops up in my head, but that I can't necessarily see until I begin.

It's much easier to change perspective and add to something than it is to stare at a blank slate, hoping inspiration eventually strikes.

"Okay."

Confused, I lift my chin. "What?"

Jonas's hands come to his leather jacket, unzipping and shucking it off. "I said okay."

My eyes bulge, and the paintbrush falls from my fingers, rolling to the edge of the frame. Hooking a thumb in the neck of his black T-shirt, Jonas tugs the material over his head, revealing a broad chest and well-sculpted hips.

Any saliva present in my mouth dries right up. My eyes scour over every rigid plane, soaking in the defined muscles and the hair trailing down his belly button, disappearing into his jeans.

"Y-you can't." I pause, forcing a swallow over the ball of nerves in my throat. "Get naked, I mean."

"If you are, why can't I?"

"We can't *both* be naked."

A slow, wicked grin appears on his face. "Why not, my little puppet? Don't think you can control yourself?"

"Please. You're the one who can't seem to keep your hands off me."

"Nor do I wish to." His gaze heats, stirring arousal in my

stomach like a thick honey. "Right now, though, I'll behave. Perhaps you can teach me a thing or two."

The double meaning isn't lost on me.

Apprehension threads through my shoulders as he toys with his bracelet, loosening and setting it aside. As he reaches for his belt, my hands lash out, halting him. Paint gets on his fingers and the denim of his pants, and both his brows arch.

I'm stretched awkwardly, my balance hinging between my grip on his buckle and my knees. One wrong move and I'll mess up the piece I've been working on since yesterday morning.

Clearing my throat, I consider my options. I can redo the painting if I fuck it up beyond repair. Nothing I haven't done a hundred times before—nearly every piece I've created has at least two versions of itself in my attempts to perfect the craft.

Or I can let him strip. Take that step into a slightly more vulnerable place with the man who's occupied most of my thoughts for the last few weeks.

The man who hates my family and tried to murder my father.

A man who's made it clear that, if we *did* get together, the sex would be very, very good.

Phenomenal, even.

The memory of his hand between my thighs at brunch resurfaces, and warmth floods my cheeks. Short tingles radiate up and down my limbs, making me feel liquid as I recall how it felt to have someone touch me when their intent was not malicious.

How interesting that a man with so much blood on his

hands is the only one who seems capable of refusing to harm me.

Still, as I slip the pin from its notch in the leather belt, there's a little voice in my head saying *yet*.

*He hasn't hurt me* yet.

But I ignore it, choosing instead to focus on the sound of him sucking in a breath. My fingers tremble as I unhook the buckle, slowly dragging the end through the metal square. His eyes stay on mine, wide and unblinking, like he's trapped and can't possibly look away.

Somehow, my chest feels the same. Caged tight and quickly running out of air.

"I was joking, love," he rasps. The words sound forced and scratchy, like he has to reach in and tear them from his throat.

Acid bubbles in my chest. There's something painfully erotic about our stance—him towering over me as I kneel before him, trying to... well, I'm not exactly sure what I'm trying to do.

Maintain what little power I have here, maybe. If I let him disrobe on his own, all it does is prove my discomfort.

If I take the initiative, it proves I'm *okay*.

Popping the fly of his jeans, I hook my fingers into the waistband and pull them down over his hips. His cock bobs free, partially erect, and I gnaw on the inside of my cheek at his size.

Far bigger than Preston even as it is now.

My clit pulses, the muscles in my thighs clenching.

Glancing up, I let his jeans pool at his feet, then push the canvas aside and sit back on my haunches, clasping my hands behind my back.

Jonas squeezes his eyes shut, drawing a stuttered breath.

"Do you have any idea what you're doing, my little puppet?"

Resentment and shame coil in my gut, and I give him a dirty look. "I've sucked dick before, you ass—"

His arm lashes out, one hand coming around my head, gathering my hair in a ponytail and tugging back at the base. My neck bends at an almost ninety-degree angle, and goose bumps spray down my arms and legs, making me shiver.

"It's in your best interest to not speak of those before me."

My mouth twitches. "Why? Ego can't handle knowing yours isn't the first dick I've seen?"

"I can handle it just fine," he says, gripping the thick shaft with his free hand, giving it a single pump in front of me. "I just don't want to. When my cock is in your face, I don't want to imagine all the others you've taken because they no longer matter."

"'Cause you're *so* good in bed?"

Tightening his fist in my hair, he pulls back even farther so I have to press up on my knees to keep my spine from snapping. When he shifts, I feel the mushroom head brush my lips, leaving behind a salty residue as it drags across them.

"They don't matter," he rumbles, his voice dropping so its low vibrations echo in my chest, "because once I'm inside of you, splitting you open and filling your cunt with so much cum you choke, you won't remember anyone else existed."

*Oh, God.*

My body hums, electricity thrumming through my bloodstream as he leverages my face, moving it left and right to massage the underside of his cock. As he moves me, my nose brushes his balls, and the urge to taste him becomes overwhelming.

Maybe it shouldn't. This whole situation feels dirty, but my pussy responds in kind, pulsing wantonly as he degrades me.

"I said I wasn't going to fuck you," Jonas grits out, his cock growing as he continues.

"Doesn't seem like you meant it."

Licking my lips, I let the tip of my tongue swipe against the base of him, then flatten and drag it along the thick vein running up the middle. He grunts as I reach the crown, curling around it before he pulls me off.

"No," he agrees, fitting himself against my mouth again. "I lied."

Parting my lips, I let saliva pool under my tongue before easing forward, wrapping my lips around his head. He tastes clean, the scent of his natural musk making my pussy throb with anticipation.

"Do you have any idea how stunning you look on your knees?"

Pulling back, I kiss his slit, absorbing the pearly bead leaking from it. "Not as stunning as I'll look with you down my throat."

His fist jerks, and he grins. "Go on, then. Show me a masterpiece."

One of my hands comes up, and I grasp him at the base, taking him back into my mouth. I work slowly, laving from side to side as I meet where I'm wrapped around him. Flattening two fingers against his pelvis, I inch deeper, gagging when his tip meets resistance.

"*Bloody* hell," Jonas groans, clenching and unclenching his jaw.

As I retreat, mucus and spit leak past my lips, dribbling onto my knees and the floor. His cock is wet and sticky, and I sit forward, smearing the head over my chin, my tongue, my cheeks.

We don't break eye contact; his irises smolder, violet flames that flick against my skin, sending waves of heat spiraling through me like a wildfire. Delirious approval lightens his features as I move back in, bobbing up and down with more vigor, adding the pumping of my hand over his skin.

"Christ, that's—" He breaks off, choking as I swirl around his crown, sucking in shallow strokes. "Perfect, love. You feel bloody perfect."

Pride beams through me like a lightning bolt, and I drop my hand. Pushing my palms into my knees, I redouble my efforts with no other assistance, enveloping as much of him as possible into the warm, wet tunnel of my mouth.

"Is this what you think about at night?" he taunts, adding a little force behind his grip on my hair. Am I imagining his breathlessness, or is that *me*? "Sucking your fiancé off while your cunt floods the floor?"

Heat scorches my cheeks, and I bring my thighs together. Wetness collects between them, and I'm pretty sure if I slid my hand south, I'd feel just how slick and swollen I am, but it's ridiculous that he just knows.

My pride wants me to hide my attraction better. To not let him know how he affects me, but Jonas Wolfe has seen right through me since the night we met.

It's a completely unnerving feeling, realizing you're not as formidable as you thought.

"Fake fiancé," I say around him, my words garbled and sloppy.

Jonas grunts. "Good girls don't speak with their mouths full."

With my lungs on fire, I get back to work, hollowing out my cheeks each time he reaches the back of my throat. His hold on my hair sends spots across my vision as he begins dragging me faster up and down, and I retch noisily as he coaxes me farther.

"Deeper, love. Just like that. *Fuck*." His approval makes my toes tingle, and I chase more, licking and sucking and gagging until it feels like I might actually have bruised my esophagus. "This is what I think about, you know. When I fuck my fist every night, it's to the thought of my little puppet on her knees, letting me command her strings."

I let out a moan as he picks up the pace, focusing on not throwing up. His hips piston into me, his pelvis bumping my nose with each thrust, and I give up on trying to control it, letting him lead with occasional breaks to breathe.

"Usually you're tied up in my fantasies. Completely and utterly helpless as I discover all the ways I can shove my cock into your tight little body."

The image of being bound does something strange to me, almost freezing the fire in my veins. I reach up and grab onto his hips, trying to push it from my mind as he gets closer.

"You're *always* touching yourself, though. Making yourself come while I use you." With his free hand, he takes his thumb and wrenches my right eyelid open, forcing me to look up at him while he defiles me.

The lewdness of the act and his words works alongside the adoration in his gaze, and the unease from a moment ago subsides into something warm and fuzzy. I sweep over my ribs and down between my legs, obeying even though he didn't explicitly ask.

His vibrant gaze grows dark as my fingers land on my clit, spreading my arousal around as I begin rubbing.

"*Yes*," he hisses, his thrusts growing erratic and harsher, "fuck yourself, love. Come on your fingers and imagine your cunt squeezing my cock."

Moaning, I push slightly in, pumping slowly and keeping the heel of my hand on my clit, as he seems to swell in my mouth.

"That's it," he coos, throwing his head back at the same time the first ropes of cum splash against my tongue. "Feel how I'm filling you up, my little puppet? Don't you waste a bloody drop."

As if on cue, I gag as his semen collects, teasing the back of my throat as I hold it there. Pushing my finger in deeper, I let out a ragged moan as one tears through his chest, and with the added friction of my palm, I follow him over the crest of oblivion within seconds.

My face is sticky when he finally lets me go, and I remove myself from him with a dull pop.

"Show me," he says, and I frown, not sure what he means. His hand comes up, stroking my jaw. "Open your mouth and show me what I gave you."

Using my tongue to push some of the warm liquid around, I open my mouth and stick my tongue out. His thumb caresses my cheek, and the aftershocks of my orgasm have me panting, satisfied yet somehow ready for more.

"Beautiful." With a sigh, he drops his hand and moves back a step. "I think you were made to take my cum, love. You did perfectly."

I grin, swallowing the load with a slight wince, then wipe my mouth with the back of one hand. "Careful, my ego might just swell to match yours."

"Swelling isn't always bad," he says, voice low. "In fact, why don't we—"

A sudden crash against the back door cuts him off, and then a light flashes through the windows, shining against the far wall. As if someone's on the other side of the glass, though it's impossible to see how dark it is outside.

For a second, neither of us moves. We blink at each other, still half-drugged by our orgasms.

Jolting upright, I dive to the couch where my robe is and pull it to me, covering myself from a potential intruder. Jonas steps into his jeans quickly, never removing his eyes from the back door.

"What was that?" I ask, unable to hide the quiver in my voice.

It's not like this part of the island sees a lot of guests, and even less so at two in the morning. The shadowy figure I've seen a few times now comes to mind, filling me with a heavy dread as I try to consider who it could be.

"Wait here," Jonas says, holding his hand up like I'm a dog. I scoff, starting to push off the couch, and his head whips in my direction. "*Wait. Here.*"

He creeps over to the door, peeking out the windows from the side, before reaching for the doorknob. I begin to protest, given that he doesn't have a weapon, but he just ignores me and opens it anyway.

When he disappears into the night, I try not to think about how my last memory of him might be the way his cum tastes on my tongue.

# 24

I SHOULDN'T BE outside without a shirt or a way to defend myself.

I know it even as I open the door, but I'm still just buzzed enough from the alcohol and Lenny's sweet, glorious mouth that I don't stop to think it over.

Waves lap at the shoreline behind the beach house, each crash of water into sand louder than the last. Aside from that, I don't hear anything else.

Don't *see* anything, despite the obnoxious sound of something hitting the window just moments ago. No one's in the immediate vicinity, and as I stalk around the perimeter of the property, I come up empty.

And much more paranoid.

Heading back inside, I pause with my hand on the doorknob, glancing down at the far end of the porch. Something dark catches my eye as it contrasts with the light wood, and I walk over, bending down to inspect.

A flashlight.

Suspicion weaves through my stomach as I look around once more, scanning the beach for even the slightest sign of life. The breeze picks up, whispering across my bare skin and setting my nerves on edge.

In my line of work, I've seen a multitude of unwelcome visitors over the years. People who track me down with the intent of seeking justice for those they've lost at my hand.

Aside from the Andersons and mine and Lenny's brothers, though, no one knows we're out here. At least, they *shouldn't* know, but the fact that someone's clearly been around has murderous rage coursing through my nervous system.

Careful to only grab the handle, I pinch the light between two fingers and stand up, taking it inside. Lenny's standing just beyond the threshold, clutching the lapels of her robe to her neck.

"Did you find something?" she rushes out, hurrying to my side.

I walk into the kitchen and set the flashlight on the counter. She looks at it, then up at me, green eyes narrowed. "What's that?"

"Certainly, you've seen a flashlight before."

Her expression flattens. "I *mean*, where did it come from? Is it yours?"

"No, Lenny, I don't typically leave my belongings unattended." Starting down the hall with the light, I swipe my shirt from the floor and pull it on, heading for the front door.

"Wait, where are you going?"

"To figure out who's been traipsing around my bloody property."

Lenny shifts, toying with the tie of her robe. "Do you... so, you think someone's out there?"

"Hence the swift departure."

"And you're just gonna leave me here?"

My hand tightens around the knob. "You're plenty safe in the house, I can assure you."

Rubbing her arms, Lenny fiddles with a strand of hair. "What if I'm not? What if someone breaks in while you're gone, even though you have those weird bars on the windows, and I can't escape?"

"Because of the bars."

She nods, glancing down at her toes as they curl into the floor. I watch her for several beats, noting the rapid rise and fall of her chest, as well as the soft, vulnerable expression on her face, and a strange feeling wells up inside me.

Like I've been raked over hot coals and left to tend to the wounds on my own.

"All right," I tell her, forcing irritation into my voice so she doesn't get the wrong idea. As if this is more than just the simple fact that I don't care to see my investment harmed.

I'm sure it has nothing to do with the fact that her fear makes me uneasy, because it's not something I've seen from her before.

Lenny scrambles up the stairs, returning a few moments later in a pair of jeans and an old Nirvana T-shirt of mine. I cock an eyebrow as she tugs at the hem, clearing her throat when she reaches the bottom of the steps.

"It was the first thing I grabbed," she says, and I don't respond because I can't admit what I want to.

That she looks delectable in my clothing.

That I wouldn't mind seeing her in it for the duration of our little arrangement.

But enough lines have been crossed tonight, and I don't want to add fuel to the fire.

We get to the Range Rover, and I go to her side and pull open the door, but she stops at the trunk, folding her arms over her chest.

"I don't think you should drive."

Snorting, I release the door and take a step toward her. "Dare I ask why?"

"You were drunk when you came home, or at least had been drinking. It's not safe."

"Hmm." My legs carry me closer, not stopping even as I breach the confines of her personal space. She sucks in a little breath that I feel in my cock as I back her up against the vehicle.

Lashing out, I grab both of her wrists in one hand and bring them up, forcing her to bend her elbows so I can press them into the vehicle above her head.

"Are you saying you took advantage of me a few moments ago?"

She blinks. "*What*?"

I smirk, pushing my hips into hers. So close I can still smell myself on her breath, though it's replaced with a hint of mint. "If I'm too drunk to drive, doesn't that also mean I was too drunk for you to strip me down and let me use your throat like a cunt?"

The slightly aroused flutter in her eyes evaporates immediately, and her body goes rigid against mine. She struggles, twisting her hips and wrists in an attempt to escape, and her breathing grows uneven like the edge of a serrated knife.

Horror, finite and resolute, flashes across her face as I grip tighter, not quite sure what's happening.

"Let *go* of me," she spits through clenched teeth, some saliva hitting my chin. As she rears her head back, I think she's about to let a wail into the night air, but instead her neck snaps forward like a whip.

Her forehead cracks against my mouth and my teeth slice into the inside of my bottom lip, flooding the cavity with the taste of copper.

Mind swimming, I stare down at her, blanking completely for a moment. The assault refuses to compute, giving her enough time to recover and jerk back to repeat the motion.

She hits again, and this time it knocks me off-kilter; I stumble back a step, stars dancing in my vision, and she darts back to the beach house.

One second ticks by as I raise my finger to my lips and bring it away covered in blood. In the next, I spring into action, lunging after her, my long legs eating the distance between us twice as quickly as she can move.

There's no time to consider how to trap her. I simply barrel into her body, and we land in a sweaty, angry heap of tangled limbs on the ground.

A scream rips out of her throat, vibrating my chest as it rests against her back.

"What in the bloody hell is happening?" I snap, trying to shove my hands beneath her as she attempts to crawl away.

"You're *sick*, and I want you to stay away from me."

Her arse pushes against my groin, and I feel myself stir behind my trousers despite the circumstances.

Maybe even because of them.

"Well that's too damn bad now, isn't it? I told you weeks ago that you're stuck with me as long as we're pretending."

"I want out," she sobs, wrenching her face to the side. It's caked in dirt and tears, and there's a tiny cut on her forehead dripping blood. "This was a stupid idea, and I think we should stop."

"Unfortunately, I don't really care. We're in it deep, my little puppet, and I don't particularly feel like letting you go."

Again, she screams, and this time I manage to get my hands on her hips, pulling back enough to flip her over. Fury lines the delicate ridges of her face, creasing her forehead as she glares up at me.

"Now," I say, brushing the hair from her mouth, "care to explain to me what in the hell just happened?"

She doesn't say anything for a moment. Just stays totally still, watching me with wide, guarded eyes that look like sea glass in the porch light.

My palms dig into the ground on either side of her head, but I feel it against my knee when her hand shifts. Sliding my gaze downward, I try to swallow down my amusement when I realize what she's holding.

A paintbrush, medium-thick and broken into a shiv-like device at one end. My sweet little puppet's go-to defense mechanism, the weapon that makes her so uniquely *her*.

Slowly, she lifts her hand between us, knuckles white from how hard she's gripping the handle. Touching the sharp end to my chest, she still doesn't speak. The wood tip stabs through my shirt and into my skin, but just barely;

she'll need more leverage if she wants to actually do any damage at this angle.

Chuckling, I wrap my fingers around her tiny palm, urging her to push harder as I rock my hips into her. Her swallow is audible, and she parts her legs—just slightly, but enough that I feel the shift.

"Interesting form of foreplay," I murmur, biting back a moan as she swivels her pelvis up, meeting the roll of mine. "But you always were a bit murderous, weren't you?"

"You don't know anything about me," she says.

"I want to. Desperately." Cocking my head to the side, I give it an incredulous shake, because I can't believe the sentiment, nor that I'm admitting it.

"Because you think I'm weird?"

"Because I think you're *terrifying*."

With a sigh, she releases the pressure on the paintbrush, and I'm racked with the sudden, inexplicable urge to lean down and kiss her. To seal this night between us as some kind of monument, attaching it to our relationship indefinitely.

I dip down, allowing the tip of the brush to stay notched against my pec, and I don't feel the movement of her free arm. My focus remains solely on her pretty, puffy lips, and the image of my cock sliding between them not even an hour ago takes root, blotting out all logical thought and self-awareness.

When the blunt object smacks into the side of my head, it takes a moment for the ringing in my ear to catch up with my sudden loss of vision. A grunt falls into the air, whisked away on a sea breeze, though I'm not sure who it belongs to.

The object comes down again, something dull but thick, and this time it sounds as if something in my skull cracks.

Pushing off of her, I clutch at the wound, my fingers coming away slick as I feel around beneath my hair. I'm too stunned to speak, and as soon as my eyes meet hers again, she manages to wiggle out from under me before I can comprehend what's just happened.

A large rock falls to the ground in front of me as she jumps to her feet, and this time when she bolts, I let her.

# 25

## Lenny

My first thought is to run back into the beach house, but then I don't want to think about how Jonas will retaliate. Attacking him was definitely not something I saw coming, but the urge to free myself became overwhelming, and my body moved before my brain could catch up.

Fight or flight kicked in, and any progress I've made at overcoming my issues seemed to take a complete backseat. The most impulsive of impulses—violence.

I duck past the back of the house and keep walking, through the fields of tall grass and wildflowers, the broken paintbrush wrapped tight in my fist. By the time I make it to the main road, my feet ache in my Prada flats and I'm shivering, even though it's not actually that cold.

Shock seems to have a chokehold on my system, though, and when my feet touch the pavement, I just stand and stare at it for a few seconds. Definitely not a good idea coming out here alone, and while I could probably make it downtown by sunrise, I realize that I don't really want to.

Turning around, I consider trying to retrace my steps and go back the way I came.

Maybe Jonas won't be angry.

Biting my lip, I touch the cut on my forehead, wincing as it smarts.

*Sure, Len. He'll probably welcome you back with open arms.*

Pulling my phone from my pocket, I open up my contacts and hit Cash's name first. Even though he's back in Boston, he's the most likely to be awake right now, and the most likely to come get me.

He doesn't answer.

Headlights shine against me as I hit Palmer's number, and my stomach flip-flops as I wait to see what the car does. Tension clogs my throat as it passes, fear that whoever was at the house has followed me, but they don't even slow down.

Heaving a sigh of relief, I bring the phone back to my ear and get Palmer's voicemail.

I can't call my parents. They'd never let me live it down, and Daddy would have me moved back into the mansion before lunch. Mama would use this as another opportunity to try and drive a wedge between Jonas and I, fitting Preston in the middle like he isn't a major factor in why I left in the first place.

Technically, I could call a taxi, but even then I'm running the risk of paparazzi seeing me and running with some convoluted story. In fact, the longer I stand here, the greater that risk becomes, and I start to panic at the idea.

My finger taps a button at the last second, before I can consider the consequences, and when a white pickup truck turns onto the street a half hour later, I feel *stupid.*

A pang of guilt and shame ripple through my chest as the truck comes to a stop at the curb. After a pause, the driver's door swings open, and Preston climbs out, stuffing his hands in the pockets of his blue jeans.

Immediately, I regret the decision. Should've known Mama would send him.

My feet shuffle back a half-step, and he catches the movement, freezing in place. Irritation sweeps his features, and he lets out a sigh.

*Always a fucking sigh.*

"When are you going to stop pretending you're afraid of me, bug?"

I swallow. Shake my head. "I'm not pretending, it just makes you feel better to think that."

"Then why the fuck was I asked to come out here? Your mom doesn't seem to think you're scared."

*Why would she? She doesn't know the truth.*

He pulls a flashlight from his pocket, turning the bulb so it blinds me, and everything inside of me locks up, like a piece of machinery that's been shut down mid-production.

Flashlights aren't uncommon, sure. I know that.

*But what if...*

"Did you get into a fight with a wild animal?" Preston asks, scanning me head-to-toe.

I just stare at him. Mouth dry, unable to formulate the words to tell him to leave.

In the grand scheme of every mistake I've ever made, this is probably the biggest.

Well. Second biggest.

How painfully interesting that this man is at the center of both.

Another set of headlights flash as a new car comes down the road, this time from the opposite way Preston came. Dread seizes my heart, squeezing it until it feels like I might combust on the spot.

When the black Range Rover comes into view, it comes to an abrupt halt directly in front of Preston's truck. A beat of silence passes, and Preston lets out an annoyed sound.

"We're good, buddy. No need to fulfill your Samaritan duties, we were just leaving."

I grimace, pinching my eyes shut, knowing who the driver is before I even hear that velvety British accent.

The driver's side door opens, and the sound of boots smacking against pavement reverberates in the air. My throat constricts, and I wring my hands together, trying not to choke on my own bad decisions.

Jonas rounds the front of the car, but I don't look directly at him. *Can't*, with shame forcing my neck down and making me nauseous.

"Puppet," he says, and even though it's still a nickname, the sound lacks any heat behind it. His voice is flat and devoid of emotion, furthering the spiral of apprehension wreaking havoc on my insides. "Get in the vehicle, would you?"

My brain sends signals to my feet, but they remain in place. When I finally drag my chin up and meet Jonas's eyes, a chill runs down my spine. I can't see their shade, but somehow I *feel* his anger, like some sort of beacon to the weight of it.

"She called *me*," Preston says. "Clearly, she's not interested in going with you."

"You mistake me for someone who cares about her interests."

"As her fiancé, don't you think you should?"

Slowly, Jonas turns his head, fixing his stoic look on Preston. "I care about what's best for her. Your concern for *my* fiancée is noted, and not appreciated."

"What the fuck is that supposed to mean?"

Jonas doesn't answer. Just returns his focus to me, rolling his shoulders. "In the car, Lenny."

Still, my natural temperament tells me to resist. Straightening my spine, I cross my arms over my chest and don't move.

"Oh, bloody hell." Jonas takes a step forward, and a flash of what transpired earlier stamps my vision, clouding my judgment.

The feel of his body against mine, of him holding me captive with that look in his eyes like he wanted to strip me bare and fuck me against the vehicle.

Then, the immediate bucket of cold water when he suggested I'd taken advantage, and every memory that came rushing back with the claim.

*Dirty, rough hands stroking where they don't belong, with no regard to my pleasure. Hands interested only in taking, in getting to experience Lenny Primrose at her most vulnerable.*

*Preston's whiskey breath mixing with mine, equally as saturated, although I swear I didn't have that much to drink.*

"Either get in the car, or I'll put you in myself."

My eyes narrow. "You can try."

His lips curve, the lights from behind him making the gesture seem a million times more sinister. "Think you can outrun me again? Consider it carefully. It's not likely I'll be bested twice, love."

Preston moves forward, partially putting himself between Jonas and me, and a laugh burns in my throat.

Jonas stays still for a while, but eventually shoves his hands into his pockets and backs up. "Have it your way."

With a one-fingered salute, he turns and walks to the driver's side, getting into the car and slamming the door shut.

Clearing his throat, Preston looks at me. "Come on, bug. Let's go."

When he reaches for my hand, I recoil. Disgust flares in my stomach, tangling in my internal organs—with myself and him, for a multitude of reasons.

But I refuse to continue down a path of self-destruction by going with Preston.

"Don't *fucking* touch me," I snap, shoving him away when he tries again. Anger surges through my chest, and tears sting my eyes, but I clench my jaw to keep them at bay.

He blinks. Drops his hand. And for the first time in months, the first time since he hurt me and let others join in, he does something to acknowledge the truth.

He *laughs.*

It's low and throaty, probably not audible to Jonas in the car, but it slaps me across the face regardless. Steals the air from my lungs, making me feel like I'm drowning all over again.

"Do you really think you can stop me? Nothing's changed, except now you have a rabid guard dog. But you're still *mine*, and if I want to touch you, I will."

"Put your hands on me and I will bite them off."

Another laugh, and this time he leans in, turning so Jonas can't see him cup my jaw. I push him away, but his hand returns, fingers digging into my cheek.

"God, I miss your fire. Sure made holding you down while my friends made you their bitch a lot more fun." Sighing, he releases me. "Mark my fucking words, you stupid slut. I am not letting you go."

Bile teases the back of my throat as he walks away, getting into his truck and taking off. I cradle my stomach as I make my way to Jonas, yanking the door open and hiking my leg up over the threshold.

He takes off as soon as I've cleared the vehicle, before I've even closed myself fully inside. As I buckle, I stare at his knuckles, bleached white as he grips the steering wheel, whipping the Range Rover in a U-turn and heading away from Preston and town.

We don't turn down the road to the beach house, though, instead continuing on when it forks and heading even deeper to the other side of the island. My cheeks are warm, hot with embarrassment, and the silence doesn't help.

"I didn't call him, you know."

Jonas doesn't look over at me or acknowledge my words. His tongue runs over his bottom lip, and I wonder how bad the cut is there, considering the small one on my forehead.

My eyes roll over his face, then up around the back of his head, and my heart sinks further into my body, like an anchor falling to the ocean floor.

I'm not sure how much time passes, but eventually he pulls up to an iron gate with a huge, Gothic-style house behind it. One I've only seen in pictures before.

With a frown, I glance at the Asphodel and back, my brows creasing in the middle.

Shutting off the ignition, Jonas steels me with a heavy, hooded gaze that I feel down to my toes. It burns so hot as it sears through me that it leaves me feeling cold, eliminating the oxygen from my body.

"The next time I find you alone with him," Jonas rumbles, "he's dead."

# 26

"A BABYSITTER? ARE YOU SERIOUS?"

Elena juts her hip out to the side, adjusting the hold she has on her infant daughter, Noelle. The baby tugs at the ends of her mother's hair, babbling softly before sucking on her fist.

Crossing his ankles, Kal leans back in his leather armchair, swirling the ice around in his tumbler. His four year-old, Quincy, is snuggled into his side and sound asleep, her dark curls plastered to her head with sweat.

"You'll have to excuse my wife," he says, taking a drink. "She's very passionate about being watched."

Setting my old-fashioned aside, I drop my face into my hands and groan. "I feel like I'm way out of my element here."

"Your element is murder for hire. Of course, you're not comfortable supporting your fiancée," Elena points out, walking over to her husband. She snatches the glass from his hand and deposits their baby in the free space on his lap, who immediately reaches for his face.

"I'm *trying* to support her, but she won't tell me what's going on. All I know is she has issues with her parents, and she hates her ex."

"Preston Covington is an asshole." Elena downs the rest of Kal's alcohol, leaning against the stone fireplace.

Most of the Asphodel has been changed over the years, renovated to reflect a residence rather than the hotel it used to be, but certain aspects like the massive fireplace and the ancient Greek art hanging on the walls remain the same.

Since his marriage and subsequent children, the bloke's put a bit more effort into making it homey, adding colorful throw pillows and toys neatly lining the corners of almost every room. I find it endlessly entertaining based on how staunchly against putting down roots he once was.

The man used to be worse about keeping personal effects than me, yet now there's a family photo of them posing with puppies at the county fair sitting on the mantle.

Funny how everything changes so swiftly when you're in love.

"How do you know Preston?" I ask, pausing to retrieve my phone from my pocket. A message from Alistair sits on the lock screen, right below one from Lenny, whom I haven't spoken to in the days since the *incident.*

After showing up here with her in tow, I'd gotten out and

she'd refused, perhaps thrown by the threat I made regarding her ex.

Perhaps I wouldn't have made such an extreme claim had she not nearly gone off with him. After everything else that transpired that night, finding them together felt the most agonizing, like she'd reached into my throat and attempted to thread my intestines through my esophagus.

"My sisters know his people because of sorority connections." Elena gives the tumbler back to Kal, who places it on the end table, using his free hand to wrestle Noelle's fingers off his nose. "His parents are big donors at Boston U, and I guess because he's also an alumnus, he's a big shot on campus. Guys like that are always trouble."

"Weren't there also rumors about how he treated Lenny?" Kal muses, lifting his daughter up to blow a raspberry on her cheek. "I don't keep up with the tabloids, but I do recall being asked about the breakup at some city council meeting months ago."

Elena narrows her hazel eyes at him, tapping her thigh just past the hem of her black skirt. "When were you at a city council meeting?"

He brings Noelle back down, looking at his wife over her head. "When I had to go to discuss zoning regulations for a piece of property I bought years ago."

"I don't remember being told about this."

"That's because you rarely recall the conversations we have when my dick is inside of you, and yet it's your favorite time to talk."

"Bloody hell." Pushing to my feet, I wipe the exhaustion from my eyes and shrug back into my jacket. "You two were a lot more interesting when you disliked each other."

"You didn't come here for interesting; you came here to

get me to spy on your girlfriend and make sure she doesn't go anywhere or do anything bad."

"*Fiancée*," I grit out, though I'm not sure why I bother making the distinction when I can tell neither of them fully believes the stance, anyway. "I just thought she could use a friend, all right? If she won't open up to me, perhaps she would another woman."

"Oh." Elena's face falls, and she purses her lips. "Well, that changes things."

Later, after I've got the details of the arrangements with Elena and Lenny set up, I head to The Flaming Chariot. Alistair's already there, drinking tea in my office chair like he belongs there.

"You look cozy, brother."

He sucks on the end of a cigar, nodding as the door swings shut. "Lock up, will you? This is hardly a matter for prying ears."

I take the empty seat across from my desk, toying with the bracelet on my wrist as I wait for elaboration.

Alistair clears his throat. "The Aplana Island Art Society is hosting a gala at their gallery soon. I thought perhaps you and the future Mrs. might like to join?"

"You're phrasing it as a question, but it doesn't actually feel like I have a choice."

"There's always a choice, Jonas." He inhales, blowing out puffs of smoke in the next second. "I do think you should attend, however. Show yourselves off as a couple to more than just her family and the few wankers who do write-ups on you. Plus, it will help to have a united front in front of my colleagues."

The idea of dragging her out and about sounds as appealing right now as a lobotomy, but I can't tell Alistair that I'm having issues. In all the years I've worked for him, finishing a job has never been a problem, and I have no intentions of ending that streak now just because the girl involved is so unbelievably unnerving.

"Perhaps you're just *frustrated*," my brother comments, sticking his cigar in the ashtray near my desktop.

Furrowing my brows, I shake my head, realizing I must have said that last bit out loud. "If you mean sexually—"

"Of course, that's what I mean. For Christ's sake, Jonas, if you don't want to shag the Primrose princess, at least stop by a fucking whore house and get your dick wet. This is important, you know."

"Getting my dick wet is high up on your list?"

"I'm just saying that you can't think straight if all the blood is constantly rushing south."

Running a hand through his hair, he shifts his gaze to the desk in front of him, the muscles in his jaw tightening. When we were young, Alistair and I didn't get along; he's three years older than me, and his mum depicted our dad in a bad light because of the way their relationship ended, leaving her alone with a toddler.

It was only when I became an adult that we began spending any amount of time together, after he approached me to "handle" some issues he was running into with adversaries at his alma mater. It was petty crime at first—little things like busting the fraternity president's kneecaps because he was trying to sabotage Alistair's political aspirations, or embezzlement of department funds into investments that would eventually secure his mayoral campaign.

Like most crimes, the small orders began to spiral out of control. The busted kneecaps became broken femurs and missing fingers, and then I joined the ranks of my father when I killed because someone else asked me to.

A partner at Primrose Realty, though not on the official payroll. I suppose the bloke took himself off in an attempt to distance himself from the atrocities committed by the company, but the underground world doesn't forget.

Nor does it forgive.

Hence why my father wound up on the receiving end, and I got caught. Our connections came to light, damaging the Wolfe family reputation that had only been thrust into the spotlight because of my brother and me in the first place.

Perhaps that's why I feel such a strong urge to correct my mistakes.

For the shame brought to our family.

Exhaling, I push to my feet, and Alistair's eyebrows arch. "Leaving already?"

"Apparently, I have a gala to plan for."

And while I know I should go straight home and let Lenny know about the event, I don't. Can't bring myself to for some inexplicable reason—something terrible, caught between betrayal and desire when it comes to the little puppet I've let into my life.

Can't stop thinking about her kneeling before me like a mortal praying to her god, or how she used that weakness against me later to escape.

To be quite honest, that part is not what bothered me, though.

It was the resistance. The terror.

In that moment, she felt more like a stranger than the night we met, and I've been trying to reconcile that sensation —something vile and hollow—with the warmth I've otherwise experienced. It's been utterly maddening, and I'd be lying if I said the juxtaposition hadn't driven me over the edge of sanity once or twice since.

The problem with her is that I've known all along she would be trouble.

I just fear I've miscalculated what kind she'd be.

# 27

## *Lenny*

My hand slips as I lean over the canvas, and I catch the heel of my palm on the material, watching the large brush I'm holding drive right through it.

Sitting back on my heels, I blow out a long breath, trying to stabilize my emotions. If I let them snowball out of control, the urge to indulge becomes damn near impossible to manage.

Lifting my chin, I glance at the kitchen island across the room where Jonas stands, swiping on a tablet as he reconfigures the parameters on his security system.

He wears a disconcerted frown, his forehead wrinkled in

the middle as he glares at the device. Not once does he glance up, or even look as if he's tempted to.

Guilt boils in my chest along with every unspoken apology I owe him. My heart wants to say the words, to beg his forgiveness, but my brain is too damn stubborn.

Being wrong is embarrassing. It's *difficult*. That's why so many people double down on their mistakes instead of owning up to them; digging a hole in loose soil is much simpler than climbing out and filling it.

Growing up, Daddy never once admitted when he was in the wrong even though he so often was.

I didn't see it back then.

Maybe I didn't want to.

Mama and Daddy were the closest thing I had to friends, and seeing their true colors would've meant a very lonely existence for me.

Plus, when I went along with their mistakes, they liked me more. Gave me extra attention, because I would parrot whatever they wanted to hear. Whatever fit their narrative.

Eventually, you regurgitate the misinformation so much, and your credibility suffers. You go from child to pet, from respected to subhuman.

That's why when Preston told Daddy about what I'd supposedly done, he didn't believe me.

Called me a liar when I refuted the claims, and then made his own up about me that the media ran with. Because who doesn't love a good train wreck?

I was Aplana Island's favorite screw-up for weeks. My face graced every front page, every online forum, every celebrity news channel. A shiny little toy for them to poke fun at and wonder how low I would go, and if I would drag the Primrose name down with me.

So, I ran. Fled the island and its scrutiny, much to Daddy's dismay.

To him, fleeing meant admitting guilt, even though in his eyes I was already tainted.

But in Vermont, he couldn't control me or the narrative. When I came back, I didn't give him the chance to reclaim it, and yet here I am about to throw all of that away because I can't fucking say two simple words.

Pulling the brush from the canvas, I let out a groan when it tears even more. The painting is completely ruined, and for some reason, it being beyond repair is my snapping point.

Picking the frame up, I get to my feet and scream. Frustration bleeds through my pores, covering me in hot goose bumps as I lift my knee and bring the canvas down over it, cracking it in half.

The wood frame splinters, though the canvas itself doesn't do anything more until I tear it apart, ripping out the staples and throwing the broken, torn bits to the floor.

Chest heaving, I look across the room and find Jonas still staring at his tablet. Annoyance creeps up my spine, sliding between the vertebrae like soft tissue and shoving me into the kitchen. My hand whips out, yanking the device from his hands, and I throw it at the office doors.

Pressing his lips together, he steeples his fingers and drags his gaze up to mine. The blank expression reflecting back makes me distraught, and I grip the edge of the island to keep from reaching for the knife block and stabbing him.

Wouldn't want to prove his theory about me being murderous. The man's ego is already the size of fucking Texas.

"Feel better?"

"No," I snap, smacking the countertop. "No, I don't feel better. Do you realize how fucking rude it is to cold shoulder someone?"

His blink is lazy. "Is it as rude as beating them over the head with a rock?"

"Worse."

"Ah. Worse." He shifts, leaning back against the kitchen sink, folding his arms over his chest. The veins in his forearms bulge, his pecs jumping beneath his Henley. "Do explain, love." *Why is he so fucking calm all the time?*

Everything he does and says, every reaction he has is met with a particular precision, and while logically I make out that it's probably a very useful skill for his job, the side of my brain driven by anxiety and chaos hates it.

For once, I want to see him lose control.

"I just..." Clasping my hands together, I squeeze until my knuckles ache. "I didn't—"

"Didn't what?" He pushes off the counter and stalks toward me, not stopping until he's standing directly in front of me. I have to crane my neck back to meet his violet eyes, laced with potent fury as they penetrate my soul. "Didn't think there'd be consequences for your actions?"

Swallowing, I drop my gaze to his chin. His index finger hooks beneath mine, tipping my head so I'm forced to look at him.

"What were you expecting, love? For me to fall at your feet and worship you?"

Heat scorches my cheeks. "No, that's not—"

His free hand comes up, fingertips grazing the side of my bare thigh. I've been wearing clothes to paint ever since the *incident*, too ashamed to act normally around him.

"I'll do it." He skims the cuff of my jean shorts, slipping beneath the denim.

"What?" I breathe, my focus splitting between his caress and his words.

"Drop to my knees and eat you until you're trembling. Until tears stream down your cheeks and you beg me to stop, only to hold my head between your thighs because you're a filthy little liar, and you wouldn't *really* want me to stop. Not before you could soak my tongue."

"Jonas," I say, but it comes out as more of a sigh when he reaches for the button on my shorts, popping them open. "I just wanted you to stop ignoring me."

The back of his palm sweeps over my pubic bone, making my abdomen tense up. His nose brushes my temple, his other hand sliding up to tangle in my hair, and it feels like he's everywhere. Twisting and teasing, setting my body aflame when all I really wanted was his attention.

*Well, Lenny, you certainly have it.*

"If I don't ignore you, I won't get anything done." He tugs on my hair, stealing a gasp from my lips. "All I can think about anymore is how bloody magnificent you looked with my cock in your mouth, and how I'm dying to return the favor."

Slipping farther, he pushes beneath the elastic band of my panties, ghosting over the smooth skin until he reaches my clit. I suck in a sharp breath, my hand coming up to clamp down around his wrist, over the bracelet he always wears.

The W-shaped charm hanging off the leather catches my attention. "What's that?" I ask, using all of my strength to keep him in place.

Jonas glances at the jewelry, frowning. "It used to be my father's."

My chest pinches, a core memory flashing through my mind—Daddy's bald head, shaved because they had to remove bullet fragments from his skull. The awkward, mangled flesh that I couldn't help but stare at every morning at breakfast when he came home, and how it'd been sliced through during the surgery.

Even the jagged incision didn't obscure the letter, though. A W burned into the side of his head. Larger than the charm on Jonas's bracelet, but complete with the same hollow finish and the roses and vines weaving inside.

Up until now, the reality of the man I've asked for help has been nothing but a distant idea. One I've been writing off in order to focus on staying out of Daddy's clutches, and the conscious effort I've been making not to let my nightmares haunt me during the day.

But the truth is, this man is dangerous.

He kills people for a living. Almost killed my father.

Probably still wants to.

And yet, I feel... *safe* with him.

Secure enough with myself to let him touch me like this, when even the thought of being with anyone sexually made me violently ill mere months ago.

Maybe it lies within the fact that Jonas has already seen me at my lowest. The night we met, when my emotions were high and barely computing, as I stood coated in someone's blood.

All he did was clean up the mess. Made it possible for me to accept what I'd done and move on in private, which would've never happened if I'd gone to Daddy. He would have announced my actions to the world, used them to spin some sort of victim-positive sentiment on behalf of Primrose Realty.

Jonas cleaned up quietly, quickly, and left me alone to deal.

There was no pressure.

No judgment.

Then again, maybe it's just easier because he doesn't know the full story.

Maybe being with someone loses its edge of vulnerability when that person isn't aware that you're fucked up.

Or maybe he's just worse than me.

My tongue sticks to the roof of my mouth as Jonas's hand retreats, toying with the fabric of my jeans. I watch him carefully, noting the distinct lust in his hooded gaze, but also looking for signs of unease or resentment.

Something that might make holding onto my own anger and bitterness easier.

"I'm sorry," I whisper finally, registering how fucked up it is that I'm just accepting this but also not giving a single shit about the morality of it.

This is the reality I asked for when I approached him weeks ago.

This, him, is exactly what I wanted.

"You didn't kill him." Jonas chuckles, brushing some stray hairs from my face.

My heart cracks inside my chest, fissures of sadness appearing in the muscle. His tone indicates that *someone* did, though his hesitance makes me feel as if he is unsure who, and I can't think of anything more sad than not knowing the identity of someone who changed your life so drastically.

The way I've always known his.

"That's not what I'm apologizing for."

# 28

I've never been big on apologies.

Don't like giving them, and I'm not a fan of receiving them either.

Especially considering that more often than not, they're just words. And words have no correlative meaning unless you assign them one.

Slowly, I pull myself away from Lenny, crossing my arms over my chest. Her soft green eyes are unflinching as she tips her head back, meeting my gaze, and for a moment I expect tears.

A little lubrication to make swallowing her pride easier.

She drags a hand through her golden-brown locks, twisting the ends around her fingers, and draws in a shaky breath. I tense, waiting for the onslaught of emotion, prepared to reject it.

Instead, I get nothing, and for some reason, the sudden silence irks me more.

"You're sorry," I repeat, prodding her along.

"I am."

"Okay." Pausing, I wait for more, but the little puppet just continues staring. "Well, I don't accept."

Confusion knits through her brows. "Why not?"

"Why should I? The simple act of regurgitating a sentiment is hardly enough to make me believe you. If you're sorry, prove it."

Her mouth parts, and there's a dark shift in the air. Something unnatural that pulses between us, an undercurrent of despair I haven't felt in her presence before. It's like the calm before a storm, when everything becomes very quiet and very still, and you know disaster is imminent.

Reaching up, I cover her lips with my palm and give a shake of my head. "I don't mean some sort of spiel you've rehearsed. You give me the truth, or..."

She mumbles something against me, the vibrations tickling my skin. I pull back just enough for her to speak. "Or?"

Shrugging, I resist the urge to press her against the island and kiss her until neither of us remembers the word sorry. I bite down on the inside of my cheek, wanting nothing more than to apologize and take responsibility for her, just so I can spread her out on the counter and feast on her flesh.

*Jesus Christ, Jonas. Get a hold of yourself, you wanker.*

The image of her standing on the side of the road with

her knobhead of an ex flashes across my mind, pressing against the sore spot on the back of my skull, and I remind myself that I can't do it.

"You're an artist," I tell her, tapping her nose with my pinkie. "I'm confident you'll think of something."

Pulling back, I untangle myself from her warmth and walk over to the office door. Scooping the tablet up, I smirk when I see that not even the screen is cracked, and I turn it back on, heading out to the back porch to continue surfing through hours of footage.

With my legs propped up on the railing, I rock on the wooden swing, scrubbing back to over a month ago as I try to figure out who's been lurking.

I'm not sure what the purpose of my new security system was if they can't even pick up a simple intruder, and I don't particularly like the idea of Lenny being completely defenseless in the event of an invasion.

Now, I'm regretting not just bringing her to my house in the first place. At least it has an underground bunker and more than just one official bedroom.

A futon is no place for a man of my size, and yet since moving Lenny in I've been sleeping on one, too stubborn to face the consequences of joining her at night.

Especially now that I've tasted her, albeit briefly, and I know what she looks like swallowing my cum. There's no way I'd be able to sleep beside the little puppet and not wind up fucking her like some kind of drug addict.

Something in my chest pinches, and I reach up to rub the spot.

Is that what I am now?

Addicted to a girl I barely know?

Perhaps that's why I crave her repentance so eagerly, because if she feels bad about our situation, I don't have to.

The glass door leading to the kitchen slides open behind me, and Lenny steps out onto the porch a moment later, hugging her biceps.

"I'm not used to this, okay?"

Balancing the tablet on my knee, I sit back, looking up at her. With the sun shining in the sky, its warm rays extending through the clouds, she looks like an angel. Though I know her to be anything but.

"I don't know what you want me to say."

"Ah, but you do. I've explicitly told you what I wanted to hear."

Her face flushes crimson, matching the shade of the low-cut blouse she has on. "You want my truths."

"What's that old saying? A confession for a concussion."

"That's not a saying."

My legs drop to the ground. "No, but I believe it's a fair trade-off."

Throat bobbing on a swallow, she turns her head and looks out at the ocean. She's silent for several beats, and for a moment I wonder if I've lost her. Pushed too hard, so she's slipped from the life preserver and into the bottomless sea.

"Did I really give you a concussion?" she asks quietly.

Setting the tablet aside, I reach up and rub the scabbed spot on my scalp. "Possibly. I didn't check. I'm a grown lad, and I've had much worse."

"Lots of people die from head trauma."

"Your father didn't."

Whipping her head around, she presses her lips together. Swallows. Wrings her paint-stained fingers together like she's tweaking, or perhaps nervous. Despondency colors her face, flushing her tan skin, and I lean forward, grabbing her hips and pulling her between my spread legs.

Sitting back, I prop my hands behind my head and wait.

I haven't a bloody clue what I'm waiting for, but her discomfort scrapes at the dead edges of my soul. Begs for patience.

"Do you wish he had?" She drops her arms to her sides. "Died, I mean."

Keeping silent, I just raise an eyebrow. She knows that isn't relevant—and, judging by the way she won't meet my eyes, knows the answer, anyway.

Her little nostrils flare, evidence of her anger returning, and I feel the gesture in my cock.

Finally, with a deep, resolute sigh, she speaks. "I dated Preston Covington for three years. Daddy loved him, and I loved Daddy, so when he suggested setting us up, I was all for it. Preston was cute, and he existed in the same circles as us, so I thought it would be an easy fit. Thought he'd be able to understand the pressures and that he'd give me some breathing room from the compound I'd spent years rarely ever leaving."

My throat grows scratchy, and my hands come down, my fingers hooking in the hem of her shirt. Twisting, because I can already tell I don't bloody like where this is going.

She keeps her eyes on my chin. "Technically speaking, it *was* easy, and he did give me a little more freedom. Daddy would let me leave without a major security presence, and Preston would take me on these big lavish dates and introduce me to all these important people. The media loved us together, and it looked great for Daddy's company."

I scoff, though she seems too lost in her memories for it to register.

"What Daddy didn't know, though, is that Preston had a gambling problem, and owed some very bad people a *lot* of money. And I think that's why he sought me out in the first place..."

My brows furrow and my fingers slip under her top, smoothing against her soft stomach. "What do you mean?"

Pursing her lips, she just stares for a moment, before pinching her eyes shut. "The public sort of got to watch me grow up, although through a very distorted and distant lens. I think some people grew attached to the narrative of me, and some people liked that I came from money and seemed demure and easy-going."

"Ah, clearly they don't know you the way *I* know you." My hands slide farther up, skimming beneath her ribs, reveling in the shiver that ensues.

She shakes her head, slowly. Sadly. "I wasn't... I'm not like that, the girl you met at that party. I've never killed anyone before in my life."

"Well, we all start somewhere, love."

"I've never *wanted* to kill anyone," she insists, though I do recall the glint of excitement in her eyes when I stumbled upon her and the corpse. How she'd been filled with something bright and fiery, even then. "They made me that way."

Freezing, my hands stop their roaming. Rearing my head back, I squint up at her, waiting for elaboration.

"Who did?" I prompt when none comes.

"Preston. His friends. I agreed to... help pay off some of Preston's debts, and things kind of got... out of control."

Nausea churns hot and toxic in my gut, threatening to incinerate the lining of my internal organs as they mix together. White-hot vitriol spills into my bloodstream, staining my vision red.

My jaw clenches so hard I can feel a crown loosen on one of my molars. "What did they do to you?"

"What didn't they do?" She chews on her lip, then slowly brings her hands up to mine, pushing them higher up into her shirt so I'm grazing the undersides of her tits. Fuck, they feel amazing, but I also recognize the shift for what it is; a distraction.

"Lenny," I warn, as she divides my fingers, bringing them up the curved flesh to brush over her nipples. "We aren't done talking."

"No more," she whispers, leaning into my touch, and fucking Christ, I'm a piece of shit, because I let her.

Bloody fucking hell, I let my little puppet take comfort where she can. It's like she's reached up and handed me her own marionette, asking me to continue the show.

Behind the zipper of my trousers, my cock throbs painfully. Desperately, weeping for this woman. This far-too young, devious and damaged piece of collateral.

A pawn in every man's life that she's ever been a part of, and even though I've been up front about my intentions, that doesn't make them less impure.

Doesn't make her less used.

And yet, as she guides my fingers, kneading her breasts with my hands as a barrier, I find that I don't care about intent.

Just like I don't really care about her apology.

*Does a man who's done far more for far less even deserve one?*

Locking my ankles around hers, I use my knees to pull her in, and she squeals, bracing her palms on my shoulders. Pushing her blouse up slowly, inch by devastating inch, I reveal more and more of her to my hungry eyes. By the time the fabric sits over her breasts, baring their heavy swell and dusky-pink peaks, I'm salivating.

"Okay," I say, blowing cool air over one nipple, watching it pebble before sluicing the flat of my tongue against it. She gasps, arching into me, and I let out an involuntary groan. "No more for now."

Her skin is soft, ridiculously smooth, and I dig my fingers into her hip as I anchor her in place. My lips part, gently teasing once, twice, redoubling my efforts when she shivers.

When I take her tit as far into my mouth as I can get it, letting her crawl into my lap to get closer, *closer*, so she can rub her cunt on my cock, I reason that I don't need to hear the rest, anyway.

I can fill in the blanks, and I've already made up my mind.

Preston Covington will not survive me.

# 29

## Lenny

IGNORING my brother's glare is an art form I've perfected at this point in my life.

Unfortunately, it's the only one.

Slapping my emergency credit card onto the boutique counter, I meet Cash's thousand-yard stare head-on. "If you have something to say, spit it out. You're being weird."

Cash watches, rapt, as the cashier swipes the payment. Then he shakes his head, stepping out of the line again. "Did Dad finally give you your allowance back?"

"No."

His eyebrows hitch. "So, who's paying for this?"

"Uh, hello?" I take the black card as it's returned, waving it around in his face. "Cold, shiny, hard plastic."

A flat expression graces his features. "I know you're referencing a movie, but I refuse to acknowledge which."

"Mean Girls," I say. "Palmer would've gotten that."

"Yes, well, maybe next time I'll invite him. I'm sure he'd be much more inclined to spend his lunch hour waiting while you tried on dresses that, I think, you're never even going to wear."

We pause at the glass doors of the building, and I frown. "Why won't I wear them?"

"For starters, they look like Mama's dresses. Either you're missing her more than you claim, or you just wanted to blow some money."

He's not wrong, really. After the half-confession I managed with Jonas yesterday and the make-out session that followed, my options of relief were limited. Since I haven't really been keeping snacks, and I didn't feel inspired to create anything, I figured a day in the city was a good alternative.

The problem with retail therapy and growing up with money, though, is that when I splurge, my purchases don't typically serve a purpose. Like now, the dresses I've just bought are ones I don't even like, with collars and floral patterns, while I'm wearing another of Jonas's t-shirts.

This one has the fire-breathing Minotaur logo for The Flaming Chariot, and it's tied up so the bottom rests beneath my breasts, and the lacy red corset I have on under is still plainly visible.

I could tell from the second we met up that it made Cash uncomfortable, possibly because he's the only one aware of the nature of my arrangement. Or maybe because wearing someone's clothes suggests you're sleeping with them, and Cash has never been good at accepting me as a sexual being.

Either way, I'm ignoring his unease because I refuse to let it ruin my day trip to Boston.

"Do you realize what happens when people don't pay their credit card bills?"

"I'm not *destitute.*" The cashier hoists my bags onto the counter, and I hook my fingers in the handles. "I did have some money of my own before Daddy ex-communicated me, you know."

A little nest egg put in my name when I was younger by Mama, who swore up and down that I'd need it one day.

Sometimes I wonder if she knew just how spectacularly our family would implode, like a volcano on the verge of eruption.

"And when you've spent it all on food and clothes you don't need? What then?"

Pushing open the boutique door, we step out onto Washington Street, where crowds of people are gathered outside storefronts eating lunch and enjoying their afternoon.

Someone in the distance shouts my name, and I look down the row of metal patio tables to see a man in a Hawaiian shirt waving with one hand and a camera in the other.

"Lenny, baby! Long time no see! Can we get a statement from you?" He advances quickly, eyes bright and frenzied as he snaps pictures.

Unclenching my jaw, I plaster on a tight smile. "On what?"

"My sources say you're no longer involved in the family business, and that your relationship with Jonas Wolfe has severed your connections with your parents. Take your pick."

"My official statement is that's all bullshit," I say sweetly, knowing men like this get off on the light abuse, because they think it makes their invasions of privacy okay.

The man chuckles, getting extremely close even as we continue past him. He doubles back around, breaking into a sprint to catch up.

"Rumor has it that you're not even really dating Jonas," the man huffs. "Just using him for his money."

"Do you realize my net worth probably dwarfs what he has in the bank?"

"Well, do you think you'll get back with Preston, then? Someone in your tax bracket? Or do you think he's done with you after your cheating scandal?"

My eye twitches and this time Cash's palm comes down on my shoulder, squeezing me into his side. "Get the fuck out of here."

"Hey, don't shoot the messenger!"

We stop in front of an outlet store, and my brother yanks open the door. I pause, spinning around as the pap tries to follow us inside. "Maybe the messenger should try not being a dick."

Shoulder-checking him as I turn around, I pull the glass closed as I enter the store after Cash. He motions over a security guard, letting him in on the situation, and the bald man takes up a spot at the entrance to ensure no trespassers make it in.

My lungs compress painfully as we're closed in, irritation sliding over me like a second skin. *Cheating scandal*, my ass.

As if Preston didn't fucking *trick* me into fucking his

friends. Get me drunk and then force me into painful positions, all while he took their money and watched.

Hurt wells up, scorching a path down my sternum, and I reach up to press my hand against it. Trying to push it away, like I learned to in Vermont.

*The abuse only has control over you if you let it.*

Besides, I know Daddy's the one who leaked about me cheating. Wanted to salvage his relationship with Covington Pipelines and keep Preston on his good side, so he sabotaged his daughter and then blamed her for it.

No matter how many times I claimed otherwise.

No matter how much proof I gave.

My story, my experience, didn't fit Daddy's narrative, so he refused to share it.

And I've been rotten inside ever since.

Straightening my shoulders, I stuff the resentment down where the sun can't reach and help it grow, and jog over to where Cash has wandered.

"Regarding the money situation," I say as we enter the home section. "I don't know what I'll do. Hope I don't run out, I guess."

"You should look into investing, or selling your paintings—"

"No," I say quickly, cutting him off.

Sighing, he drags a hand through his hair, stopping in front of a throw pillow display. I reach for a fluffy pink one, and then one with orange sequins—more shit I don't need but am going to end up getting, all because that pap left me flustered.

"I don't understand why," he says. "You're *good*, you know. Galleries and dealers are probably dying to buy an original Swan Primrose."

Chucking one of the pillows at his head, I roll my eyes. "I don't paint to sell, though. My artistic vision doesn't include profiting off my stuff. It's just…"

"A release," he finishes, sticking the cushion under his arm. "I get it."

Blowing out a breath, I move to the next aisle over, bending to look at the fall candles already sitting out. "Not everyone makes money off their passions, you know? I mean, we can't all make careers out of arguing with people. Maybe I'll just sell my body."

"Something tells me your fiancé wouldn't be very fond of that," comes a lilted voice from behind us.

Cash and I spin around, surprised at the intrusion into our conversation. Elena Anderson stands near a self-help kiosk, her hands resting on the handlebar of a black and pink double stroller.

One side houses a toddler with jet-black hair pulled into two curly pigtails, flipping through a picture book, while the other has the sleeping baby she'd been wearing at the beach house the day we met.

My heart squeezes in my chest, a momentary flare of jealousy burning through me at how effortless her life seems.

She glances between Cash and I, one of her perfectly arched brows quirking.

I force a laugh, discomfort weaseling its way to my extremities. "Jonas might not like the sound of it, but he'd probably enjoy the income."

Her golden eyes narrow. "Is Jonas aware that he has such premium pussy in his midst?"

My head snaps back, a warm sensation forming on my cheek like I've been slapped. At my sides, my hands curl into fists, and that dangerously familiar volatile twinge ripples in my chest like a plucked rubber band.

"Excuse me?"

Cash's palm comes down on my shoulder, and he squeezes. "Maybe we should consider the fact that we're in public right now. And not Aplana public, but *Boston*."

Frowning, I take a quick sweep of the area through my peripheral vision, noting at least three different sets of eyes on us. One person even has their phone pointed in our direction, poised and ready to capture anything that happens.

"Jesus, that was bitchy. I'm sorry." Elena slumps forward, leaning over the stroller. The toddler looks up at her and grins, before going back to the sensory patches in her book. "I just left lunch with my sisters, and they're... well. A lot. Add in these two hellions, and I'm having kind of a shitty day."

The diamond ring on her left hand glistens in the fluorescent lighting. "Is your husband not here?" I ask, recalling hearing things about his possessive nature, and how he doesn't like leaving her alone.

Again, jealousy pinches my insides, but I ignore it.

Elena laughs, sweeping her dark hair over her shoulder. "Kallum doesn't come to Boston. He prefers to stay an ocean away from his in-laws."

"You're from here?" Cash's eyes narrow as he studies her face. "Oh, shit. Elena *Ricci*?"

She gives him a quick once-over. "And you are..."

"Cassius Primrose. I was finishing up my JD at Harvard when your father went to trial."

"Also, my brother," I offer, nudging him with my elbow. His eyes are wide and reverent like she's some kind of goddess in his midst. "Cash is an environmental lawyer, so I'm not sure why he knows about your dad."

Cash snorts. "It's not every fucking day a big-shot Mafia don gets indicted on seventy-five felony charges." At that, he cringes, giving her an apologetic look. "Sorry."

She gets a little faraway look in her eyes but shakes it off with a shrug. "No big deal. I have much bigger fish to fry than to worry about what trouble my papá's in."

"What about your mom?" he says, stuffing his hands in the pockets of his black dress pants. "Last I heard, she was still AWOL."

"Uh, yeah." Elena shifts, tension creasing her forehead. In the stroller, the baby starts sputtering, indicating she's on the verge of waking up, so Elena uses her heel to rock her back to sleep. "No clue where Carmen is. Weird how people can just disappear, isn't it?"

The three of us just stare at each other for a beat, some unspoken understanding passing between us—or at least, between Elena and me. Something that says people don't just *disappear.*

Not unless you want them to.

Clearing her throat, Elena gives me a tight smile. "Well, it was nice seeing you two. Lenny, maybe one day we can get together over coffee, get to know each other? Since our men are such close friends, I'm sure we'll be seeing a lot of each other."

"Jonas and your husband are good friends?"

Her eyes narrow, and she puts one hand on her hip. "You don't know your fiancé's friends?"

My gaze darts around the area, picking up on the eavesdroppers. A soft gasp comes from somewhere, but when I search silently for the source, I come up empty.

"Well, obviously I know them. I just mean... you know. Since they're both so closed off, it's hard to consider them as more than acquaintances."

Pursing her lips, she processes my reply, nodding after several awkward beats of silence. I'm not sure she believes me, but she nods anyway.

Maybe she just wants to get away from us. "Right. So, dinner?"

# 30

Few things have a more melodious sound than that of a grown man's tears.

Screams come in close second, but there's something about the tears that reaches me on a molecular level. It's basal and totally tantalizing, and my favorite thing about my job is that I get to test out all the ways I can provoke the response.

Some men, like the scrawny bloke sobbing into the floor in front of me with his naked arse in the air, break immediately.

They're no fun.

Raising my pistol, I fit it against the back of the boy's head, giving him one last chance to confess his greatest sin.

I already know it, of course. The fact that he had his hands on Lenny at all didn't bode well for him in the first place, but knowing that they were there without her consent...

*Pop.*

Blood and flesh fragment as the bullet tears through his skull, ricocheting across the room as it sails out the other side.

Turning my attention to Samuel, a slightly overweight fellow with a square jaw, I bend down and press my thumb into the brand on the side of his neck. He screams into the silk tie hanging from his mouth, and I sigh.

"Your screaming is going to alarm my customers," I tell him, glancing at the locked office door. "Perhaps that's on me for once again choosing to do this here, but I don't want to take the blame, you see? So, I'm going to shift it onto you. Let that guilt eat away at your conscience. Feel free to give me a confession in return."

Tugging the tie from his mouth, I watch his face transform from unbridled fear to unadulterated fury.

My eyes narrow, watching as his mouth twists up. "If you spit on me, mate, I'll be forced to cut out your tongue. Have you ever choked on your own blood? It's not the most pleasant experience, I'll tell you."

He groans, his hands straining against the metal cuffs they're bound in behind his back. "Why are you doing this?"

"Oh, bloody hell. Listen up this time, would you? I know you had non-consensual relations with my fiancée."

"Fuck, man, I haven't put my dick in a girl in almost a year—"

Gritting my teeth, I swap the pistol for my branding iron, fisting the handle and whipping my arm forward. The end slices across his face, and the sound of his cheekbone splitting echoes in the air around us.

"Lenny Primrose doesn't ring a bell, then?"

He spits out a tooth. "Oh, *shit.*"

I take the iron to the other side of his face, creating a symmetrical mess of broken bone and flesh. "That's what I thought. So, tell me what possessed you to touch something that belongs to me?"

"She didn't belong to you at the time."

"Semantics, really." In truth, I don't appreciate his reminder, because all it does is reiterate that even now, she isn't *mine.*

Not that I want her to be.

I just don't want her to be anyone else's, either.

The thought of anyone seeing her the way I've gotten to over the last few weeks, naked and completely in her element hunched over a painting, or humming to herself as she snacks when she thinks I'm not looking, sets my entire soul on fire.

A fire I have no idea how to tend to, except by fanning the flames and hoping they don't spiral out of control.

Still, when I grab a fistful of Samuel's short hair and rip his head back, I'm aware that I'm very slowly losing it, anyway. Whatever control I had where Lenny Primrose is concerned grows thinner with each day, and I don't know how to stop it.

She should be scared of me.

I should be staying away from her.

Neither of us seems to know what's good for us.

"L-look man, I didn't mean anything b-by it," he

manages. "Preston said she was game and that we could have a go at her if we paid. No one knew she was drunk until we'd already started. She hadn't even had that much to drink, and she *agreed*—"

"Sam, Sam, Sam." Sighing, I wrap my arm around the back of his neck, slapping my palm down over his mouth. "Not the answer I'm looking for. I already know you're a piece of shit, now tell me who the brain behind your operation is."

His brows furrow, and I sigh. *Bloody pillock.*

"Who does Preston owe money to?"

My hand slides up slightly, and he sucks in air. "Mr. Primrose! Tom. H-he loaned Preston money for some business venture, or something, and Preston l-lost it. It was a *lot*, too. More than he was ever going to get for his whore."

His words cause a stutter in the rhythm of my heartbeat, sending ice water through my veins.

Depending on the amount, it sounds like Tom was planning on using Preston for some seedy operation, and Preston likely lied to Lenny about it being from gambling. They were probably working on a laundering front, or some shitty investment that'd wind up bankrupting a company and seeing its assets go up in flames.

It's the exact scenario I saw play out over a decade ago, only this time with new players.

This time, there's no hospital to be destroyed. No innocent patients left to fend for themselves, or money to be collected from insurance after the fire.

This time, my father isn't around to play patsy.

But I am.

If Tom wants to reignite old flames of war, I'm game.

My collateral is certainly worth more to him this time

around.

With an exasperated sigh, I release Samuel and swipe the pistol off the floor, aiming it directly at his forehead. His face screws up and then come the tears.

*Blimey, those tears.*

I'm tempted to close my eyes for a moment and let them sink in. Tempted to lick them off his face and see if they taste as good as they sound.

But I don't. That would be ridiculous.

"Bro, what the fuck?" he wails, thrashing against his cuffs all over again. "I told you what you wanted to know. Let me go!"

"Unfortunately, I'm not a fan of your answer. Do make sure to plead your case again, though. God might be more lenient on your poor, wretched soul."

*Pop.*

"HOW COME you don't sleep in the bed with me?"

Lifting my head from the Chinese takeout menu in front of me, I find Lenny standing in the doorway to the guest bedroom. Her hair is wrapped up in a terry cloth towel, and she's clad in nothing but a white satin robe that makes her sun-kissed skin seem even brighter than normal.

Sitting up on the futon, I have to forcibly remove my gaze from the curve of her thighs, exposed just enough that I'm tempted to go over and unveil them completely.

"Believe me when I say it's better for the both of us that I have my own space."

Lenny leans against the door frame. "Are you a cover hog, or something? Secretly hiding a tail?"

"No."

"Then... I don't get why you're in here when there's a perfectly good bed across the hall." Picking at the edge of her robe, she looks down at the flood. "Do you not want to sleep with me?"

My cock jerks to life. "Do I want to sleep with you, or do I want to *sleep* with you? Those are very different questions, and the answer varies based on my mood."

"Your mood?"

"Certainly."

Tossing the menu to the floor, I get to my feet and slowly approach her. The pulse at the base of her throat flutters, and I imagine what it might feel like beating beneath my palm. Battering against her skin and my hold with the will to live, struggling for air as she comes violently on my cock.

"For example," I say, not stopping until our bodies are flush, and I turn hers into the frame, pressing her back into it. "If I've had a good, but tiring day, perhaps I'd be inclined to climb under the covers with you and behave. Maybe we could cuddle, maybe there'd be some light petting. But mostly, we'd sleep."

Bringing my hand up her side, I skim over the soft curves of her hips, the concave shape of her abdomen, and over her shoulders. My hand comes to her throat, fingers spreading, wrapping, as I feel that pulse against my palm.

"What if..." She trails off, her gaze dipping to my mouth for a moment, before immediately snapping back. "What if you're in a bad mood?"

Tracing the seam of her mouth with my free hand, I pluck at her plush bottom lip, a smirk tugging at my features. She swallows, the sound rumbling in my chest, and I move forward so she can feel the evidence herself.

I catalog her every inhalation, her every twitch and facial expression, gauging at what point I cross a line.

Part of me expects her to be less open. For her to crack under the pressure and shove me away. Maybe this time she'd actually manage to stab me.

Clearing my throat, I trail my fingers from her throat to collarbone, slipping my thumb under one side of the robe. "If I joined you while in a bad mood, I'd probably try to exorcise some demons on you. Tie you to the bed you've begged me to be in, fuck you until you pass out."

"You'd tie me up?"

Curiosity gleams in her green gaze, and I chuckle, my cock lengthening considerably. "Like a bloody Christmas present. And I'd take my time unwrapping you. Run my fingers over every glorious inch of your skin, then add my tongue to the mix, because how could I stand not to taste my sweet, deviant little gift?"

A Trojan horse, if ever there was one.

If this was Tom's way of getting inside my head, of making me lose the plot concerning my father and the revenge he deserves...

It's working.

Fuck me, is it.

Lenny sucks in a breath as I reach into her robe, letting it fall open enough for me to thumb her nipple, eliciting a tiny sound from her throat that I want to consume.

In truth, I want to devour her. Eat her alive, swallow her whole, leaving her body too broken and bruised and satiated from me that she doesn't ever move on, even long after our little arrangement is over.

"Why don't you show me?"

# 31

"That's a dangerous invitation, love."

His fingers are cool as they sweep over my warm flesh, teasing my nipple with the ghost of his touch. The wooden door frame digs into my spine as he shifts forward, pinning me to it, but I don't even care right now.

"I know," I say in a thick voice, sliding shaky hands up his chest, toying with the curled ends of his dark hair at the nape of his neck. "That's why I said it."

Removing himself from my robe, he gently tugs the tie loose, letting the smooth material fall open.

Exposing me to him.

A shiver skates down my spine. My lungs constrict, like they're being crushed by a concrete block. Violet eyes darken as they drop, raking over me with a liquid heat I feel all the way to my toes.

Calloused fingers brush my hips, grazing without fully engaging. Leaving me desperate for more.

They slide inward, and my stomach spasms as he passes over my belly button, inching down. My jaw drops, mouth popping open, when I feel him glide between my thighs, tracing my seam with two digits.

"Perhaps we should eat first." His voice is hoarse, his breath hot as it fans over my face.

"Okay." Shaking my head, I start to pull away from him, glancing over at the takeout menu he dropped earlier. "Are you in the mood for Chinese, or—"

Gripping my chin, he jerks my face back to his, crushing our mouths together in an aggressive kiss that threatens to tear my soul in two. Our teeth clash, and he pushes his tongue past my lips, tangling and seeking and warring.

Every kiss with this man feels like a battle of wills and sanity. Like we're fighting attraction with violence and trying to see who comes out the victor.

As I sink into it, into him, I doubt it'll be me.

Jonas tears his mouth away, only to reattach himself to my throat. With one hand, he cranes my neck to the side, granting him better access to my pulse. His teeth nick and scrape on their descent, alternating between sudden bursts of pain and soft, fluid expressions of it.

A small moan escapes me as he crests my collarbone, dragging his tongue along the length of my sternum.

I don't know if it's supposed to hurt, and part of me keeps

waiting for it to get worse. For the pinpricks of discomfort to morph into agony, and for panic to set in my bones.

Pain isn't the only thing I've ever known, it's just all I can remember.

When Jonas drops to his knees, squeezing the outsides of my thighs in his large palms, I frown. He hooks a hand beneath my left knee, bending upward so I'm partially open for his perusal.

Invisible flames rain down my back, fire consuming every one of my nerve endings.

"I thought you were hungry," I whisper, too afraid to speak any louder and let my nerves show.

"Oh, I am." Turning his head, he skims his lips over the inside of my leg, his trim beard tickling my skin. "Ravenous, in fact. And it's your wet cunt on the menu."

My hand flies to my mouth as he moves in, and I take a knuckle between my teeth, trying not to clamp up. A squeak comes from low in my throat when he parts me further, cool air rushing to caress my newly exposed flesh.

"I've bloody dreamt about this," Jonas mutters, his lips not quite touching me but creating little vibrations anyway, almost as if my body is buzzing with anticipation. "About your little pink snatch and how she'd taste."

Knots thread through my insides, weighing me down while simultaneously making me feel airy. Buoyant, like if I was placed in a river I'd just float away.

When his tongue swipes in with a single, languid stroke against my clit, my knees buckle. He repeats the action, this time applying more pressure in the opposite direction, and my thigh pushes against his hold, nails digging into the wall behind me.

With his free hand, Jonas grips my foot still on the floor

and shoulders his way beneath that leg. Rough palms travel up, cupping my ass as he drapes me like a ragdoll over his body, sealing his mouth to my swollen flesh with a throaty moan.

"O-oh, *shit*." I'm not even sure if I say the words out loud, but his grunt of approval makes me feel like he hears them either way. Or maybe he feels them, the way his beard scraping against my sensitive skin has a direct effect on my brain.

I short-circuit, panting and burning without a single thought aside from the need to come.

My pulse accelerates in time with my body temperature, rising at an exponential rate and making me dizzy. God, it's been so fucking long, and *never* like this.

"What is it, love?" he says against me, circling with the tip of his tongue. "Do you like this? Me on my knees while you ride my face?"

"I'm not riding you," I manage, arguing the finer points of things just because they're all I can grasp right now.

He grins into my skin, teeth scoring lightly across my clit. "Let's remedy that, shall we? Better hang on."

My ass relies entirely on the support of his forearms as he dives back in, sucking and laving until my insides coil so tight, I think I might burst. Thighs quivering, I struggle to stay upright, shoving my fingers into his hair as he spears into me, massaging my entrance with a wet succulence I can hear perfectly.

A flush creeps up my throat as the lewd sounds fill the hall.

Gasping for breath, I fist his hair until my knuckles ache. He dips in and out, opening his mouth wider so he can delve deeper, and his sticky breath on my damp skin creates a friction I start to crave. My hips jolt, moving as if with a mind of their own, rolling slowly into his motions.

"There you go," he says, retracting himself from my pussy just enough to offer praise. "Feels good, doesn't it?"

Knocking my head into the wood behind me as he plunges back inside, I nod, fervent as electricity creeps up my spine. Bliss collects at the base, radiating in hot waves through my limbs, and I pull his hair tighter, pinching my eyes closed.

"Jonas," I whimper, so wet at this point I can feel it dripping down my thigh, though I'm not sure if it's him or me or both.

Either way, I suppose it doesn't matter, because he laps up the moisture before it can make a mess.

"*Fuck* me, you are beautiful. So terribly desperate to come, aren't you?"

As I nod again, his fingers dig into the meat of my ass, encouraging me to grind harder. His lips capture me, rapid-fire lashes against the bundle of nerves making me cry out.

One of my arms twists up, clutching at the door frame in an attempt to keep myself in place, and his hand slides up my side, pausing at my lips before breaching them. Two fingers press down on the flat of my tongue, and I gag at the intrusion, saliva flooding my mouth immediately.

It pools over, spilling down my chin as his feast grows louder, rougher, angrier.

"Give it to me," he commands, sucking so hard I feel my soul begin to unravel. Withdrawing his fingers, he snakes his hand between my legs and pushes in, eliciting a startled moan from my throat. "Come on my tongue like you're trying to drown me."

His words and the rhythm of his strokes send me catapulting over the edge, and I explode into a frenzy of frayed nerves and kaleidoscope colors. My core clenches, my pussy convulsing around him as I writhe, grinding my tailbone on the wall.

After a moment of trying to catch my breath, I slump back, my hands falling limp at my sides. Jonas grins from between my legs, pressing soft kisses into my skin as he retreats.

"You taste just like I imagined," he says. "It would not take much to get addicted."

My face, already flushed from the orgasm, heats up. "No one's ever..."

His brows shoot into his hairline, offense etching itself into his forehead. "Gone down on you before?"

"Preston said it was weird." I shrug, trying to play it off.

"He said it was *weird*?" Shifting, Jonas's forearms latch beneath my thighs, his hands hooking in my ass again, and he pushes to his feet.

I squeal, grabbing onto his head to keep from falling, but all it does is press him closer to my sensitive pussy. My clit pulses, ready for round two as he heads across the hall into the bedroom.

A single lick has my back arching. "Jonas."

"I'm just showing you that the only thing *weird* about me eating your sweet cunt, would be if I didn't want to."

His weight is suddenly gone from beneath me, and I go sailing through the air, my back landing on the mattress.

"Let me be very, very clear, my little puppet." Slamming his palms down on either side of my head, he looms over me, a predator who fully intends on enjoying every bit of his prey. "I want to eat it. I want to spend breakfast, lunch, and dinner drenching my chin between your thighs, doing my best to get my fill of you."

Parting my legs, he fits his pelvis against mine. The friction causes me to buck up, and he repeats the motion, drawing a moan from my chest as his entire length rubs my clit.

"And when I've gotten my fill—a great feat, mind you, because I don't think I'll ever not be starved for your taste—I'll spread you out, tie you to my headboard, and fuck you full of *me*." *Jesus.*

My tongue darts out, sweeping across my bottom lip. "Threat or promise?"

And for the first time since I met him, Jonas Wolfe *smiles.*

# 32

As I STARE DOWN at Lenny, watching her green eyes absorb every little detail about me, I realize this is it.

The time and place where I solidify my commitment to a hit. Up until this moment, I've skirted around what I want to eventually do with her father. Dodged my intentions with the girl herself, because the longer I denied my end goal, the longer I could pretend with her.

There's no coming back from this. Frankly, it would be difficult enough to recover from the fact that I just had my tongue inside of her, but the full act of shagging bears far more consequence.

It makes this fake relationship somewhat legitimate—at least, one facet of it. Which means, if I kill her father, the fallout will be massive.

Catastrophic.

And yet…

My cock jerks against my zipper as she runs her toes over my calf, arching her hips in a slow grind. Already wanting more.

"Someone's greedy," I mutter, bending to say the words into her collarbone.

"Or has bad impulse control and wants to get a move on before her brain convinces her this is wrong."

Frowning, I push her robe off her shoulders, dragging my teeth in the path of exposed skin as the fabric falls. She lifts up, slipping her arms out before folding them over her chest.

The gesture has her tits bulging obscenely, and while I appreciate that view, I don't want obstructions.

"Careful, love. You're going to give me a complex." Sitting back on my knees, I kick her legs further apart and reach for her wrists, pulling them from her chest.

She resists, a little smirk forming at the corner of her mouth. "Please, we know your ego's big enough to take it."

"Perhaps," I agree, yanking harder. She unlatches at once, and I move quickly, pinning her hands up above her head. "The real question is, can *you* take it?"

A ripple travels down her throat as she swallows. "Your ego?"

"No."

With my free arm, I manage to work the button on my fly free, shimmying the denim down over my hips. Freeing my cock from the confines of my boxer briefs, I give it a slow pump and try not to come on the spot.

Fisting just beneath the crown, I slip the tip through her arousal, collecting it on my bulbous head. She's soaked, so it only takes one pass through before I'm massaging her clit and making her gasp for air.

"*Jesus,*" she hisses through gritted teeth.

"Still no." Clucking my tongue, I pull the silk tie of her robe free and climb up the length of her body. Straddling her chest with my knees on either side of her, I take one of her hands and fit a looped end over her thumb.

Extending past that, I continue wrapping the tie around her wrist and the front of her hand so it intersects at her knuckles. Unhooking her thumb, I tug the end through the loop and underneath the strap against her palm.

"What are you—"

"Exactly what I said I was going to do. You might be used to getting let down, but I'm a man of my word, love. If I say I'm going to tie you up, I mean it."

Lenny watches with wide, cautious eyes, and I can tell she's curious but erring on the side of resistance. Still, she bites her tongue, though I'm not sure if it's because she's trying to prove herself, or because she actually likes the idea of being helpless to me.

The robe tie isn't as long or sturdy as I'd like, but I don't particularly feel like heading to the shed outside for something proper.

I want her bound and at my mercy as soon as bloody possible.

"If I say I'm gonna break you open with my cock until you're crying from the pleasure, I *mean* it."

Now, she's a buffet laid out before me, all breathless and sweaty and *pink*. Her cheeks, her tits, that sweet paradise between her thighs.

As I pull the tie through the headboard and back out, repeating the same binding on her free hand, I'm salivating at the thought of getting to bury myself there.

"Relax," I say, my ass hovering over her chest. With her arms extended backward, any movement tightens the cuffs around her wrists. "It's just you and me, puppet. Kick at me if you want to stop."

Taking my cock in my hand, I give it a slow, lazy pump in front of her face. She licks her lips, eyeing my strokes with a hungry look that has my bollocks tingling already.

With my free hand, I reach behind me and roll my thumb over her breast, flicking the peak until it hardens like a diamond beneath my touch.

Her hips shift and her legs press together, as if trying to relieve the sudden ache there.

"Look at you. Completely helpless, just waiting for me to fill you up. Is something wrong?" I taunt, pushing my crown to her lips. "You're squirming an *awful* lot."

Eyes alight, she pokes her tongue out, teasing my slit and coaxing out a bead of precum. "I'm fine, it's just that I'm..."

"Sopping and needy?"

She pauses, tilting her head back. Then, "*Yes*."

With a moan, I surge forward, catching myself on her lips. "Open."

Eager, she complies immediately, taking me with the finesse of an emotionally and sexually starved madwoman. Which is none, really. Her jaw seems to unhinge to a degree in order to accommodate my girth, and she gags when I'm about halfway, producing a sloppy wave of saliva that floods around my cock.

Pulling out, I give her a second to breathe; she spits

everything out, letting it dribble past her chin and over her neck. Making room for more.

"God," she cries out, laving over my tip before I push back in.

"Incorrect again." My hips flex, the warm constriction of her mouth drawing a groan from my chest. "Though if this is your idea of worship, I'll be yours. You can pray to me anytime if that means choking on my cock."

Again, I yank out for a moment's reprieve, and she gasps. Twisting her wrists, Lenny grabs hold of the tie, pulling so hard she almost slides out from under me.

This time, when I feed myself back into her, I push until I'm in her throat. Her mouth brushes my pelvis, and *fuck* it feels so bloody good. She swallows around me, her muscles waxing and waning along my shaft, and I have to fist the headboard to keep from collapsing.

"Jesus," I snarl, my jaw clenching tight. "You look absolutely devastating with a cock in your throat. Such a pretty little slut."

Hollowing out her cheeks, she swings her pretty green eyes up, seeking mine. I stare down at her from between my biceps, my hips pistoning of their own accord. Fucking her throat in earnest while she lies there enduring it.

Perhaps enduring isn't the right word, because her gaze is feverish, and there's an urgency in her permittance. Like she's allowing me this edge because she wants what's to come after.

*Pun intended.*

Desire curls up around my spine like smoke, and my bollocks begin seizing. Threatening release.

I feel it cresting and my eyes fall closed, waiting for it to barrel through, but then I'm gritting my teeth and grunting, forcing it away at the last second as I rip myself from her mouth.

Her chest heaves, and she blinks rapidly. "What the hell?"

Chuckling, I shuffle backward, dragging the underside of my cock through the pool of glistening spit that she's covered in. Smearing it over her tits, I scale the rest of the way down her body until I'm back between her legs.

One of my hands grabs her hip, and in the next second, I'm flipping her onto her belly. She shrieks and tries to catch herself on her elbows, but the tie gets shorter in this new position, making movement awkward.

Yanking so she's bent in half with her lush arse in the air, I bring the flat of my palm down on the underside of one cheek.

"Ow—*oh*," she grunts, changing her tone when I smooth over the site, soothing her inflamed skin.

"Pink is a good color on you," I say, dipping my fingers into her cunt and curling against her inner walls. "But I do think I prefer red."

The next spank is met with a stuttered gasp, and Lenny turns her face into the comforter with a sob. Her knuckles go white as she grips the tie, and I land another series of slaps to her flesh, reveling in the light outline of my hand as it welts.

"You're so close, love," I say, driving deeper as her walls begin spasming, chasing the high of imminent release.

"*So close*. Oh, god, Jonas, that's—"

"Don't do it yet, puppet. Not until I'm inside you."

"Fuck, I can't... I'm..."

A horrific groan tears from her lungs as I quickly remove my fingers and position myself behind her. Pressing my hand into her lower back, I angle her arse at a perfect level and kick her knees farther apart.

She's dripping when I fit my cock against her opening, the glistening crescent shape of her upside-down cunt making me harden to a point of pain.

"Say please, puppet."

Her whimper is broken. "*Jonas.*"

"*Say it.* Use your words and tell me exactly what you want."

Shifting, she rubs herself against me, wetting the tip with her arousal. She drops her voice, desperation coloring her tone, and glances over her shoulder. "I want your cock. *Please.* It's so big and I want to be so fu—"

Something primal and animalistic takes over me, and before she's even finished begging me to fill her, I do it, plunging in to the hilt in a single thrust.

Lenny clamps down around the intrusion, almost as if she's trying to push me back out, but I dig my nails into her hips and stay put, letting her get used to me.

"Holy *shit.*" A strangled sound comes from her.

Focusing on a spot on the wall above the bed, I flare my nostrils, trying not to move. Even when she relaxes slightly, the vise grip on my cock melting into something soft and manageable, I remain still.

After a moment, she pushes back. Wiggles around a bit. "Jonas?"

I let out a breath. "Yes?"

"Are... are you okay?"

My fingers tighten on her skin, little patches of red sprouting beneath my touch. I don't know how to tell her that she feels like fucking Heaven, sending waves of euphoria spiraling through my chest.

At the same time, she's hell, too; wicked, delicious sin crafted especially for my taste buds and served on a silver fucking platter.

Glancing down, I pull my hips back a bit and then snap them forward, watching my cock disappear into her.

"Perfect," I say, in lieu of an answer, because how can I explain it? As I saw in and out, my pace gradually picking up as the imminent need for release subsides, I realize I've never fucked anyone before and had it feel like this.

Like she could save me or condemn me, and the entire fate of my soul rests in her hands.

Or, cunt, I suppose, depending on how you look at it.

"Fuck." Her word is a whisper, puffing out between salacious grunts as I begin fucking her faster. "Oh, god, don't stop."

Sweat beads along my hairline and a tendril of it swoops into my eye. My hands grow clammy, slipping as I try to hang on, riding her like a broodmare. Each thrust draws a different gasp from her, saturated in raw lust and tears. *Bloody hell, she's a mess.*

That shouldn't do it for me, but there's something *alluring* about the fact that she's so far gone, so lost to the throes of pleasure, that such a basal instinct takes over. It's as if her body doesn't know how else to react, so it defaults to tears and spit and sweat, and soon Lenny's sobbing into her bindings, begging me to come.

"You feel so *good*," she moans.

"Yeah?" I increase my pace, cracking my palm against her unmarred arse cheek, watching it ripple as I fuck her. "Tell me this is the best you've had."

"Yes, yes!"

"Tell me my cock was molded specifically for your cunt.

That it fits her so well, you can't imagine ever taking another as long as you live."

"Your—it fits perfect—" Propping my knee up, I shift so I can drive deeper, and that's when she begins unraveling. The thread holding her composure snaps, and her cunt begins spasming around me, clutching and trying to keep me inside. "Oh, my *god*. Jonas!"

"That's it, love. What a good girl, squeezing my cock like that. *Fuck*, you're incredible."

Something primal erupts from deep within her, and she pitches into a fit of full-body convulsions. Her legs shake as she comes, her inner walls kneading and coaxing.

I'm right there with her, my own release barreling through me like the bullet from a shotgun, firing at will. Clarity sparks at the last second, and I manage to pull out just in time.

Grabbing my cock, I beat my shaft furiously until I'm coming, hard, panting and grunting and exploding, painting her arse like one of the canvases sitting in the living room downstairs.

Exhausted, I let out a breath and collapse beside her on the mattress. Dragging a hand over my forehead, I wipe off some sweat and try to regulate my breathing.

Lenny tugs on her restraints, but remains quiet, with her head turned away from me. I reach up, undoing the tie and pulling it back through the headboard, and she goes totally limp.

Alarm washes through me, though it takes me a moment to find my voice. My mouth is dry and my tongue is stuck to the roof of it, but I swallow anyway. "Are you okay?"

"Dead," she mutters, still not moving. "You killed me. Congratulations."

Pride swells in my chest, and I chuckle. "All in a day's work."

We lay there in silence for a while, though eventually I get up and retrieve a wet wipe from the washroom, cleaning her up before she can protest. When I'm through, she pads butt naked to the toilet, rejoining me minutes later in bed as she flops onto the mattress, closing her eyes.

"I can't believe I let you tie me up," she whispers.

Smirking, I brush some of the hair from her face. "Why not?"

One eyelid peels back, but just for a second. "I'm not... usually into not being able to move. It reminds me of..."

My hand curls into a fist, a sick feeling lodging in my stomach. Is it possible that everything she just experienced was through the lens of her past?

"I see."

"Before I went to Vermont, I had a lot of nightmares." With a deliberate sigh, Lenny rolls onto her back, folding her hands over her chest. I reach down and tug the duvet cover over us, which she pulls up to her chin. "I think I developed claustrophobia, or something, after the whole... *incident*, because my dreams were always about being confined or trapped."

She sighs. "Then, when I left Aplana, they just... stopped. No extensive cognitive therapy, or a significant length of time. I just woke up at my aunt's cattle farm and didn't have another nightmare."

"Cattle farm?"

"Don't ask why I went there. I still don't know."

Pressing my lips together, I reach for her, yanking her into me. She goes willingly, and even though I'm not a cuddler or a dater, I let myself break the rules.

Just for tonight, I tell myself.

Just for right now.

There's nothing wrong with indulging her for a little while.

*Consider it a perk for agreeing to her contract in the first place.*

"He was nowhere near my mind, if you're wondering."

She says it quietly, into the hollow of my throat. Almost as if she sensed I wanted to ask but couldn't bring myself to admit it.

"Just you and me, huh?" I ask, gripping her chin and making her look up.

When she nods, a tiny smile pulling at the corner of her lips, I crash mine onto hers, wanting to prolong the make-believe for just a little while.

# 33

## Lenny

My WRISTS ARE raw when I wake up.

Scratch that.

The slightest stretch reveals that it's actually every muscle that's raw and achy, as if they've been wrung out and left to dry. Rolling over, I find Jonas sprawled out on his stomach beside me. His arms are stuffed beneath his pillow while his legs tangle with mine, and pieces of his hair stick up in opposing directions.

He looks... *cute*. Innocent and unburdened in a way I've never seen.

Still terrifyingly handsome, but when he sleeps, there's a

softness to the sharp edges. Something that proves he's human, and not wholly consumed by his demons.

Emotion wells up in my throat, heavy and pointed the longer I watch him. Ignoring it, I quietly slip from the bed and head to the shower. After scrubbing my scalp with some tropical shampoo, I rinse and move on to my body, carefully cleaning between my thighs.

The memory of Jonas splitting me in half with his cock rushes to the surface of my brain, combining with the steady spray of hot water, and my body grows impossibly warm. Confining, almost, like a wool sweater I can't escape—but also don't really want to.

"Sore?"

Startled, I drop my washcloth and spin around, panic seizing my chest. Jonas stands on the other side of the glass door, his body distorted because of the frosted pane, arms crossed over his chest.

Releasing a breath, I nod. "A little, but nothing I can't handle."

Humming, he pulls open the door and steps inside. "Resilience is an attribute you seem to possess in spades."

My face flushes at his words, and I turn toward the tile so he can't see.

His palms skim over my hips, and I reach out, bracing my hands on the wall as he nestles his erection against me.

"Hiding already?" he murmurs, taking my earlobe between his teeth. "There's no need to be embarrassed, love. I've seen everything. Quite enjoyed it, actually."

I don't respond for a moment, unsure of what to say. It's not my body I'm trying to shield, but the organ inside my chest that's been battered beyond repair.

A heart can only take so many fractures before it shatters, and Jonas Wolfe could break mine without even trying.

"I'm not embarrassed," I say finally, and only when his fingers drift to my pussy, dragging the words out of me.

"Then turn around and let me see you."

Swallowing, I nudge his hand away and face him, pressing my back into the wall. The tile is icy on my skin, a stark contrast to the heat otherwise crawling through me.

His violet eyes sweep over me, leaving sparks of electricity in their wake.

"It's different in the daylight."

Pinching my chin, he forces me to look up. "Better," he says, pinning me against the tile.

Grabbing my hips again, he hoists me up, and I lock my legs around his waist as he notches his hard cock against me. Slick with arousal and aided by the shower spray, he slips in easily, and though there's a twinge of discomfort as he stretches and stretches, it ebbs off into a heady pleasure when he's fully seated.

He fucks me slow this time, but no less rough, each flex of his hips punctuated by the guttural sounds of our collective moaning.

"So." *Thrust.* "Much." *Retreat, and thrust.* "Better."

Mama's eyes narrow at me from across the table as she cuts into her baked potato. I watch her knife glide back and forth, separating skin and the mush inside, trying to understand the reasoning behind it.

It's a *baked fucking potato.* The pieces are already manageable, and yet I've witnessed this process countless times over the years.

Bringing the fork to her mouth, she takes a tiny bite. Chews far longer than necessary.

Palmer sits beside her, sipping a beer, eyes volleying between us. Guilt lines his facial expression, and I resist the urge to reassure him that everything's fine, because it's not. When he invited me to supper, I was under the impression that it would be just the two of us, and yet my arrival at the little fine dining eatery near the north marina proved otherwise.

I groan, slumping in my chair. "What are we doing, Mama?"

Her blonde brows hike. "Eating, dear. Or, *I* am, anyway." She looks down at my plate of untouched salmon and asparagus. "Are you avoiding your entree because it's not junk food?"

"No." Indignation puffs in my chest. "And I don't only eat junk food."

"Well, I should certainly hope not." She takes one more bite and puts her plate down, dabbing at her pink lips. "Your metabolism may be high now because you're young, but eventually all that salt and processed sugar will catch up with you. Then what will Jonas think?"

"Mama," Palmer scolds softly, setting his glass on the table. "Just 'cause Daddy wanted you thin and bony doesn't mean that's what every man wants."

"Excuse me for trying to be proactive." She shrugs, taking a sip of sangria. "You'd better find a way to lock him in, is all I'm saying. Men tire very easily, especially those who run in your father's circles."

Stomach full, I push my plate away and clasp my hands in my lap. "Jonas isn't a part of Daddy's circles."

She scoffs behind her glass. "That's news to me."

"Are you drunk?" Palmer asks.

Sighing, she adjusts the collar of her kelly green blouse, straightening her shoulders. "No, but I am beginning to wonder if Helene knows what she's marrying into." Glancing at me, she cocks an eyebrow. "You must understand the danger that comes written in that man's DNA?"

"And yet, I feel safer with him since moving in than I ever did at home."

Not entirely true, but she doesn't need to know the details. Every day that passes, it feels more and more like I'm being watched—to the point where I've stopped venturing outside past dusk, just in case some wild beast is hiding in the ocean, waiting to attack.

*Or worse.*

I spend more of my time actively not thinking about it, though, because if I did, my entire life would be reduced to sheer panic.

And when anxiety wins out, you don't get anything else done.

I didn't spend weeks in Vermont reading books about affirmations and hanging out with my cow-obsessed aunt to backpedal like that.

"Preston is the better choice," she says, reaching across the table for my hands. Cradling them in her cold fingers, her tired eyes grow pleading. "You two were good together, and he loves you so much."

"Preston loves himself, and that's about it." The diamond ring on her left finger glints in the overhead lighting, a reminder that she's likely only inserting herself so furiously because Daddy asked her to. "Besides, what happened to '*we can't help who we love*'?"

"We can't," she agrees. "But we *can* help who we marry."

"Mama, honestly." Palmer frowns at her, leaning back in his chair and stretching. His white T-shirt rides up, and she glares until he tugs it back into place.

"I'm just looking out for you, dear." Our waiter drops the check at our table, and she thanks him, but doesn't make a move to grab it. "I'm sure Jonas is very… *fun*, but you need to be practical."

Anger burns bright in my stomach, slowly pressing up against the back of my throat. She looks so sure of herself, so confident that she's on the right side of history. Because just like with Daddy, the possibility of being wrong doesn't exist to her.

When it comes to creating our own realities, my parents are so far removed from the truth that they're on an entirely different planet, looking down at everyone else from their thrones.

"Here's the thing, Mama." Leaning forward, I take her hands in mine and suck in a deep breath, trying to channel some inner strength I'm not quite sure I'm capable of. An ache flares between my legs, reminding me that even if I don't *feel* strong, my body is proof otherwise.

Proof that trauma doesn't define me. That whatever hold Preston and Daddy once had on me hasn't ruined my ability to heal.

That my body is *mine* and mine alone, regardless of whoever decides they have access to it.

It's on the tip of my tongue to tell her what happened, but when I open my mouth to do so, the words don't come.

Silence bleeds into the air, and the two of them stare back at me, clearly waiting for some huge revelation.

Snapping my jaw shut, I shake my head. "You know what? It doesn't matter. Let the Preston shit go, Mama, and tell Daddy the same. I'm through being his little PR gopher."

She has the gall to look affronted by my tone, ripping her hands from mine. "Goodness, he's already affected your manners, I see."

"Actually, that's on me. I'm no longer interested in being polite with people who don't return the favor."

Pushing my chair back, I swipe my purse from the table and stand up, making the dishes clatter loudly. A few other customers glance over, and I even see one pull their phone from their pocket as soon as they realize what they're witnessing.

I can already see the headlines: *Sweet Little Lenny Primrose Loses it in Public Again*, or *Real Estate Heiress Terrorizes Restaurant, Threatens to Overturn Tables.*

Never mind that neither of those are—or ever have been—remotely true, they also blatantly oversimplify a much larger problem, which is the fact that they've invaded my privacy for clicks in the first place.

And yes, that's the way my world works. Being in the public eye means they see everything, and there's always a comment to be had, but that doesn't make it an easier pill to swallow.

Reaching into my purse, I pull out a wad of cash from the emergency stash I keep hidden in my dresser, tossing it onto the table by the check. "Thanks for dinner, Mama. Maybe next time you can just kick me in the stomach and save yourself the trouble."

Palmer scrambles out of his seat as I turn to leave,

jogging to catch up. We walk down the street to where his Audi sits in a pay-lot, and as we climb into the vehicle, he shoots me an apologetic look.

"Could've been worse, right?"

Leaning my head against the seat, I turn to look at him. "*Could* it have been?"

He quiets, tapping his fingers on the steering wheel. After a prolonged silence, he turns the car on and backs out of the space, and within minutes we're en route to the beach house.

The sky darkens as we drive across the island, pinks and oranges splashing against the clouds and making the ocean look ethereal. I try to imprint the picture in my mind so I can emulate it later, but annoyance still simmers in my gut, tainting the image.

Palmer pulls into the drive a little while later, switching into park before turning toward me. "Look, I don't know what happened with you and Preston—"

"Oh, god, not you too."

Snorting, he shakes his head and runs a hand through his hair. "No, no. I don't care who you fuck or marry, swan. I care that you're *happy*, and if you say this Jonas character makes you happy, then nothing else matters. Not even his *rumored* profession."

Squeezing my thighs together, I think about the way everyone used to whisper about the things Jonas Wolfe is capable of. That he kills for the Mafia and lacks even a modicum of remorse, and supposedly doesn't have a caring or kind bone in his body.

And sure, most of that may be true, but even that isn't the full story.

"Anyway." Palmer taps my nose, drawing me back to the

issue at hand. "My point is, I'm happy to see you thriving, and that you got away from whatever demons were weighing you down before."

I glance at him, something in my chest pinching tight. "What are you talking about?"

"Do you think people don't take notice when the light in their lives goes out?" He gives me a sad smile, and it doesn't meet his dark eyes. "For those of us living in the dark, it's obvious."

Blinking, I search the angular features of his face—so similar to mine in structure, but more worn from overuse. Like he's been battling his own storm clouds and was long before my sky grew gray.

I'm not sure what to do with his assumption that I'm *better*, even though I want to believe it. Part of me does, knowing full-well that my urges have lessened and the nightmares have ceased.

Still, some traumas weasel their way into your soul, and they don't ever uproot. No matter how hard you pull or how deep you bury them.

Getting out of the car, I tell Palmer goodbye and make plans to see him again this weekend. Jonas doesn't appear to be home, so the beach house is dark, and I push my finger into the biometric scanner at the front door, letting it process my print.

An eerie feeling washes down my spine, icy hands skimming along the bone, as I step inside and flip on the lights. Throat tight, I scan the foyer and down the hall, kicking the door shut with my heel.

"Hello?" I call out, in case Jonas is here and I happened to miss his Range Rover.

I'm met with tense silence, and after a moment, I shake

off my unease and move on. Like the foyer, the living area and kitchen are empty, and I let out a sigh when I see no signs of intrusion or missing items.

Walking to the windows on the back wall, I draw the curtains over the iron security bars. My stomach growls, begging me to grab a snack, so I pop some popcorn and take it with me to my workspace on the other side of the room.

Bending down, I pull an unopened box of charcoal over and pull my sketchpad from beneath the couch cushion, shoving a handful of popcorn into my mouth.

I'm halfway through chewing, completely concentrated on the piece in front of me, when the office door swings open, and someone who is definitely *not* Jonas lets out an ear-piercing scream.

# 34

"How many people are left on this spiritual quest of yours?"

Zipping the black duffel bag closed, I give Alistair a flat look. "You mean the one you *paid* me to start?"

Taking a big drink from his insulated water bottle, he glances from me to the corpse at our feet. "I don't remember taking a hit out on the comptroller's son."

"Right. Just anyone who might oppose your senate nomination."

He shrugs, stuffing a hand in the pocket of his athletic trousers. "That's just good sense."

Good sense would be leaving me alone right about now,

but Alistair's never been one to observe social cues. Not because he can't read them, but because ignoring them makes people uncomfortable, and he loves having an edge.

And the gossip blogs wonder why he hasn't dated in over a year. Not since his boyfriend went off to become a stuntman in Vancouver and broke his heart.

Made him meaner.

Having just left the gym, Alistair insisted on stopping by my house upon seeing me parked outside for the first time in weeks.

"In any case," he says, rolling back on his heels, "there's been a massive rise in missing persons reports lately. Chief of Police called me yesterday, asking if I'd be willing to make a statement on it."

"So?"

"*So*, are you trying to tell me it's a coincidence that the missing people are all connected to a Mr. Preston Covington?"

"I think it's interesting that you seem to have so much information about a case you say you were just told about a day ago."

"Due diligence, little brother." He watches as I bend down with a nylon rope, maneuvering the comptroller's son —whose name I've already forgotten—into the fetal position. "But truly, what's your endgame here?"

"None of your bloody business."

His eyes narrow. "See, that's not true, is it? Our fates are quite intertwined, Jonas. You get into trouble, and it inevitably bleeds over to me. I'm the one who stands to lose something from the fallout."

Clenching my jaw, I cinch the rope tight, tying the corpse's wrists to his knees before rigor mortis can set in.

"There won't be any fallout from this. It's just a little rubbish pickup."

"For your fake girlfriend?"

"*Fiancée*," I snap. Alistair's head cocks to the side, and I kick myself internally. *Why does the distinction matter when it's all pretend, anyway?* "It's not anything she asked me to do."

"Oh, good. You're just killing on another's behalf without even telling them first. I'm sure that'll be a great addition to the vows at your imaginary wedding. Have you completely abandoned the list I gave you?"

Blowing out a breath, Alistair drags a hand through his inky hair and stalks to the kitchen sink off the living area. He dumps the remaining water in his bottle, then refills it from the tap before returning to my side.

"What's gotten into you?" I ask, dragging the folded corpse into the corner where a hollowed-out concrete block sits on a plastic tarp. "You're dodgier than normal."

"I'm fine. Just a bit concerned you're losing sight of our long-term goals."

It takes some serious finagling, but I manage to stuff the dead bloke's body into the block, then reach for the blue plastic wheelbarrow at my side. Pulling on a pair of latex gloves, I check the consistency of the concrete batch I made just before Alistair showed, then aim the mouth of the barrow at the container.

"Our long-term goals?" I shake my head. "You asked me to date her, Alistair."

"I didn't ask you to care for her."

"Well, that's too bloody bad, isn't it?" His glacier-blue eyes widen at my words, mirroring the size of mine.

The mixture pours out, filling the empty spaces rapidly, then leveling out as it overtakes the body. Once he's adequately submerged, I drop the wheelbarrow and wipe the front to keep anything from dripping onto the floor.

"So, that's it? She bats her pretty lashes or spreads her tanned legs, and you give up everything you've been working for?"

My hand whips out as I whirl around, grabbing one of the branding irons from the fireplace and shoving my brother against the wall. His skull smacks against a sconce, knocking it out of place, and I bring the brand up to his face.

It's still hot from where I spent the last hour decorating the comptroller's son's skin, and I know he feels the heat on his cheek, though he doesn't even flinch.

Just stands there, letting me crush his windpipe. Not a single flicker of emotion reflects in his eyes, and I realize why it was easy for him to enter the world of politics, and why he's always insisted on outsourcing his dirty work.

Alistair simply doesn't *care*. About anything, or anyone, and certainly not enough to get his hands a little muddy.

One thing brings him satisfaction, and it's the ability to get under someone's skin. To goad them into a reaction because the man's not capable of emitting one himself.

Lessening the pressure on his throat, I press the edge of the iron W to his jaw, testing him.

Still, he just stares. Motionless. Almost bored.

Like some sort of bloody sociopath.

"If you speak of her like that again," I spit, my rage reaching a boiling point, "I'll feed you your tongue and make sure those are the last words you ever utter."

His right eye twitches, like he's resisting the urge to roll it. "I didn't realize how deeply involved you've become."

It's a taunt more than anything, the insinuation that I've come to care for Lenny beyond the confines of our contract and sex life wrapping itself around my neck until I'm choking for my next breath. With an irritated huff, I push him aside and turn away before I do something I'd probably regret.

Besides, we worked tirelessly to get to a point of ease between us. No need to ruin that progress because we're both arseholes.

He is, after all, the only family I've got.

"Nothing has changed."

As I clean up, he stands off to the side and stares at the wall. I look over a few times while I scrub the wheelbarrow clean, half expecting him to have moved away at some point, but he never does.

After a while, he finally seems to slip back into himself, and he straightens up, giving his head a little shake.

It's like watching a reverse exorcism, and he becomes slightly more animated as he pins me with an arrogant smirk. "But you care about her, no?"

I don't bother answering. The leaden ache in my chest each time I think about the little puppet waiting for me back home, proves that anything I say would be a lie, anyway.

Alistair sucks on his bottom lip, releasing it with a pop. "You're bound to hurt her, you know. That's the Wolfe curse."

This time, he doesn't wait for a response, leaving quietly a few minutes later.

When I lock up a little while after his departure, I take a moment to look around the house, double-checking to make sure everything is still in its rightful place.

It feels odd that I've been away so long, but the smell of formaldehyde and industrial-strength cleaning solution that's practically embedded into the walls relieves some of the nostalgia.

Half an hour after I've left, I'm parked in front of the beach house, and I spend a few moments just twiddling my thumbs, staring at the front door.

In truth, I've thought of little else since I brought Lenny to bed several nights ago, and I've kept her in it every night since.

If my mind was preoccupied with the vixen before, now that I've defiled her over and over, it's as if there's no room in my brain for anything else.

Normally when I complete a kill, the outside world ceases to exist, and yet when I grabbed the comptroller's son this afternoon and held him face-down in a dirty puddle outside my pub, Lenny's face had been everywhere.

Is it because I'm seeking revenge on her behalf? Ending the lives of the men who had a hand in ruining hers?

Or is it more than that?

*Worse* than that?

An ache flares to life in my chest, and I rub absently at the spot, trying to massage it away. Scrubbing a hand over my face, I dismount from the vehicle and head up the front walk, noting that the curtains in the living room are drawn, and there are no lights on upstairs.

Either Lenny's asleep, which seems unlikely given her history of waiting up for me, or she's painting. My cock jerks to life at the thought, already hungry for her even though it's been less than ten hours since I last had her naked and writhing beneath me.

Now that I've had one taste, though, I can't seem to stop.

Insatiable is one word for it.

Completely and utterly *deranged* is more accurate.

Throwing open the front door as it unlocks, I peer down the hall, kicking my shoes off.

"Lenny?" My voice echoes off the walls, harsh against my eardrums, and I'm met with terse silence.

Frowning, I shuck out of my leather jacket and hang it on the hook on the wall. Maybe she's absorbed in whatever she's working on, and hasn't heard me come in. Starting down the hall, I whistle lightly, fully expecting her to be on her knees near the sofa with her hands speckled in paint.

Instead, my floor is covered in popcorn, as if an entire field was cooked in the open comfort of my living room. Charcoal streaks across the hardwood, broken pieces littering Lenny's workspace, while the pages in her sketchbook are torn and her easel is broken.

Paint splatter marks the floor, the sofa, the wall by the fireplace—a cacophony of color I try blinking away, but each time it gets louder and louder. The room is positively destroyed, glass shards from an overturned end table sprinkling through the kitchen, and all I can do is stare.

Confusion worms its way through me, and I step farther into the room, scanning with widened eyes.

As I reach the sofa, I freeze in place, immediately recognizing the waves of golden-brown hair spilling down a slender back. The ponytail she left earlier in is no more, the strands having been pulled out and yanked on, creating a frizzy texture.

My heart stutters inside my chest as I take her in, and my throat grows impossibly tight. Is it possible the crimson stains aren't actually paint at all?

For a split second, there's no movement, and all I can see is her, but then her head whips around and those green eyes meet mine. A disturbingly powerful wave of relief washes through me, and I slump slightly against the sofa back.

"Bloody fucking hell, love." I breathe out a chuckle,

running a shaky hand through my hair. "I thought you were in—"

She shifts again, confirming my previous immediate fear: she's not alone. With her knees outstretched, Lenny straddles the narrow hips of a dark-haired woman, and as she sits back, I see she's got one of her broken paintbrushes held to the base of the woman's neck.

Sucking in a deep, steadying breath, I take a moment to appreciate her lithe form in action; just like the night we met weeks ago, she looks terribly comfortable holding a weapon to someone's throat, and I'd be lying if I said it didn't stir arousal hot and fiery in my gut.

As I continue my perusal of her, simultaneously cataloging her triumph and seeking signs of harm, my chest feels like it caves in.

There are bright pink scratches decorating Lenny's bare arms, and blood collects at the corner of her mouth, but it's not any of that I'm paying attention to anymore.

Not when I reach the other woman's face.

My chest burns, like some omnipotent being has reached in, stolen the air directly from my lungs, and then set them on fire. I can scarcely catch my breath, my gaze boring into the wide, teardrop-shaped eyes I haven't seen in over twenty years.

"*Mum*?"

# 35

I FORGOT how old I was when my mum left us.

Purposely put it out of my mind in order to avoid the grief.

Loss is difficult enough, and it becomes a thousand times more insufferable when it's the kind that could have been avoided. The kind that could be *remedied*, if only someone cared enough to return.

Mine didn't. So, I spent a lifetime pretending she didn't exist at all.

Aside from the beach house itself, I've kept no connection to her—not a single photograph, or article of clothing, or note scribbled and stuffed into my lunch pail before school every morning.

Even my memories now are hazy at best. Try hard enough to convince yourself that something never happened, and eventually in your mind, it didn't.

In order to get over my mum's abandonment, I forced myself into the belief that she had never been around in the first place.

A tactic I found infallible, given the years that passed without a single point of contact.

Until now, apparently.

Her black hair is shorter than when I last saw her, cropped to her chin and fanning out beneath her head. Everything else looks the same, from her bronzed skin to the bright, yet hollow look in her dark eyes.

Lenny's eyes bulge comically when I question the identity of the woman she has pinned to the floor. The hand wrapped around her brush wavers, but doesn't move away, the sharpened end still pointing right at my mum's neck.

"This woman broke in and claims she's your mom," Lenny explains as if I haven't just outed the other woman. "But I know that can't be true, because you told me your parents are *dead*."

"Oh, *sirts*." My mum has the audacity to sound pained, using my childhood nickname as if it might endear me to her.

Instead, the word grates over my skin like a jagged strip of metal, and nausea rolls through my internal organs. My jaw tightens until it numbs, sparks of tingly pain radiating up my cheek.

*How* dare *she*.

Crossing my arms over my chest, I focus on Lenny. "I also said the house was haunted."

"No," she corrects, narrowing her gaze at me. "You said it *wasn't*. Specifically. God, did you lie about that, too? Are there ghosts living in the attic?"

"We don't have an attic."

"That's not—" Huffing, she cuts herself off, beginning to dismount. "Look, I'm really sorry—"

"Don't move," I snap, interrupting her apology.

Her brows knit together, suspicion drawing them in. "What?"

I jab a finger in my mum's direction. "We're not letting her up until she explains what the bloody hell she's doing here."

"If you would just let me explain—"

"Absolutely not. The only way I'll hear an explanation from you is if I'm rotting in the afterlife with that as my punishment."

Lenny hesitates. "Maybe you should hear her out..."

Gripping the back of the sofa, I lean forward slightly, looking directly into her eyes. They don't blink, that sea foam green color of her irises slightly soothing my anger the longer I stare.

Unwilling to let it slip away entirely, I glance back at my mum on the floor. It floods back like a tidal wave, invading the shore with no regard for anything in its path.

"All right." Raising an eyebrow, I nod for her to continue. Lenny starts to get up again, but I hold out my hand. "No. She'll explain where she's at, or I'll let you stab her."

Lenny gives me an incredulous look, but I ignore it, silently imploring my mum to continue. She blows out a breath, opening her mouth to speak, but I grow impatient and cut her off again.

"How in the bloody hell did you know I was here? How did you even get inside?" I glance around, noting that none of the broken glass appears to have come from any entrance points. Another thought occurs to me, and I recall the flashlight I found on the porch. "Have you been *stalking* me?"

Licking her lips, she shakes her head. It's a fraction of a movement because of the way she's being held, but I see the denial, nonetheless. "I *didn't* know."

"So, what? You just showed up randomly after all this time, and it *happened* to be while I'm staying here?"

"In two decades, I've never seen you step foot inside, so how was I supposed to know today would be any different?"

Everything else in my world slows down, crawling to an abrupt halt. I stare at her, trying to place her presence on the island, but come up short.

"What do you mean, you've never seen me come inside?" Taking a step away from the couch, I toy with the bracelet on my wrist, something pinching in my chest. "How would you know what I've been doing?"

The room gets silent. So much so that I can hear the waves outside slapping against the sand, even through the thick glass windowpanes. My tongue sticks to the roof of my mouth, anxiety and despair coming together like a tsunami in my veins, making it difficult to breathe or swallow or think.

Lenny shifts, discomfort evident in the tension on her face.

My mum exhales, wiggling her fingers where they're pinned by my fake fiancée's knees. "I never *really* left you, *sirts*."

Sharp, irrefutable pain shoots across my middle, nearly doubling me over with its force.

"Really?" A laugh tumbles out of me, but it doesn't sound normal, even to me. It's low, forced, and painful on the exit. "Because I don't recall seeing you. Or hearing from you. In fact, what I *do* remember is calling you over and over and *over* for weeks after you left, until your line was disconnected. I remember writing letters until my fingers were calloused and my knuckles were blue, only to have every *single* envelope returned to sender."

Fire rages in my throat, making my words come out strained and broken. Singed, the way she left my heart and soul years ago.

"I remember attending Dad's funeral *alone*, even though everyone swore you'd show up. '*Oh, Mileena loved your father more than anything. She'll be there.*'" The memory tastes acidic on my tongue, but I spit it out anyway. "And I thought, okay. Surely if she loved Dad as much as everyone says, she'll be there."

Tears well in her eyes, and I laugh again, just to keep my hands idle. What I really want is to walk over and wrap them around her throat, then squeeze until my heart stops cracking.

"*Sirts*," she whispers, somehow equally as broken, as if she has any right to be.

I point a finger at her. "*No.* You don't get to call me that. You don't get to show up and reinsert yourself back into my life, or even exist on the outskirts. Get the fuck out of this house."

Taking that as her cue, Lenny scrambles to her feet and comes over to me. She stands at my side, not touching, but close enough that the warmth of her seeps into my skin, like a balm to the coarse parts of my soul.

My mum pushes into a sitting position, draping her forearms over her knees. The hoodie she has on sports a small tear at the hip, and I wonder if it was there before her altercation with Lenny.

"Unfortunately, I won't be leaving."

"No? That's fine, I have no qualms against taking out the rubbish."

Starting around the sofa with malice directing my movements, I grab her bicep and begin pulling her to her feet. She doesn't even struggle, coming right up like the delicate little weed she is, but when I move toward the back door, she resists.

My nostrils flare. "I don't think you want to test me, *Mileena.* I'm not the little boy you abandoned years ago."

"I know," she whispers, and I hate how disappointed she sounds. Hate that it seems to cut me open, slicing through my heart even though I don't want it to.

Pushing my tongue against my cheek, I give a curt nod. "Great. So, leave."

"This is my house, Jonas. I'm the owner, the title's in my name, and I'm not going anywhere."

"You've got to be kid—" Biting off the end of that sentence, I pinch the bridge of my nose and release her. My entire body hums with pent-up fury, begging to be released.

From behind the sofa, Lenny clears her throat. "Maybe we should give your mom a chance to settle in. You know, without anyone trying to kill her."

"Let her *settle in*?" Exasperation bleeds from my tone. "She's not a bloody house guest, love. Just a pest."

"If you try to remove me, I'll have you arrested for trespassing."

Jaw clenched, I stare at Mileena until my vision blurs, red with the rage of a son who grew up without his mum, just for her to return out of the blue and begin demanding things from him. A boy whose mum apparently stuck around enough to watch him grow but didn't bother reaching out.

Perhaps a man better than me would be rejoicing that she's come back at all, but all her presence does is remind me that she left in the first place. Took off in the middle of the night without even so much as a note saying goodbye.

It devastated my father. Drove him to be reckless and stupid, especially when it came to his involvement with the Primroses.

If not for the blanketed distraction that my mum's abandonment caused, perhaps my father would still be alive now to see her return.

My stomach flips, bile pressing at the base of my throat.

He'd have been ecstatic.

"*Fine.*" Throwing my hands up, I shrug and step away from her. "You stay, I'll leave."

"Jonas—"

But I turn without waiting to hear more, bolting up the stairs and heading for the bedroom to take off my boots and jacket. Carding my hands through my hair, I tug at the ends, slivers of pain radiating on my scalp as some of the strands get yanked out.

Soft, delicate footsteps sound on the stairs, and then the scent of vanilla fills the air. I suck in a deep breath, inhaling her right to my lungs and wishing I could streamline her into my veins.

"I can't *believe* you told me she was de—"

Whirling around, I lunge at Lenny, pushing the door

closed as I shove her up against it. She squeaks, her legs instinctively wrapping around my waist as my arms bracket her head in place.

"Dead to me still counts," I say, pressing our foreheads together.

Her hands come to my face, fingers cupping my jaw. "Not really."

Annoyed, and quickly growing more agitated by the second, I palm the base of her skull and crush my mouth to hers. My tongue forces its way inside, sweeping over her teeth and tangling with hers, warring for dominance. She lets out a tiny moan at the intrusion, and the vibration from it surges straight to my cock, which I grind into her.

When she breaks away, she's breathless. "Jonas, we should probably talk about this."

"After," I insist, my voice gruff and hardly recognizable to even my ears. Trembling hands reach for her blouse, and I sink my fingers into the lacy fabric, pulling until it tears.

"Hey!" She fists my hair as I uncover her tits, bending down to roll my tongue around one nipple before sucking it into my mouth. Gasping, she arches into me. "That was La Perla."

Releasing her with a wet pop, I switch to the other, delivering a bite on the swollen underside. "I'll buy you the entire store as an apology."

"The *whole* store?" Her hips shift, grinding slowly against me and making my cock leak.

Tearing myself from her chest, I straighten back up and capture her mouth, kissing her so hard that her head bounces off the door. Fumbling for her skirt, I push the velvet hem up her thighs, baring the scrap of silk fabric between them.

"I'll buy out their bloody stock," I say, shoving her underwear aside and hooking two fingers inside her.

Back bowing, one of her hands slaps the door as she strains against the invasion. Squelching sounds fill the air as she drenches my hand, writhing along with the frenzied pace I set.

"*Goddamn,* listen to how soaked you are. Is that all for me?"

She nods. Whimpers, the sound eviscerating any pieces of self-control I've been hanging onto.

"Do you like the idea of being spoiled, my little puppet? Your cunt certainly seems to."

The heel of my hand grinds against her clit as I plunge in and out, curling and massaging until she's fucking shaking. She tightens her thighs, trying to gain leverage and push me in deeper, so I add a third finger, stretching her even more.

Fishing the shreds of her top from where they're still tucked into her skirt, I push the material aside and palm one of her breasts, teasing her flesh until it's hot and puckered beneath my touch.

"I wish you could've seen how *smashing* you looked when I walked in on you downstairs, holding that weapon to Mileena's throat." Dropping my head, I skim my lips over the pulse in hers, flicking the tip of my tongue over it. "I knew you were murderous but seeing it in action is another thing entirely."

Lenny breathes out a laugh, clenching around my fingers. "Violence gets you going, huh?"

"Only if it's yours."

Moaning into her skin, I drag myself up to kiss her again. And again, and *again*, until she's pulsating and quivering, a blubbering mess on the brink of absolute catastrophe.

When she comes, that's what it feels like: a raw, gut-wrenching cataclysm, sweeping away the last vestiges of my soul that try to insist there's nothing here between us.

She climaxes, and it's the most serene, truthful experience, even as a riotous sound rips out of her chest and into the air.

It's exactly what I always expected: complete and utter *absolution.*

Her cunt floods my hand, drenches my trousers, and I feel cleansed of all my sins.

Withdrawing slowly, I fish my cock out and give it a rough tug. She blinks, head lolling in her post-orgasmic fog, and reaches for me, wrapping her fingers beneath the crown. I groan, jerking at her touch, so bloody hard I can barely see straight.

"Put me in, love." My words are ragged, rife with pure lust as heat unfurls in my gut.

Straightening her spine, she adjusts her hold, positioning me at her entrance. My hips flex forward, sinking inside slowly, *so fucking slow*, as her nails dig into the back of my neck.

"Oh, god…" she exhales, dropping her head against the door. "You feel so good. So *big.*"

My chest heats, arousal spreading like jelly through me. "And you take it *so well.* Who'd have thought such a sweet little snatch would stretch so wide and easy for my cock?"

"Made for you," she murmurs, her words jumbling as I draw my hips back, slamming into her to the hilt. She cries out, and I swallow the sounds.

"Say it again," I command against her mouth, gripping her arse in my palms. My thrusts grow brutal, punishing, and the door rattles with each.

"My pussy was made for you," she moans, kissing me back with a fervency I feel all the way in my bollocks.

They draw up as I piston in and out, coaxing my cock along her inner walls. I curse under my breath, biting down on the inside of my lip to try and stave off the release building in my spine.

"O-*oh.* Yes, Jonas, *fuck. Harder, please.*" Lenny starts to spasm around me with each stroke, and I hold her tighter, stabilizing her so I can increase the force of my thrusts. "Gonna come," she chokes out, clamping down on my cock before she's even finished the last word.

I fuck her through it, my breaths erratic and the grip on her arse bruising, on the verge of passing out as she crests the hill of release.

After it rolls over her and she's left panting, I whirl around and cross the room, tossing her on the bed. Her tits bounce as she lands, and I scramble up beside her, brushing the hair from her face and pointing my cock at her.

Fisting it tight, I pump my shaft rapidly, matching the pace I set when I was inside of her. My climax barrels up and out, pulling soft groans along with it, and she opens her mouth at the last second, holding her tongue out.

Hot, thick ropes of cum land on her face, collecting beneath her eyes and over her nose, spurting across her lips and tongue.

"*Fuck,*" I say, pinching my eyes closed as I paint her like the bloody Mona Lisa, my vision wiping out completely as I milk myself dry. "So bloody beautiful all messed up for me, love. If I could keep you covered in my cum forever, I believe I would."

The last drops drip onto her smooth skin, and I sit back with an exhausted breath. Sweat glides down my back, so I slip from the bed and discard my clothing, watching Lenny for signs of distress.

One of her eyes is covered, so she reaches up and drags her fingers through it. Her tongue sweeps out, savoring what's on her lips, and my cock kicks against my thigh.

"Lenny..."

Ignoring me, she continues cleaning herself, pushing the thick liquid into her mouth, before opening wide. "Aaaah." She smiles, swirling it around, and I have to grip the bedpost to keep from taking her all over again.

With a devious glint in her green eyes, she coats her index finger and brings it between her thighs. Keeping her gaze on mine, she pushes in slowly, adding my juices to hers.

"Careful, love. You're playing with fire."

Grinning, she withdraws her hand but doesn't look at all remorseful. "Maybe I want to get burned."

My chest aches with awareness, frissons of heat providing evidence toward that very possibility. That we aren't at risk of catching fire; we're already *there*, engulfed in flames with no end in sight.

Walking over to the bed, I lean down and scoop her into my arms, then carry her bridal-style into the bathroom after making sure Mileena hasn't followed us up.

We clean quickly, and then are back in the bed within minutes. I draw her backside against my front, burying my face in her neck with a sigh.

"So," she says after a moment. "Your mom's not dead."

"Believe me, before tonight it was better to assume she was."

Lenny stays quiet for a beat. "Better or easier?"

I pull back slightly. Brush my lips under her ear. "Aren't those the same thing?"

"No." Her voice is soft. Like she's afraid speaking too loud might shatter the sense of contentment in the air around us.

Sighing, I roll onto my back, yanking her with me. She nestles into my side, and it strikes me at how naturally we've fallen into this facet of domesticity. If you didn't know our relationship was fake, you might not even believe it.

I'm having a hard enough time, myself.

"She disappeared on my father and I when I was a kid. No reasoning, no goodbye. We just woke up one day, and she was gone." My eyes rove over the ceiling, darting around so the memories don't take root. "It was bad enough being this loner kid with a dad everyone knew was a criminal. Then, she ditched us and everyone wanted to make out like it was my problem. Like I was..."

"The reason she left?"

Sharp pain ripples behind my irises, and I turn my head, pressing my lips into Lenny's hair. I nod, and she blows out a breath, tracing little designs on my chest with the tip of her finger.

"And you think you'd be betraying your younger self if you listened to her side of things?"

I don't respond, because in truth, listening to Mileena isn't something I'm interested in at all. Betrayal aside, I don't even know her enough anymore at this point to care what she has to say.

Whatever explanations or apologies she wants to wield are two decades too late.

"She called you something downstairs."

"*Sirts*," I say, swallowing over a knot that lodges in my throat. "Armenian for 'my heart.' Roughly."

"Does that mean you know Armenian?"

"No. A few words, maybe, but I wouldn't be able to hold a

conversation or anything. Mileena was born in the States, and her parents died when she was young, so she grew up mostly with native English speakers. I remember, though, the lullabies and bedtime stories she used to tell me. Those were authentic. Passed down from her parents and grandparents."

Lifting her head, she cocks an eyebrow. "Can I hear something?"

"Lenny."

Hooking her finger around my nipple, she pouts. "Come *on*, please? I thought you were into spoiling me."

"Buying you lingerie I can rip off and speaking in a language that's dead to me are very different things."

Blinking, she just waits.

Gritting my teeth, I sigh, fisting the sheets at my sides. Racking my brain for something, anything, to satisfy her. Threading my fingers through her hair, I tilt her head back so she's looking up at me, and utter a soft, "ցաւդտանեմ. *Tsavt tanem.*"

*Let me take your pain.*

I've been trying to do it without her even knowing.

My throat tightens as the words leave my lips, and I've never been so grateful in my life for an interpretive barrier. Not because I don't mean them, but because I've never bloody meant anything *more*, and the notion that Alistair was right doesn't sit well with me.

How is it possible that I've come to care for this girl, when she represents the very things I despise?

Her eyes hood, lashes fluttering. "What's it mean?"

Pressing my lips together, I shake my head. The lie tastes like sulfur, but I say it anyway. "I have no idea."

# 36

## Lenny

When I wake up the morning after Jonas's mom shows up, I'm not at all surprised to find him sitting on the edge of the mattress, lacing up his combat boots.

Water droplets cling to his damp curls, and I see the pink indentations from my fingernails scoring across his neck. Heat rises in my chest like rolling smoke, and I sink further beneath the duvet, rotating my ankles to work some of the kinks out of my leg muscles.

Jonas turns his head. "Are you all right, love?"

"Are you?"

"Right as rain."

My eyes narrow. "I've never heard you use a metaphor."

"I hate to say it, puppet, but you might not be the most observant lass on the planet."

Throwing the blankets back, I sit up, indignant. I'm completely undressed because of last night, but I don't even care. "Did you just call me stupid?"

"No." After letting his eyes trail lazily over my bare breasts and pussy, he leans over the bed, pushing the covers aside to reveal a white shopping bag. "I'm saying sometimes you have a one-track mind. Which I don't mind. Just means you're dedicated to quality."

Ignoring him, I peel open the bag, snorting when I see a replacement corset top inside. Running my fingers over the black satin, I shake my head. "What'd you do, get overnight shipping?"

"Where there's a will..." Jonas comes over to my side of the bed, perching beside me. "There's more."

Excitement bubbles in my chest, and I push the top aside to find a pile of black lace at the bottom of the bag. "Oh," I say, pulling out the suspender belt and its matching thigh-high stockings, bra, and thong. "You... what am I supposed to do with these?"

Amusement swims in his violet eyes. "Wear them, preferably."

Dropping them into my lap, I just stare at the expensive material for a long time. Hours could pass, and I would have no idea as my thoughts scatter, struggling to collect themselves.

I've never gotten a gift from someone else.

Not something I didn't ask for, anyway. No one's ever

taken the time to seek something out that they think I'd like, and even though it's obvious he'll get enjoyment out of the set, I can't deny that the color and style is identical to the stuff I wear on a regular basis.

A knot forms in my throat, and I clear it repeatedly, trying to alleviate the pressure in my windpipe. It feels stupid getting choked up over something so simple, but my body reacts anyway as my heart swells.

"Thank you," I mutter, smothering my grin.

Hoping he doesn't notice how deeply my face is flushed, or the vulnerability seeping from my pores. I stare down at the gift, my heart fluttering like an untamed beast inside my chest.

*This certainly doesn't feel fake anymore.*

Jonas chuckles, fingering the edge of the belt. "Don't thank me for being selfish. I just want to see what they look like on before I shred them off of you."

"Wouldn't it be easier if I started out naked?"

"Easier, but not better." He reaches into his jacket pocket, pulling out a little pink envelope and handing it to me. "Besides, you can't go to this naked. I'd have to murder anyone who looked your way, and they frown on that at these events."

My face flushes, his possessiveness such a contrast to Preston, who wanted to share and parade me around any chance he got. Unwrapping the envelope, I turn over the card inside and read the black cursive lettering at the top.

"A gala?"

"Political fundraiser. My brother's a big donor to Aplana's Art Society, and every once in a while they throw parties in his honor. Personally, I don't get it, but he got us invited, and it'd probably be good publicity for us, right?"

My stomach twists, because I've been to these parties before. Daddy will most likely be in attendance, especially if it means scoping out potential political candidates. He likes to schmooze early so they're easier to get in his pocket.

"Okay."

Jonas hesitates, and it looks like he wants to say more, but his gaze drifts to the alarm clock on the end table, and he exhales. "Okay. Now, I'd better get a move on before Mileena wakes and tries to rope me into another round of confession."

"Are you really just going to avoid her?"

"Seems that way, doesn't it?" Chewing his bottom lip, he reaches out, swiping his thumb over one of my nipples. "I'd much rather spend my time devouring you. Already, she's proving to be a bloody nuisance."

"Some nuisances go away if you ask them nicely."

He smirks. "You didn't."

"Yeah, well." I flop back on the bed, yanking the covers back to my chin. "You kept accosting me. What was I supposed to do?"

His deep, rich chuckle is the last thing I hear before I drift back to sleep. My body isn't used to the amount of physical exertion it's been undergoing lately, so I spend another few hours in bed before pulling on a pair of black jeans and one of Jonas's t-shirts, tying it at the side to make it fit properly.

When I get downstairs, Jonas's mom—Mileena?—sits at the kitchen island, gnawing on the corner of a granola bar as she reads the newspaper. She perks up when she hears footsteps, her face brightening as she turns.

I'm struck by how little she looks like her son. Her hair is black and her eyes are a deep brown, while her skin is deeply tanned and unmarred by age. In fact, she hardly looks old enough to *have* a thirty-three-year-old child.

Coming to a stop at the bottom of the stairs, I cross my arms and glare. Her features slacken when she sees me, disappointment evident in her frown lines.

"Jonas has never had an overnight guest before," she comments, going back to her paper.

Walking over to the counter, I glance at the bowl of snack food I keep there, tempted to alleviate the nerves fluttering around in my stomach. Instead, I turn to the fridge and grab a bottled water, taking a long sip, keeping my eyes on her.

"Sounds like he's never really had a mom before either, and yet here we are." She snickers to herself, and the sound irritates me. "Don't make me regret not stabbing you last night."

"Honestly? Kind of wish you had." She leans her elbows on the counter with a sigh. "Clearly, my son is perfectly fine without me. He's got every right to be upset, too. I was a terrible mother and leaving only solidified that fact."

The water bottle crackles as I squeeze it in my palm. "I don't know if I'd say he's *fine*."

"Apparently, he goes around telling people I'm dead. I think it's safe to say he's not terribly torn up about it."

I study her as she stares at her fingers, twisting a gold ring on her right hand. It's not possible to remain impartial after hearing the thick emotion in Jonas's voice last night, and seeing how her arrival fucked with him, but I try to anyway.

"How did you get in yesterday?"

Tucking a piece of hair behind her ear, she shrugs. "I have a key."

"But the alarm didn't even go off. We never got a notification that anyone had opened the door."

"You have an alarm system?" Glancing around, she frowns, her brows knitting together. "Here?"

"Yes. There's a fingerprint scanner at the front door and everything."

Her eyes shift to the foyer, as if she expects to see cameras, then she looks over her shoulder at the bars on the windows. "Well, that sort of explains the bars. Though I don't understand why they're inside."

"To keep me from escaping." Mileena's brown eyes widen, and I force a laugh, realizing too late what I've said. "Ah, no, sorry. That was a joke."

Silence ebbs between us, heavy and pointed as several seconds tick by. I try to place her somewhere—not because she looks familiar, but because the shadowy figure that I *know* has been lurking around the house could have been her size and shape.

Could also have been someone different, but I never got a good enough look at them. Still, what are the odds we'd have *two* trespassers?

If it were paparazzi, they'd have made themselves known.

Anyone else wouldn't want to.

Rubbing her chin, Mileena tilts her head, watching me with a curious look in her eye.

"How well do you know my son?"

"Well enough." Then, deciding to just double down on the lie entirely, I add, "Since he's my fiancé and all."

Hand freezing on her jaw, she goes very still. "*Fiancée*? My... Jonas is engaged?"

Emotion saturates her words, dripping like hot wax and burning my skin. Maybe I should feel bad for telling her that, but my parents think we're engaged, so why not add Jonas's to the mix?

Besides, it sounds like she deserves to know how badly she fucked up. I'm not sure how Jonas would feel about me taking her punishment upon myself, but considering he got aroused by the idea of me killing her, something tells me he probably wouldn't mind.

I *am* sure that he wouldn't appreciate me leaving her there on her own, but I have a lunch date with Elena and, frankly, I don't want to stay with this stranger.

Swiping my keys from the fireplace, I note that she cleaned up the mess from last night and appears to have slept on the sofa, if the folded blanket and throw pillow are any indication.

Pausing at the door, I turn and give her a last lingering look. "How long have you been back?"

Mileena sighs, placing her granola bar on the counter. "I just got in last night. Usually, I stop in once a month to... check on things," she says, her voice growing soft at the word *things*. "But work's kept me tied up for a while."

"What do you do for work?"

"What do *you* do for work? Mooch off my son?"

I snort. "Primroses don't mooch."

*They lie, cheat, and steal. But mooching is beneath us.*

With that, I spin on my heel and leave her there with her jaw hanging open. I'm not sure if the entire Wolfe family has beef with mine, but her immediate shock is enough of a reason to believe the rivalry runs deep.

Much deeper than any of the rest of us knows.

A little while later, I'm eating shrimp scampi port-side at

an experimental yacht restaurant, waiting for Cash to get off the phone with one of his firm partners. Elena sips a martini, eyeing me from across the table as I scarf down my plate.

I'm past the point of being comfortably full when I push back from the table, and I wipe my face with my napkin. "What?"

Elena shrugs, wrapping a strand of dark hair around her pinkie. "Nothing. You just seem hungrier than usual."

Since we met up that day in Boston a few weeks ago, we've had a dozen lunch dates; despite my initial apprehension regarding making friends, as that skill wasn't one I grew up utilizing much, Elena and I sort of hit it off immediately.

She's warm and inviting, but there's also this alluring darkness to her. An edge I've not seen in many people, especially any my age, that I find somehow comforting. Like I can embrace the broken, ugly parts of me in her presence, and all she'll do is show me hers in return.

Don't get me wrong, the woman seems to have her own host of secrets. I suppose you can't be involved with the Mafia and live transparently.

Not to mention, her husband is completely terrifying. The one time I met the man who Aplanians call Dr. Death, he just stared at me and then disappeared down the hall with their kids.

But his friendship with Jonas definitely makes sense.

I take a drink of my water as Cash comes back to the table, intruding on our lunch because he insists on checking up on me nowadays.

"Not hungrier," I tell Elena, setting my glass down. "Just nervous."

"Is his mom that intimidating?"

"No, she's just... I don't know. Imagine spending your life

thinking about someone close to you a certain way, getting used to that idea of them and eventually coming to terms with it, only to one day have that notion totally wiped. Almost a clean slate, except you can still see the dirt they left behind in the first place."

Cash stabs a piece of his Caesar salad. "She fucked him up that bad?"

"Apparently."

"Parents will do that," Elena says into her glass, and I remember her comment about her mother's disappearance, and wonder if that's what destroyed their relationship.

Or if it was something else entirely.

"Imagine if we sat down and wrote out every single transgression our parents bestowed onto us." Cash looks at me, scoffing. "We'd be writing until we die."

"What are you talking about?" I ask. "What did they do to you?"

He makes a face. "You don't think you have some sort of monopoly on the Primrose family trauma, do you, swan?"

Heat scorches my face, and I sit back in my seat, brushing some hair off my shoulder. The summer sun beats down on us, reflecting off the rippling water around us, and I write off the sweat beading in my palm as the summer air.

I *don't* think that, but my brothers were never held to the same standards as me. They didn't need to be, because for the most part, anything they did could be easily explained away. Whereas for me, a girl, my actions in public were always being judged more harshly, and a single slip-up could have detrimental ramifications.

The worst thing either of the twins ever did in our parents' eyes was when Cash got a DUI riding his bike around campus, and Palmer opened up to the island about his sexuality.

They even managed to come to terms with the latter, as difficult as it is for bigoted Southern Baptists to do.

But me? I'd messed up *once* in my entire life, a decision that spiraled completely out of control and beyond the realm of what I'd intended, and Daddy not only held it against me, but *used* it as fuel.

Paraded my pain around for everyone to see.

Made me a bad guy, because it was easier to write off the end of my relationship with Preston Covington and my "descent into debauchery" as a colossal mistake.

If he'd owned up to it, that would've meant severing ties with business partners and friends. People Daddy refuses to disassociate with, even though it was my sanity on the line.

So, no. Not a monopoly on Primrose trauma, but I've definitely received the lion's share.

"Well, I don't know about you guys," Elena cuts in, disrupting my thoughts. "But nothing *good* has ever come from the sudden reappearance of an estranged parent. Trust me on this; it'll be a bloodbath, one way or the other."

The rest of lunch is rather quiet, as we shift into stories about Elena's daughters, and some big pharmaceutical case Cash has coming up, but I just sit back, wringing my fingers together.

Anxiety threads through the muscles in my stomach, and since I've eaten too much, I do my best to focus on not puking.

After a while, though, the nausea morphs into something else.

Something dark and sinister, as I think about my father and the men he let get away with hurting me.

Richard Stiles's horrified face comes to mind; how he'd seemed so shocked on the balcony when I fought back. It was almost as if someone had told him I wouldn't, and I've always wondered *who*.

I think deep down, though, I've always known.

# 37

THE MAYOR'S mansion dwarfs the natural beauty around it; the grounds are traditionally landscaped, with perfectly manicured hedging and an array of pine and maple trees native to Aplana Island.

It's got beautiful gray-stone walkways and a cherub fountain out front, making it look as stately as any other in the country despite being relatively new.

When you get to the house itself, however, the modern architecture, with its squared roof and block-style doors, it just doesn't blend well.

Strangely appropriate, I suppose, given my brother's the

current inhabitant, and he's always seemed incapable of fitting in.

*That*, I fear, is the real Wolfe curse. We were brought up with such a specific purpose, that venturing beyond it is incomprehensible.

I show up unannounced the morning after Mileena shows her face on the island, escaping the house before she can wake and drive me to insanity all over again.

Her comment from last night about the house being in her name makes me uneasy, so I'm bringing my concerns to the man who convinced me not to let the bank foreclose in the first place.

Alistair's in a meeting when I force the lock to his front door and head to his office upstairs—I use the term *meeting* liberally, given my brother's pants are around his knees while his cock is in another man's mouth.

Though not just *any* man; this one I recognize immediately as Isaiah Fredrickson, aside from Tom himself, Isaiah is the last remaining name on my father's hit list. CFO of Primrose Realty for over a decade, and the initial person to report my father as the reason behind company assets that suddenly vanished.

Smacking his palm against the ornate wooden mantle across the room, Alistair grunts and shoots me a dirty glare. "Don't you knock?"

"Knocking is a privilege not reserved for secret-wielding swine," I snap, pulling my Glock from the inside of my jacket.

Twisting a suppressor onto the end of the barrel, I cock and aim, putting a bullet through the other man's neck before he even has a chance to spit my brother's cock out.

Blood splatters against the fireplace and the white

armchairs positioned in front, and across the light blue button-down my brother has on. It sprays his neck and chin, and his entire demeanor flattens.

He swears under his breath, spinning away from the mess and stomping to the half-bath connected to the office.

"There are *cameras* in here, you nutter."

"Oh, piss off. You think I'd come in without dismantling them first?" I walk over to Isaiah's slumped form, wiping the silencer on the handkerchief I pull from his suit jacket.

"Could you not have waited for me to finish?"

"Worrying about you busting a nut is not on my list of priorities." I pause, tucking the gun away. "What in the bloody hell were you doing, letting that filth touch you?"

"Ah, I didn't realize what a snob you are, little brother." Bending down, he scrubs his face clean with a hand towel, then clicks his tongue as he inspects his shirt in the mirror. "This was brand new, you know."

"Add it to the list of clothing items I'm having to replace lately."

Sighing, I plop down in one of the armchairs beside my newest corpse. Kicking my feet up on the glass coffee table, I prop my hands behind my head and let it loll back. The smell of death is hot as it permeates the air, shifting drastically from the damp sheen of sex that existed when I showed up.

"Right. Well, if you'd bothered to stop and ask questions before coming in guns blazing, you'd have learned I was *using* Isaiah."

"Quite well, I'd say. How lucky for you that your reconnaissance allows for such liberties."

"We can't all be assassins. So little would actually get solved."

Smoothing my palms over my thighs, I resist the urge to mention it was *his* encouragement that kept me in the field in the first place. Without him, I'd probably have been happy enough running The Flaming Chariot.

Maybe it wouldn't have satisfied me, but I was never really given the chance to see, either.

"Nothing to solve, Alistair. Dad's dead, Tom Primrose is responsible. At this point, an investigation isn't going to change anything."

Unbuttoning his shirt, he shrugs out of it, walking to a Victorian-style wardrobe in the corner of the room. He pulls it open and slips a crisp white dress shirt from its hanger, looking over at me.

"Don't you want to know *why*?"

"No," I say, my eyes flicking to Isaiah's body. "My priority is justice, and a prison sentence is more than these people deserve."

Alistair exhales long and slow, leaving the top two buttons of his shirt open. His leather necklace peeks out, reminding me of why I came here in the first place.

"Speaking of explanations… were you ever going to tell me that my beach house is still Mileena's property?"

Sinking into his desk chair, he pulls the straps of his suspenders up, forehead creasing in surprise. "*Mileena*? Your mum?"

"She showed up last night, so I'm regressing."

"She *showed up*?" Swearing again, he adjusts his cufflinks in short, jerky motions. A button pops off in his haste, and he clenches his jaw, staring at the surface of his oak desk. "She wasn't supposed to make bloody contact."

My muscles tense up, like they've been injected with silicone and are rejecting the addition. "Pardon?" A stiff laugh works past my lips, and I touch my fingers to them, trying to tamp down the anger boiling in my throat. "Did you... did you *know* she was around?"

He stills, his Adam's apple bobbing on a swallow. Steepling his hands together on the desk, he meets my gaze head-on, unflinching despite the resentment rife in his blue eyes. They're suddenly heavy, laden with one of the only emotions I've ever seen him expel: *regret*.

"Your... Mileena contacted me not long after Dad's death. She's, ah..." He reaches up, scratching the back of his neck. "She's the one who gave me the list."

"*Bollocks*. How in the bloody hell would she have gotten a hold of that? She would've had to have seen him before..."

My heart drops to the pit of my stomach like a concrete balloon. A numbing sensation washes over me, and my vision slackens as I surrender to the struggle.

The struggle to piece together this convoluted puzzle, which just yesterday seemed to only involve my father and a corrupt businessman.

"I'm just the messenger." Alistair holds his hands up, shrugging, and my hand twitches, itching to put a bullet between his smug fucking teeth.

*Just the messenger* is an awfully convenient way of absolving yourself of any wrongdoing, which is something my brother excels at. Getting other people to take the fall for his messes.

Suspicion curls like smoke in my chest, filling the cavity and threatening to suffocate me. I push to a standing position, eyes narrowed, and he just stares back.

Unblinking and unbothered, as if my entire world hasn't been flipped on its axis and then turned back around all in the last twenty-four hours.

"How long have you been working with her?"

"I'm not—"

"*How. Long.*" It doesn't come out as a question the second time.

Alistair sighs. "Nine years. She said the list just showed up in her mail one day."

Hollow amusement rises like a tide, pushing through my lungs in the form of a breathless chuckle. Shaking my head, I reach for my Glock, sliding it out of my jacket slowly as I approach his desk.

He slips a thumb beneath his suspender strap, a neutral expression on his face. It irritates me even more that his regret seems to have been short-lived, and there's not even an ounce of fear to make up for it.

Pushing my tongue into my cheek, I lift the gun and point it at him.

"Have you even spoken to her?" he asks in a practiced, monotone voice. "Listened to her story?"

"I'm not interested in entertaining the ramblings of a liar. That includes yours."

My wrist cocks back, and the barrel of the gun flies through the air, whipping across his nose. The familiar, deliriously sickening crack of bone echoes in the air, and his hands fly to cover—or maybe protect from another blow.

Blood trickles out from between his fingers, and satisfaction settles in my gut.

But it's the empty kind that only leaves you wanting more, and since I'm not actually interested in killing the bloke, I turn on my heel and leave. For the first time ever, I don't stick around to clean up the mess for him.

Shortly after, I find myself staring at the gate to Primrose Manor. Not directly in front of it, since the bald security guard watches my every move like a bloody hawk, but on the road just beyond the stone property wall.

Tapping my fingers on the steering wheel, I reach into the center console and pull out the list Alistair gave me weeks ago. Every name is crossed off except Tom's, which is written in thick, bold ink and circled in red.

Then I dig even deeper into the console, unlatching a secret compartment at the bottom. The Polaroid is warped and coffee-stained, but I studied it so many times as a child that I know every single detail anyway.

A beach day with my mum and dad, behind the very house I've been staying in. The one that apparently still belongs to *her*. My father's unsettled, having launched himself into the frame so he could make it before the self-timer went off, and my mum's arms are wrapped around me.

The picture of innocence. Of love and warmth and happiness, even though it's arguable that we were never close to that. How can you be, when your foundation is built on secrets and deceit?

Besides, the next day, she was gone. Shattering whatever illusion of normalcy I'd been able to concoct despite my father's career and leaving me to deal with the consequences.

Scoffing, I toss the photograph to the side; it flutters to the floor of the passenger seat, face-up so Mileena's haunted eyes continue staring at me.

Yes, I lied to Lenny when I said I hadn't kept anything.

But I also lied to her about my feelings. I've *been* lying, and I suppose that makes me no better than the rest of my family, except that there's still a chance for her to escape.

After she finds out what I've done, she'll likely be dying to.

No pun intended.

A presence at the back bumper of my vehicle snags my attention, and I put my hand on the pistol in the passenger seat, ready to once again shoot first and ask questions never.

My mood has only soured since leaving Alistair, with betrayal sawing my nerve endings into dust, leaving me a mass of agony and paranoia. Jaw clenched tight, I curl my fingers around the gun and roll my window down, aiming as soon as a pair of khakis appear.

"Jesus, man, watch it. You're gonna shoot my dick off, and I happen to like that appendage."

Agitation stabs at my chest. "Preston."

His sudden intrusion is completely unwelcome, but he doesn't seem to care as he rocks back on his heels, grinning.

"What brings you around, Wolfe? Returning your merchandise?"

Lenny's story about what he pulled with her resurfaces in my mind, and my rage from before reinvigorates. Temptation swims in my veins to get rid of the problem once and for all, but I ignore it.

Normally, I'm not into making a spectacle of things, but add in the fact that this man had unfettered access to my little puppet, and he *abused* it, and I'm willing to make an exception.

For now, I hold back.

"An hour ago, I shot and killed a man in a more public space than this. I suggest treading wisely, Covington, or I'll be more than happy to introduce the two of you."

"That what you came to do? Finish off your future father-in-law?" He pauses. "Offing my friends isn't cutting it for you?"

My thumb swipes back, unlocking the safety.

So, he's aware I've been picking people off but still approaches. Interesting.

"Look," Preston says, running a hand over his blond hair. "What if I said I could help you?"

"I'd say I don't need, or want, your help."

"Your previous track record with Tom begs to differ." He shifts and starts to lean into the window, but pauses, choosing instead to just hook his fingers over the door. "I know you're not *really* dating Lenny, and I know the details of your contract."

My eyes flicker to his face.

"She promised you money, right? On top of the publicity? A sizable donation to your brother's senate campaign."

Still, I stay quiet. I really hadn't read the contract—at least, not past the parts I absolutely needed to. We hadn't discussed the outcome beyond public image, and I had Alistair look over the document, because the only thing that interested me was getting close enough to Lenny's father to kill him.

Revenge is the only thing I was *supposed* to want.

Preston gives an incredulous laugh. "Like father, like daughter, I guess."

"Watch it, Covington."

For a moment, he just stares at me. I can see the wheels turning in his mind, cogs falling into place to create a well-oiled machine. Eventually, he nods, like we're in on some shared secret.

"Didn't mean anything by it, really. Just that, you know. There *is* no money. None Lenny can give you, anyway."

I scrub a hand over my beard, my irritation spiking. The kid apparently has no idea how close I am to offing him. "Get to the point, mate."

"All Primrose assets are tied up with Tom. Even the stuff Lenny thinks belongs to her, like former endorsements or sponsorships, it's all *his*. Don't ask how he made that happen, because I still don't understand, but it is what it is."

"What's that got to do with me?"

"Well, Tom doesn't even have control of his own shit. It's in his name, but it's not *his*, if you catch my drift." I blink, growing bored very quickly, and Preston rolls his eyes. "We're talking the fucking Mafia, man. They own his ass, and he owes them a fuck ton. We're talking millions. He lent me money, and now I'm on the hook as well."

"Okay..." Not surprising, given the man's past affiliations, though this is the first I've heard of him being indebted rather than working alongside them. If the organization is anything like the 'Ndrangheta my father associated with, the entire Primrose empire is likely in danger.

"They're coming after him. I have no clue how long he's owed them shit, but I know last week someone turned over my apartment in Southie, and I only walked away because I'd happened to not be there."

Sucking in a breath, he shakes his head, something akin to vulnerability flickering on his face. "If they don't get their money, they'll come for you too. And Lenny. Anyone they can shake change from."

"I don't think you need to worry about my safety. I'm perfectly capable of handling myself."

"But *Len*?" His use of a nickname makes my blood boil, and I grind my teeth together. Nodding, he points a finger at me. "See, I can tell, dude. You like her. Your relationship may be fake, but the way you're clenching your jaw at the thought of her getting hurt? Your feelings are real."

Exhaling harshly, I yank the gun back, slide the safety

back into place, and turn on the vehicle. "Thanks for the psychoanalysis, but you've greatly overextended your hand here, Covington."

"Fine. But don't come crying to me when she's dead. You could've avoided all of this."

A knot forms in my throat, hot and angry, at the thought of a single hair on Lenny's head being out of place for any reason outside of me.

And even though I'm confident I could scrub our existences off the face of the planet, send us into hiding to avoid whatever fallout is bound to occur from this, I'm not confident that she'd agree.

Then what?

I'm alone, again.

Preston turns and begins walking away, and I clutch the steering wheel so tight that it feels like my knuckles could snap.

"Fine," I grit out, hating myself for this. "What did you have in mind?"

# 38

"JESUS, LOVE." My eyes pinch shut as wave after wave of pleasure rocks through me. "You get any better at that, and I might be convinced you're trying to kill me."

Lenny's eyes curve up at the corners as she lets out a soft gag around my cock. Pulling back, she lets her drool pool down, slathering my shaft and her fingers wrapped at the base.

Running her tongue along the thick, purple vein on the underside, she coaxes a shiver from deep in my bones, and I clutch her hair tighter.

"If it doesn't feel like I'm trying to suck the soul from your body, I'm not doing it right."

Diving back in, she bobs up and down the length, holding a few seconds each time she hits the back of her throat.

I'm hanging on by a loose, frayed thread, the taste of her cunt from moments before still fresh on my lips, propelling me toward release.

"Bloody hell," I groan, fisting the bedsheet with my free hand. Lust blurs my vision as she flicks the tip of her tongue against my slit, then smacks the flat of it with my crown. "Such a pretty little slut, taking me in your mouth like this. You love being a good, filthy girl for me, don't you?"

She nods, enthusiastic as she redoubles her efforts until it's me on the edge of a cliff, more than willing to jump off and find God.

"Your warm, wet little mouth is gonna make me come, love. That what you want? A belly full of me?"

Moaning, her cheeks hollow out, and her hand comes up to cup beneath my shaft. As she alternates between massaging and sucking, increasing her pace, I unravel spectacularly.

My knuckles blanch as release rolls up my spine, hot currents of ecstasy coursing through my bloodstream.

I come hard, back bowing as I guide her all the way down my cock, fitting her lips against my pelvis. Her tongue swipes back and forth in short jerks, teasing me as I spill down her throat.

The tiny swallowing sounds she makes prolong the orgasm, and I come for what feels like an eternity, my cock pulsing to the point of pain. Sliding off slowly, Lenny closes her lips around my tip and disconnects us.

"Did you swallow?"

She shakes her head, and my cock twitches.

"Show me."

Taking me back in her hand, she poises her mouth over me, opening and coating me in the mixture of cum and saliva. It trickles down, and she leans in, using her tongue to mop it back up.

"You taste so good," she murmurs, holding my gaze. When she's on her knees like this, she doesn't break the contact—like she needs the connection, needs to *see* that I'm enjoying what she does.

Then she gets on top, or I throw her onto her back, and she refuses to meet my eyes.

Grabbing the back of her head, I drag her up to me. "Let me see."

As I seal our lips in a salty, sloppy kiss, her knees sink onto the mattress on either side of my hips, and then she's lifting her arse and reaching beneath to thumb me inside of her.

She sinks down, her cunt hot and snug around me, and we let out a simultaneous breath of content. Rolling her hips gently, she works to get me back to the edge, gnawing on her bottom lip and bracing her hands on the headboard behind me.

Pulling back, I cup her cheeks, waiting for her to glance up from where she watches our bodies connect. Normally, that's enough, but right now there's something in me screaming for *more*.

"Lenny," I whisper, chest tight. "Look at me."

A shake of her head brushes some of her golden-brown hair off her shoulder. I bend, pressing an open-mouthed kiss just above her clavicle, and then try again.

"Look. At. Me."

After a moment, she does, those sea glass eyes dark and wide with unspoken emotion. I press my forehead against hers, dropping my hands to her hips so I can guide her into slower, deeper movements, meeting each grind with an upward thrust of my own.

Bottoming out in her over and over, I keep the pace up until we're both panting, spiraling quickly toward a second release. "This is exactly where you belong, love. Riding my cock, flushed with pleasure, and dirtied up from a previous round. Our living room may be filled with art, but you're the most bloody beautiful creation I've ever laid eyes on. The museums and galleries should be *envious*."

She moans, pulling me in for another kiss, and then she rocks harder, faster, her cunt choking me as it flutters. Holding onto her as she begins to let go, threading her fingers through my hair, I help her ride out the waves of euphoria as they seize her body and soul.

My cock swells inside of her, and my bollocks draw tight, so in the next second, I'm shoving her off of me and painting that glorious pink cunt.

Flopping back on the mattress, Lenny spreads her legs as I spend myself on her. She's sweat-slicked and clearly exhausted, but she reaches between her thighs anyway, massaging my cum into her skin like it's her favorite moisturizer.

With a tired grunt, I slink off the bed and peek out into the hall, checking to make sure Mileena isn't around. The last few days, she's made herself pretty scarce, though like a bloody raccoon she returns every night begging to talk to me.

I've grown quite bored with it, in all honesty. I might not be able to kick her out of the beach house, but I'll be damned if I'm subjected to whatever blasted story she's spent the last twenty or so years concocting.

Besides, it really *doesn't* change anything. Damage inflicted is not so easily erased, no matter the amount of time between the initial hurt and eventual recovery.

Coming back, I clean Lenny's mouth, chin, and neck, before swiping carefully between her legs.

She lets out a little breath, and I watch as her chest rises and falls with it, realizing that the sentiments I spewed moments ago weren't simply the delusional recitations of a sex-starved fiend, but the complete, unadulterated truth.

Words don't even do her justice.

Nor do they any longer accurately encapsulate how brightly she burns in my world, like an exploding sun wiping out all of humanity.

My hand stops moving, and it feels like my heart falls through my stomach, landing with a resounding thud.

*Fuck.*

"You know," she says after the silence grows to an uncomfortable decibel. "I think I'm clean."

Startled from my reverie, I blink and return to reality and force a chuckle. "You're probably right."

She shifts her eyes to the ceiling. "I talked to my dad yesterday."

"Oh?"

"He offered me ten million dollars, equity in Primrose Realty, and said he was prepared to fly me across to Europe so I could attend the best art schools in the world."

My fingers curl into my palm. "If?"

"If I come back. Date Preston, make him look good again. Apparently, my character has been defamed, though I'm not sure who started it." She blows a strand of hair out of her face. "It's a good offer, even though it's way less than what my inheritance was going to be. I should probably feel lucky that he's willing to give me anything at all, at this point."

Preston's claims from the other day poke at the back of my brain. It's easy to offer the world to someone when you know there's no way you'll ever be able to follow through with it.

Lifting my hand, I run my knuckles over her cheekbone, smoothing away a smudge of paint under the corner of one eye.

"But it just made me think... I left because I *didn't* want any of that. Going back now would feel like erasing any kind of progress I've made, just to make Daddy happy."

"What would make you happy? College? Traveling?"

*Me?*

*I could make you happy if you'd let me.*

She shrugs, leaning into my touch. My heart kicks against my ribs, wondering if she'll voice my thoughts.

Disappointment stabs the organ when she doesn't. "I don't know. But I think I'd like the chance to figure it out."

THE EVENING before Alistair's gala, I find Mileena rocking slowly on the back porch swing. One of her hands curls around the chain hanging from the ceiling, and there are three suitcases sitting beside her, stuffed to the brim.

"*Sirts*," she greets, not even needing to turn around and see who's there. Almost like she can sense me, even after a lifetime apart. Clearing her throat, she glances sideways as I approach. "Sorry. I... old habits die hard, and all."

"Yes, well. Not hard enough it seems."

An awkward silence descends. "Your fiancée is nice. We didn't get off on the best foot, and I'm not sure she likes me, but she's sweet. Very good at painting, too... not that I know a lot about art. But she's been decent company."

*And I haven't.* I tug at my necktie, trying to loosen it as it becomes suffocating, and nod at her luggage. "Are you going somewhere?"

Pursing her lips, she gives me a quick once-over. "You look..." Trailing off, she scoffs and shakes her head. It's then I notice the brown bottle in her hand, sans its label, and she tilts her head back to take a sip. "So different."

"The passage of time does that to people."

"It's not just that." She frowns, twisting a piece of hair between her red fingernails. "Your clothes, your attitude, your... job. God, you kill people for a living, Jonas. Murder for hire, just like your father."

"And his father, too. Don't forget, Wolfe men are hardly new to this career field." Leaning against the wooden railing, I stare out at the ocean, wishing I didn't feel such a vast disconnect between us. That I could pick up the pieces where she tossed them. Be the bigger person and forgive.

My father taught me how to tie a Windsor knot, build a bookshelf, and make homemade cold brew.

He taught me how to kill. How to aim a sniper and discard a body so it would never be found.

But he died bitter, paranoid, and angry.

At the people he'd worked with for years for betraying him.

The woman he loved for leaving.

Angry in general, and that's the emotion I attached myself to. Collected wrath like lucky pennies and used it as fuel for as long as I can remember.

No one ever taught me how to stop.

Mileena frowns. "I'm sure you think I'm passing judgment—"

"Sounds like it."

"—but it's not you I'm upset with. It's me." Drawing a shaky breath, she bends and sets her bottle on the ground, pulling her legging-clad knees to her chest. "There is no way I will ever be able to atone for my sins or to get back any of the time I've lost with you. I know that. I've grieved, Jonas."

"Oh, piss off with that sorry sob story, Mum. What did you lose?"

"I didn't get to watch you grow up—"

"Because of a bloody choice *you* made."

"Do you think it was easy?" she snaps, pointing at me. "For me to leave? My baby?"

"Then why did you?" I shout, slamming my fist against one of the wooden pillars holding the porch roof up.

The outburst is sudden, an explosion of hurt and rage erupting from me like hot lava. Normally, it's the kind of thing I settle with violence, but even though I wouldn't mind wringing her neck, I realize as the hurt verbalizes that I want the bloody explanation more.

"You didn't come back. Didn't reach out." My throat burns, flames caught in the passage. "I was just a kid, and you left. Where the fuck was my goodbye, Mum? What kind of coward does that to someone she loves?"

Her hands shake in her lap. "There was so much going on back then. I was young, and scared, and—"

"*I* was young. *I* was scared. Confused, broken, hurt. Do you know how many nights I spent standing at our front door, praying that you'd come back?" Scoffing, I just shake my head. "Of course, you don't. How could you, when you were gone?"

With ice in my veins, I drag a hand through my hair. Press a palm to my chest, beneath my suit jacket, trying to calm my erratic pulse.

"I prayed every bloody night. For you to return, then when that didn't work, I tried bartering with God. Said I didn't need you to come home, if only he'd let me know you were okay. That you were safe." Glaring at the night sky, I huff a bitter laugh. "Kind of fucked, isn't it? It seemed like such a simple request, and yet..."

With a shrug, I wave my hands around. "Nothing. I was abandoned by my mum and my belief system within months of each other. And you wonder how I could've ended up any other way."

Tears well in her eyes, and I snap. Stalking over to her, my hand whips out and my fingers dig into her cheeks, squeezing roughly. "No, you don't get to fucking do that. You don't get to cry or make me feel bad for being upset. *You* hurt *me*. Not the other way around."

A sob still manages to work its way from her throat. Disgusted, I shove back, and she crumples against the chain, burying her head in her arms.

My heart rages inside my chest, beating so hard against my ribs that I'm afraid it might actually break free.

"I know," she says quietly. "I know I hurt you, *sirts*. You have no idea how sorry I am for that."

Snorting humorlessly, I put my hand on the kitchen door and pull it open, pretending I didn't hear the apology.

"I was young. *Young*, Jonas, when I had you."

Closing my eyes, I take a deep breath and pause at the threshold.

"Your father didn't know, but I was only sixteen when I got pregnant." Her voice falls to a barely audible whisper. "I lied to him. Said I was eighteen, because I knew when we met that he was far too old for me."

My mind flickers to Lenny, how I told her all those weeks ago that she was too young. I try to imagine my father saying the same thing.

Imagine the heartbreak he could've avoided.

"I'm sure you're about to ask why," Mileena says. "And the short answer is that I was a dumb kid. My parents were gone, I'd been living in what was essentially a halfway house for troubled teens, and I just wanted out. So, I used what little money my parents left me to forge official documents, and then booked a flight to London."

She glances over, her eyebrows creasing together like she'd expected me to leave. When it becomes clear I'm interested enough to stay, she nods to herself and continues.

"He was such a gentleman, your father. Caring, suave, totally charismatic. I fell for him immediately, even though the few friends I'd made in the city warned me not to. They said he was dangerous. Involved in organized crime." She pauses, staring off into the distance. "I grew up hearing horror stories about people like that. My parents moved to the States specifically to avoid that life and the things it entailed, but Duncan seemed so... *normal.* So, I stuck around."

"Then you got pregnant," I supply, filling in the dots. "And couldn't leave."

She nods. Just once, but it's a knife to my heart all the same. "I had no money, nowhere to live, no way to care for you by myself. I know it sounds selfish, but I did what I had to do to survive and keep you safe."

Letting the door slide shut, I step back and cross my arms over my chest. "I don't begrudge you the things you did out of necessity."

"I know, but you think I left because I wanted to. I *didn't*, Jonas. Leaving you and your father was the hardest thing I've ever had to do, but I wasn't... I wasn't okay, mentally. After I had you, I started noticing changes in myself. Emotions and thoughts I didn't have any control over. Thoughts like..."

Her voice shakes, cutting off.

My stupid heart pinches.

"Thoughts of harming you, or myself. I couldn't take care of you because I was so *numb,* and just didn't feel like doing it. The doctors diagnosed me with postpartum depression a few weeks after you were born, and it was nice to get a diagnosis, because I could research it and find out how to get better."

Silently, I wait.

"Only, it didn't. It never got better, and eventually spiraled into a chronic thing. I could be okay for a little while, and then I'd fall into these major depressive episodes, where all I wanted to do was die. I couldn't..."

Another sob racks her body, and she covers her mouth with the back of her hand. "I didn't want to subject you to that, so I left. Not exactly a shining moment of mine, but when you're young, every decision, every thought, is life or death. I had to choose life. I'm sure you don't remember, but it had already stolen so much joy from us at that point."

When she finishes, the air feels thicker. Heavier, now that it's laced with the burden of truth.

I'm not sure what to do with the information or the fact that it hasn't shifted anything for me. I still don't know how to forgive her.

"I didn't know because you didn't tell me." My words are quiet, competing with the ocean waves to be heard.

She chews on a fingernail. "I'm sorry," she says, voice just as soft, yet so bloody loud I can barely think straight. "I only did what I believed was best. And I failed you still."

We stare at each other for a few moments, and I can tell she wants me to accept it. To say I'm over it, and that we can move on and start anew.

But the truth is, I hold grudges. Let them fester like infected wounds in the chambers of my heart, diseasing my soul because it's better that way. Keeps me from continuing to get hurt.

As I turn back toward the door and head inside without saying anything else, a little thought peeps up, knocking the breath from my lungs as it slams into me.

*Better, or easier?*

Easing the door shut behind me, I find Lenny standing in the kitchen with a blueberry scone hanging from her mouth, eating over the sink. Pausing to admire the outline of her curves in the sleeveless, skin-tight navy gown she has on, I walk up behind her and press my lips against her ear.

"You look divine, love," I murmur, and she almost drops the pastry. "Though I quite prefer your mouth stuffed with something *else*, this is good too."

She jolts forward, swallowing. "Yeah, well, scones are good for that, as we both know." Tossing the pastry onto a paper plate, she spins around in my arms, reaching up to adjust my tie. "Everything okay? I heard yelling out there."

Sucking in a deep breath, I consider lying again. But when I look into those green eyes, I can't bring myself to do it. "Not really, but... I don't know. Maybe one day it will be."

Even if I don't know what exactly that means, it feels more truthful than anything else I've ever said.

# 39

## *Lenny*

For some reason, I'm not expecting the whole of Aplana Island to turn up at this gala.

When Jonas and I arrive, there's a faux red carpet set up outside the gallery, a white brick building with massive windows and skylights. It sits across from the courthouse and newspaper offices, though it's one of many places I've not even ventured inside of before because of the strict rules Mama and Daddy always enforced.

Funny how Daddy seems keen to support my art now that he thinks he can use it as leverage against me.

What's not funny is the fact that as we leave the Range Rover with the valet, my parents are the very first people I spot. Fear and anxiety collide in my throat as we approach, making it difficult to breathe.

"Relax," Jonas whispers into my ear, slipping his arm around my waist. He pulls me flush with his side, smoothing circles over my hip with his thumb. "They can't touch you, remember? You left them and are better off for it."

That doesn't really help. It feels like I grow smaller the more we walk, and suddenly my heart is far too large for my chest. "What happens when this is all over, Jonas?"

Coming to a halt at the curb, he turns me to face him. "What are you on about?"

I gesture wildly between us, not sure what he isn't comprehending. It's obvious to me, so why is he pretending?

"We're on borrowed time here, you know?"

"Our contract doesn't have an expiration."

"So, what? You just want to be fake engaged forever?" I laugh, but my face heats with shame, and it feels like I've been dipped in the thick of it. "Kind of unrealistic for a guy who doesn't date, don't you think?"

Asking that question feels like I'm cutting myself wide open and begging him to stop the bleeding.

But I still want to know the answer, either way. Even if it hurts me.

He opens his mouth to respond, a strange, unreadable look passing over his face like a dark storm cloud, but someone cuts him off before he has a chance. Pulling me back against his side, he grips my hip so tight that I can feel bruises forming, but I don't ask him to let up.

I like the reassurance, even if it is a little hollow.

Mama and Daddy make their way over to us. Behind them, people line the red runway, posing for pictures and stopping to speak to photographers and reporters. As if any one of them are important enough to warrant such attention.

"My goodness, Helene," Mama coos as she approaches, grabbing my cheeks and leaning in for air kisses. Jonas doesn't let me budge, though, and after a moment, she releases me and pulls back to peruse my outfit. "What an... interesting fashion choice. A little warm, isn't it?"

The thrifted faux-mink coat I grabbed right before we left the house felt like a good idea at the time. Something to hide my insecurities in, since I've fallen out of the habit of these publicity events.

Running a hand over the soft white material, I shrug, giving a pointed look at the alligator boots she's paired with a bright pink pantsuit. "It may be warm, but it's not more interesting than yours."

Daddy clears his throat, grinning down at me in his gray three-piece. It's a fake gesture, one I could spot a million miles away, but he leans into it regardless. As if the majority of my life wasn't spent cataloging those gestures, taking mental notes so I'd know what to do in the spotlight myself, and so I'd know when he needed reigning in.

Now, the only person around to keep him on his leash is Mama, and she was never any good at that in the first place.

Malice lines the dark rings around his irises, and my limbs tense up. Being in public and not being clued into Daddy's emotions or thoughts beforehand is more unsettling than I thought it would be.

Not to mention, he looks like the cat that caught the

canary. Eerily similar to the way he'd seemed after I told him about Preston and his friends, as if the wheels were turning, figuring out how to spin things to fit his narrative before I'd even finished talking.

"Wasn't sure if you'd show tonight or not," Daddy says.

I frown. "Why wouldn't I?"

"Events like this used to be our thing. Wasn't sure if you were feeling up to it or not, given the sudden shift in company." His eyes flicker to Jonas, but they don't remain. "I remember what happened last time I let you attend a function without me."

My spine stiffens, and Jonas grips me harder. Since I didn't tell him about Daddy's involvement, I doubt my fake fiancé's aware of the reference, but still.

Other people could be.

Still, Jonas doesn't seem satisfied being left in the dark. "What happened last time?"

Daddy's boisterous laugh fills the air, and he claps Jonas on the shoulder, drawing the attention of several different reporters. Their cameras turn our way, flashing over and over until I start to feel sick.

Or maybe it's the situation in general making me nauseous.

Either way, bile teases the back of my throat, and I'm about three seconds from puking everywhere.

"You know how girls get sometimes when they've had too much to drink." Daddy shakes his head, like this is some big inside joke we're all a part of. "Can't blame her for stepping out on the poor kid, though. Not everyone can be tied down to one person, like her mother and I."

A snort catches in my nose, and I cover it with a fake

sneeze. I suppose being faithful is easy when you're too busy being evil.

And right now, my father has never looked more so. There's something sinister in his gaze, dark and contrite as he looks at me.

It sends malcontent slithering along my spine.

I feel Jonas look at me, but I don't dare meet his gaze. "She certainly seems content enough."

"Oh, I've no doubt. That's how they all start, and it's how they get you." Daddy's eyes narrow at me, pinning me in place. "Mark my words, son. She'll break your heart."

"Could I have a word, Daddy?" I snap, extracting myself from Jonas's grip. He doesn't look like he wants to let me go, but since we're in public, he seems to think better about protesting.

Daddy frowns as I walk away, following after he says something in Mama's ear. I stop just out of earshot, and he folds his arms over his chest as he comes to stand in front of me.

"What's your problem?"

His eyebrows shoot up. "Excuse me, little girl?"

"No, *not* a little girl. An adult, actually, who would really appreciate it if you'd stop trying to manipulate her every chance you get." I grip my biceps, hugging myself.

A muscle in his jaw thumps. "Big words from a girl who has nothing without me."

The complete disregard for my previous statement burns, though I guess I shouldn't be surprised. All he's ever done was ignore me.

Pressing my lips together, I glance down at the ground, noting the shoes he has on. They're old and scuffed, a pair of

Italian loafers I had Mama special order for Father's Day years ago, with little swans engraved on the sides of the soles.

Back when I was still okay with being the butt of the joke, because I didn't know any better. Just wanted to stay as close to my father as I could.

Sadness swells in my chest, rising in my throat like a flood. Everything changed in such a short amount of time that it feels like it's all just starting to catch up. Memories from the night my world shifted resurface like waterlogged corpses, crawling over my skin like a thousand tiny bugs.

Daddy's voice, stern and low, when I tried to tell him what happened. The disappointment etched on his face when I used the word rape, and how it felt like a slap in the face when he asked what I'd been wearing.

If I'd been drinking.

Worse, the absolute mortification that came when I woke up to my name smeared across the internet, with intimate details of what happened up on dozens of blog sites. Statements from Daddy and Preston, talking about how unhinged I had become, and how I was having an early quarter-life crisis, and that was why I'd cheated.

*Me. Cheated.*

How I wished for the earth to crack wide open and consume me.

For that alone, I could never go back to the way things were. Not even if he returned my inheritance in full or issued an actual apology.

Some things are too heinous to come back from.

Not everyone deserves forgiveness.

He sighs. "All right, Helene. You want to play hardball? I'll double my previous offer. Come home tonight, and we can just put all of this behind us."

"No."

His mouth turns down at the corners, and he reaches out, grabbing my forearm. "It's no longer up for debate, missy. You will stop shaming this family by whoring yourself out to that Wolfe boy, and you will return home this instant."

I try to jerk away as his grip becomes harsh. "Let go of me!"

"Stop making such a scene, or I'll make it a point tonight to let everyone know the *truth* about your relationship." My eyes swing to his, and a wicked smile pulls at his lips. "Yeah, I'm not stupid. I'll tell everyone about how he's using you to get back at me, and you fell for it because you're a naive little girl. A slut who—"

Neither one of us sees the punch coming, but before Daddy can finish his sentence, Jonas's fist is connecting with the side of his head. Dozens of gasps can be heard as his skull whips to the side, and even Mama lets out a high-pitched scream.

Grabbing him by the shoulders, Jonas pulls Daddy back into an upright position, but even the grip he has on Daddy's neck seems violent.

"You're lucky I don't gut you right here," Jonas says in a low, dangerous voice. "But I don't want to ruin my brother's night, even if you deserve to be rotting six-feet deep right about now."

Embarrassment clings to my pores, trying to soak into my skin as I stare at the two of them. With a harsh shove, Jonas releases Daddy, who practically tumbles into Mama's arms.

I try not to let the shame take hold.

Try not to let Daddy win.

I do, I swear.

But even as Jonas whisks me away from the scene as Mama calls for a paramedic, I manage to steal a last glance over my shoulder. Pain lodges deep in my chest like a weed, rooting deep and making it difficult to concentrate the rest of the night.

Inside, the gallery is vast and beautiful, the middle aisle punctuated by beautiful sculptures while paintings by local artists line the walls. Jonas and I mostly stick to a corner in the back, and I breathe a sigh of relief when Elena and her husband make an appearance, giving me some reprieve from the concern in my fake fiancé's gaze.

He hasn't spoken a word since.

The air in the room seems to evaporate when they arrive, their presence alone enough to make everyone stop what they're doing and stare, if only for a second.

She's in a short, black cocktail dress while he's dressed in an all-black suit, Hades and Persephone themselves gracing humanity.

"Jeez, who died?" Elena says when she and Kal find us. A waiter passes by with a tray of champagne, and she swipes two from the platter, sliding one to me across the tall, circular table we're standing at. "I thought art galas were supposed to be fun."

"The fun is really in the interpretations." I point at a piece across the room. "See, that one with the blues and grays? The overall tone sort of screams *heavy*, while the intricate line work, the short brush strokes, say that while the subject matter that inspired the piece may be loaded, the artist's vision might not have been. They might have been trying to relay the calm in the middle of a storm."

Everyone looks at me, and I shrug, taking a sip of my

champagne. "That's just a guess, though. One interpretation. I could be way off the mark."

"What about that one?" Elena nods at a piece in the corner, but there are too many people in front of it for me to see it.

Curious as to what's sparked everyone's attention, I walk over to the exhibit and push my way to the front.

My lungs seize up as I take in the canvas, immediately recognizing the watercolor style of the little ballerina dancing on top of a pond. Surrounded by swans, she spins on the water, driven to performance because of the crowd.

Or, perhaps, in spite of it.

It's not the original painting—I have about six different versions that I've worked on over the last few weeks, each one with a different sheen of brightness and transparency.

Superimposed on this much larger canvas, though, I can't help noticing how different the hues and use of white space look, as if made for this exact medium.

Someone taps my shoulder, and I glance behind me, expecting to see Jonas; instead, a tall man with inky hair and the coldest, iciest blue eyes I've ever seen stands at my side, though he's staring at the painting.

*Mayor Wolfe.* Despite how close I've gotten with his brother, this is the first I've ever seen the man in person. His jaw is clean-shaven and disturbingly sharp, the kind of devastating beauty you see in marble sculptures.

Somehow, he's even more immobile and intimidating.

He's wearing a tan suit and an impassive expression, and his finger stays on my shoulder. Almost like he's forgotten he reached out in the first place.

"How much?" he asks finally. His voice is just as deep and velvety as Jonas's, though accented differently. Still uniquely

British, but with a hint of another dialect blending in, blurring his syllables.

I pull my shoulder back, watching his hand fall. "What do you mean?"

Slowly, his gaze slides to mine. "You're the artist, right? How much are you selling this for?"

My eyebrows knit together, confusion lacing my insides. "I'm not."

"You're not," he repeats in a flat tone. "Then why in the world did my brother insist on showcasing this piece? Do you have any idea how many dealers and curators I've had asking about it?"

"*This* painting?" I look at the watercolors again. "Why? It's not... I'm not even professionally trained. I don't know what I'm doing."

"There's a beauty in that, sometimes. A... uniqueness often lost with experience." Mayor Wolfe shrugs, glancing past me. His entire demeanor shifts when he does, his face going totally stiff.

I turn my head, searching for the cause, following his line of sight to a girl standing in front of an abstract marble sculpture. Royal blue hair spills in waves down her back, exposed through the crisscrossed straps of her hot pink minidress, but that's all I can really make out.

She laughs at something someone else says, her shoulders shaking, and it seems to infuriate the mayor.

After an incredibly awkward silence, he finally seems to snap back to reality, clearing his throat. "In any case, I did this as a favor to my brother, but you've garnered serious interest." He pulls several cards out of his pants pocket, holding them out for me to take. "Call any one of those numbers, and you'll see. Or don't, I don't bloody care one way or the other."

With that, he leaves me standing there. I try not to watch him leave, but my eyes are almost glued to him as he stalks across the gallery floor, pausing at the marble sculpture just beside the girl.

They don't seem to speak or interact at all. If you weren't paying attention, you probably wouldn't notice just how close he is, or the way her shoulders tense at his presence.

A minute later, he turns on his heel and walks away, disappearing into a hallway that leads to a cafeteria, the restrooms, and the offices. I wait, watching the girl for a long time, until finally, she takes off.

In the same direction.

Shaking my head, I try to wrap my brain around the events of the night. We're only a few hours in, and I'm already exhausted from the mental gymnastics.

Glancing up at the painting, then at the cards in my hand, I frown.

Fake fiancés don't do this kind of thing, right?

They don't buy things from a thrift store that you left behind or have lingerie special-ordered from expensive shops just because.

They *definitely* don't put your paintings up for auction. Even if that's not technically what this is, the business cards I'm holding beg to differ.

And for some reason, I feel violated. Like he's stripped away my choice of not putting my personal hobby on display.

But there's also something innately wholesome about it, I suppose. A belief in me he sees and wants to show the rest of the world, no matter the cost.

When I spin around, I have every intention of finding Jonas and laying into him, but he's no longer in the corner with Kal and Elena.

Heading in the same direction that Alistair just took off in, I clutch my chest, searching for an outside exit. *Air, Lenny. You just need some air.*

I turn down a corridor, pausing when I hear hushed voices. Familiar voices.

"...what do you think people are gonna say when they realize how these missing people are connected? They aren't nobodies. They have families and loved ones who are *going* to raise suspicion, and it's not gonna look good for you when they realize what you've done." *Preston.*

My eyes roll so hard into the back of my head that a sharp pang shoots across my skull. Of course, he's here.

Jonas's voice washes over me like a bucket of ice water. My fingers clutch the archway I'm standing beside, and I strain to hear.

"I don't bloody care how it looks. Alistair will either excommunicate me or deal with the fallout. Politicians survive scandal all the time, and it's not like anyone operates under the impression that my brother's a good guy."

"So, that's it? We had a deal and you're just backing out?"

"Are you daft? I'm not *sharing* Lenny with you, Covington. The *deal* was I'd put on a little show for you and your friends, and that was it. You're overplaying your hand here, lad, and I'm not interested. Find another way to pay her father off, I'm out."

Footsteps start in my direction, and I slap my palm over my mouth to stifle my gasp, sliding back from the doorway.

"Well, maybe I'll just have a little chat with Lenny. Let

her know how you've been going around killing people in her honor."

My eyes widen, bulging out of my head, and bring my free hand up to cover the other one, pressing harder. *He's what?*

Silence. "Maybe I'll just finish the job. Make sure you don't get to say anything to her ever again."

Preston laughs, and the sound sends a shiver through me. "Killing me doesn't resolve her father's debts."

"No," Jonas agrees, and I glare at the wall, completely lost. "But I bet she'd sleep easier at night."

"There's something wrong with you," Preston says, and it sounds like there's some shuffling. A thud makes the wall I'm leaning against vibrate, and I inch away from it, fear coursing through me now at the thought of being caught eavesdropping.

"There is." A choking sound echoes through the empty hall, and I back up even more. "Remember that when I come to collect."

The gargling suddenly stops, and then it's silent again. After a moment, I hear footsteps scurry down one end of the hall, growing softer as they seem to get farther away.

Blowing out a breath, I drop my hands and turn to investigate; a scream rips from my throat as I collide with a broad chest, and Jonas reaches out to steady me.

His expression is unreadable, and it makes my stomach sink for some reason.

"What are you doing out here?" he asks, jaw tense.

"Are you..." I swallow, the words searing the inside of my throat like a serrated knife. "Is it true? What Preston just said?"

He doesn't answer. His violet eyes darken as he tilts his head, taking on that dangerous blue hue.

Like an anchor tossed to sea, my stomach drops even more, heavy and burdensome as discomfort rests at my feet.

"The stuff I told you about him, and his friends? Have you—"

"Have I what, Lenny? If you're going to make accusations, spit them out."

Removing my tongue from where it's stuck to my cheek, I push away from him, glaring. "Are you *murdering* people for me?"

Stuffing his hands into his suit jacket pockets, he just stands there. Staring.

"Oh, my god." Bile scorches up my esophagus, begging to be set free even as I swallow and swallow, trying to repress it. Spinning away, I start back the way I came, but he chases, grabbing my wrist and yanking me back. "Don't *touch* me. Don't you fucking dare, Jonas."

He ignores me, pinning both my wrists between us. In a flash, he's reached into his pocket and pulled out a pair of dirty handcuffs, and within seconds I'm shackled and helpless.

"I was *helping* you, love. Finishing what you bloody started on the balcony at your parents' house. Those bastards didn't deserve to live, not after what they did to you."

Tears sting my eyes, spilling over and streaming down my cheeks. I continue thrashing, my mind very quickly spiraling out of control as every emotion I've pressed down over the last year seems to come to the surface, collapsing together like the creation of the universe.

An ugly, raw, *painful* universe I never wanted to be a part of.

That people forced me into.

And here, this man I thought I could trust with my secrets, my shame, pushes me further into it.

"I didn't ask you to do that," I sob, feeling like my chest has been ripped open, my trauma displayed for all to see, even though it's just the two of us here.

But it hurts, oh god does it hurt, as the memories rush past, forcing me to relive them one by one.

"You never would've asked," Jonas chokes out. "And you shouldn't have to, Lenny. You deserve to have someone in your corner without having to beg them to show up in the first place."

The sobs grow in volume. In ferocity. I struggle to draw in a breath, sheer terror seizing the bones in my body, locking them up tight.

"That wasn't your battle to win." I punch against his chest, once twice, the handcuffs making the movement choppy. "That pain was *mine*, and you commandeered it. Stole it from me, and for what?"

"Because I bloody love you!"

I hiccup, staring up at him through blurry eyes. He exhales, bending to press his forehead against mine, and his fingers gingerly trace my jaw.

"Look," he murmurs, his minty breath washing over my face. "I don't know when it happened, or what it means, but bloody fucking hell, love. If you hadn't noticed, I've been quite enamored with you for some time now."

My heart skips, hopeful in spite of the complete meltdown I just had. Am still having, albeit internally while he rambles.

"You might have been dealing with it on your own, but I... I couldn't. I'm not strong enough to sit idly by while men who hurt you still roam this earth."

Another hiccup from me, and I let his words soak in. Try to take them at face value, even though my brain is begging me to do anything but. It says not to trust him—that all the work it's done over the last year is for naught if we're just immediately going to fall in love with someone else.

Love hurts, my brain says.

But it also heals.

And my heart is a damn fool to its temptations.

My heart wants *him*.

His thumb strokes over my skin, and I suck in a deep, cleansing breath. Pinching my eyes closed, I nod. "Okay."

Shock colors his face. "Okay?"

I shrug, tapping him with my restrained fists. "I'm resilient, remember?"

He laughs, tilting my face back for a kiss, and even though I don't return the gesture, he doesn't mention it.

When he pulls back, I clear my throat. "Do you think you could grab me a paper towel from the bathroom? I don't really want to go back inside looking like this."

There's a split second of hesitation, but he glances at the handcuffs and seems to deem it acceptable. It might help that the bathroom is right across from us, but either way, he tells me to stay put and disappears behind the wooden door.

I consider it.

Staying put.

But then I think about what he said.

About how the men who hurt me are still roaming this earth.

Acting as if nothing ever happened.

So, I bolt.

Kick my heels off and head for the exit Preston went out of, trying not to cringe when Jonas's shout reverberates down the hall.

As soon as my bare feet hit concrete, a large arm wraps around my waist and a hood comes down over my head, and then I don't hear or see anything at all.

# 40

I DON'T KNOW why I run.

Even before I've made it out of the building, I know she's gone.

Scouring the entire premises of the gallery, I search for her, my skull feeling like it's been cleaved in two with each second I spend not finding her.

Eventually, I circle back around to the parking lot, beating my fist on the hood of a random Hyundai as I try to regulate my breathing. Panicking does me no good—in fact, all it does is cost me precious time.

I'm teetering, trying to determine whether she's hiding or

not, when my phone rings. Pulling it from my pocket, I don't even bother checking the number, immediately barking "*What?*" into the receiver.

"My, my. You should really get that temper of yours checked out, Wolfe. It'd be such a shame if you succumbed to something as treatable as high blood pressure, leaving poor little Lenny bug to fend for herself on this planet."

Rage simmers in my soul, spiraling outward until my insides are bleeding with it. "Preston."

He cackles, the sound maniacal and harsh. My grip on the phone tightens, making my palm ache. "See, I know you said the deal was off, but I already had plans for her. Just had to wait long enough for you to fuck up, and I knew she'd come running."

"Let me speak to her."

"Mm, no can do, *mate*. We're on a tight schedule."

A muffled shriek comes over the line, and I recognize it immediately. Every muscle in my body turns to stone, torn between relief that she's alive, and the horror of not knowing what he's doing to her.

Presumably, his goal is to let his friends and colleagues finish what they started all those months ago. Pay for the privilege of fucking her.

"If you harm a single hair on her head—"

"Gonna do a bit more than harm them, my friend." Shuffling comes over the line, and he grunts, a distinct smacking sound cracking in the air.

"Hurt her and you will regret it. This entire bloody island will."

Preston hums, the sound grating against my nerves. "Well, you'll have to find me, won't you?"

*Click.*

Red splashes across my vision, and I throw the phone as the dial tone bleats out. It whips against a nearby truck, shattering before it falls to the ground.

"What the hell is going on?"

Alistair's voice comes from behind me, and I whirl around, my hands already reaching for his neck. I stop at the last second, freezing in place as I realize we have an audience —Kal and Elena, and a portion of the catering staff stand in front of the building, watching us silently.

I haven't spoken to my brother since Mileena showed up. Frankly, I hadn't been planning on coming to the gala at all tonight, if not for the fact that I'd put Lenny's painting on display. In retrospect, however, the betrayal I felt then pales in comparison to the violence pumping through my veins now.

Dragging a hand through my hair, I tilt my head and glare up at the moon. "She's gone."

Shifting his weight from side to side, Alistair tugs at the collar of his shirt. "Ah, I'm sorry to hear that. She seemed nice—"

My chin snaps forward, and my eyes narrow into slits. "I don't mean she *left*, you pillock. Not everyone leaves me, you know."

"I know," he agrees quietly. "I never did."

His words set my sinuses on fire, and I rub my palm over my jaw, ignoring them.

For now, anyway.

There's no time to dissect that.

"You let her get kidnapped?"

Elena stomps over, eyes wide. Kal's on her heels, and he catches her around the waist as she launches herself toward me, holding her back.

"Little one," he warns in a low voice.

"Don't *little one* me," she snaps, struggling against him. "We were literally in a public place. How could you let that happen?"

"I didn't *let* it happen. She took off. Freaked out because I told her I love her, I guess."

Kal frowns. "Why would that freak her out?"

Shrugging, I shake my head. "Maybe because—"

"Oh, my god! I knew it!" Elena jabs a finger in my direction. "It freaked her out because you were never really engaged. I fucking told you. Kallum, you owe me twenty dollars."

The patience very quickly exits my body, flooding outward. "It doesn't really matter how we started, does it?" I give them a very pointed look. "The outcome. That's what we're focusing on, and right now the woman I love—your *friend*—is in very real fucking danger. So, either volunteer your assistance or piss off."

She snorts, and Kal slides his hand over her mouth. "You have his number?"

I glance at the shrapnel that is my phone. "You have time?"

Back at The Flaming Chariot, Kal contacts the cybersecurity team he works closely with. I'm expecting the CEO to pick up after the first ring, but instead it's a woman; her heart-shaped face comes into view on the computer monitor, rose pink hair pulled into a bun as she eats ramen with chopsticks.

"Well, well. Just when I was starting to miss that angry face of yours."

Kal rolls his eyes. "I just saw you last weekend."

"Semantics." She looks around the screen, raising a blonde brow. "Whoa. You have friends?"

My hand curls into a fist, and Kal blows out an irritated breath. "Jonas Wolfe, Riley Kelly. Hacker extraordinaire."

"Oh, don't tell my brother that. Or my boyfriend, cause he doesn't know I track his phone when he goes to New York." She pauses, as if waiting for judgment, and then continues. "Not because I don't trust him, but you know, what if he gets a bagel without me? Or if he gets into—"

"Riley." Kal applies her name like a brake. "Not why I called."

Sighing, she pushes her noodles aside. "Whatcha need?"

Eventually, the girl manages to get a trace on Preston's phone, except it pings to about four different locations. Downtown, the marina, an apartment in Boston, and Primrose Manor.

My insides tighten as we stare at the yellow blips on the map, trying to decide where to check first. And as much as I want to believe he wouldn't, my eyes keep flickering to the biggest dot of all.

The place where all of this began.

Alistair looks over at me, as if sensing the spot I can't drag my gaze from. He clears his throat, nodding at the screen. "You know she's there."

I nod. Just once.

All the confirmation we need.

I don't know how I know, but the gut doesn't lie.

"Well." He yanks a desk drawer open, pulling out the

branding iron I keep inside. Holding it out, he lifts a brow. "What're you waiting for, brother?"

My hand curls around the metal, and a delirious wave of excitement courses through me. The kind that rears its head when vengeance is imminent.

Looks like Tom Primrose is getting his war, after all.

# 41

## Lenny

When I was little, Mama really doubled down on that whole "if life gives you lemons, make lemonade" shtick.

She'd say that not all lemons are created equal, and that it was up to my brothers and I to find the good parts of the bad lemons and make use of them.

Lemonade can't ever be too sweet, she'd tell us, while enjoying the very sweet, pampered life she'd been given.

It's difficult to reconcile someone's lessons when they've never had to learn any the hard way.

Besides, all the sugar in the world couldn't make up for the rotten pieces of Preston. I'd rather die than try to find any redeeming qualities in him, especially now that I'm kneeling in front of the stone fireplace at Primrose Manor, still fucking handcuffed, waiting for him to do something while he paces behind me.

My chin smarts from where he backhanded me in the car, and I've imagined about thirty different ways I could kill him, if I could *just* get my hands free. No amount of sweat seems to do the trick, even though at this point it's dripping down my spine, soaking into the soft fabric of my dress.

An uneasy thought occurs to me, and I remember the lingerie I have on underneath the gown. The black lacy set that Jonas gave me and asked me to wear, and now probably won't even get to see.

Sadness spirals behind my eyelids, and I blink it away, trying not to provoke Preston.

At this point, my silence is just to prolong the breaths I have in my body.

I can panic later.

Sighing, I bring my hands to my chest as Preston comes over. He fists my hair, and I feel dozens of strands rip from my scalp as he wrenches my neck backward.

He spits on me.

No sneer, no warning, no taunt. Just gargles in his mouth for a second and purses his lips, scattering his saliva over my skin. Then he smears it across my face with his palm, and I feel dirty.

More than that, though, I'm angry. That's the emotion I settle on as he attempts to sully something Jonas and I enjoy, though I'm not sure how he knows.

I guess Preston always did have a knack for knowing what buttons of mine to push.

"Just getting you lubed up," he says, pinching my cheek until I wince. "We don't want the boys going in dry, do we?"

Remaining silent, I watch as he walks over to a metal, rectangular case on the floor by the grand piano, bending down and unlatching it. I can't see what he pulls out, because he's only got one floor lamp turned on so we're surrounded by shadows, but whatever it is, he stares at it for a long time.

Turns it over slowly, inspecting every little inch.

My palms grow clammy and my knees begin to ache. "Shame what happened to the rest of your *boys*, huh?"

Preston's head whips around, and he glares. "Don't tell me Lenny Primrose condones violence now." He chuckles, pushing to his feet while keeping his mystery object hidden behind his back. "Oh, bug, think of how much more fun it'll be this time if you fight back. I bet I can charge double, and have your dad paid back in no time."

My eyes flicker to him. "What?"

He gasps, pressing his fingers to his lips. "Oops, did I let the cat out of the bag? Goodness, I certainly hope that doesn't put a damper on your relationship with dear ol' Daddy."

"What do you mean, you'll be able to pay him back?"

Clicking his tongue, he moves in front of the fireplace, switching the mystery object so it's still hidden from my view. "I really shouldn't say."

As my mind swims with possibilities, trying to keep up with his nonsense, he just sighs.

"Oh, fine. I'll bite since I did bring it up." He speaks to me over his shoulder, while he messes around with the fire. I hear it crackle and spit as he toys with the flames, but when I crane my neck to get a better look, he moves with me. "I know you think I'm this evil mastermind who set out to hurt you, but the reality is much simpler than that. Your dad paid me to do it."

I roll my eyes, resisting the urge to laugh, cry, and puke all at once. "You're such a fucking liar, Preston."

"Normally, yes." He shrugs, unbothered. "Don't tell me you never wondered why he didn't take you seriously in the first place. What kind of overprotective dad doesn't launch into immediate investigation mode when his precious angel tells him she was brutally assaulted?"

"What kind of person casually talks about the assault he orchestrated?" I snap, his words bringing the memory once again to the forefront of my brain. My fingers hook into the neckline of my top, and I focus on my breathing, trying not to have a panic attack again.

Turning around to face me again, Preston holds up one hand. "Hey, I didn't really orchestrate it. Your dad offered me a lump sum if I could get you in a compromising position. He brought the guys in. I mean, some of them were my friends, but for the most part they were just looking to bang Ms. Prim-and-Proper."

"Why would he do that?" Shaking my head, his words still don't compute. Daddy's a lot of things, but... *evil*? No way. "Why would *you* do that?"

Stepping forward, Preston finally slides his other arm out from behind his back, revealing an elongated metal rod that looks a lot like a fire iron. The blunt, odd-shaped end glows orange, like he's been holding it to the open flame this entire time.

I swallow, eyeing the bar. So much is happening right now that my nervous system struggles to keep up, but this new addition makes my chest feel like it's caving in.

"'Cause you agreed to it."

"When I thought it was just going to be you and one other person." Shame floods my bones, incinerating the strength in my marrow. "You lied to me and said you needed money, and that if I did it, you'd be off the hook."

"That part was true. I just needed more money than I initially thought. Apparently, you can't gamble with the mob and not pay up. Your dad offered me a way out, so I took it."

"You drugged me. *Raped* me."

"Whoa, now. Easy with the R-word, Lenny bug. That's a serious accusation."

My eyebrows shoot into my hairline, and exasperation wraps around my sternum, pulling tight. "You're insane. Literally a fucking *insane* person. I hope Jonas cuts your dick off when he gets here."

"Ah, yes, your knight in a dirty leather jacket." Sighing, Preston continues walking toward me, wielding the iron like a baton. He stops just in front of me, lifting the metal so I can see the flat shape at the end.

It's a W, hollowed out and engraved with tiny roses and thorns inside. I squint at the shape, trying to place its familiarity in my mind.

"When all this is said and done, that psycho assassin's getting pinned for this, too. Gonna make sure to mark you up with his brand, so everyone knows he came back to finish you off. Won't be hard, since your scar will match the one he leaves on all his other victims."

*Daddy's head.* The scar he got the night of the assassination attempt that helped police identify Jonas in the attack.

It's the same W as the little charm on the corded bracelet he wears.

The Wolfe family insignia.

"You're not marking me."

Preston smirks. "We'll see about that."

As he advances, he tilts the iron, aiming for my collarbone. My fingers twitch, the idea of him scarring me like this physically, in such an intimate way, pushing vomit up my throat. I choke it down, jerking back when the heat brushes my skin.

"*Wait*!" He pauses, narrowing his eyes, and I exhale slowly, looking down at the metal just centimeters away.

Silence fills the air in the house just as much as the shadows, and I realize that it's entirely possible Jonas won't find me here.

Even if he does, the odds of breaching the security system and making it to us before Preston has a chance to hurt me more are slim.

I don't want the mark of the man I love tainted by the one who broke me.

Pinching my eyes shut, I send a silent prayer to God, the universe, whoever's listening that Jonas can appreciate the dedication I have to this no-longer-fake arrangement.

Especially if I don't make it out of this alive, which the devious glint in Preston's gaze tells me is a genuine possibility.

I have no idea when this man went from grade A douchebag to psycho killer, but I don't really have the luxury of time to think about it, either.

Inhaling, I open my eyes again. Look up. "I can do it."

"Do what?" He shakes the iron. "You want to put his mark on your body?"

"Yes. I'll do whatever else you want, just... just let me do this."

He doesn't respond for several seconds. My knees are

screaming at this point, begging me to get up off the hard ground, but I ignore them. His eyes scan my face, searching for signs of deviance, I assume, but finally he backs off with a hoarse laugh.

"Always knew you were a bit of a freak. If you think this'll help him sleep at night, have at it."

Grabbing a pair of bolt cutters from a gardening bag he brought in from the garage, he fits them on the chain linking my cuffs and severs it. Adjusting my top, one of my hands drops into my lap, while he forces the iron into the other.

"Hurry up, before it cools down. I want this to hurt."

Internally, my eyes roll, and I turn my wrist so the W faces me. My hands tremble so violently, it's hard to position the shape correctly so it misses bone, and my entire face flushes as the heated metal draws nearer.

Gritting my teeth, I remind myself why I'm doing it.

That I'm taking back my power by not letting Preston inflict more damage.

*For Jonas.*

The first brush of the scalding iron against my skin yanks a whimper from my lips, and as I press in slowly, nausea bubbles like a cauldron and makes me dizzy.

Raw, searing pain ripples along the length of my collarbone, and the pungent scent of melted flesh floods my nostrils, suffocating me. I hold it there for as long as I can stand it, until my fingers are numb and my vision starts to blur from the sheer magnitude of the pain, and then I drop the iron to the floor.

A choked sound crawls from deep in my being, and I collapse forward with my hands on my knees, gulping down air.

Preston bends, brushing a few strands of hair from my

face as he leans in to inspect. “Holy shit,” he breathes, a smile in his voice. “You actually fucking did it. What a crazy bitch—”

Before he can finish the sentence, the hand that had no role in my branding lashes out, striking him across the face once. He falls back on his ass, shocked, and it takes a second for it to set in what just happened.

Somewhere in the house, Daddy’s grandfather clock chimes. Footsteps carry through the halls, though I’m sure no one else is here.

As Preston scrambles back up, my hand whips out again, this time turning so the broken paintbrush wrapped in my palm slices across his cheek.

I’ve never been so happy to keep it tucked inside my dress.

Blood beads in the wound, and he lets out a cry as I jump up, hauling my foot back to drive my heel into his groin.

“*Fuck*,” he groans, doubling over with his arm over his lap. “I’m gonna fucking kill you.”

With a grin, I grab the iron and ignore my body’s aches.

“You’ll have to catch me first, fucker.”

And then the lights go out.

# 42

## Lenny

MY BROTHERS and I learned the layout of our house as soon as we moved to Aplana. Navigating in the dark was a necessity for the three of us, albeit for different reasons.

It feels strange for me to be tiptoeing around now when the end goal isn't just to stuff my face with junk food.

This is life or death, and I never would've imagined that skill would come in handy, but here we are.

Or, here I am, anyway. Sliding my palms along the walls and using muscle memory to keep me from tripping up.

I don't know what happened to the power, but I'm not staying still so I can find out, either. I've discarded my heels, tucked my paintbrush back into my dress, and hold the iron against my leg as I walk, on high alert.

Preston's footsteps don't come for a long time, and even when they do, they echo through the corridors, announcing his presence. Though for some reason, he never leaves the immediate downstairs, occasionally coming over to the main staircase to stand silently, but then he always retreats back to the living room.

Almost as if he's waiting me out.

Unfortunately for him, I will not be returning downstairs. If I can hide somewhere, I *know* Jonas will make it to me before anything else can happen.

Which makes the burn mark on my chest feel very stupid, but whatever.

It'll heal.

Probably.

And if not? Well, at least there can be no denying my feelings for Jonas Wolfe anymore.

Still, the brand *hurts*, so I move as silently as possible to a half bathroom in the very back of the west wing of the mansion. Pushing the door open slowly, I crouch down and pry open the sink cabinet, digging around for antibacterial ointment or a bandage.

I find a little packet of *something*, but since it's practically pitch black in here, I can't confirm the contents. Tearing the paper open, I lift and smell, trying my best to detect scents present in a cream that would make the burn worse.

The ointment has a neutral scent, though, so I squeeze a generous amount onto my fingers and gingerly press them to the site. My body locks up, rejecting the contact, even as the cream seems to soothe the inflammation.

Measuring the size of the bandage against my palm, I

open it up and fit the gauze against the half dollar-sized mark, breathing a small sigh of relief when it's over.

Getting to my feet, I exit the bathroom, holding my breath as I plaster myself to the wall. No footsteps can be heard, so I start around the corner and head for my old room.

My hand grips the doorknob just as someone shoves into my hair, yanking me back with a startled squeak.

There's a single, split-second where I think Jonas has finally found me.

That I'm saved.

But it's Daddy's voice that comes.

His hand that slaps down over my mouth as he shoves me into the door.

"Did you really think it'd be that easy, Helene? That you could ever just walk away from your duties to this family, and not have severe consequences?"

When I don't answer—hello, can't answer—he cracks my skull against the wood. My vision darkens at the corners, bright speckles of light flashing behind my eyelids.

"You'll go back downstairs, and you'll finish what you started with Preston and his friends. You'll let them fuck you until you bleed, or get pregnant, or whatever the hell it is they want to do to you, and then you'll be returning to the compound as soon as they're done. Got it?"

Sliding his hand away, he shakes me a little. "Do you fucking understand, Lenny? All this time you thought your role was to be my little helper. The face of Primrose Realty." He laughs, and the sound makes me physically ill. "I was just priming you to see how much you'd be able to take. See what you'd tell people. Turns out, your mother and I raised you better than we realized."

My eyes burn, tears threatening to spill over as his disgusting words assault me. The fractures in my heart seem to split, shattering until there are a million little pieces—so many pieces, that I fear it can never be put back together.

"Why?" I whisper, my voice utterly broken.

Reality is supposed to be what you make of it, but I don't remember asking for this.

"Because they're willing to pay, baby girl. And our world revolves around the almighty dollar. You just don't know it yet, because I've been protecting you all this time. But it's time I fed you to the wolves, otherwise you're never going to learn your lesson."

Well. There's my confirmation.

Preston wasn't lying.

Violence thrums through my veins, and my body practically hums along with it. My brain lags and my heart is out of the question, so I focus on what my gut is saying.

The easy thing to do would be to try and endure. To hold off until Jonas and my maybe cavalry arrive, but who knows what shape I'll be in at that point?

*Easier is not always better.*

I struggle against him, trying to get my hand up enough to knock him loose with the iron, but then he's reaching for my throat and crushing my windpipe.

"Stop being such a pissy little brat," he snarls, nails cutting into my skin.

Then, he shifts, freeing one of my arms, seemingly unbeknownst to him. It slides up my chest, snatching the brush hidden in my cleavage.

Curling my fingers around the handle, I suck in a deep breath, ground my feet into the floor, and hope that one day I'm able to come to terms with my decision.

Relying on pure adrenaline and instinct, I rear my arm up around my head and drive the handle into the side of his throat. A brief pause ensues, and I feel him reach up to clutch the wound, but then I pull it out and repeat the motion, adding even more force behind it.

Then I do it again.

And again.

And *again.*

Until finally, his hand falls away from my throat, and I hear his body hit the floor.

I stand still for several minutes after, staring at the door even as my father's blood drips down my scalp, trailing a path along my spine. Over my shoulders. It clings to me, along with the lead weight of his threats—followed quickly by the ghost of promises made when I was younger.

That he'd never hurt me.

That he wanted me to be happy.

The paintbrush falls from my hand, and I lean against the door. I want to sink into it, to become one with the wood so maybe everything would hurt a little less.

I'm not sure how long I stand there, but the voice that breaks through the darkness coaxes the first of many tears from my exhausted, dirty body. Like lightning striking a storm cloud, igniting everything it touches.

"Well." That smug British accent skates over my skin. "Better you than me, love."

Pushing off the door, I launch myself into Jonas's arms before waiting to make sure he'll catch me.

He does.

Naturally.

They wrap tight around my waist, and he buries his head

into my neck. I wince, pain ebbing where the brand brushes against him.

Pulling back, he cradles my face with calloused hands. "Are you all right, love?"

I shake my head, tears rolling over his fingers. "No," I whisper, wishing more than anything that I could see him. Take some sort of comfort in those violet eyes and let myself get lost in their depths.

But if the lights come on, that means I'd see my father, too.

So, instead, I pray they remain off a little bit longer.

Scooping me into his arms, Jonas fits his shoulder against the wall, as if using it to judge his movements. I lay my head against his chest as he carries me, and my eyelids get so heavy that I decide to rest them for a moment.

When I open them again, I'm lying on the sofa in the living room. The lights have been restored, my dress has been discarded and replaced with an oversized T-shirt, and the fireplace warms my toes. Jonas sits on a stool at my side, glaring at the branding iron on the floor.

Across the room, Preston sits with his back against the wall. His wrists are handcuffed, and his arms are bound with a thick nylon rope, while packing tape covers his mouth.

Not to mention, he's completely naked, and his hands are positioned, so he holds his flaccid dick between them. Humiliation colors his skin in reds and purples, and the glare he sends me could probably kill if I wasn't already dead inside.

Looking at the man by my side, though, feeling warm in spite of everything that has happened tonight, I remind myself that it's not true.

That the damage they did isn't permanent, because I'm no longer allowing it to be.

"He'd been watching us," Jonas says through clenched teeth. "I kept seeing things outside, shadows at night, but I didn't think to look. Didn't think it'd be anyone, because the security cameras never picked up on anything. Then, when Mileena showed up, I figured it'd just been her creepy arse."

Drawing a deep breath, he shakes his head. Scrubs a hand over his face. "This brand isn't even one of mine. He copied it. Watched us together. Watched *you* alone in my house. Knew where you'd be, what you'd be doing. He... he saw *everything*, Lenny. Like some sick Peeping fucking Tom."

Pushing into a sitting position, I tuck my hair behind my ears and crawl to him. Without hesitation, Jonas yanks me into his lap and releases a shuddering breath against my throat. He pulls back, tugging the neck of the T-shirt down a bit, cursing under his breath.

"And now he's done this to you. Hurt you—"

"No," I interject, gripping his chin. "I did that. He had no part in it, except that he threatened me with it in the first place."

His violet eyes are wide as they roam over my face, and he squeezes my hips. "You burned my initial into your skin?"

I nod, biting my lip as his gaze seems to darken.

"Well, that doesn't change the fact that he tried to take you from me." His hand skims along my spine, leaving a trail of fire in its wake.

"But he didn't."

"The impact does not negate intent, in this case. I want him to suffer."

Nodding again, I realize I'm barely even paying him any attention. My body's so content, fit tight and snug against his after the uncertainty from this evening, and my heart feels so fucking full that nothing else is really registering.

"Lenny." He stills my hips, which I didn't notice were even moving until he pinches me. "What are you doing?"

"I don't know," I admit, swallowing.

And I don't, really. This isn't a normal response to trauma —or maybe it is.

Maybe your response has more to do with the circumstances themselves and your personal reaction to them, rather than the rightness of the situation.

My pelvis shifts and I feel him grow thick and stiff beneath me. "*Lenny,*" he admonishes, and a small vein bulges against his forehead. "Stop it."

Shaking my head, I reach down and tug the hem of the shirt up my thighs, revealing my bare pussy. Frowning, I give him a look. "Hey. Where'd the lingerie go?"

"Thrown out."

"Rude. I didn't even get to see your reaction to it." I pout, my fingers fumbling with the buttons of his white dress shirt, yanking it from his black pants. "Have I ever told you how much I like you in a suit?"

"Maybe tell me when we don't have an audience, and you're not in shock or healing from physical wounds."

I blow a raspberry with my lips, then lean forward and lick the seam of his mouth. Frissons of heat coil tight in my core, and I sit up straighter, looking him directly in the eye.

"This will hurt him," I say, pleading.

"This shouldn't be about him."

"It's not." When I reach for his belt, he doesn't stop me. "Just an added bonus."

He's silent as I work him free, and I grin when he pops

out, heavy in my palm. Preston starts making noises, struggling against his binds, but I don't bother looking at him.

Just like I didn't want the brand tainted, I don't want this moment to have his presence stained on it.

With a resigned sigh, Jonas grunts, lifting me up. He fists his cock, positioning it at my entrance, grinning when he slips a finger through my arousal.

"Are you ever not wet for me, love?" I shake my head, and he blows out a breath. "Tell me you want this."

"I do. I need it."

The tip pushes in, fishing a gasp from my throat. He stretches slow, so fucking slow, keeping his eyes on mine.

"Tell me you belong to me. That you're sorry for running off."

"Well, I'm not really sorry for that, though." I pause, and his brows furrow. "I got you back in the house, didn't I? And here we are, finishing wars that never should've belonged to us in the first place."

Grunting, he shunts in deeper, and my fingers claw his neck. I wish I could make my home in his bones, but I suppose this is as good as it gets for now.

"It was stupid and reckless," he says, and I'm not sure if he thinks that I planned to be kidnapped, or what, but I also don't care. The only thing that matters is the way he feels pushing into me, fucking me slow, sending me off the edge of oblivion already.

"Our entire relationship was based on stupid and reckless."

He bottoms out, and I let out a ragged moan as sparks collect in my core, pulsing outward. Rolling my hips, I tilt them so my clit grinds against his pelvis, and his head lolls back.

"We have about thirty minutes before the police show up. After I had the power cut, they were called," he says, guiding my movements, taking me faster and harder. "Be a good girl and make me come, okay? I want to fill you while that piece of shit watches, and then I want to slit his bloody throat for ever touching you in the first place."

My nods are fervent, matching the feverish pace I set. I slam down over and over onto his cock, the force of my thrusts so powerful that I can feel him in my chest.

My orgasm crests quickly, though whether it's because of the adrenaline or because of Jonas in general, I can't say.

I also don't care.

The consequences of my actions will still be here, long after I come.

"Fuck, love. You look so bloody perfect on top of me. Keep going, just like that."

Obeying, I grip his shoulders tight, using it as leverage. Rocking up and down, back and forth, I feel sweat bead on my forehead, and then Jonas is gritting his teeth again and fisting my hair, tugging my head back.

"Say you love me," he commands, forcing my pace to slow. His cock drags against that sweet spot inside me, and my entire body feels like a single pulse point, on the very verge of bursting.

I moan, my pussy spasming around him. "Why?"

"Because I know you do, and I want to hear it." He licks a path up my neck, nipping at my jaw. "Don't come until you've said it."

Squeezing my eyes shut, I try to stave off and ride through my climax before it hits, hoping he comes first. But then he shifts, dropping a wet thumb to my clit and adding counterclockwise motions to the brutal pounding of his hips from below.

And I just can't hold it in any longer. "I love you," I cry, my world exploding into thousands of tiny blissful shards, some glass and some wooden, and all just as dangerous.

"Fuck," he hisses, and this time when he goes to move me off of him, I lock my knees and stay put.

"Come inside me," I whisper, my lips on his ear, and he follows me right over the edge. He pulses, emptying himself, and I feel his hot cum flood my pussy, drawing a second wave of euphoria from me.

We're a mess of sweaty, tangled limbs as our collective high wears off, and I can feel the despair from before trying to settle in. Running my fingers through his hair, I sigh.

"I do, you know. Love you. I don't think this relationship has been fake for a while."

Chuckling, Jonas gently pulls me off of him, and I try not to whimper at the loss, even as his cum runs down my thigh. "I'm not sure that it ever really was."

He's right, in a way. It started off completely unconventional, and maybe a little cold at first, but there has never been another person I've felt such a strong, visceral connection to.

No one else has ever been willing to save me, when it was all I ever really wanted to begin with.

That unconditional kind of love that you'd risk your life on a battlefield for.

We sit there quietly for a long time, until sirens can be heard in the distance. Pushing up, I glance over at Preston, who seems to have fallen asleep—or maybe passed out since there's a massive stab wound in his side that I didn't see until now.

It's no longer bleeding, but he's still covered in blood, and I wonder if he's even alive.

Sliding off of Jonas's lap, I pull my T-shirt down and walk over slowly, trying to reconcile this man with the one I thought I knew for three years. How could I have gotten it so wrong?

Then again, my father was once my absolute best friend, so I suppose you can only know a person as well as they want you to.

Preston's eyes flutter open as I bend down in front of him, looking at the myriad of weapons laid out like a buffet. I feel Jonas come up behind me, his presence warm at my back.

"I thought you might want to decide how he dies," he says, and my heart swells ten times.

That shouldn't be romantic, but goddamn.

The man just gets me.

Picking up a long, slender kitchen knife, I grip the handle tight in my hand and sigh, looking over my ex one last time. Disgust and anger boil inside me, blocking out any other emotions right now, and I cock my head to the side.

"Any last words, Mr. Covington?"

His cuffs clink together as his hands move, and I smirk when he lifts his middle finger.

"Yeah," I say, reaching down and pinching his dick between two fingers, bringing the sharp edge of the blade to the underside of the crown. "Fuck you, too."

# EPILOGUE

"THE FACE THAT LAUNCHED A THOUSAND SHIPS." Lenny frowns, moving backward across the room as she taps a brush against the corner of her mouth. "That kind of sounds like an insult, don't you think?"

I don't look up from the floating shelf I'm working on mounting, though her every movement registers in my peripheral anyway. Ever since the night I found her at Primrose Manor months ago, covered in her father's blood, I can't stop paying attention.

"Girl started a whole war just because she was pretty." Lenny shakes her head, holding her thumb up for reference to the wall where she's painting a Helen of Troy mural. "Tell me that's not the most dramatic thing you've ever heard."

"More dramatic than the time you decided to renovate the entire beach house out of boredom?"

Hands on her hips, she turns to me with narrowed eyes. Gorgeous, sea foam green that I wish I could deep dive into and drown in.

"You told me to pick a passion project for my portfolio. I fail to understand how you didn't see this coming."

*Fair enough*. Especially since the only reason she decided to start community college courses was because I encouraged her to.

The events at Primrose Manor sparked a huge wave of controversy surrounding her family, even though the bodies inside were given manufactured fates, per the request of Mrs. Primrose. According to official records, Tom suffered a heart attack and died peacefully in his bed, while Preston went missing during a yacht outing.

His body has yet to be recovered, but only because I burned him alive after Lenny made him a eunuch.

The press cared far less about either of the deaths than we anticipated; in fact, most of the controversy came when Mrs. Primrose put the compound up for sale and high-tailed it back to Savannah, leaving her three kids behind without a word.

Since I'd already been there, done that, I suggested Lenny explore her newfound freedom.

After weeks of watching her sob into her pillow every night, sometimes only showering when I picked her up and made her, and an endless stream of Elena or her brothers stopping by to keep her company, she finally went to therapy.

A few weeks later, she'd enrolled in some online courses for an interior design program, stating that she wanted to try and combine her love of shopping with that of art.

Which is why I'm standing in our spare bedroom building a bloody bookshelf instead of fucking her on the couch downstairs, or on the kitchen island, or on the back porch in celebration of my mum finally moving out.

She'd technically already moved to a cottage on the south side of the island some months ago, but she retrieved the last of her things from the crawlspace today.

Things between us aren't what she was probably hoping for, but I am trying, at least. It's more than I think she deserves, but I'm limited on family.

And if, by some bloody miracle, Lenny decides she ever wants to bear my children, I think they deserve to have a grandmother in their lives, even if she couldn't be the mother in mine when I needed her.

Still, my intention upon returning from my pub today was to christen as many surfaces in the house as possible in celebration of our official engagement.

Alistair, surprisingly, was the one to goad me into doing it. He's become something of a sap over the last few months, and I dare say I know why, although he's yet to admit it.

I won't push him on it. We're still working on our relationship, too.

The diamond ring on Lenny's finger glitters in the bedroom light, and I reach out, grabbing her wrist and tugging her into me.

My lips trail up the side of her neck, and she sighs, leaning into the touch. "Mm," she moans, tilting her head to give me better access. I bite down on her pulse, making her jolt, and then bring my hand up to push aside the raggedy shirt she has on.

Though slightly faded, the W etched into her skin is still plainly visible, and each time I see it, I'm filled with a primal haze of lust.

It's insane, sure, but I love knowing that if anyone ever touches her again, they'll know who they're fucking with.

"All right," she says, reaching up to tangle her fingers in my hair. "We can take a break, I guess."

"Oh, thank fuck." In seconds, I have her naked and writhing on the floor, my tongue spearing between her thighs.

She trembles violently, and as I look up at her, I swear that I've never seen anything more bloody beautiful.

Devastatingly alluring and completely terrifying, Lenny Primrose (soon to be Wolfe) could easily start another war in her lifetime.

And I would be at the helm of the very first ship, leading the charge into battle.

Simply because she's mine.

# ACKNOWLEDGMENTS

Keeping it short and sweet this time around, because honestly... six books in, and the support behind the scenes hasn't changed all that much. Hopefully you all know how much I appreciate you in general, but if not, here... we... go:

To my family: thank you for all the love, laughter, and dysfunction, and for supporting me even though you don't read these books. Thank you, also, for not reading them, so that I never have to explain to you why I know about semen allergies or the exact steps to DIY branding.

To Emily: I don't know what I would do without you. Thank you for inspiring me, keeping me sane, and sending Tik Toks even though I continually forget to reply to them. I would reference the Kanye Era, but that hasn't exactly aged well, so I'll just leave it at this: love you the most.

To Jackie, Cat, Ellie, and Rosa: you guys are the best behind-the-scenes team a girl could ask for. Thank you for making my books pretty on the inside and out, and for trying to keep my life on track.

To my Sirens and the ARC ladies: thank you so much for being the OG hype teams, and for all you do to promote my books. I literally couldn't do any of this without you, and I will forever be honored that you love my work enough to want to shout it from the online rooftops.

To the bloggers, reviewers, silent readers, and everything

in between: thank you for making the Monsters & Muses series such a success so far. Since publishing Promises and Pomegranates, my life has changed so drastically, and it's all because of you.

To Lord Byron, Poe, and Arrow: thank you for existing.

## ALSO BY SAV R. MILLER

**King's Trace Antiheroes Series**

Sweet Surrender

Sweet Solitude

Sweet Sacrifice

**Monsters & Muses Series**

Sweet Sin

Promises and Pomegranates

Vipers and Virtuosos

Oaths and Omissions

Arrows and Apologies

Souls and Sorrows

Liars and Liaisons

Standalones

Be Still My Heart

## ABOUT THE AUTHOR

Sav R. Miller is a USA Today bestselling author of adult romance with varying levels of darkness and steam.

In 2018, Sav put her lifelong love of reading and writing to use and graduated with a B.A. in Creative Writing and a minor in Cultural Anthropology. Nowadays, she spends her time giving morally gray characters their happily-ever-afters.

Currently, Sav lives in Kentucky with her dogs Lord Byron, Poe, and Arrow. She loves sitcoms, silence, and sardonic humor.

For more information on announcements, bonus material, and Sav's other books, visit savrmiller.com or become a Sucker in her Facebook reader group: www.facebook.com/groups/savrmiller/


facebook.com/srmauthor

x.com/authorsav

instagram.com/srmauthor

tiktok.com/@authorsavrmiller

threads.net/@srmauthor

Printed in the USA
CPSIA information can be obtained
at www.ICGtesting.com
LVHW021919120524
780071LV00002B/81

9 798985 920307